WICKED KING

KINGS OF TEMPTATION

SIENNA CROSS

Paperback ISBN: 9798335274678

Cover Design: Joy Design Studio

❀ Created with Vellum

To all the women who find it perfectly acceptable to be forced into an arranged marriage with a wicked Italian mobster…

~ Sienna Cross

WICKED KING

CONTENTS

DICTIONARY

Chinese

Bà - dad

Bǎobèi – treasure

Lǎodà – Triad leader (formal)

Lǐngdǎo - leader

Nǎinai – grandma

Xiānsheng – respectful way to address a man, like Sir or Mr.

Yéye - grandpa

Italian

Cazzo - fuck

Coglione - asshole

Dio - God

Madonna, sei bellissima - God, you're beautiful

Merda - shit

Ti prego - I beg of you

Tagalog

Nanay – mom

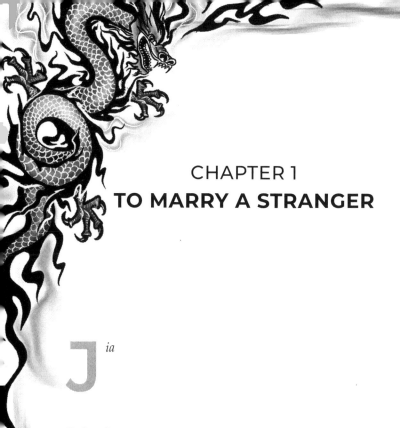

CHAPTER 1
TO MARRY A STRANGER

J *ia*

Today, I marry a stranger.

Worse, I marry the man who is responsible for my brother's death.

A pair of mismatched eyes bore into mine—one as brilliant as the enthralling seas of the Caribbean and the other as murky as the darkest pits of hell. His hand tightens around my own, like a steel band chaining me to a dismal future.

I heave in a breath and attempt to focus on the priest's words, but the ancient scriptures blur in the background in a muffled rush.

No, Marco Rossi is not exactly a stranger. I've known the wicked mafia playboy for a few months now. The Italian mobster and CEO of Gemini Corporation is infamous within the dark world I've been forced to inhabit due to the blood that runs through my veins.

As a Guo, and the daughter of the former head of the Four

Seas, one of the notorious gangs of the Chinese Triad, I somehow always knew this day would come, and yet, I'm still completely unprepared. How does one marry a man you despise to save your family's honor?

The melodic tune spun by the enormous organ and the large choir casts its spell across the crowded cathedral. The delicate scent of jasmine fills the space, a scent that typically brings with it a sense of peace, but today is unable to quell the brewing storm within. Despite decades long hatred between the ruling families of lower Manhattan—the three legs of the legendary Triad: the Red Dragons, the Golden Star, and my own, Four Seas, along with the feuding Italians: the Valentinos and Rossi's—they all sit shoulder to shoulder to celebrate this grand union. And complete farce.

I strangle the bouquet in my fist, the fragrant jasmine bitter today. In spite of the harmonious melody echoing around me, my heart is a frantic drumroll beneath my breastbone. Despite the high neckline of my pristine wedding gown, I'm certain my future husband can see its mad pounding beneath my fair skin.

Either that or he simply can't take his eyes off my cleavage through the sheer lace.

Dirtbag.

The philandering Marco Rossi is well-known among Manhattan's female elite. I'm sure he's screwed half of the city's debutantes. Likely many of the women seated in this very cathedral. He even graced the cover of *The New Yorker* last month as one of the city's most eligible bachelors. Women grovel at his feet, hang on every precious word that tumbles from his perfectly bowed lips and drop their panties without a second thought. It's disgusting, really.

I hazard a quick glance at my fiancé and take in the piercing wild eyes from beneath a tumble of dark hair, wide set jaw, and flawlessly carved cheekbones. Physically, he's enthralling, and logically, I understand why females throw themselves at the mafia god, but that smug smile... I want to rip it right off his ridiculously handsome face. He really thinks he's a prize. As if being shackled to him for an eternity makes me the luckiest woman in the world.

And I'm simply supposed to forget that Qian is dead because of him and his brothers?

The fingers of my free hand curl into a fist at my side and the platinum glints beneath the stained-glass windows of the magnificent domed ceiling. My gaze travels from the meaning-less wedding band up my hand, to the long, lace sleeves that reach down to my wrist. It's the height of summer, the temper-ature in the city reaching record highs, but as always, I cover my forearms and the shame they bring.

God forbid anyone ever saw... *Bà's* wrath would have only intensified.

My future husband clears his throat and his eyes dart to mine, as if somehow in that instant he's read my darkest, inner-most thoughts.

I stare up at the face of the man I'll be forced to wake up to for the rest of my life, and a wicked smirk twists his lips. Lust. Desire. Vengeance.

Something snaps inside me.

I refuse to spend the remainder of my existence at the hands of this possessive man. I suffered enough under my father's tyrannical hold, and I would do anything to ensure I never endure that torture again.

There is only one option: I'll kill Marco Rossi the first chance I get.

One Month Earlier

. . .

Sitting at the drafting table with my pencil pressed to the paper, I stare out the window at the buzz of traffic below. The Meatpacking District on a Monday morning is alive with energy, a different kind than exists a few dozen blocks north in Midtown. My tiny loft sits above the small warehouse space that houses my one-of-a-kind designs and the myriads of fabric samples I've managed to amass in the last year. I'm so close to finally realizing my dream without a penny of my family's tainted money.

My own fashion line.

CityZen: combining urban, chic apparel with a relaxed, modern vibe.

My storefront isn't even open yet, but I have two mannequins perched at the windows wearing my hand-sewn fashion. I've actually had a few people wander into the store looking to buy the designs.

Now, if I could only focus. My gaze flutters to the vase on the table filled with fresh jasmine. The sweet scent has always calmed my nerves, reminding me of my mother. Tearing my eyes away from the white blooms that signify purity and hope, I stare at the blank page, willing the image in my head to come to life on paper. I hit a wall, much like the red brick one staring at me from across the street.

Damn it. Focus, Jia.

The creak of the front door opening spins my head toward the entrance. I can't quite make out the door around the brightly graffitied brick wall that separates my bedroom-slash-office from the living area of the industrial loft. I spent hours creating that masterpiece along the auburn bricks when I moved in—a glorious crimson and gold dragon, my spirit animal and star sign in the Chinese zodiac.

"I come bearing caffeine!" My best friend's voice echoes across the high ceilings, bouncing off the metal rafters.

"You are a life saver, Ari." I reach for the skinny latte and take a sip. The first one always tastes like heaven. "You know you're not getting paid for this, right?"

She smirks. "One day, you'll be a huge designer and all the mean girls from FIT will be standing in line to get a Jia original. I'm totally content with working pro bono for now."

"I can't take advantage of you like that…"

"You're not. I'm offering my help for *free*. We had all our classes together, you know I'm no good at the creative stuff, but I am damned good at the business side. I guess Daddy was right and I should've gone to UPenn, instead." She shrugs. "Oh well, their loss is your gain." Squeezing my hands, she offers a reassuring smile. "We can do this. I know we can. I believe in you."

Unwanted emotion stings my eyes, and I blink quickly to chase it away. *Show no emotion, Jia. You must be strong and never show any signs of weakness.* My father's words echo across my mind. Even from the grave, they hold power over me. Too much power.

Tugging down my long sleeves, I give my best friend a smile. "Thanks, Ari. You don't know what your support means to me."

She peers over my shoulder, standing on her tiptoes to examine my drafting table. "I can see you're in desperate need."

I groan and spin back to the empty canvas. "I'm having a hard time connecting with my muse today."

Arianna slumps down on my bed, her cute blonde bob whipping strands of hair across her heart-shaped face. "Is there anything I can do to help?"

I love my friend. She's amazing and has been there for me since the first day we met at FIT. New York's elite fashion institute isn't exactly known for its warm and fuzzy feel. It's cutthroat and beyond competitive so I'd really lucked out when I stumbled across this gem of a human. Still… I hate getting her involved in my messy family life.

I'd filled her in on bits and pieces of our sordid connection with New York's sketchy underground, but I'd never told her I was the granddaughter of the infamous Four Seas' founder. She knew my brother Qian was involved with the crime syndicate but never the extent of it.

"Come on, Jia, spill." She takes a sip of her iced coffee, and those expressive emerald eyes pin to mine. "Is this about your brother?"

I exhale a sharp breath and crumple down into the chair. He was killed only three months ago, caught in the middle of a shootout with the Italian mafia. I'm still fuzzy on the details. And numb. My brother and I hadn't exactly been close since we were little. For as long as I could remember, *Bà* had treated him differently. He was being primed to take over the family business. And me? I was simply supposed to sit there, be quiet and look pretty. The best possible future for me was finding a decent match for marriage. One that would propel the Guos and the Four Seas into greater notoriety.

"Pretty much," I finally mumble to my friend. "Any way you can turn back time?"

"I wish. Then I'd go back and never agree to that date with Matty." Her lips pucker. "Not only was he a cheap bastard who wanted to split the cost of dinner, but he also tried to get in my pants on the subway." She makes a retching sound. "Come on, now. If you want to get some, at least splurge on a taxicab."

An unexpected laugh tumbles out as I watch her re-enact the story. I wish my problems were that trivial.

She waves a hand, and her smirk falls away. "In all seriousness, what can I do?"

"Nothing. I don't think there's anything either of us can do." I shrug and spin around toward my work in progress.

I've been summoned to appear in front of the Chinese Triad tomorrow afternoon. As the only living heir to the great Qian Guo, my father, not my brother who shared his name, I still officially represent the Four Seas in the eyes of the ruling families.

Clearly, I want nothing to do with their dark, illicit dealings. I have absolutely zero interest in assuming the role of head of the Four Seas. I need to focus on my legitimate business, my future. Something I never would have had if *Bà* hadn't died a few months before my brother.

I'm finally free, and I refuse to let anyone drag me back into the darkness again.

CHAPTER 2
ENDLESS DANCE WITH DEATH

M *arco*

The damp air of the abandoned warehouse clings to my skin, heavy with the stench of rust and old seawater. My twin brother, Nico, stands at my side, his breaths measured, a stark contrast to the rapid thundering of my heart that I'm certain must be echoing through the stillness. Beside him, Jimmy and Max are crouched with guns drawn. None of us are strangers to this endless dance with death, but tonight, the air is electric with something fierce, something desperate.

A simple visit to one of our warehouses to check on inventory had turned to this. A fucking deadlock. Ever since Qian's death, the Four Seas have been out of control. Without a strong leader, their violence grows more wild, more reckless. And tonight, they have us cornered, their whispers slicing through the silence like the faint hum of a blade. Their shadows, a sea of navy, loom across the stacked crates and the moonlit floor of the warehouse.

Nico raises his hand and signals, three, two… and one—the world erupts in chaos.

Gunfire thunders, a deadly symphony of violence. I duck behind a container, the cold metal a sharp contrast to the warmth pooling in my veins. I peek around the edge, my eyes cutting through the murky darkness to meet the hungry gazes of our assailants. Fucking Lei Wang and his rebel squad. They've gone completely off the rails.

I squeeze the trigger, my gun kicking back against my palm. The bullets fly through the warehouse like vengeful spirits seeking retribution, cutting through the air with a purpose. Somewhere to my right, Nico releases a round of destructive strokes, his shots finding their marks with the precision of an artist. Funny, since my brother paints to escape the madness of the world in which we live.

"Marco, watch out!" His voice cuts through the gun blasts, and I swivel, catching the glint of a barrel in the dim light. My body moves on instinct, years of survival threading through my muscles. The shots ring out, a staccato against the lower hum of battle, but I dive behind a stack of crates.

Missed, *bastardo*.

The damned Four Seas are relentless, the growing numbers following their new rebel leader an ever-encroaching tide. They must be stopped.

Bodies fall, whispers turn to shouts, and the bloody dance continues. I hazard a glance over my shoulder at Nico. It's been a while since he's participated in a shootout. He's taken a backseat since his precious Maisy moved in. Now, my brother is completely pussy-whipped. I can't say I blame him, the redhead is gorgeous, but for me, variety is the spice of life.

Max crouches behind a tower of crates, discharging his weapon with deadly precision. My twin's driver was a sniper in another life. Now he prefers chauffeuring the CEO of Gemini Corporation around town than this sort of shit. But when you lead two lives, the upstanding CEO in the spotlight and the mafia boss in the dark shadows of night, the two tend to blend at the worst possible times.

Sirens wail in the distance, and the barrage of gunshots fall away as quickly as they'd started. Nico appears beside me and clasps my shoulder. "Let's get the hell out of here before the cops swarm the place. Gemini Corp cannot afford this sort of bad publicity."

"You don't have to tell me twice."

Jimmy stalks out of the shadows, his dirty-blond hair driven up in spikes. With my brother taking a backseat in the underground operation, his former right-hand man has started clinging to my side. "I lost Lei."

"Fuck," Nico grits out. "That asshole needs to be put down if we have any hope of establishing some sort of peace in Manhattan."

Smoke veils the warehouse like a shroud, bodies strewn across the concrete. Dodging lifeless forms, I follow my brother out with Max and Jimmy trailing behind us.

I grunt. "Peace, that's funny." As if the ongoing feud between the Italians and the Chinese wasn't bad enough, there were still the Russians and the Irish, and now the Puerto Ricans were making their move.

"You have to admit things have been better with the Kings since… you know." Nico pushes the metal door open with a loud squeal.

Nodding, I press my lips into a tight line. Our half-brothers, Luca and Dante Valentino run King Industries by day and the notorious Kings by night. Until a few months ago, my brother and I had dedicated our lives to ruining theirs. Then Nico fell in love, certain secrets came to light, and everything changed.

The streetlamp in the dim alleyway flickers as we quicken our pace with the howling sirens nearly upon us.

"I don't think we'll ever find peace with the Four Seas, not now that Qian's gone and Jia is in charge." *In charge*, that's laughable, really. The female heir of the Four Seas' throne wants nothing to do with her family legacy, which is exactly what has resulted in this shitshow.

"I think you're wrong, brother. You just need to be open to the possibility."

I shake my head and mutter a curse. Qian was bad enough, a fucking psycho who kept his father's head in a box after he murdered him to steal his throne. Before Qian was killed, he had tried to rope my brother into an arranged marriage with his sister, Jia. Nico had already met Maisy and was too far gone to even consider it. Ever since then, my twin doesn't let a day go by without hinting at an arrangement for me and the dark-haired Asian beauty.

I'd rather gouge my own eyes out than marry into that family, that girl.

Sure, she's hot as fuck, but tying myself to one woman for the rest of my life sounds like hell. I gave love a shot once and everything went to shit. Not to mention the extra bonus of inheriting the disastrous Four Seas... No, thank you.

There must be another way to keep the third leg of the Chinese Triad from imploding and taking down all the Lower East Side along with it. We just have to find it.

I slide into the backseat of Nico's BMW while Max and Jimmy take the front. I already know my brother's going to start in on his you-should-marry-Jia speech. I can feel it in the twitch of his jaw and the deep furrow of his brow.

"Don't start," I mutter as I shrug out of my jacket. There's a hole in the sleeve and a matching one on my shirt, along with a gash across my bicep. I hadn't even felt it in the chaos.

"Start what?" Nico eyes me in that predatorial way he has.

As identical twins, I can usually read my brother better than most. Despite the icy mask he wears, to me, he's an open book. And maybe now to Maisy too. I find that oddly unsettling. "Trying to guilt me into marrying Jia Guo."

The hint of a smile curls his upper lip. Or maybe it's a sneer.

"I've already told you, I'm not doing it."

"You're being selfish," he snaps.

"So were you a few months ago when *you* refused her." My eyes taper as I regard my brother. "If you think about it, this whole war with the Four Seas is on you."

He waggles a finger at me, tsking. "Technically, it was Dante who fired the gun that took out Qian."

"But it all came down to Maisy, didn't it? If our half-brother hadn't busted in guns blazing, you would've tortured the asshole to death anyway."

"True." He smirks.

"And, anyway, I don't see a ring on Maisy's finger yet. You could still marry Jia and end this."

"Absolutely not," Nico snarls. "I love Maisy, and I will spend the rest of my life with her. You have no one in your life."

"That's completely untrue! There's Mel, and Laney, and the girl from the club the other night—"

"Just stop." Nico's lips thin out. "And how many times do I have to tell you to stop fucking our executive assistant?"

I shrug. "But Mel does this thing with her tongue—"

He raises his hand, cutting me off. "You're only proving my point. It's time for your manwhoring days to come to an end. For the good of all."

A chuckle tumbles out. "I disagree. I don't think the girls would find it good at all."

"You better open the windows, Max, Marco's head is getting so damned big it's going to blow out the glass in the backseat."

His driver laughs, then Jimmy releases a chuckle. Assholes.

"It's not arrogance if it's true," I mumble.

"I find it hard to believe you're that memorable in bed." Nico cocks a dark brow.

"You've heard them moaning, *fratello*." My twin likes to frequently remind me of our adjoining *and thin* office walls. "We could always swap places like we used to do when we were kids and see if Maisy notices a difference." I shoot him a wicked grin. He's so obsessed with his girlfriend he'd never take me up on the offer, and I know it.

"Don't be a dick," he growls. "I'd never do that to my little fox."

"Lighten up, Nico. You're no fun anymore."

"That's because I grew up, as should you." His eyes narrow as they raze over me, and an uncharacteristic expression darkens his countenance. "What happened to Isa was a long time ago—"

I raise my hand, cutting him off as darkness creeps into my vision. "No," I growl. "Do *not* speak her name."

He heaves out a frustrated breath. "Fine, but I don't want to start a future with Maisy in the middle of a war zone, Marco. And I want a real life with her. I need to give her the happily ever after she deserves." His hand closes around my shoulder and squeezes. "So please, I'm asking you to at least *consider* my request."

Something about his tone and the dark shadows in his gaze tears at my insides. Nico has never pleaded with me for anything.

"Okay, I'll think about it."

CHAPTER 3

BLOOD OF THE DRAGON

J*ia*

My chest vibrates with the pounding of my anxious heart as I ascend the steps to the Red Dragon Restaurant. Jianjun Zhang, the leader of the Red Dragons, opened this establishment nearly a decade ago as a legitimate front for the Triad's not so legitimate dealings. Two crimson dragons glare at me when I cross between them, as if they're furious at me for forsaking my blood legacy. The ancestors will not be pleased.

Honor is everything, Jia. My father's voice rattles my already fragile nerves.

I draw in a deep breath, and the pungent scent of sweet and sour sauce and fried wontons invades my nostrils. The powerful fragrance ignites memories of the past, of·my mom hustling around our small kitchen. Despite her Philippine heritage, she'd always catered to *Bà*'s cultural and culinary preferences. The only thing she'd drilled into me—in secret, of course—was her devout Catholicism. As a child living in the

Philippines, she and her family had been visited by missionaries and had adopted their religion. She'd clung to it her entire life, instilling those values in me.

Though I'm not exactly practicing anymore, I still want to believe.

My hand wraps around the tarnished gold handle and I freeze at the door, my heartbeat a manic staccato. *You can do this, Jia.* Blood of the dragon and all that. Steadying my nerves, I twist the knob and march in with my shoulders pinned back and head held high. I am a Guo, after all. My father may have been a bastard to me behind closed doors, but in public, he treated me like a princess. And now, I was heir to the Four Seas.

A woman stands at the entrance foyer in traditional Chinese attire, a brilliant ruby silk dress with gold piping and a high collar that reaches nearly up to her chin. She dips her head and motions to the back of the restaurant. "They are waiting for you."

Great. I'm not late already, am I? I steal a quick peek at my watch. Ten o'clock on the dot. Figures the others would get here early just to intimidate me. I weave through the maze of mauve tablecloths and keep my gaze fixed on the double doors at the back. I accompanied *Bà* to a few meetings when I was younger, but I was never permitted to pass through those doors. Instead, I'd been forced to remain sitting at one of these tables with the hostess babysitting me.

How things have changed…

Stiffening my bottom lip, I push through the swinging doors and that thick, oily, fried scent invades my nostrils as I pass through the kitchen. To the left, another door is open and from the corner of my eye, I can already make out the two intimidating males sitting at the table. Jianjun Zhang and Hao Wei, the two eldest members of the Triad. Father had sat at that very table only last year.

"Jia, is that you?" A gravelly voice spurs my feet forward.

I peer into the back room and meet two pairs of piercing orbs. Even sitting, the menacing elder males' auras fill the small space. Behind them, a dozen men dressed in their respective gang's colors: red for Jianjun's Red Dragons, yellow for Hao's Golden Star, and to my surprise, a handful of navy clad Four Seas. Standing behind the chair presumably saved for me is a familiar face, one in which I have no desire to see today. Lei Wang.

Beady eyes fix on mine, and a slimy grin curls his thin lips. Lei was my brother's best friend. Since his murder, he's taken it upon himself to assume the leadership role within the Four Seas. He can have it, for all I care.

"Sit down, Jia." Jianjun ticks his head at the vacant chair to his right. "We have much to discuss today."

Drawing in a breath, I round the table and narrow my eyes at Lei until he releases his possessive hold on my chair. He may want the throne, but it isn't his—yet. I fold into the seat, every muscle in my body tense. Still, I keep a practiced smile on my face when I pivot toward the two males. "Let's get started, then. I'm quite busy myself."

The hint of a smile curves Jianjun's lips. He and *Bà* were close once, as close as one can be to a trusted enemy. "Since Qian's death," Jianjun begins, "the Four Seas have been in chaos. This cannot go on, Jia. Your father would have wanted you to assume the role of leadership, to carry on the legacy your grandfather began."

"Only, as a female, I was never born for this role, Zhang *xiānsheng*, as I'm sure you are aware."

"I am, but in the absence of a male heir, the duty falls to you."

"He is right," Hao interjects. "The time for indecision has ended. Our territories are at risk from a number of outside forces. The Italians pose a constant threat despite multiple treaties, the Puerto Ricans are moving in, and the Russians…"

He clucks his tongue. "We must stand united as a powerful Triad as we once did when your father was with us."

I open my mouth to interject, but Lei appears over my shoulder.

"If I may suggest an alternative?"

Jianjun and Hao both lift their narrowed gazes to me. I wave a nonchalant hand at the rude male peering over my shoulder. "Sure, why not?"

"It is clear that the beautiful Jia is uninterested in assuming her role, and I cannot blame her. Such nasty business is best left handled to the men." He tosses me a reassuring smile, and I barely restrain the urge to snarl at him. It isn't that I *can't* handle managing a gang of grown men because I'm a woman, it's that I have no *desire* to. But I keep my teeth clenched and allow him to continue, for now. "I offer myself to rule in her place. The Wangs have long served the Guos and Four Seas. It would be my highest honor to continue the legacy Wei Guo began decades ago."

Jianjun sneers, and Hao lifts an uninterested brow.

Apparently not dissuaded by their reactions to his suggestion, Lei continues, "At the very least, it should be voted upon at the next Triad council meeting."

"It will never be approved," Jianjun replies dryly. "Per our custom, the only way in which a new family may take over an established syndicate is by terminating the remaining bloodline." All eyes pivot to mine, and I choke down a gasp.

They aren't serious, are they?

Lei would have to kill me to assume the leadership of the Four Seas?

I wouldn't put it past the conniving male, not for an instant.

"Perhaps it's time to modernize our barbaric ways," I blurt. "Why should I be forced to rule or die?" What I really want to say is "fuck you all." But there are at least a dozen males with guns in this small room, and a shootout would be a bloodbath for all.

Jianjun scowls, his glare of disapproval reminding me too much of my father. "It is tradition, Jia, and we will uphold it."

"Then I formally request an audience with the Triad council," Lei announces.

The old male shakes his head and blows out a frustrated breath. "Fine, Lei. Your request has been noted." Then he turns to me, that frown carving deeper into his wrinkled jowl. "As heir of the Four Seas, you will be required to attend the meeting as well."

"Can't I just tell you my vote now?"

"No," Hao and Jianjun bark in unison. "We will preserve our traditions," Jianjun adds. "We will inform both of you when the meeting has been scheduled."

I can't help the dramatic eyeroll from taking over my perfectly schooled expression.

"And Jia," Jianjun snaps, "in the meantime, I expect you to exert a firmer control over the Four Seas." He shoots a pointed glare in Lei's direction. "The proliferating violence rampant across the Lower East Side must come to an end. We've lost too many lives on all sides in the past few weeks."

I nod, lips pressed into a tight line. I have no idea where I'd even start. I haven't been down to Qian's whorehouse—or rather, warehouse, since my brother's death. "I'll see what I can do." I remain seated despite every nerve ending screaming at me to bolt out of this awkward meeting.

"I suppose we'll have to postpone this discussion until the decision of leadership has been finalized." Jianjun sends another disappointed glance in my direction. Finally, once he and Hao stand, I slowly rise and dip my head.

The elders file out of the room with their respective men trailing behind. Once they're gone, I release the breath I hadn't realized I'd been holding. Well, that went well. The men of the

Four Seas remain, lingering behind me as I waver at the threshold.

Lei turns to me before I can gather my wits enough to take a step out. "You know, Jia, there is another way to get around this." He inches closer and sweeps a dark lock of hair behind his ear, calling my attention to the tattoo along his left temple and cheek: a series of Chinese symbols. Though I can understand my mother tongue, I'm a bit rusty when it comes to speaking and reading it.

"What's that?" I finally ask when he doesn't continue.

"If we were to be married, we could rule together without anyone's permission." A creepy smirk pulls at his thin lips, and nausea claws up my throat. I'd rather run away than ever allow this sniveling rat's hands on me.

My brother had already attempted to force me to marry one of the Rossi brothers to cement our reign across the Lower East Side. With the Red Dragons allied with the Valentinos, it was a calculated move, and a smart one at that. Too bad Qian died before he was able to force me into the marriage. Now with him gone, no one would compel my hand like that again.

Gritting my teeth, I grind out, "I could never impose on your kindness like that. Taking on a wife is quite a sacrifice."

"One I would be more than happy to assume." He leans closer, sidling beside me, and his hot breath lifts the hair on the back of my neck. "Think about it, Jia. I could finally accomplish what your father and brother never could: supremacy for the Four Seas. No more bowing to the Red Dragons or Golden Star, or worse yet, those barbaric Italians."

I swallow hard, maintaining the pleasant smile on my face costing every ounce of self-control I possess. Lei Wang is a loose cannon. I may not know much about the Four Seas or their operations, but even I know it's because of him Jianjun and Hao are so desperate for order to be established. My brother was a psychopath, and Lei is eager to follow in his footsteps.

"I will think on it. Thank you for the generous offer." I clench my teeth into a smile, but I'm certain it comes off more like a feral sneer.

The kitchen door swings open, and a familiar pair of dark eyes lift to mine. "*Yéye?*"

CHAPTER 4
DELICIOUS PREY

M*arco*

"Oh, fuck, yes. Harder, Marco, don't stop."

A symphony of ragged breaths and moans fills Melanie's tiny bedroom. I fist her long, blonde locks tighter and twist her head to the side so I can see her face as I plow into her from behind. She's on all fours on the bed, her skirt hiked up to her waist and panties around her ankles. My cock plunges into her pussy in a mesmerizing rhythm, in and out, in and out.

Dio, that feels good. Nothing like a good fuck to clear my head.

My executive assistant was on her way into the office, as I should have been, before I stopped her. Living with your fuck-buddy did have some benefits after all. •

"Hurry, I'm going to be late," she groans.

I bend over her and nibble on the shell of her ear. "I think you're forgetting who's the boss here, Mel." Grabbing a palm full of her ass, I knead her silky flesh before I yank my hand back and spank her flushed cheek. The crack echoes over our haggard breaths and she cries out, back arching.

"Yes, Mr. Rossi," she pants.

"That's a good girl." Gripping her hips, I sink deep inside her then quicken my thrusts to a punishing pace. She's not wrong; we are going to be late if I don't hurry up. As enjoyable as this is, I simply can't get out of my head today and the damned orgasm eludes me.

I'd hoped a quick fuck would get my mind off things, but even Mel's throbbing pussy isn't enough to clear my jumbled thoughts. Damned Nico. This is all his fault. I can't stop thinking about his request.

My brother has never asked me for a single thing our entire lives. Me, on the other hand, I've definitely been the needy one between the two of us. Despite being identical twins, Nico was technically born ten minutes before me and as a result, has taken the older brother role to heart. I always allowed him to take care of me. He enjoyed it on some level, so what was the harm?

But this ask is just too much.

He can't seriously expect me to marry this Jia girl.

"Marco..." Mel whines.

I blink quickly and realize I've stopped moving. She rubs her ass against me, sliding her wetness across my shaft and I start to thrust again. I'm so distracted my dick is starting to get soft.

"Come on, baby, I'm close." She grabs my hand and tugs it between her legs, rubbing her needy clit against my palm. "Don't you want me to come?"

"Fuck, Mel, I've got a lot on my mind." I jerk my cock out of her before I go completely limp and embarrass myself.

She lets out a groan of frustration and flops down on the bed.

"Finish yourself off," I hiss as I stuff my dick back into my boxers, then pull up my slacks.

Mel spins around and scrambles to the end of the mattress. "You're an ass, Marco."

"Maybe, but I'm also your fucking boss."

"And you're living in *my* damned apartment," she barks as she squirms into her panties and tugs down her skirt.

"Clearly, that was a mistake," I mutter before I can stop myself.

"You're right, it was. Get out." She buttons up her blouse, and bright blue eyes sear into me.

"You're joking, right?"

Her pink lips press into a tight line, and she shakes her head. "No, I'm not. I can't keep doing this. It was one thing when we were just screwing, but you've been living with me for months now, Marco. And nothing has changed. I don't want to sneak around anymore. If you want to keep doing this, then let's make it official." The hope in her eyes is worse than a kick to the balls.

Sure, I like Mel, but I don't do official. The only reason I've been living with her for the past three months is because my brother kicked me out of our penthouse when Maisy moved in. I've been too lazy to find a place of my own. A part of me kept wishing Nico would take me back, that surely this thing with Maisy wouldn't last.

Damn was I wrong.

"I'll take your silence as my answer." Mel huffs out a breath and disappears into the attached bathroom. The door slams behind her with a depressing ring of finality.

I stand there like an asshole for an incredibly long moment before my brain finally starts to function again. I scan the room while reaching for my duffle bag beside the bed, noticing my t-shirts strewn across the floor. Three months and I hadn't even unpacked. Mel offered me half her closet after the first week.

Maybe I have been a *bastardo*, leading her on all this time.

"I expect you gone by the time I'm out." Mel's voice seeps through the crack in the bathroom door.

"Right," I mumble back. It's not like we're not going to see each other in half an hour at the office. *Fuck*. Maybe Nico hadn't been completely off base with his incessant hounding about not messing around with our admin staff.

Once I shove everything back into my bag, I stagger out of her apartment and slam the door behind me.

Staring out onto Park Avenue and the sprawling skyscrapers surrounding Gemini Tower, I heave out a breath. The city moves in a frenetic pace, but I'm somehow still stuck. I spin my chair back around to face the sleek glass desk and reach for my phone once again. I've texted four of my consistent hook-ups and each one has denied me a temporary place to stay.

What the actual fuck?

The door to my office swings open and my brother darkens the entryway. His lips are pulled into a snarl, and his wavy hair looks like a storm rolled through. Fuck. Melanie must have ratted me out.

"How many times did I tell you not to fuck our assistant?" he roars.

Yup. Busted.

"Melanie is threatening to quit." He stalks toward me and slams his palms on my desk. The glass quivers beneath his weight. "We're lucky she's not threatening to sue us. And she has every right to because you couldn't keep your fucking dick in your pants."

"Relax, Nico. We just got into a little fight." I stand and meet my brother's burning glare. "She's overreacting. I'll smooth things over in a few days, and everything will be fine, I'm sure of it."

"I'm not," he growls.

"I've learned my lesson, okay? No more screwing around

with girls from the office." I hold up my hands, palms out. "I swear."

"I'll believe it when I see it." He pushes off my desk and presses his arms across his pristine jacket, nostrils flaring.

"What's going on with your housekeeper, by the way?" Anything to change the subject until he calms down.

"Still nothing. I've run countless background checks on Blanca, and she seems squeaky clean. No ties to the Puerto Ricans..."

"So you think Maisy just forgot to log off your computer that day when she found the girl hunched over your screen, and it truly was all innocent?"

His dark brows furrow as he snags his lower lip between his teeth. "I'm not sure, honestly, but I have eyes on her at all times now when she's in and out of the penthouse, so we'll find out soon enough."

"Speaking of the penthouse... I kind of need a place to crash."

Nico's eyes narrow as he regards me. "I've told you for months it was time to get your own place. You're an adult, damn it, Marco, not a teenager couch surfing. Are you really that frightened of commitment?"

I snort on a laugh. Frightened of committing to an apartment? No way. "I will, all right? I just need somewhere to stay for a few weeks so I can find a place."

"What's wrong with a hotel room?" he hisses.

"Seriously?" I growl right back.

"It's not like you have a lot of things. I still have the grand collection of your furniture and boxes in our storage."

"Fine, asshole. I'll get a damned room at the Waldorf again."

"Good." He steps closer, leaning across my desk and jabs a finger at my chest. "It's time to grow up, *fratello*. Find an apartment and get serious about your life."

"Just like you have?" I snap.

"Yes!"

"So it's true, then, love conquers all. Now everything is magically fixed in your life? You and Maisy are the perfect couple, and you're the perfect man?"

"Fuck off, Marco. Don't be jealous. It doesn't look good on you."

I drag my hand through my hair, tugging at the short tips. A part of me knows I'm being an asshole, but I'm too pissed to care. I can't believe I was actually considering my brother's request to marry the Triad princess and restore peace in the chaos of the Lower East Side . Well, fuck that. I'm not doing anything for this *coglione* anymore.

If he thinks marrying me off to this Four Seas heiress is going to fix me, he's got another thing coming. "Whatever," I finally mumble. "I have work to do—you know, like an adult." I tick my head at the door in a clear invitation for him to get the fuck out of my office.

"We'll speak more on this later."

"Right." The hell we will.

The moment after Nico walks out, I grab my jacket and head to the door. I need to get out of here and really clear my head. Maybe I'll luck out and stumble across a vacant apartment in my wanderings.

A few hours later with my earbuds stuffed in my ears playing my favorite songs, I've made it all the way down to the Meatpacking District. On the plus side, my head does feel much clearer. I can pick a damned apartment. It's not a big deal. I'm not a child. On the downside, my crisp button-down shirt is soaked in sweat. It's only June and already the heat in the city is suffocating.

Maybe I'll just look for a house in Montauk to rent for the summer, which will buy me some extra time to commit to an annual lease. *Dio*, is my brother right? Am I that afraid of commitment that I can't even choose an apartment?

I walk past a small boutique, and a head of dark, silky hair catches my eye. I stop midstride and peer through the window. A striking woman stands in the far corner dressing a mannequin. Her skin is flawless, a milky porcelain with high, proud cheekbones. A pencil is tucked between her ruby red lips, and she holds a sketch pad of some sort against her chest with her free hand.

There's something familiar about the woman. Is that...?

No, it can't be.

It's been months since the day we squared off against Qian and the Four Seas, and I caught a glimpse of Jia Guo. I do not remember her looking like *that*. Granted we were in the middle of a deadly shootout, so perhaps I just wasn't paying enough attention.

I tear my gaze away from the midnight-haired beauty to scrutinize the sign on the door. Closed. Too bad, I could use another shirt.

Movement in the back of the store pivots my gaze to an older man in a silk robe shuffling toward the woman. The pencil drops from her lips as her mouths splits into a smile. As she turns toward him, her eyes flicker to mine.

A pair of dark orbs latch onto my own, and an unfamiliar twinge tightens my ribcage. I pull out the earbuds with *Perfect* by Ed Sheeran playing in the background as I continue to stare mindlessly. Those pouty red lips purse as she regards me, a hint of recognition flashing through the starlit night I'm staring into. I stand there frozen as I memorize every detail of her perfectly sculpted face, then drift lower to her petite form, going from her proud shoulders to the long neck and the low cut of her blouse, which flows down to a tiny waist and a slight curve to her hips.

Dio, she's gorgeous.

The Chinese dragon tattooed across my chest twitches, as if coming to life at the sight of its formidable prey.

Maybe I'd been too hasty in dismissing Nico's idea, after all.

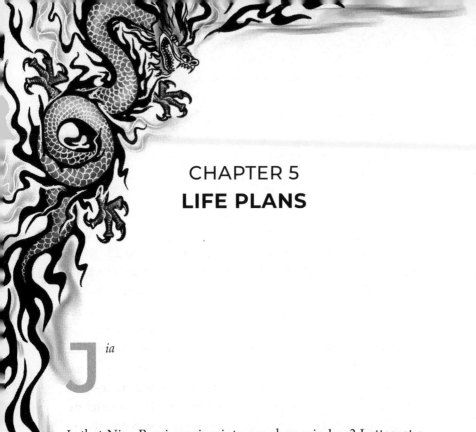

CHAPTER 5
LIFE PLANS

J*ia*

Is that Nico Rossi peering into my shop window? I attempt a casual glance from the corner of my eye so as not to alert *Yéye*. The last thing I need is my grandfather worrying about the Italian mob paying me a visit. Dark hair, sunglasses, black suit: check, check, and check. Tall, perfectly muscled, arrogant smirk: also check. My brother may have been an ass, God rest his soul, but at least he'd chosen an attractive man to sell me off to.

The last I'd heard, Rossi had found his true love, therefore reneging on my brother's brilliant, arranged marriage agreement. So why is he here now? I swivel my gaze back to *Yéye* and meet a pair of anxious dark orbs. Despite the great Wei Guo having led the Four Seas to notoriety with his infamous stoic calm, that icy mask always crumbles in my presence. Maybe it's because I am his only granddaughter and he never had daughters of his own. Three sons and he's buried each one.

A pang sears into my chest as I stare into those wizened, dark eyes and the years of conflict and struggle that wrinkled the corners. Am I being selfish by refusing to bear the burden of his legacy?

"Good morning, *bǎobèi*, are you all right?"

I glance over my shoulder and the mysterious Rossi brother is gone. My grandpa's old nickname brings a smile to my lips, despite the churning guilt. *Treasure*. My own father never referred to me as anything but daughter. He barely used my given name. Pushing back the pointless memories, I brighten my smile and nod. "Of course, *Yéye*, especially now that you're here. Though I'm still not quite sure why you came all this way."

His eyes taper at the edges as he regards me. Our mutual understanding of each other has always been a two-way street. He can read me as well as I can read him. Which means in a second, he's going to call me out on my bullshit. I'm honestly amazed he's waited this long. After he appeared at my meeting with the Triad yesterday, we'd gone for dinner, sticking only to safe subjects of conversation. Then we'd returned to my studio and my grandfather had gone straight to bed—mine, of course. I was forced to struggle through a night on the couch, which was what had ultimately brought me to the boutique early this morning.

"You know why I came, *bǎobèi*. You are many things, child, but a fool isn't one of them." He reaches for a lock of stray hair and sweeps it behind my ear. His rough thumb against my cheek is so familiar it brings an unwanted tear to my eye.

"You don't have to worry about me, grandpa. I'm fine." Or, at least, I *will be* fine. I hazard another glance through the front window, but Rossi is definitely gone. Thank the ancestors.

"Are you, though? From what Jianjun tells me, the Four Seas are in absolute disarray. The Triad will not stand for that, and you know that as well as I. You may not desire the burden of rule, but it has fallen on your shoulders, nonetheless."

I huff out a breath, those damned shoulders feeling heavier than they'd ever been.

"I don't want to frighten you, Jia, but someone will come for your throne if you do not secure it."

Jianjun's menacing words from the meeting strike up a dance in my mind. *Per our custom, the only way in which a new family may take over an established syndicate is by terminating the remaining bloodline.* I swallow hard and meet my grandfather's heavy gaze. "What do you want me to do?"

His hands close around my shoulders, the firm hold reassuring in the sea of chaos that is my mind. "As I said before, you are wise beyond your years, *bǎobèi*. I trust that you will come to the right decision. I only came to assist in the process in any way I can."

"So you left the white sand beaches of Costa Rica to navigate an international mob war with me?"

"Of course, I did, Jia. Besides, retirement can get a little boring after a while." The corners of his lips hitch, making the long silver strands of his mustache twitch. "Now, where can we go for breakfast? You have nothing edible in your apartment."

My cheeks burn, and my head immediately drops. I'm a complete failure as a traditional Chinese woman, but I know takeout like nobody's business. Grabbing my purse from the floor, I spin around and thread my arm through my grandfather's. "Come on, I'll take you for the best bagel with lox in all downtown Manhattan. My treat."

"Very well, *bǎobèi*, and while we are there, we will discuss your future."

My head dips in acquiescence, and I give my grandfather a gentle tug toward the front door. I briefly contemplate going out the back just in case any Italian mobsters are still lingering in the area. Maybe Nico Rossi came because he heard the great Wei Guo was in town. Was he here to make another deal?

With my thoughts churning, I force my feet forward. If Nico is still here, I'll have to face him sooner or later, and with my grandpa in tow, the whole encounter might be more tolerable.

I swing the door open to leave, the familiar, light tinkling of the bell overhead momentarily easing my nerves. Ari bought it a few weeks ago insisting we had to have one now that we were so close to opening CityZen. I hated to disappoint her, but with my fickle creative muse having vacated the building, we were nowhere near the grand opening. I do love that bell though.

Scanning both sides of the sidewalk, I catch no sight of Nico Rossi and proceed onto the sidewalk. I wait for the relief to set in, only it never comes. Am I that terrified of the idea of ruling the Four Seas alone that I've warmed up to the idea of an arranged marriage?

No, absolutely not.

Then again, after the encounter with the slimy Lei, the gorgeous Italian is looking less loathsome.

Grandpa nudges me in the side, drawing me from my musings. "Jia, will you tell me what thoughts are swirling in that busy mind of yours or must I guess?"

He always knows me so well.

"I suppose I'm simply considering all my options."

"Very well, as you should."

I chew on the inside of my cheek and tug on the ends of my long-sleeve blouse with my free hand, a habit that used to drive my father wild, which only made me do it more. If he insisted on marring my arms as punishment, then I would remind him every chance I got.

At this point, I can't even figure out what my realistic options are. Completely avoiding my birthright no longer seems a legitimate route. Unfortunately. I pause at the cross-walk as we wait for the light to turn red. "What do you think are the best options, *Yéye*?"

"I believe the choice is simple, child, do you wish to rule by yourself or share the burden with another?"

"I don't wish to rule at all." The traitorous words burst out before I can snap my jaw shut. Though, truth be told, it's no mind-blowing confession. My grandfather knows me well enough to have understood this all along.

"Sometimes in life we are called to assume a duty from which we take no joy."

I grunt, the completely inappropriate sound escaping my loose lips. My grandfather was born a male in the Guo family. He had the opportunity to make his own future. He wrought the beginnings of one of the most infamous Triad syndicates in the great city of Manhattan. What did he know about being forced into things?

Grandpa's long, wrinkled fingers close around my shoulder. "Jia, you may be wise for your age, but you are still *very* young. When I was twenty-three, I thought I knew everything too. It was your grandmother who reminded me every minute of every day that I knew nothing." A rueful smile curls his lips, and those dark eyes twinkle. My father used to say the only time he'd ever seen his own father smile was in the presence of his wife, and later, after she passed, only for me.

"So you think I should get married?"

My mouth must twist into a pout because his grin grows wider.

"I believe you will come to the best decision for not only yourself but also your people. It may not seem like it, but those men look up to you. Whether you like it or not, you are a Guo, and therefore you are their ruler by blood."

"Tell that to Lei Wang. He's chomping at the bit to evict me from the throne."

"That is not how I understand it. On the contrary, I heard he wishes to marry you."

A groan squeezes through my clenched lips. "He's awful, *Yéye*, just vile."

"Then I believe your choice is clear."

The light finally turns red and I step onto the crosswalk with my grandpa at my side. Right. I would just rule over a gaggle of unruly, bloodthirsty Chinese men alone? And juggle my burgeoning fashion line? It sounds like a logistical nightmare.

"Are you sure you wouldn't like to dip your toes back into the Manhattan mob scene?" I toss him a wink.

"Oh goodness, no, Jia. I've only been back to the city for one night and already I miss the tranquility of home. Over fifty years creating and leading an empire is far too long. Your *nǎinai* was right, I should have retired long ago. I would have been able to spend more time with her before she got sick…"

I tug my grandfather tighter into my side and squeeze his arm. When I was young, I believed him to be indestructible. I would see how others bowed down to him, practically kissing the floor he walked on. He mellowed over the years, but it's only now as an adult that I realize we all have our weaknesses. My grandmother was his. He walked away from everything the moment she needed him.

My father was no such hero.

"That's what I want, *Yéye*, what you and *nǎinai* had." I realize my mistake the moment the words are out. A smirk stretches beneath his wild mustache.

"And you know, treasure, that our marriage was arranged in China when we were nothing more than children."

I hiss out a breath. "Things were different back then."

"They were, and in some ways, they were much the same." He pauses and inhales a long breath, something he does to ensure he has my full attention. "I only ask that you not discount a possibility simply because it does not perfectly fit in line with your life plans. Love works in mysterious ways."

"Maybe," I mumble. I'm certain about one thing, though, love could never be mysterious enough to convince me to marry Lei Wang.

CHAPTER 6
A BET

M *arco*

A blonde head of hair zips past the elevator as I step out. I trail the tight mini skirt and translucent blouse for a long moment before mentally cursing myself. Melanie is off-limits. She is my executive assistant, and that is all. Actually, at the moment she won't even speak to me so I've been forced to tend to all my administrative matters myself.

I can't even complain to Nico about it because he'll only tell me this entire situation is my own fault. And he's not wrong. I saunter into the office and shoot a flirty smile toward Janey at the front desk before I internally chastise my complete lack of self-control. *Dio*, I just can't help myself. The young twenty-two-year-old has only worked with us for a few weeks now so I haven't had the pleasure of her company just yet.

No, not at all. *Never.* Janey is also off-limits.

Maybe if I say it enough, I'll start to believe it.

Nico is right anyway. What's that saying? Don't eat where

you shit or something? There are millions of single women in Manhattan I can fuck. There's no reason I should be limiting myself to the office. I'm doing the city's eligible bachelorettes a disservice, really.

Now, I just have to rope in my wingman.

Forgoing my office all together, I march into the next one over, my brother's. I swing the door open, and a sharp feminine gasp echoes across the room.

Oh, shit.

My brother's girlfriend is sprawled across his desk, her tits bouncing as his head bobs between her thighs, her movements against him coming to an abrupt stop.

"Mother trucker, get out!" Maisy squeals as her eyes meet mine over Nico's head.

I barely suppress a chuckle over her ridiculous curse, typical for her, and school my expression. I wish I could say this was the first time I'd caught my brother and his girlfriend in such a scandalous position, but after living with them for a few months, I'd seen it all. I'm fairly certain I'm more familiar with Maisy's body than most of the women I sleep with.

I drop my gaze, but my feet remain planted to the spot. "It's not like I haven't seen it before, Mais."

Nico's head finally pops up and he drags his girlfriend's skirt down to cover where his head had just been. He whirls at me, blue eyes dark and murderous. "Get the fuck out, *coglione*," he hisses, his chin glistening with her arousal.

I can barely hold the straight face for a minute longer. My brother is so completely whipped by this woman I almost feel sorry for him. I remember when he used to have women on their knees for him, not the other way around.

"Have you ever heard of a lock? You know you have one on your office door. For privacy..."

"Just get out, Marco."

"But I have to talk to you about something," I finally mumble.

"And it can't wait?" he snarls.

"No. I know how you two are. You'll be at it for hours." I toss him an I-swear-I'm-not-jealous smirk. "Besides, Mel needs a few more details from you, Maisy, about your charity's opening fundraiser next month."

Nico's girlfriend's eyes light up, and she practically leaps off the desk as she buttons up her top. She's so easy. There isn't anything that woman cares more about than my brother, but her new foundation for abused women comes in as a close second. And Nico being the bleeding heart that he is, has donated millions for the cause. Sometimes I wish I could just hate Maisy, but she's one of the most amazing women I've ever met. I still don't understand how Nico snared her, especially after their rather questionable start.

Maisy whizzes past me, tugging down the hem of her skirt and running her hands through her mop of wild auburn hair.

"Careful, don't trip," I call out as she passes. The woman may be beautiful but she's an accident waiting to happen.

A smack to the side of my head whirls me around to face a pair of seething sapphire orbs. "Don't be an ass," Nico hisses.

"You've got a little something over here." Smirking, I make a move to wipe at his chin, but he jumps back. "Damn, Nico, you won't even let me touch her c—"

"Don't even say the word," he snarls. "I don't want to associate anything regarding my little fox with you."

"So possessive, even of her cum." I blurt the word out before he can stop me.

Nico drags his hand through his hair, his expression lethal as he lunges for me, but I raise my hands.

"Relax, *fratello*. I'm only messing with you, damn, chill out."

"What do you want, Marco? Did you find an apartment yet?" He sounds exasperated already.

"No, not exactly. But that's kind of why I'm here."

He looses a frustrated breath and pins his arms across his

pristine jacket. Even after going down on his girlfriend, the *bastardo* still looks impeccably put together. "Speak," he grits out.

"Okay, so I'm not a dog. And I was hoping you could be my wingman for a night out on the town tonight."

His dark brows furrow as he regards me. "You're joking, right? What does that have to do with finding an apartment? And *cazzo*, that's what you interrupted me for?"

My lips quirk into a grin. "Yes. It's simple. I'll find a girl, and she'll fall hopelessly in love with me and *bam*! I've got a new place to stay for a few weeks."

"*Merda*, Marco, it's been three days, and you've already given up on finding an apartment?"

"No," I snarl. "I'm just taking a little break."

"You're completely helpless."

"I am not." Okay, I may have whined a little on that one.

Nico sits on top of his desk where his girlfriend had just been, eyes pinned to mine. "Didn't you read Jimmy's report on the Triad's activities this week?"

I shake my head. "I've been a little busy apartment hunting."

"Right." Nico grunts. "Lei Wang has formally requested a meeting with the Triad council. You know that can only mean one thing."

My thoughts flicker back to my endless walk to the Meatpacking District and those piercing dark eyes through the boutique window. "He's going to make a play for the Four Seas," I finally reply.

"That's right. That guy is ten times worse than Qian, and you know it. Having him sit at the head of the Chinese gang will be a complete shitshow." He stands again and moves closer, those eyes pleading. "We've made so much headway in the last few months since we settled the feud with the Valentinos…"

I know exactly what he's going to ask, but my answer hasn't changed. "I'm not marrying Jia, Nico."

"Why not? Have you seen her? She's stunning."

My mind swirls back to the boutique again... those fuckable ruby lips and perky breasts. My cock hardens just imagining thrusting into her wet, tight pussy. Would she be all prim and proper, or is there something lethal lingering below the pristine surface? Breaking her would be a fucking thrill.

"Marco?" Nico's voice draws me back to the conversation. He smirks at me, his gaze dropping below my belt. "I can already tell by your raging hard-on you want a taste."

"Yes, exactly, *a taste*. Why would I want to buy the cow if I can have the milk for free?"

Nico snorts on a laugh. "Something tells me the beautiful Jia wouldn't be quite that easy to coax into your bed."

"Ha! You really think so little of me?"

His eyes sparkle with mischief, and I realize I've completely walked into this one. "How about this, if you can get Jia into your bed, I promise never to bring up the arrangement again. But if you can't, you take the deal. If you think about it, it's really a win-win for you. If you marry the girl, you'll just have more time to convince her to fuck you." A wicked grin curls my asshole brother's lips.

"You're loving this, aren't you? You know I can't say no to a bet." It's a matter of pride. My body physically revolts at the idea of standing down. It's been like that since we were kids.

"Oh, I know."

A quick knock sends my brother's gaze flitting to the door. He looks to me with a droll expression. "This is how you're supposed to enter someone's office, observe." Then he turns to the door again and calls out, "Come in."

Such an ass.

A familiar face peeks through the crack in the door. "Oh, Mr. Rossi, I'm sorry, I thought Miss Maisy was here."

Nico signals for the woman to enter. "She'll be right back, Blanca, please come in."

My brother's housekeeper-slash-Broadway actress saunters in, dark curls twisted into a messy bun. The woman is undoubtedly attractive, with caramel skin, pouty red lips and darting eyes. Even the dingy housekeeper's uniform does nothing to hide those killer curves.

As I ogle the maid, I remind myself she could also be a spy for the Puerto Ricans.

Maisy rushes in a minute later, pink lip-gloss reapplied and sex hair now tamed. "Sorry for the wait, Blanca! I still need a few more minutes with Mel."

"No worries, chica." She waves a dismissive hand, then throws my brother a sheepish grin. "I'm in no rush to get back to work."

Maisy drops a quick kiss on Nico's cheek, then offers me a wave before turning to the door. Blanca follows her, the two females chattering like the best of friends.

Once the door closes, I eye my brother. "You think it's wise to let Maisy spend time with Blanca?"

"My little fox insists. Since she was the one to first catch her snooping around the penthouse, she's taken it on as her personal mission to uncover the truth." He shrugs. "I ensure Maisy's safety at all times. They're always surrounded by my guards, obviously."

"Obviously."

Nico draws closer, a dark glint in his bright blue eyes once more. "So about Jia and that bet…"

I grunt before drawing in a steadying breath to give myself a minute to consider despite my raging arrogance. Given my record, this should be a no-brainer. I can't remember the last time a woman denied me. As if my looks weren't enough— thank you Mamma and Papà—there's the Rossi name and Gemini Corp bank account. I wasn't in *The New Yorker*'s spread for most eligible bachelor this year for nothing.

"Come on, Marco, do we have a deal or not?" He extends his hand, and I eye it for another long minute.

"Just to be clear, if I get the lovely Jia Guo into my bed—no, wait, if I fuck her anywhere, you'll never bring up this arranged marriage shit again, right?"

"Right." Nico offers me that million-dollar smile we share.

"And you'll come out with me tonight?"

"Sure, why not?" He shrugs, his expression pained, like a night out on the town away from his girlfriend would be tantamount to the wickedest torture.

With a deep breath, I close my fingers around his palm. "Deal, *coglione*."

My brother's smile grows downright feral. "I can't wait to see you walking down the aisle, *fratello*. You'll make such a beautiful bride."

I shake my head. *Coglione*. "What makes you so sure you'll win this?"

"Only because before the loathsome Qian Guo was killed, he shared a tiny bit of information about his sister with me—a way of enticing our deal, let's say."

My brow lifts as a swirl of dread tightens my chest. "What's that?"

"The lovely Jia is a virgin."

CHAPTER 7
TWINS

J*ia*

"I still can't believe you made me go out tonight, Ari."

My best friend rolls her eyes as she drags me through the crowd to get to the bar. "Even your grandfather said you deserved a night out."

Well, they aren't wrong there.

The DJ's hypnotic beats float on the air of the swanky rooftop lounge. It's five o'clock on a Thursday in Midtown so the place is swarming with men in suits. Charming smiles, gel-backed hair, and Rolexes fill the glittering scene. It's not at all my style.

Give me a hip, artsy guy spouting poetry in Union Square any day.

Investment bankers, Wall Street brokers, and CEOs are much too cocky for my liking. I want a free spirit, someone who isn't afraid to break through the shackles of conformity.

Then again, I doubt I'll get much of a say at who I end up with at this point.

Ari makes it to the bar and swings her head over her shoulder, strands of short blonde hair flicking across her face. "The usual?"

"Yes, please." I squeeze between two suits to snag a small space at the bar while Ari goes after the bartender. The scent of expensive cologne and thriving portfolios is thick in the air.

The blond guy turns around, his eyes growing wide when he sees me. He's moderately good-looking, with a strong, clean-shaven jaw. "I apologize. Please, let me get out of your way." He throws me a cheesy smile, flashing perfect teeth. "Or better yet, let me buy you a drink."

"Thanks, but my friend is on it." I signal to Ari who's blatantly flirting with the bartender across the way.

"It seems like your friend is otherwise entertained. It could take a while, so please, allow me."

Lifting a bare shoulder, I nod. I'm wearing a *Jia* original tonight, one of the few pieces I'd handsewn and typically use as a sample. It has slits on the shoulders with long flowy sleeves that allow for airflow in the scorching Manhattan summer. If I was being honest, my love for clothing design stemmed from necessity. Being forced to wear long sleeves year-round severely limited my spring and summertime wardrobe choices. I created my first design at twelve with a pair of kiddie scissors, and just like that, I knew what I wanted to do with my life.

Without asking for my preference, the Suit hands me a glass of white wine a few minutes later. I take a sip and my mouth puckers. *Bleh, Chardonnay.*

"I'm Brian, and you are?" He clinks his bottle of beer against my glass.

"Jia."

"It's a pleasure." He takes my hand and rubs his thumb

across the top, flashing his gold Rolex. "And may I say, you are the most beautiful woman in this bar."

"That's very kind of you. I'm sure you say that to all the ladies." I place the glass back on the bar, the idea of stomaching another sip too revolting. I've never been a white wine girl and Chardonnay is my most hated variety.

"Jia! I got them!" Arianna appears with a drink in each fist and hands over my dirty martini.

Brian's eyes go wide as he regards my beverage of choice. *Yeah, maybe you should have asked, idiot.*

"Well, thanks for the drink, Brian." I click my martini against his beer and shoot him a smirk. "See you around." Weaving my arm through Ari's, I tug her away from the bar.

"Why didn't we stay and talk to the cute blond?" My best friend complains as I drag her through the crowd.

"Because I'm not interested in spending all evening talking to guys whose only desire is getting me into their beds. I came to have a drink, relax, and hang out with my best friend."

She tucks me into her side and squeezes. "Not that I don't love that idea, but girl, you're twenty-three, don't you think it's time to cash in that V-card?"

"Ari..."

"Okay, okay, I'll stop. It's your choice, and I fully respect your decision."

We've had this conversation at least a hundred times since we met in college. At first, choosing not to have sex was a personal one. I just hadn't found anyone I liked that much. Then, after *nanay* died, it was a way to hold onto the religion my mom loved so dearly. Waiting until marriage seemed like a small sacrifice to make after all she'd endured.

Now, with the looming prospect of an arranged marriage, maybe Arianna is right. What if I end up having to marry Lei? Bile oozes up my throat at the thought of his hands on me. Then again, that Brian guy was not a much better option.

As we weave through the lounge in search of two seats, a

dark gaze bores into me from across the rooftop. I lift my chin to meet a pair of mismatched eyes, one the darkest brown, so dark it's nearly black, and the other a vibrant sapphire. My brows knit as I take in the handsome face that comes with those mesmerizing eyes.

Nico Rossi?

His dark hair falls in wild tumbles across his brow, and a smirk curls the corners of his full lips. A sleek black jacket molds to his perfect form, and on him, the suit doesn't look quite so loathsome.

Why the hell does this guy keep popping up?

"Oh, Jia, now that guy," Ari whisper-hisses, "he would be worth giving it up to. He is totally eye-fucking you."

"No," I rasp out. "Absolutely not." I curse myself for not being completely honest with my best friend. I simply couldn't find the words to tell her my brother had been trying to force me into an arranged marriage with his enemy just to secure the Four Seas notoriety.

And now it was happening again, and I still couldn't tell her. I'd hinted at bits and pieces, but she had no idea I was a week away from becoming the leader of one of the infamous Chinese gangs of New York.

"Why not?" she whines. "Okay, you don't have to sleep with him. Just go talk. He's so freaking hot!"

As if the beautiful Italian mobster hears my friend, he stands and stalks toward us. The man moves with the grace of a panther, each step silent and deliberate, exuding an air of lethal confidence.

"O.M.G., he's coming this way, Jia."

I gulp down a long sip of my martini and heave in a breath. Nico Rossi is responsible for Qian's death. Despite the angelic smile and devilish good looks, the man is a monster. *You will remember that, Jia.* My father's voice swirls through my subconscious.

He presses closer, those enigmatic eyes pinned to mine, and

my chest heaves at the effort of drawing in a breath. What is this sorcery? I don't recall reacting this way on the brief occasions I'd met him a few months ago.

He weaves around a blonde, and the woman's eyes light up as he passes, her lips curling into an inviting smile. She whirls around after him, but he waves her off, eyes never unlocking from mine. Endless moments pass as he looms ever closer, my heart a battering ram against my ribs.

When he finally reaches us, Ari lets out an embarrassing squeal, earning a smirk from the notorious Rossi. He pauses in front of me, preening like a peacock, as I stand immobile, strangling my martini. "Finally, I have the pleasure of officially meeting the lovely Jia Guo." He reaches for my free hand and presses a kiss to the top. Soft lips caress my skin, igniting a wave of goosebumps up my arm.

Once he releases me, I find the wherewithal to process his words and actually summon some of my own. "Finally?" I blurt.

"Yes, I've heard a lot about you from my brother."

"Your brother?" I realize I sound like an idiot, but I'm so damned confused.

He ticks his head over his shoulder at the table he's just walked away from. Another dark-haired male sits beside a redhead, their foreheads pressed together as they whisper to each other.

"I'm *Marco* Rossi." That deep tenor wraps around my body, more lethal than any hands could ever be.

"Marco?"

"Yes, I'm Nico's twin brother."

For shit's sake, there's two of them?

Ari snakes between us and throws her hand out. "Twin you say? I'm Arianna Davila. Is your brother single by chance?"

Marco, *not* Nico, throws his head back and a warm laugh rumbles his broad chest. "I'm afraid not." He points to the table once again. "Unfortunately, my brother has already found his true love."

That's her, that's the woman. She's the reason Nico Rossi reneged on the original arrangement with my brother. It's all true.

"Unfortunately?" I blurt, again, positive now that I sound like an idiot.

Marco's eyes swivel to mine, a flicker of amusement playing in the shadows. "I've seen what love does to powerful men, Jia, it's not a pretty sight."

The burning embers deep in my core shrivel and then all but die with those dismal words. Thank God. I need a rush of reality. Despite that intriguing smile and the fact that he's Marco and not Nico, he's still a Rossi. Both he *and* his brother were responsible for Qian's death.

I swallow down the rest of the martini in one gulp and narrow my eyes at the grinning murderer. "Anyway, we were just leaving."

"We were?" Ari squeaks. "But why? We just got here."

"Because my grandfather is waiting for me at home."

"Your grandfather?" Marco's mouth curves into an *O* before he schools it back into that practiced smile.

Shit. I shouldn't have said that out loud. The return of my grandfather could signal something big in the underground world these men rule over.

"He just came for a visit," I add. "To mourn my brother's loss. You knew Qian, didn't you, Marco?"

He swallows hard, his Adam's apple bobbing. "Not well, unfortunately," he murmurs. "My brother handled most of the interactions between our organizations." His gaze flickers to Arianna and his mouth slants into a hard line. Smart man. "I'm sorry for your loss," he whispers a long moment later.

"Thanks." I cross my arms over my chest and turn to Arianna. "Can we please go now?"

She holds up her full drink and takes a long slurp from the straw. "I'm hurrying, I'm hurrying."

"Don't rush, Arianna," says Marco, before his eyes chase to mine. "I can take her."

"That's not happening. I'd rather grab a cab."

"But why? I have a car parked right out front." He signals down the fifty-odd stories below to Park Avenue.

I stand on my tiptoes and lean in close, so my lips nearly brush the shell of his ear. "Because I'd rather walk the sixty blocks in stilettos than sit in a car with the man responsible for my brother's death."

His eyes widen to the size of mismatched brilliant full moons. "I wasn't—it wasn't me…"

"I don't care about the specifics," I hiss. "You were there. You were involved."

"Jia…"

I spin away before his fingers can wrap around my upper arm.

"Wait for me!" Arianna shouts, but I don't stop. I can't stop, not with the tears welling in my eyes.

I just need to get out of here.

CHAPTER 8
A WHITE KNIGHT

M *arco*

"Fuck," I snarl as my traitorous eyes follow the tempting Jia through the crowd.

"Nice to meet you," Arianna calls out over her shoulder as she scampers behind her friend. "And sorry about that!"

The girl has no reason to apologize. If she wasn't in such a hurry to get away from me, I would've told her exactly that. Jia obviously hasn't let her friend in on the other life we lead. And shit, if the virgin thing wasn't hard enough to get around, there's no way she'll ever sleep with me if she holds me responsible for Qian's death.

And it's total bullshit. I wasn't even the one to pull the trigger.

Trigger. The word bounces around in my skull as my thoughts start to travel to a dark place. I squeeze my eyes closed, banishing the painful memories. I never thought about *her*. I couldn't allow myself to if I hoped to function…

I stomp back to the table where Nico and Maisy are kissing and giggling like fucking schoolgirls. So much for my wingman.

"Excuse me," I grind out.

Nico finally tears his lips off his girlfriend's and offers me a snide smile. "Well, that was a fortuitous encounter."

"Only it wasn't lucky for me at all because it only served to confirm Jia's absolute hatred." I slump down on the lounge chair and hiss out a breath. I'm never going to win this bet. "She thinks it's my fault that Qian's dead."

Nico's lips thin. "Well, that's unfortunate."

"This is all your fault," I snarl. "And thanks for the backup. Great wingman you turned out to be."

"You seemed so confident in your abilities that I didn't think you'd need wingman services."

"Oh, stop, both of you." Maisy slides to the end of the chair and straightens her blouse, then places her hand on my twin's knee. "It's not Nico's fault, Marco. If anyone is to blame, it's me. What happened to Jia's brother at the warehouse that day was because of me."

Nico's arm encircles Maisy, and he gently tucks her into his side. The move is nauseatingly sweet, as is everything with these two. "Qian caused this. There's no one to blame but that *bastardo*. Not a soul threatens my little fox and lives." He presses a kiss to Maisy's forehead and I barely restrain a groan. "Don't worry, brother, not all hope is lost. You still have three more days until the Triad council meeting to convince Jia to sleep with you." He throws me a smirk, and my fingers curl into fists to keep from choking the *coglione*. I'm so fucked.

Two days left before I lose this damned bet. I spent all day yesterday following Jia around like a stupid, lovesick puppy, trying to find an in, some way to coax her into my bed before

I'm stuck with her for life. After twelve hours of surveillance, all I'd discovered was that she spent all day in her studio poring over her design table. I still have no idea what she's drawing or why. The only plus is that I learned her caffeinated beverage of choice is a skinny latte with one pump of sugar-free vanilla. That's certainly not a sure-fire way into her pants. Fucking fantastic.

An entire day of trailing her and I hadn't even caught a glimpse of the notorious founder of the Four Seas. If Wei Guo is still in town, he's hiding out in Jia's apartment or some other Triad safehouse. With the council meeting in only two days, surely he'd remain in the city to attend. The question is what exactly are they convening to discuss?

I finally reach my destination in the Meatpacking District and slow my pace as I peer at the red-brick boutique across the street. The big windows reveal an empty shop except for the petite woman in the corner. The raven-haired beauty brings a white flower of some sort to her nose, and a smile drifts across her delicate lips. Then, she takes a sip of her skinny latte and sketches something on an easel. Maybe Nico and her would have made a decent pair after all, with their creative minds and apparent love of art. Something about that thought makes my chest tighten in a weird, terribly uncomfortable way.

I eye the quiet shop, and my brows furrow. The store is clearly closed, so why is she in there? Jerking my phone out of my pocket, I type out a quick text.

Me: *Find out who owns the property on 875 Washington Street.*

Jimmy: *Will do. You got a lead on the last heist?*

Me: *What are you talking about?*

Jimmy: *…You didn't hear about Lei's guys breaking into the Red Dragon's warehouse in the Lower East Side and stealing half of their shit?*

Fuck, of course I hadn't. I'd been too busy following

around a beautiful ghost. Jianjun Zhang isn't going to stand for this.

Me: Of course I know. But this isn't about that. Just do it ASAP.

Jimmy: Consider it done as soon as I finish up surveilling the Puerto Ricans.

Shit... what's going on with them? Maybe I have been a little too preoccupied. I'll have Nico catch me up on everything when I return to the office.

I pocket my phone as two figures appear across the street, jerking my attention away from Jia and her mysteries and all the other questions now circling my mind. The males, wearing navy from head to toe, slow as they reach Jia's boutique. They peer around the corner through the window, and the hair on the back of my neck rises.

One of the males slides his hand into his pocket and pulls out something metal that glints beneath the early morning sunlight. I squint to try to make out the details but cars zip back and forth across the road, blocking my view.

The guy throws the silver thing through the window, and the sharp crash of glass breaking sends my feet into motion without my even giving it a thought. I race across the street, the blaring of horns as I weave through traffic nothing compared to the mad thrashing of my pulse.

By the time I reach the sidewalk, smoke fills the small shop. "Jia!" I wrap my hand around the door handle and try to wrench it open, but it's locked. *Fuck.* "Jia!" I pound on the door as the dense cloud of gray consumes everything inside. "Open the door!" Eyeing the broken window, I mutter a curse as I stare at the shards of shattered glass around the opening. I'm not meant for this white knight shit, I failed at that long ago. The dark thoughts spiral once again, but somehow, I manage to keep them from sucking me under. It's not the same. Jia isn't *her*... And when you think about it, I don't owe this woman anything, really.

Still, I survived a brutal house fire when I was only a kid, and no one deserves to endure that.

Reaching into my jacket pocket, I jerk out the silk pocket square and cup it against my mouth. I use my free arm to cover my face to avoid the broken glass, kick in more glass to widen the hole and squeeze through the opening. A jagged shard slices across my side as I push through and I bite back a snarl. "Jia! Where are you?"

Moving through the murky space, I realize there are no flames, no actual fire. Only that thick, foul-smelling smoke. I scan the room, and a figure on the ground catches my eye. Shit. Bending down, I forgo the covering over my mouth and scoop Jia's motionless form into my arms, cradling her against my chest. Her eyes are closed, her breaths faint. *Fuck, not again.*

The toxic fumes sting my eyes as I scan her pale skin for a wound of some sort. "Jia?" Nothing. Holding my breath, I navigate the seemingly endless fog, dodging mannequins, and rush toward the front door. Balancing her on one arm, I blindly search for the lock. As my fingers finally close around the cold metal, I release the breath I've been holding and barrel through the door onto the sidewalk.

Sucking in a breath of fresh air, I drop down to the ground and gently lay Jia across my lap. "Come on, breathe. Breathe, damn it." Her chest refuses to rise, and a terrifying blue tint encircles her lips.

Pinching her nose, I cover her mouth with my own and blow a breath. Then another, watching for the rise of her chest with each of my breaths. The wail of an ambulance sends my heart skyrocketing up my throat.

"Jia!" A vaguely familiar old man appears around the corner, his eyes wide as they land on us.

It's Wei Guo, her grandfather; it has to be.

Jia takes a deep breath and begins to cough as he drops to his knees beside me and pulls the girl's head into his lap, murmuring in Mandarin. Her breaths become more even, the steady rise and fall of her chest oddly reassuring.

"She's going to be okay," I mutter.

The old man dips his head. "Thank you."

I nod and rise as the ambulance pulls up along the sidewalk. I need to get out of here. The last thing I need is to break down in the middle of the busy street, or worse, be involved in bad publicity for Gemini Corp. This was clearly a gang-related incident and as the co-CEO, I can't be implicated. My company has been under enough scrutiny, and the mob rumors certainly don't make it any better.

I dart down the street, but I can't keep myself from looking back as the paramedics lift Jia onto the stretcher. Her grandfather stands beside her, and even from across the block, I catch her dark lashes fluttering across porcelain skin.

Jia's okay. She's going to be just fine.

Not that I care...

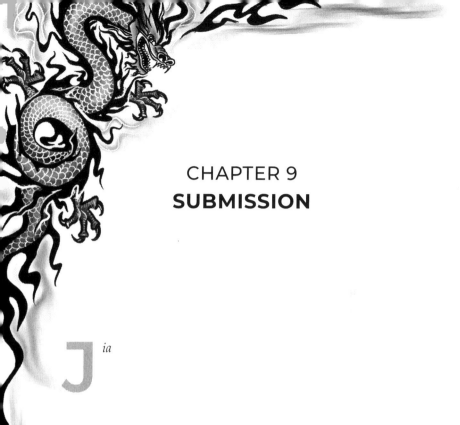

CHAPTER 9
SUBMISSION

J*ia*

The howling sirens echoing through the inside of the ambulance only intensify the pounding in my skull, but I squeeze a smile out nonetheless and lower the oxygen mask. I try to sit up straighter on the stretcher, but my lungs heave from the effort. "I'm fine, *Yéye*, I promise."

My grandfather watches me intently, the mask of calm broken and shattered into a million pieces.

A male paramedic squeezes within the tight confines of the back of the truck and checks the beeping monitor over my head before he drops his gaze to mine. "You should keep that oxygen in place for a few more minutes, at least. You inhaled a lot of that smoke."

A rebuttal perches on my lips, but I swallow it down when I see the worry in my grandfather's dark eyes. So instead, I pull the mask over my mouth once again, and take long, full breaths.

A nasty pungent scent fills my nostrils, the toxic smoke clinging to my clothes. But beneath it, a more pleasant fragrance lingers. Bergamot and cedarwood, if I'm not mistaken. *Nanay* always said I had a nose for perfumes, like a scent hound. The hint of a smile tugs at my lips at her memory before the unceasing beeping jerks me to the present, and the sweet recollection is immediately eclipsed by anger.

I'm embarrassed and pissed off more than anything. When the glass shattered in my boutique, I'd caught a glimpse of the fleeing men in navy before the space was consumed in smoke. The organization *Yéye* had created all those years ago is making a statement. If I didn't bend to Lei's will, I'd be eliminated. The message couldn't be any clearer. I should be afraid after Jianjun's menacing words about succession within the Triad, but instead, all it's done is fuel the rage.

That asshole Lei Wang thinks he can intimidate me into submission. Well, he's grossly underestimated me. Not only will I attend the Triad Council meeting, but I will also vote against his petition to rule. With *Yéye* at my side, surely I'll have the necessary votes to overrule the traitor.

And then what? My father's voice haunts the dark recesses of my mind. *You will rule by yourself?*

It's the last thing I want, but perhaps, *Yéye* is right, and there are times in life when you must take on responsibilities you don't particularly desire.

The paramedic reappears in the back of the truck, checks the monitors again and heaves out a frustrated sigh. "I still think you should be seen at the hospital before we release you."

I pull the oxygen mask down as I shake my head. "I'm fine, really."

"Your oxygen level is back to normal, so I can't force you to go, but I'd still recommend it, especially since you were unconscious." The man eyes my grandfather.

"If my granddaughter says she's fine, then she's fine."

The paramedic shrugs and begins to detach the array of wires and tubes. "If you have any shortness of breath or headaches, you should go to the emergency room right away."

"Will do." I give the man a smile as I sit up.

"And the police are waiting outside for your statement."

I groan internally as *Yéye's* wary eyes meet mine. As soon as the paramedic jumps out of the back, my grandpa barks out a command in Mandarin.

Tell them nothing.

My language skills might have been rusty, but that much I understood. Nodding, I slide off the stretcher, and *Yéye* helps me out the back. An NYPD squad car is parked behind the ambulance, and a detective leans against the hood of the vehicle.

He's a young guy, early thirties, at most, with sharp eyes and a decent smile. He steps forward and offers a hand. "Ms. Guo?"

"Yes."

"I'm Detective Jackson, and I'm going to need you to answer some questions."

"Must she do so right now?" *Yéye* grumbles. "My grand-daughter has been through a terrible ordeal."

"I understand that, and I'm sorry, but the sooner we get this over with, the more quickly we can find the men who did this."

Poor guy has no idea that that's the problem.

After we finish the grueling line of questioning and file the report with the NYPD, I'm utterly exhausted. Still, as I sit with my grandpa in my small studio sipping tea, I can't help but think back on the detective's questions and my grandfather's blatant lie.

Placing my cup down on the table, I glance up at *Yéye*. "Why did you tell the police you were in the boutique with me when it happened?"

According to the statement he gave the detective, he said

he'd walked out for a minute and returned to find me unconscious. When in reality, I'd snuck out of my apartment long
before he'd woken, and I'd been alone in the boutique at the
time of the attack. I was lucky he'd heard the commotion and
come down to save me.

His silver brows furrow, expression turning pensive.
"Because I was not the one who carried you out of the building, *bǎobèi.*"

"You didn't?" I blurt. "Then how did I get out?" The last
thing I remembered was scrambling for the door when I got
dizzy and fell.

His lips curve into an expression I can't quite decipher. "As
unbelievable as it may sound, it was Marco Rossi."

"What?" I gasp.

My grandfather nods. "I did not wish to implicate him in
the attack."

"But why? What was he doing here?"

"I do not know. I did not have time to question him before
the ambulance arrived." He pauses and sucks his lower lip
between his teeth. "It seems we owe the man a debt of grati-
tude for saving your life."

Oh, God, no. Anyone but the cocky mob boss.

Instead of voicing my thoughts, I smile and nod and bring
the teacup to my lips once again.

"You must be careful, *bǎobèi.* Two days remain until the
meeting, and it appears Lei Wang is attempting to sway your
decision."

"Clearly," I hiss.

"I assume his tactics have not done anything to soften your
heart in his direction?"

"Of course not," I snap, a little more harshly than intended.
Modifying my tone to a more respectful one, I add, "How
could I be with a man like that?"

"Perhaps, it seems ruthless to you, but to us, who have

been honed by the harsh edges of this brutal world, it shows strength."

My brows slam together, righteous indignation coursing through my veins. "So you'd have me marry Lei after he tried to kill me?"

"It's not ideal, *bǎobèi*, but at least you would not have to rule alone. It is a solitary duty to hold, Jia. I wouldn't wish it upon you."

"Anyone but him…" I murmur under my breath.

The hint of a smile twitches the corners of his mouth. "That is what I had hoped you would say." He rises, and I shoot up after him, but my head spins and I fold back down on the couch.

"Where are you going?"

"There is an important matter I must attend to." He reaches for his jacket on the hook by the door and offers a reassuring smile. "Stay here and do not open the door to anyone but me. Until the meeting on Monday, you are to remain at home. I do not trust that Lei Wang is quite finished with his wooing."

"Wooing?" I screech. "You're kidding me." God, why couldn't I have been born into a normal family?

Grandfather pulls the jacket on and turns for the exit. "Lock the door. I will be back soon."

As soon as the door closes, I slowly rise and stagger toward the entryway, bolting the lock shut. My head still hurts, and a bruise is forming above my brow. I must have hit it pretty hard when I passed out. My fuzzy thoughts float back in time, and the hint of a memory struggles to the surface. A feeling of safety. Strong arms wrapped around me, quiet whispers, and that scent. Bergamot and cedarwood.

Burying the errant thoughts to the far corners of my psyche, I stagger back to the couch and flop down. I suppose a lazy Saturday wouldn't be the worst thing in the world. I just have to survive two days. Then come Monday, I'll assume the throne of the Four Seas.

Rubbing slow circles into my temples, I try to imagine what that would mean. Gritting my teeth, I steel my resolve.

If Qian could do it, so could I.

CHAPTER 10
SOME PERKS

M *arco*

"Well done, *coglione*. I didn't think you had it in you." Nico peers into my office, darkening the doorway. My brother wears the typical smug smile we share, only where mine is a practiced mask, his boasts a well-deserved confidence.

"Had what?" I push out from behind the glass desk to cross my leg over my knee.

"The great Wei Guo of the Four Seas paid me a most interesting visit yesterday."

"Oh, did he now?" My heart lodges in my throat at the mention of his name. The legends I'd heard of the ruthless leader were completely incongruous to the worried, frail old man I'd met on the sidewalk.

"Why didn't you tell me you saved his granddaughter?" asked Nico. "He's ever so grateful, and we now find ourselves at a significant strategic advantage."

"Glad to hear it." I grab the ballpoint pen off the desk and twirl it between my fingers to keep my thoughts from the motionless Jia hung across my arms. There was something about seeing the fiery woman so helpless that I couldn't quite get out of my mind, or it was just my fucked up past rearing its ugly head. I'd spent all night unable to sleep, wondering if she was okay.

Which is very unlike me.

He steps farther inside my office and plants his ass on the black leather chair across from my desk. I barely repress a groan as my brother makes himself comfortable. "May I ask what you were doing outside Jia's boutique at just the right time?"

Her boutique? Damned Jimmy never got me the intel I'd asked for on the owner of the building. That was important info.

"Freak coincidence," I mumble.

He heaves out a breath of relief and slumps back in the chair. "Ah, so you haven't succeeded in luring her into your bed? I thought perhaps that was why you were there..."

"Nope."

A shit-eating grin splits my brother's lips, and my fingers curl into fists. "Guo confirmed it was Lei's rebel gang who attacked the girl. As such, the old man has forbidden her from leaving her apartment until he personally accompanies her to the Triad council meeting tomorrow. That's going to make things quite difficult for you to get into her panties, isn't it?"

"Fuck you, Nico. You set me up. You knew the girl was a damned virgin. Hell, you probably knew she hated us because of Qian, too. How could I possibly win this bet?"

He leans forward and slams his palms onto my desk, and the glass trembles at the impact. "You can't. Instead of going through all this rigmarole, you simply should have agreed to marry her in the first place."

"No," I growl.

"It's too late now, brother. It's going to happen whether you like it or not."

"How can you do this to me, Nico? After everything we've been through?" I drag my hand through my hair, yanking on the dark tips. Sure, Jia isn't the worst woman in the world to be forced into marrying, but *Dio*, I don't want to get fucking married. I tried love once, and it didn't work. I don't want kids, I don't want any of it.

"I'm doing this for you. For us."

I jump up and slam my own hands against the glass, meeting my brother's glare across the desk. "That's bullshit."

"This strategic alliance will serve to encourage peace across the Triad and the Italian mafia. Luca and Dante have agreed to back down as well. This is exactly what we all need."

"No, this is what *you* and those weak assholes need. The three of you have found love, started families, and now nothing else matters. Don't you dare push your fucking agenda on me. Don't pretend it's for *my* own good. This is all about Maisy, Rose, and Stella. I can't believe my own brother and even my asshole stepbrothers are all pussy-whipped." I hiss out a frustrated sigh. "It's always been you and me, Nico. What the hell happened to that?"

"I grew up, *fratello* and discovered there's so much more happiness to be had in this world. Call it what you will, but it *is* happening." He stands and turns toward the door, his foot-falls pounding a manic beat matching the tempo of my pulse.

"And if I refuse?" I call out behind him.

Nico spins around and shoots me a narrowed glare. "Then you can say goodbye to all of this." He whirls around, arms spread wide as he motions to my office.

"You can't do that. I'm the Co-CEO of Gemini Corp."

"You're right, I can't do it myself, but I sure as hell can vote you out with the help of the board. *And Melanie.*"

Fuck.

"After the stunt you pulled with her, the board would have you out on your ass so fast, your head would spin."

"*Cazzo*, Nico, you can't be serious. We built this company together from the ground up."

He nods, and something like regret flashes across my brother's blazing blue eyes. "I know. Every painstaking instant is permanently ingrained in my mind, *fratello*. Papà deserting us, the foster homes, the abuse, growing up penniless. I remember *everything*. I refuse to ever go back to that. We both deserve so much more, and trust me, this is for the greater good. For *you*."

My stomach bottoms out, hitting the soles of my Ferragamo loafers. I, too, vowed never to go back to that life long ago.

Nico pivots toward the door again, and this time, I don't stop him.

Dozens of objections swirl in my mind, but none of them are worth shit.

I stand at the glass sliding doors, my fingers pressed to the flawless, crystal pane, and stare out onto the sprawling sea of skyscrapers. The entire great room feels like a fishbowl with floor-to-ceiling windows showcasing the chaos of the city below. The Midtown penthouse is a few short blocks to Gemini Tower, and despite the exorbitant price, it's perfect.

The realtor hovers behind me, chattering on about the amenities. I already pay a boatload for my exclusive membership at Palestra, one of Manhattan's most renowned clubs, simply to rub shoulders with the island's elite. Nico had insisted I join, and I must admit, the number of deals we've struck in sweats nearly outnumber those in oppressive suits in the boardroom.

"So what do you say, Mr. Rossi?" The pretty blonde scoots

closer and cocks a perfectly plucked brow. "As I mentioned, all the furniture is included so you could move right in within the week."

I'm so distracted by the prospect of signing this lease and haunted by memories of the other night, I barely noticed how attractive she is. Her full breasts spill over the lace camisole tucked beneath her fuchsia jacket. My cock hardens as I imagine bending her over the pristine leather couch and fucking her until she screams my name. Maybe that will make the one-year lease commitment less daunting. And better still, the distraction could erase that dark-eyed gaze I couldn't get out of my head.

I slowly turn toward her and lift a mischievous brow. "You were speaking of amenities… what other perks come with this specific apartment?" If I'm going to be tying myself to one woman for the rest of my life tomorrow, I might as well get in one last carefree fuck while I'm single.

She inches closer, batting dark lashes coated in heavy mascara. "I'd be happy to go over everything again. More than happy to do anything you like, actually." She pulls her full lips into a pout. "As long as you sign on the dotted line."

I close the remaining distance between us in one long stride, and a gasp parts her pretty pink lips as I tower over her. I can already picture them wrapped around my cock as that blonde head bobs up and down my shaft. My hand juts out and wraps around her throat, thumb circling the sensitive indentation as I drag her body flush against mine. "Anything?" I growl.

She swallows hard. "Yes, Mr. Rossi."

"Good. Then get on your knees, shut the fuck up and take my dick like a good girl." A feral smile crawls across my face as she drops to the floor and her tight skirt rides higher up her thighs. I unzip my slacks, and my cock springs free.

The woman's eyes widen, a bejeweled green that sparkles beneath the abundance of light streaming in through the glass.

Her mouth curves into a capital *O* as she takes me in. I've been told I'm well-endowed...

"You think you can handle all of me, Miss Raquel?"

Her head bounces eagerly.

"Are you wet yet?"

Again, her head dips, but her eyes remain fixed on my erection.

"Good, because after I fuck your mouth, I'm going to take that pussy. Is that all right with you?"

"Yes," she purrs. "So all right."

"That's what I like to hear. Talk about a full-service real estate agent." I inch closer, and I imagine dark eyes staring up at me, instead of the green. Jia. *Fuck.* I jerk back as Raquel reaches for me, a tumble of unexpected emotions slamming into my chest.

"What's wrong, Mr. Rossi?"

"I, um, I can't do this." I shove my cock back in my pants and stagger back a few more steps. "Get off the floor," I growl.

"Did I do something to upset you?" she murmurs as she tugs her skirt down, rising.

"No. This was a mistake." I drag my hand through my hair, my heart kicking at my ribs. What the hell is wrong with me? "Send all the necessary documents to my assistant, Mel, at Gemini Corporation. I'll recommend your real estate services all the same."

"Whatever you say, Mr. Rossi." She grabs her purse, and I stalk out of the penthouse.

Nico was wrong. There are no perks to this responsible homeownership shit...

CHAPTER 11
DRAGON QUEEN

J *ia*

Inhale. Exhale. Inhale. Exhale. I stare at the potted jasmine on the windowsill and breathe in its sweet scent. My thoughts instantly travel back in time to *Nanay*. God, I wish my mom was here today; she would know exactly what to do. My heart pinches, the pang of her loss still present years later. It has been nearly a year since *Bà* passed away, and I still felt nothing.

Nanay had filled our home with happiness, much like the fragrant jasmine, and I've kept the longstanding tradition in her memory. Purity, fidelity, and hope. The jasmine—or *sampaguita*, as the locals call it—is the official flower of the Philippines, where she was born. Such a modest, simple bloom and yet, its fragrance outshines the most colorful, grandest bouquet.

The quiet shuffle of footfalls draws my attention back to the present. "Are you ready, *bǎobèi*?"

Tugging down the sheer sleeves of my ruby top, each embroidered with the silhouette of a Chinese dragon, I nod. I strategically chose the colors of my attire today, forgoing the Four Seas navy for a brilliant crimson. Blood of the dragon. I am a Guo, and today, I will take my rightful seat as head of one of the most feared syndicates in the city.

I have no idea what I'm doing, clearly, but what is that saying? Fake it till you make it.

And I will do whatever I must to avoid being forced into a marriage with the abhorrent Lei Wang or to allow him to ruin my grandfather's legacy with his band of rebels.

"*Bǎobèi?*" *Yéye* inches closer, soft lines crinkling the corners of his eyes. He looks tired, and for the first time I can remember, he actually appears his full eighty years. He wears the traditional *Tangzhuang*, a silk jacket with a Mandarin collar, frog-button closures, and embroidered intricate, gilded patterns. Unlike me, he opted for the customary navy of the Four Seas. Maybe I should change... I glance down at the dragons coiled along my forearms and slowly shake my head. No. This is the image I will portray today.

"I am ready, grandfather."

"Good." His frail fingers curl around my shoulders, and those dark eyes find mine. "You know, Jia, I am so very proud of you. You have honored our ancestors by willingly assuming your duty as blood heir. Despite what may happen today, you have fulfilled your task in every way. I would like you to remember that."

I nod, something about his words inciting another wave of trepidation.

Two quick knocks at the door send my heart into a freefall. Hiding out for two days in my studio since the attack has my nerves on edge.

Before I can take a step toward the door, *Yéye* shuffles in his cotton slippers around the brick wall to the entrance. "I will answer, child."

"Be careful," I whisper, unable to settle the unease churning in my belly. This is Lei's last chance to *woo me*, or rather, eliminate the competition before the vote. The door creaks open, and I peer around the colorful graffitied wall that separates my bedroom from the living area.

My breath catches at the sight of the broad-shouldered Italian filling the doorway. Marco Rossi's mismatched eyes sail across the living room and pin me to the spot. In a dark button-down shirt and a jacket carelessly flung over his shoulder, he looks unfairly attractive, like he just stepped out of a *GQ* spread.

"What is he doing here?" I finally hiss out, once I've gotten my tongue to cooperate.

Yéye whirls around, a serene smile on his face. "Mr. Rossi has kindly offered to escort us to the Triad council meeting today."

I eye the towering male and that prickle of unease blossoms. "Why would he do that?" And why would he be allowed at the assembly of some of his greatest enemies?

"I was concerned about you after the other day." The closest thing I've ever seen to sincerity crawls across Marco's wickedly handsome face and the effect it has on my breathing is devastating. It disappears an instant later, replaced by the typical arrogant smirk, and my lungs once again begin to function.

"That's very kind of you, but completely unnecessary. We are more than capable of making it to the council meeting on our own."

He steps inside my apartment, and the hair along my nape prickles at this invasion of privacy. Having Marco Rossi in my studio seems much too intimate. His darting gaze scans the room, lingering on the crimson dragon graffitied across the brick wall. "I disagree." He presses his lips into a thin line, smothering the smirk, then turns to *Yéye*. "As does your grandfather, which was why he agreed to my request to accompany you."

Eyeing my traitorous grandpa, my lips pucker at this rather distasteful turn of events. How could he? Does he not remember this man was directly involved in Qian's death? That the Italians are our enemies?

Grandpa clucks his tongue, a stern expression carving into his sallow cheeks. "*Bǎobèi*, it is ill manners to reject such a polite gesture."

I bite back the slew of foul gestures poised on the tip of my tongue and nod demurely. My grandfather and I may share a special relationship and unique understanding of each other, but in public, I am expected to behave like a typical, respectful granddaughter. Questioning his motives would be entirely unseemly, and yet, I can't seem to stop my thoughts from churning or spilling free.

"Of course, grandfather," I finally manage. Dipping my head, I force my feet forward and pluck my purse from the countertop.

"I like the red," Marco whispers as I pass. "It's a good color on you."

"Thanks," I hiss and stomp toward *Yéye*. Just because Marco is escorting us does not mean I have to speak to him.

When we reach the ostentatious black limousine, a driver steps out of the front seat and holds the back door open.

"Please, after you, Jia." Marco offers a cheesy smile.

"In Asian cultures, we honor our elders," I snap and whirl back toward *Yéye*. "After you, grandfather."

He passes beneath Marco's outstretched arm, a faint smile curling the mustache above his lip. He's actually enjoying this. How could my grandfather find this obnoxious man entertaining?

"How about now, spitfire?" Marco dips his head into a mocking bow once *Yéye* disappears into the back.

"Don't call me that," I snarl.

"Why not? It's a compliment. I like my women feisty."

A completely unladylike snort erupts. "I will never be *your* woman, and I could give two shits what you like."

A low whistle puckers the perfect bow of his lips. "I was right, a real spitfire, just like the dragon on your blouse." His gaze lingers along my forearms, and I quickly knot them across my chest. The material is translucent, and if one stares too closely, he could see…

"What would you know about dragons, anyway?" I blurt, drawing his eyes away from my sleeves and the humiliating secret they hide underneath.

A cheeky grin flashes across that scruffy jaw, and he tugs at the collar of his black button-down shirt, revealing the hint of a vibrant tattoo. He unfastens a button, and my eyes nearly pop out of my head.

"What are you doing?" I screech.

"Relax, spitfire, I'm only going to show you a peek. I don't give this shit away for free."

I barely restrain the eyeroll. This cocky man thinks he's God's gift to women. Still, I can't help my gaze from trailing the dark hair peeking out from beneath his shirt. Under the wild, barely trimmed jungle, the head of a dragon emerges, and not just any dragon, but one disturbingly similar to the one I painted in my studio.

"Year of the dragon," he murmurs with a grin.

"How lucky for you." I spin around and slide into the car, not waiting for the grinning bastard to rebutton his shirt or to attempt more polite conversation.

A moment later, he slips in beside me, shirt fully buttoned once more, his long legs and broad shoulders consuming nearly half the back seat.

"Perhaps you'd prefer to sit next to my grandfather." I motion across the way to where *Yéye* sits quietly watching.

Marco stretches out his legs and leans his elbow against the tinted window. "No, this is just fine." He eyes me, that piercing gaze blazing a trail from the gold cross on my neck, down over the swell of my breasts, across my silk blouse, and settling on my black slacks. I hastily cross my legs, the burn of his gaze inciting a swell of unwanted heat between my thighs.

I scoot to the opposite end of the seat, putting as much distance between us as the car allows. Thank God it's a limo so I'm not forced to be squished against the insufferable man.

A tense silence settles across the vehicle, and I suddenly realize I haven't thought about the approaching meeting or my dismal future for one second since Marco Rossi showed up at my apartment. I peek at the mob boss from the corner of my eye and settle into the supple leather headrest. At least, he is good for one thing.

But now, I have to focus. I draw in a breath and call on the inner peace I vainly search for in my frequent attempts at meditation. In a few short minutes, I'll be stepping into the dragon's den, and I must prove myself to every male in the room.

It's time for the rise of a new Dragon Queen.

CHAPTER 12
I CAN'T WAIT

M *arco*

Hmm… the innermost sanctuary of the infamous Triad. It's a hell of a lot shittier than I'd imagined. The pungent odor of garlic, fried oil and hot chili peppers pervade the dank hallways as I follow Wei Guo and his lovely granddaughter past the clamoring kitchen of the Red Dragon restaurant. Compared to our Park Avenue penthouse boardrooms, the Triad really needs to step up their game.

A door at the back of the kitchen looms open with navy-hooded males on each side. I move between Jia and her grandfather, my hand poised on my gun. If Lei tries to pull something, I'll jam a bullet between his eyes so quickly it'll make his head spin.

One of the Four Seas guys narrows his eyes at my approach. "What the fuck are you doing here, Rossi?"

He looks familiar, but I can't keep track of all these assholes. If I'm not mistaken, he's one of Lei's men. "I was invited." I shoot him a smirk and motion over my shoulder. Wei Guo trails just a step behind, having dropped back as we approached the door, and is now probably hidden by my substantial form, but that traditional Chinese attire is a dead giveaway.

The guy's head immediately drops, and he mutters something in Mandarin.

Wei barks something in return, and the sea of males parts as Jia breezes past us and through the doorway, with me, then Guo following. Well, that went better than I imagined.

A small room with flickering neon lighting coalesces, but despite the poorly lit space, I can still make out every satisfying detail of surprise on Jianjun Zhang and Hao Wei's faces. I would assume that Jianjun, as eldest, is typically the man in charge, but with the honorable Wei Guo behind me, the hierarchy has changed today.

The heads of the Red Dragons and Golden Star slowly rise, each dipping their chins to the retired leader of the Four Seas. "It is truly an honor to have you in attendance, *xiānsheng.*" Jianjun's bow is so deep I'm not certain his spindly legs will hold as he rises.

"The honor is all mine," the old man replies, staring straight at the two leaders without bowing, clearly still the most powerful on the food chain, regardless of his retired status.

"While we are most privileged to have you attend the council meeting, I must ask why Marco Rossi is here." Jianjun regards me with barely veiled animosity. The Red Dragons have managed a sort of peace with my half-brothers, the Valentinos, but that treaty obviously doesn't extend to my brother and me.

"Mr. Rossi is my guest," Guo answers. "Given the most recent incident at my granddaughter's boutique, I do not find the request out of place."

A heavy silence descends over the small space, and I take

the opportunity to scan the rest of the attendees. Lei lingers in the shadows, engulfed in a sea of navy-clad lackeys but his beady eyes lock on me, then on the woman at my side. My twitchy fingers brush the cold metal of my gun. I dare you to make a move against her again, fucker. I offered Guo to bring along Nico or even Jimmy, but he felt getting only one of us in would be difficult enough. Two would be considered an outright affront to the Triad.

"As you wish, *lǐngdǎo*." Jianjun signals to the circle of men surrounding the table, and in perfect synchronicity, each one folds into a chair. The rainbow of crimson, navy and brilliant yellow fills the dingy space, and expectant eyes lift in our direction.

Jia stands frozen beside me, and despite the show of fiery temper earlier, a barely perceptible tremor vibrates through her body. If it weren't for my arm brushing her shoulder, I never would've noticed. Her face remains a mask of calm, in spite of the inner turmoil. I don't blame the girl; I admire her really. What twenty-three-year-old woman would want this responsibility?

I barely want it at thirty, and I chose this life.

Jia is being forced into it.

If her crazy brother hadn't killed their father, and then come for us, the seat of the Four Seas throne would likely still be occupied for years to come. Fate sure is a bitch.

The scuffle of slippers draws my attention back to the present, to Wei Guo lumbering around the room toward the remaining two empty chairs. Jia doesn't move, her feet remain planted to the spot. I hazard a glance from the corner of my eye, but she seems to have gone completely comatose. My hand drifts to her lower back, and with a gentle push, I steer her around the table behind Guo.

She moves as if on autopilot, and I'm not certain she even feels the gentle pressure I'm exerting, because if she did, I'm fairly certain she would have slapped my hand away by now.

Instead, she almost leans into my touch as we scoot past the other attendees. The unexpected contact sends an unfamiliar sensation blossoming in my chest.

When we reach Jia's designated seat, I'm oddly reluctant to release her. Guo must notice my hesitation because his brows furrow as he regards my unmoving hand. He clears his throat rather forcefully, and I'm snapped from the spell the touch of her body has cast over my muddled brain.

In a lame attempt to compose myself, I pull out the chair and offer her the seat. Jia finally nods, the first sign of life I've seen since we walked into the Red Dragon restaurant.

"Now that we are all here," Jianjun begins the moment her perky ass is in the chair, "we may begin this special meeting of the Triad council." His narrowed gaze darts in my direction. "I hope I must not remind all in attendance of the sacred nature of this assembly nor of the critical importance of secrecy as to all matters discussed."

I slowly dip my head and offer a reassuring smile. I may be a *bastardo* in some respects, but I am a man of my word. Guo had already sworn me to secrecy regarding all aspects of the council meeting when we reached our agreement.

The rest of Jianjun's words blur in a mix of English and Mandarin. Most of the discussion is incredibly boring and my mind begins to wander as I stand behind Jia, my hands wrapped around the back of her chair. I'm only here for one thing after all, and my part doesn't come in until the end.

I'm shocked at how calm I feel as the head of the Golden Star drones on about an influx of overseas shipments. I expected anger, fury, or at the very least, anxiety. Instead, an inexplicable serenity has come over me as I accept my fate.

From the corner of my eye, I steal a quick glance at Jia. The pinch of her lips, the furrow of her brow, and the steady thrumming of her knee speak the complete opposite of serenity. A tiny, stupid part of me wishes there was a way to ease her anxiety. But would my news only make it worse?

Most likely.

Dipping my head to Jia's ear, I whisper, "Are you okay?" The words flow of their own accord as I lean in close.

"Fine," she grits out before shushing me.

An eternity later, Jianjun's sharp eyes pivot in our direction. "And now, the final topic of discussion, the future leadership of the Four Seas." His gaze swings toward Lei and the circle of men surrounding him. "Lei Wang has decided to challenge our most sacred tradition and requests to leave the fate of the Four Seas up to a vote. He believes he can serve as the leader the organization needs."

Lei stands, his shoulders pinned back and an arrogant sneer on his thin lips. "I would be honored and privileged to serve the Four Seas, much as the great Wei Guo had done for many decades."

The old man hisses what I'm certain is a curse in Mandarin, and the boastful peacock deflates a notch. I barely suppress a smile in Lei's direction.

"As you all know," Jianjun interjects, "we do not alter our sacred traditions on a mere whim. In order for this request to pass, Lei must garner a nearly unanimous vote of ninety percent of the attendees."

It'll never happen. There's a reason why the Triad sticks to its ancient ways.

"Now, the time has come to cast your vote." A man moves around the table and deposits a slip of paper along with a pen to each of the nine council members, Jia included, as the only living heir of the Four Seas, and Lei as the former leader's right-hand man.

The near silent scrawls fill the tense space, and a trickle of sweat slithers down my spine. An endless moment later, all the scraps of paper are collected and handed over to Jianjun. He stares at the slips, slowly thumbing through each one. His face is a blank canvas, not a twitch betraying the result.

Jia is so still I'm fairly certain she's stopped breathing. Is some part of her hoping Lei will be victorious? As awful as that would be for us, at least she wouldn't be forced to rule.

The sharp squeal of chair legs scraping across concrete jerks my head toward Jianjun as he stands. "The vote has come to an end." He turns a satisfied smile toward Lei. "Our traditions will hold true. Your request has been denied, Lei Wang, as you have failed to secure the necessary votes."

Lei's lips twist, but he manages a respectful bow. *Impressive.*

"Now, what is to become of the Four Seas?" one of the males in navy asks, clearly one of Lei's men.

Jia jolts up, her chest heaving but a defiant mask firmly in place. "I will rule the Four Seas per my birthright."

A chorus of murmurs ripples across the room.

Wei Guo stands and the calm pervading my insides suddenly vanishes. My heart kicks against my ribs in a desperate attempt to flee its skeletal binds. My lungs tighten, invisible bands lacing around my organs until I'm suffocating.

Oh shit, I can't do this.

As if the old man can feel my fear, he slants a narrowed glare in my direction and plants his hand on my forearm. His long fingers tighten around my jacket, and I'm trapped.

"My granddaughter is right." Wei Guo levels every male in the room with a biting glare. "Jia Guo is next in line to lead the great Four Seas, and I trust you will respect her as you have all the males before her. The true spirit of the dragon bleeds through her veins."

A faint smile tips up the corners of Jia's lips, and the mad chaos battering my chest slightly subsides.

"However," he continues, "it is my belief that even the strongest can be made more powerful with the appropriate ally standing by their side."

Jia's eyes grow wide, the profound midnight suddenly a bottomless abyss.

Guo jerks me forward so I'm wedged between him and Jia, the move surprisingly quick for such an old man. "There will be a new alliance forged in marriage between the Guos and the Rossies. Together, our two enterprises will work side by side to the mutual benefit of all."

Jia's mouth curves into shock as a gasp escapes that pouty mouth. Damn it, I know I'm an asshole, but all I can picture are those luscious lips wrapped around my cock. The dread surging in my gut dissipates a little more as heat streaks below my belt.

Dio, I can't wait to fuck my new wife.

CHAPTER 13
SHOCK OF BETRAYAL

J *ia*

No. No. No. This cannot be happening.

The shock of betrayal steals the air from my lungs, a sting so brazen I'm left standing there with my mouth gaping like an imbecile. I can't even summon the courage to glance over at the asshole beside me. Marco must have known.

God, how long had *Yéye* been planning this?

I attempt a glare at my grandfather, but the big Italian brute blocks my path. It takes every ounce of self-restraint I possess not to shout and curse at my traitorous grandpa. The public affront would not be tolerated in our world. But how could he do this to me? Hot tears sting my eyes, a whirlwind of fury, anger and indignation battering my insides. Why would he pretend to give me a choice, when in the end, I truly had none?

"Relax, spitfire, you don't want to cause a scene." Marco's breath sails across the shell of my ear, his shoulder brushing mine.

"Don't fucking talk to me," I hiss.

The corner of his lip curls, confirming what I suspected. He knew all along. Of course my grandfather would go behind my back and seek out a marriage arrangement with whom he considered a suitable male. How could I be so stupid to think otherwise?

"Well, this is quite a surprise." Jianjun clears his throat and motions for the rest of us to sit.

No, shit. The words nearly spill out. In my frenzy, I hadn't taken a moment to assess the expressions of disbelief painted on the faces of the circle of males around the table. The look of utter outrage carved into Lei Wang's countenance makes this almost worth it. *Almost.*

Jianjun turns his wary gaze to my grandfather who seems entirely unruffled. As if marrying off his only granddaughter to the Italian mob is a normal occurrence. God, I'm so angry. *And hurt.* I shove down the pain tightening my ribcage and focus on the rage. Anger is strength, while the hurt won't help me at all. It will simply make me weak, and now, I must be stronger than ever.

"How quickly will this arrangement take place?" Jianjun finally asks.

Hao Wei quirks an interested brow as the question hangs in the air.

Yes, how long do I have? Enough time to plan an escape?

"The details have yet to be solidified," *Yéye* replies. "But once they are, rest assured you will all be invited to the grand celebration."

Celebration? Is he completely delusional? Maybe my grandfather inhaled more of that poisonous smoke than we thought. My mind jumps back in time to the attack at CityZen. Was that why Marco had saved me? Was he simply assuring his prized wife would be around long enough to perform her duties?

"And you, Mr. Rossi," Jianjun barks. "You are prepared to take on the obligation of running yet another organization?"

Marco nods, a grin flashing perfect teeth. He wraps an arm around my shoulders, and a shudder creeps up my spine at the unexpected touch. "Rest assured I will leave most of the day-to-day responsibilities of running the Four Seas to my lovely future bride. I have more than enough on my plate with my own enterprises."

My jaw unhinges, and I pivot ever so slightly to face my fiancé for the first time since the announcement. His answer is completely unexpected.

"Still," Jianjun continues, "I would feel better about this new arrangement if we could all sit down and discuss its ramifications."

"To my knowledge, there was no such discussion when the Valentinos brokered peace with the Red Dragons," *Yéye* interjects. "Why would this be any different?"

"Because neither Luca nor Dante Valentino were handed over the reins to one of the essential legs of the Triad. They merely struck a business deal. This marriage is so much more."

I couldn't argue there.

This is *forever*.

My stomach roils, gut churning until I'm certain the measly contents of my belly are about to make a reappearance. I bolt out of my chair and race to the door before I can embarrass my entire bloodline. The pungent scent of fried oil smacks into me as I whirl around the corner and reach the kitchen, and I completely lose control of my innards.

Buckling over just a few steps past the kitchen, I heave out the toxic tangle of nerves. Bile splatters across the floor and splashes up my legs. My knees tremble as another wave of nausea pushes up the remains of my breakfast.

My hand shoots out to reach for a wall to steady myself, but a steel band laces around my waist, nearly forcing more out before a hushed whisper calms the raging storm. "I've got you, spitfire." The deep tenor is so entirely unexpected, my heart staggers.

Spitting out the foul taste in my mouth, I wipe my chin and hazard a glance over my shoulder. There's no need, really. I know exactly who I'll find. The scent of bergamot and cedarwood somehow trumps the overpowering smells of the kitchen.

Those mismatched eyes meet mine, and instead of the cocky flash I expect, something deeper lurks beyond the jeweled surface. "I've got to say I've never had that sort of effect on a woman." He smirks and that arrogant smile falls back into place.

"Let go of me," I hiss.

"You sure, spitfire? I don't want you to slip and fall into that mess." He ticks his head at the pool of vomit at our feet.

To my horror, bile is splashed across his designer black loafers. Oh God, I will never survive this day.

"Yes," I growl. "I'm perfectly capable of standing on my own."

"If you say so." His steel grip falls away and despite the tremor in my legs, I'm able to remain standing by holding onto the wall. Not my finest moment, but anything is better than leaning on the smirking bastard.

He simply stands there with his hands shoved into his pants' pockets as I attempt to put myself together. I hoped *Yéye* would come after me so I could have a minute alone with him, but the rest of the attendees remain apparently unmoving in that room. I wonder what else is being said.

"You don't have to stay here with me," I bark as I run my hand through my hair, sweeping the stray wisps behind my ears.

He shrugs. "I don't really want to go back there either."

"Why don't you just go home then?"

"Because I promised your grandfather I would get you both to and from the meeting safely."

"You really think Lei would come after me now? I couldn't imagine him ever daring to cross the great Marco Rossi..."

A glimmer of amusement sparks in those unique irises. "Listen here, spitfire, I understand that you're angry about being kept in the dark, but trust me, I'm a pawn in this just as much as you are."

I snort on a laugh. "I bet." Shaking my head, I bite down on the string of curses poised on my tongue. "You're a man. You have no idea what it's like to be a woman in this world. I had no say in this. None, whatsoever. How long have you known?"

His lips thin into a hard line.

"Just tell me, damn it."

"My brother has been trying to persuade me on the merits of this arrangement for months now."

"Months?" I squeal.

"But nothing was set in stone until a few days ago when I lost a bet with my brother—"

"What?"

He drags a hand over his face and heaves out a sigh. "It doesn't matter—"

"Like hell it doesn't. You're telling me I'm forced to marry you because of a stupid bet with your twin?"

"It's not like that, Jia. This would've happened either way. You know Qian was on the verge of a strategic alliance with Nico months ago."

"But then you killed him."

"*Cazzo*, Jia, I didn't kill him—"

I shake my head, cutting him off again. "You may not have been the one to pull the trigger, but you were there. You were all there – the Rossies, the Valentinos, you're all to blame."

A wave of heavy footfalls jerks my attention to the procession of males filing from the meeting room. *Yéye* is one of the last to exit, speaking in hushed whispers with Jianjun and Hao Wei. They pause by the door, and I count the seconds until I can lay in on my grandfather in private.

I expected this from Qian, I would've expected it from my father, but never from him. His betrayal lashes at my insides, tearing my gut into bloody ribbons.

I'm so angry and hurt I don't even notice Lei circle back. He stands before me with a circle of men behind him. "You made the wrong decision today, Jia," he grits out.

Before he can utter another syllable, a streak of darkness flashes across my eyes and by the time I blink, Lei is pinned to the wall. Marco looms over him, his thick fingers tight around Lei's throat. "And you made the wrong decision in daring to speak to my fiancée," he growls.

I gasp at the venom in his tone and the murderous glare smoldering in those piercing eyes.

Lei's men tighten the circle around Marco, but he cocks his head over his shoulder with a vicious smile. "Get any closer and I'll snap his neck before any of you idiots have time to pull out a gun."

The males murmur curses, but the half a dozen men step back.

"Now, let's get something clear right from the start, Wang," Marco snarls, flashing his teeth. "Jia is mine now, and anything you have to say to her goes through me. Do you understand?"

I'm impressed Lei isn't pissing himself beneath the intimidating glare of the enormous Italian. Instead, his already thin lips squeeze into an even thinner line.

"She's in charge of your shitty little organization now, and if you try any of this rebellious garbage, I'll personally see to it that you are punished. No one threatens my future wife and lives." His fingers tighten around Lei's throat and a choking sound erupts through the smaller man's clenched teeth. "Are. We. Clear?"

"Yes," he forces out.

Marco smacks Lei on the cheek and grins. "Good boy." Slowly releasing him, he whirls around at the circle of Four Seas rebels. "Now get the fuck out of here and behave yourselves. Jia will be in touch soon."

CHAPTER 14
HIS TROPHY

J *ia*

I can't help but stare in shock and a tiny bit of satisfaction as Lei and his men scurry off like sewer rats before the subway barrels into the station.

The subway, a.k.a. my new fiancé, hovers ominously behind me until the door of the restaurant dining room swings closed behind them. Marco turns to me, that smirk firmly carved along his chiseled jaw. "Do you think Lei will be a problem?"

I think my new fiancé is giving me way more credit than I deserve. But I sure as hell will not admit to that. I have no fucking clue what that asshole is capable of. "Most likely," I bite back. "And I'm more than capable of defending myself, by the way. I don't need you to fight my battles."

"Whatever you say, spitfire."

"And stop calling me that," I hiss.

"Then stop acting like one." He grins, and all I want to do is wipe that snide smile right off his face.

"Are you ready, *bǎobèi*?" *Yéye* pokes his head around Marco's broad shoulder.

"And you, don't you dare call me that either, you *pàntú*," I whisper. *Traitor.*

My grandfather's eyes widen as he scans the empty kitchen. I might be furious, but I'm not insane enough to speak to my grandfather that way in front of others. Marco doesn't count.

"Careful, *bǎobèi*," he murmurs.

"If I truly were your treasure, you never would have done this to me without at least asking!"

"It is exactly because I treasure you so much that I arranged this deal with Mr. Rossi."

I knot my arms across my chest. "Then we have very different opinions on the definition of the word, *Yéye.*"

"Perhaps you two can carry on this conversation in private," Marco whispers.

My grandfather dips his head. "Yes, your fiancé is right."

That word from *Yéye's* lips only ignites the fire in my veins. "How could you?" I snarl as we turn toward the double metal doors that lead to the dining room.

"It is clear that you are upset and not thinking logically. We will discuss this at home, child."

My head whips back and forth in frustration, and before I can control my tongue, I spit, "You are no longer welcome in my home."

My grandfather's silver brows twist as Marco releases an odd, strangled sound. "I'll go see where Jimmy is with the car," he mutters before stepping around us.

Yéye's gnarled fingers curl around my forearm. "I will not tolerate this disrespect, Jia. I understand that you are surprised by the turn of events, but I implore you to act appropriately. We are still in public beneath the gaze of watchful eyes."

Those unshed tears sting at the back of *my* eyes. I blink quickly to compel them back, but it's no use. "How could you, *Yéye?*" A sob sends tremors racing across my shoulders. "I trusted you implicitly. You said it was my choice."

His rough hand cradles my cheek and the tears fall faster. Oh, God, please have mercy and don't let anyone see me like this. The kitchen is still empty, and I can only hope it remains that way. This sort of outburst would be completely unseemly for the new head of the Four Seas.

"You are strong and yet so stubborn, *bǎobèi.* I fear for you as a woman. I know it is unfair, but it is the way of the world. With Marco Rossi at your side, you will be unstoppable. I'm certain of it."

I shake my head, my lip trembling. "I don't want to marry him."

"He is a good man, Jia."

A grunt escapes, and I only cry harder. "He murdered Qian."

"And Qian murdered your father, and then Marco saved your life." He heaves out a breath, his shoulders suddenly seeming frail compared to the impossibly broad ones that held me only moments ago.

Right. Of course. And Qian tried to kill Nico's girlfriend. What a fucked up, twisted world I'm now forced to navigate.

"Rossi has agreed to allow you to rule the Four Seas as you wish with minimal interference. He is wealthy, powerful, and obviously attractive. I may be an old man, but even I can see that. He will treat you well; I will see to that."

I stiffen my lower lip. I would see to that too. I'd never let another man lay a hand on me again. Or they'd suffer the same fate…

"Come, Jia, we can speak more on the ride home." Grandfather tugs me toward the door, and this time I follow after sweeping the remaining tears from my cheeks.

Jianjun Zhang and Hao Wei still linger in the dining

room. Both dip their heads at our approach, and I hope I don't look too splotchy. This meeting has been a total disaster.

"I hope you are not still unwell, Jia?" Jianjun offers a tight smile.

"Much better now, thank you. Must have been some bad lox." Lame, I know.

"I am sure your grandfather will bring you up to date on the discussion after you left. There is much to be decided now that you and Rossi will head the Four Seas."

"Jia will be the *lǎodà* of the Four Seas in keeping with Triad tradition," Grandpa interjects. "Rossi will merely exist as enforcer."

Great, so *Yéye* doesn't think I'm strong enough to control my own men. Judging by the sneer hitching up Jianjun's lip, none of them do.

"As you say." Both males dip their chins at my grandfather once again. "Please let us know if there is anything we can do to facilitate the process."

"Thank you." *Yéye* returns a faint bow and steers me toward the red door.

"And please, let us know when the wedding will be," Jianjun calls out from behind.

Oh, God, the wedding.

Another bout of nausea threatens to claw its way up my throat. I swallow hard, refusing to throw up again.

Yéye holds the front door open, and I draw in a breath of fresh air, somehow managing to keep the nausea at bay. The black limousine pulls up along the sidewalk, and my stomach cramps again.

Do not puke, Jia. As it is, you'll never live this day down. Throwing my shoulders back, I march toward the sleek limo. Before I can wrap my hand around the door handle, Marco leaps out and holds it open, hinging at the waist for my grandfather.

A pleased smile curves *Yéye's* lips, and I'm not certain I'll survive the car ride home with these two.

"I think I'll walk," I blurt.

Marco's eyes widen before his head swings back and forth. "Nope, I don't think that's a good idea, Jia."

"So, now that you're my fiancé, you're going to think for me too?"

He huffs out a frustrated breath. "We're far from your apartment, and it's not safe, not until we're married."

"Like I'll be safe then? Will the ring you put on my finger be bulletproof? Because the gold band certainly didn't protect my mother." I snap my jaw shut the moment the words are out. Why am I spilling my soul to this man? Few outside of our trusted inner circle knew that *Nanay* was killed by one of my father's enemies. He believed it made him look weak, unable to protect his own wife. He was right.

"Fine, if you insist on walking, then I'll go with you."

"No," I hiss.

All the same, Marco knocks on the front passenger window and the tinted glass slides down. "Take Mr. Guo to Jia's apartment. We'll meet you there."

"Sure, boss."

The engine revs and the limo slowly maneuvers into traffic.

"You really shouldn't have," I growl as I march toward Canal Street.

"And miss out on the opportunity for a lovely stroll with my future wife?" He tosses me a toothy grin.

"Please don't call me that," I grumble.

"You might as well get used to it."

"What about you?" I bark. "You're ready to give up your Most Eligible Bachelor status?"

"Ha, I knew it! You *have* heard of me…"

"Of course, I have. Every woman in New York City has heard of your philandering ways."

"Are you jealous?" That damned smirk grows wider.

"Ugh, no! More like revolted."

Darkness creeps across his features, and the relentless smirk falls away. "Well, you'll have to find a way to get over it, spitfire. Because like it or not, we're stuck together."

"It's not too late. You can tell Grandfather you changed your mind."

"I gave him my word, Jia."

I pick up the pace, desperate to get away from this man who isn't half as horrible as I need him to be. "But I had no say in it! Don't you understand?"

"*Dio*, you are infuriating," he growls, his hand wrapping around my arm. He jerks me to a stop and pins me in that dark gaze of his. "This is happening, Jia, and the sooner you accept it, the better for everyone."

I glare up at him, and even standing on my tiptoes, I still have to look up. But that doesn't deter me. "I won't accept it. You'll have to drag me down that aisle kicking and screaming."

"Don't tempt me, spitfire. I'll throw you over my fucking shoulder if I have to."

"Fuck you." I shoot him the middle finger and take off faster down the busy street. I must get out of this somehow. I refuse to marry this man and spend the rest of my days as his trophy.

CHAPTER 15
THE LITTLE SPITFIRE

M *arco*

Cazzo, this woman will be the death of me. I march after Jia, keeping a few yards between us. The last thing I need is for the little spitfire to start running. In the chaos of the morning commute, I could lose her—or worse, be forced to make a scene and actually throw her over my shoulder.

My stupid cock twitches at the thought.

He's deluded enough to think he has a chance with her.

I've been on my damned best behavior, but still, she wants nothing to do with me. Now, I'll be forced into a lifetime of monogamy with a woman who despises me? Fuck that. I did not sign up for this shit.

My angry footsteps eat up block after block and by the time we reach Jia's boutique, I'm fucking furious. Jimmy is stationed just up the street, the limo double-parked and blocking traffic, but I couldn't care less. "Jia, wait!" I shout as her petite hand wraps around the handle of the front door.

She spins around, her dark eyes tapered at the edges. "What?"

"We're not finished."

"Oh, yes, we are."

I step into her, pinning her against the glass door of her boutique and a faint gasp is expelled through those full ruby lips. Caging her in with my palms to the glass on either side of her head, I glare down at my future wife. Not a hint of fear flashes across those midnight orbs. Instead, she glares right back at me, her jaw clenched tight. Her lips pucker and a light sheen from the sprint across town makes her skin shimmer beneath the sun's brilliant rays. *Dio*, she's beautiful when she's pissed.

Fuck, what was I going to say?

"We're finished when I say we are," I growl, but some of the fire has already dribbled out of me. *Merda*, what is this sorcery?

"You expect me to cower at your feet, Marco Rossi?" Her chest heaves against my own, her perky breasts spilling over the low cut of her blouse. "You are nothing but a weak little lamb compared to my father. I will not bow down to you, not today and not ever." The venom in her eyes is so potent I wonder what the hell her sire did to her to inspire such hatred, because this cannot solely be about me.

"I never asked you to cower," I hiss.

"You never asked me *anything*. That's exactly the point. You powerful men are all the same, you just take and take. You think that because you carry a gun and a loaded bank account, you can get away with anything. Well, I promise you, it won't be that easy with me, Mr. Rossi."

"I have no doubt about that," I grumble, leaning back an inch so that her damn peaked nipples don't rub my chest again. My cock is already so hard it's wedged against my zipper, and it's only exacerbating my foul temper.

Jia's hand moves so fast it's a blur as she slips her slender fingers beneath my waistband and jerks out my gun.

She twirls it around her index finger, the sleek black muzzle flashing like a beacon. "Now I'm one the one with the gun, Mr. Rossi... so does that mean I have all the power? Will you get down on your knees for me?"

"Jia, put that down!"

She cocks the Glock, and I stare at her completely unbelieving. Would this crazy-ass woman really shoot me in broad daylight with Jimmy in the car ten feet away and her grandfather likely just upstairs? Not to mention the dozens of bystanders littering the streets of the Meatpacking District.

The click of a car door opening sends my heart shooting up into my throat.

"Jia, what are you doing?" Wei Guo's voice is sharper than glass.

Guess he never made it up to Jia's studio after all.

Jimmy leaps out next, his revolver pointed at Jia's head.

"No," I shout at my right-hand man. "What the fuck is wrong with you, pointing that thing at my fiancée? Put that away *now*." My tone brooks no argument, and Jimmy holsters his weapon as he stalks closer, a scowl darkening his features.

The shuffle of her grandfather's approaching footfalls only deepens the furrow of Jia's brow. "Stay back, *Yéye*," she grinds out.

The little spitfire presses the muzzle to my stomach and Jimmy hisses out a curse behind me. My abs tighten at the invasion of metal, but I don't flinch. I stopped fearing death ages ago. In fact, some days, I welcome it. The errant thought startles me. I don't often admit the grisly truth even to myself.

"I will not stay back until you give Mr. Rossi his gun," the old man calls out. "What are you thinking, child?" he barks.

Jia's lip quivers, but her eyes remain fixed to mine, lethal rage pounding through the blazing darkness. Her finger closes around the trigger.

Wei Guo steps up to us, but there's no hesitation from my new fiancée. The gun remains pressed into my gut. "Jia!" He hisses a few sentences in Mandarin, but she doesn't relent. Knowing little about Chinese culture except for their extreme respect for their elders, this appears completely out of character for the seemingly submissive granddaughter.

"I won't do this, Yéye."

"You will, bǎobèi, because you are an intelligent, mature woman, and you know that my decision is what is best for all."

She shakes her head, tears blurring the impenetrable darkness.

The old man's hand closes around the gun, and somehow, he manages to pry her finger from the trigger. Once he's done that, I reach for my weapon and rip it the rest of the way free of her grasp. I should be furious, but instead, I'm slightly impressed. And way too turned on.

Wei Guo weaves his arm around his granddaughter's slim shoulders and steers her toward the alley that leads up to her apartment. I stand there in the middle of the sidewalk in stunned silence.

"You sure about that one, boss?" Jimmy sidles closer and drags a hand through his dirty-blond locks. "It looks to me like you just agreed to let the devil into your bed."

"Don't talk about my future wife that way, coglione," I snarl. "Or you'll be the one with a muzzle in your gut."

"Shit, relax, boss, I was just messing with you."

"I'm in no mood."

"Clearly," he spits and marches back toward the limo.

Now what the fuck am I supposed to do?

My gaze trails after Guo and his granddaughter, already half-way down the alley. Technically, my duty is complete. I got them to and from the Triad meeting safe and sound. I should just go home and figure out how the hell I'm going to survive my engagement to the little spitfire with my balls still intact.

But for some goddamned reason, my heels are rooted to the ground.

Cazzo… I glance up over the windows of the boutique to the apartment above, and a shadow creeps across the glass.

What the hell?

My shoes are pounding the sidewalk before my brain has a minute to process what I just saw. I whirl around the corner, but Jia and her grandfather must have already gone inside the building.

Pumping my arms, I race down the alley and wrench the door handle. *Merda*, it's locked. "Jia! Jia, don't go inside!" I shout and pound my fists into the glass door.

Fuck this. I pull out my Glock and smash the glass with the butt of the gun. It shatters in a hundred pieces, crystal shards raining down across my loafers. *Dio*, first vomit, now glass? Just a few hours with this woman, and she's already ruined my favorite pair of Ferragamos.

I snake my hand in through the broken glass and unlock the door, then race up the steps to the fourth floor, my heart a cacophony of drumbeats vibrating my ribcage.

When I finally reach her floor, cursing the damned walk-up, I sprint down the empty hall. Shit, they've already gone inside. Am I completely losing my mind, had I imagined that shadow?

A shrill scream answers my unspoken question and my heart drives up into my throat for the second time today. Dashing across the quiet hallway, I focus on my footfalls, trying my damnedest to keep them light despite the anger compelling every step.

When I reach her door, I pause, fingers clenched around my gun. Drawing in a steadying breath, I don the icy mask I wear for battle, the one I learned at the ripe old age of ten. Life in foster care may not have been an actual war, but it sure as fuck felt like it to a kid. I swing the door open with my gun trained at eyelevel. I'm greeted by a lethal stillness.

Scanning the small studio, I level the muzzle of my gun over every exposed inch of the place. Only two possible hiding spots remain: her bedroom behind the graffitied wall or her bathroom.

A muffled gasp sends my heart dropping back into my chest and kicking at my ribs as fury pounds through my darkest depths. No one touches my future wife and lives to see the next sunrise. "Jia!" Her name pops out before I can stop it.

"Ma—"

Another shuffle and then a curse, a male voice this time. "You bitch!" The groan reaches my ears and rage thunders through my veins, drowning out the symphony of my ragged breaths and thrashing pulse. An unnamable, overpowering feeling roars through my body, piercing my soul.

I dart around the brick wall, a growl exploding through my clenched teeth at the sight.

A Four Seas asshole with a knife pressed to *my* fiancée's throat.

CHAPTER 16
A SLOW DEATH

J*ia*

"Let go of her." Marco's feral growl tears through the apartment like a thunderclap, shattering the tense silence and reminding me of the feral beast that lingers just below the surface. Perhaps I pushed my luck with him a little too far today.

And look where it got me...

I hazard a quick glance at *Yéye* unconscious on the bed, a dribble of blood streaking down his temple. The moment that bastard struck my grandfather, all worry for myself vanished. I'd been awful to him. If something happened to him before I had the chance to apologize... I swallow hard, my throat bobbing against the blade. No. I can't think that way. *Yéye* is the only family I have left. Shoving down the dismal thoughts, I tell myself my grandfather has survived much worse than this.

From the corner of my eye, I glare at the coward hiding in a hood and pressing a knife to my throat. If you're going to attack the new *lǎodà* at least have the balls to show your face. "Do it, I dare you," I snarl.

"No!" Marco's beastly roar vibrates my very being. "If you shed a single ounce of her blood, I'll exsanguinate you drop by drop, until you're writhing in excruciating pain, the mere husk of the piece of garbage you once were."

A tremor of fear ripples through the man holding me against his chest. A part of me wonders if its Lei, but it's doubtful. He'd never risk being caught. He would simply send one of his devout followers. Another chicken shit.

I already managed to knee the coward in the balls before he had a chance to draw his weapon, but now he holds me in a more precarious position. So I release a string of Mandarin curses that would have my mother blushing with shame.

Marco's dark gaze lances into mine, the storm of emotions playing across those jarring eyes stealing the remaining air from my lungs. If I didn't know better, I would think he actually cared.

But that's just silly. All I am to him is a pawn in this game played by powerful, lethal men.

He stalks closer, and my captor's arm tightens around my waist. "No closer," he hisses.

The voice sounds vaguely familiar, one that I've heard, possibly even today, but I can't quite place it.

"This is what we're going to do, *pezzo di merda*," Marco snarls, his gun trained at my assailant's head. "You're going to release her when I count to five, and I'll reward you with a quick death. Drag this out, and I swear to you, you'll be begging for a bullet to the skull."

"I can't do that."

"You scared of your boss? You think Lei is scary? You haven't seen shit, *bastardo*. I'll tear you apart limb by limb, then I'll use your bones to beat the life out of every member of your family until I exterminate your entire bloodline."

A faint gasp parts my lips at the violence in his tone, and the thrill that those words incite low in my belly.

Marco creeps closer, those eyes like lasers penetrating the shield I've fought so hard to mold and strengthen. I don't know how it's possible, but his gaze seems to be locked on both me and the bastard holding me captive at the same time. "Did Lei threaten you, force you into this?" he growls.

The soon-to-be dead man shakes his head.

"Then who?"

The male's lips press into a tight line.

"This is your last chance." Marco's hand tightens around the gun, knuckles white from restraint. "I've been more than patient considering you're holding my future wife captive, and I'm about a second from losing my shit."

Wife. Wife. Wife.

That single word pulses, a maddening tempo ricocheting across my skull.

There's something about the possessive edge to his tone that has warmth flooding my chest and sinking dangerously low beneath my belly button.

"One… two…" Marco begins the slow count, and the air in my tiny studio is suddenly so thick and oppressive it's suffocating. "Three…" His gaze is feral, like a captive wild animal intent on freedom even if it means tearing its own limb off.

Screw this.

My captor is so mesmerized by Marco's icy tone that, for an instant, he completely forgets about me. I manage to gain an inch of space and jab my elbow into his side, the most ticklish part of any human according to *Nanay*. Who knew this bit of knowledge my mom imparted would serve me so well?

The bastard flinches, the pressure on my throat increasing for a second before a shot rings out. Warm liquid spurts across my face, and the steel band around my neck falls away. The traitor crumples to the ground, a bullet wedged through the slit of his navy hood and right between his eyes. Blood dribbles down the dark material and pools beneath his head painting the floor of my bedroom a deep crimson.

I blink quickly but can't seem to tear my gaze from the gruesome sight. He deserves a coward's death for his dishonorable ways. Marco's towering form looms over me, folding around me like a blanket of shadows. I never thought I'd feel comfort in his presence, but somehow, for this one moment, I allow myself the indulgence.

"I thought you promised him a slow death…" I murmur, eyes still intent on the growing puddle of blood.

Marco's multi-colored gaze snaps to mine, the surprise in his expressive irises nearly worth the whole ordeal. "I couldn't risk it," he replies. "If I'd hit his leg and he'd managed to draw that knife across your throat—" His words fall away, darkness carving into his features. He remains perfectly still for an achingly long moment, as if he's traveled to another place, another time.

His thumb brushes my cheek, the touch surprisingly gentle and for an instant only he and I exist. "Blood," he murmurs, as I'm trapped in that hypnotic gaze.

"My grandfather," I blurt.

"Right." The glossy curtain over Marco's eyes retreats along with his hand, and the shrewd mafia enforcer is back. He jerks his phone out of his pocket and barks at the person on the other side of the line, "Get Dr. Pacetti here ASAP, Guo is injured, and I need a clean-up crew."

I fold down beside *Yéye*, worry cramping my belly. A trickle of dried blood darkens his temple, but at least it's stopped bleeding.

"What happened to him?" Marco asks.

I tick my head at the body sprawled across my floor. "That asshole hit him with the butt of his gun when we walked in. He caught us by surprise."

"Did he hit his head when he fell?"

"No, I caught him."

"Good." He slips between my knees and the dresser, my tiny bedroom dwarfed by this enormous male, and disappears into my bathroom.

I perform a quick mental check to make sure I don't have any panties or bras hanging from my shower and breathe a sigh of relief. Luckily, laundry day is tomorrow.

Marco reappears a moment later with a damp washcloth in his hands. "Do you have ice?"

"Yes, right." I jump off the bed and race to the kitchenette. God, you'd think I'd been the one hit on the head. How did I not think of ice? When I return to my makeshift bedroom a moment later, Marco leans over *Yéye*, gently wiping the dried blood off his face.

My heart pinches at the unexpected sight, and I just stand there watching for an embarrassingly long moment. Marco cocks his head over his shoulder and holds out his hand. "Ice?"

"Oh, right." I hand over the Ziploc bag, wrapped in a kitchen towel. He presses it against *Yéye's* temple where a dark bruise has already begun to form. Anger singes through my veins at the attack. I understand that they're pissed at me, but why take it out on my grandfather? "What are we going to do about this?" I snap, more harshly than intended.

Marco cants his head back. "Excuse me?"

"How are we going to retaliate?"

A wicked smirk flashes across that strong jaw. "*We*? I thought you wanted nothing to do with me, spitfire."

"I don't." I knot my arms across my chest and glare down at the infuriating man. One minute he's kind, almost human, and the next, he's that cocky dickhead again. "I just thought you'd want to defend the honor of your newest alliance."

"Mmm…" He rubs his chin, the scrape from his nails across the five-o'clock shadow echoing through the silence. "I suppose I could consider it."

"I want them to pay," I hiss.

"You're the new *lǎodà* of the Four Seas, so do it. Make an example out of Lei Wang."

"But I thought you—"

He holds up his hand, tsking. "Per the conditions of our arrangement, I'm merely the enforcer, Jia. Show those men who's in charge."

CHAPTER 17
CHAINED TO YOU

M *arco*

My foot taps out a beat on the old wooden floor, my knee bouncing so damned high I cross my leg over it to conceal the nervous tell. The doc sits with Guo and Jia in her bedroom, finishing up the last few stitches across the old man's temple. I bring the bottle of water to my mouth and gulp it down, wishing it were something stronger. My damned nerves are frazzled, and there's nothing like a good whiskey to settle the raging storm.

Fuck. I don't remember the last time I was this worked up.

The look in Jia's eye while that asshole held a knife to her throat would be permanently carved into my subconscious. *Cazzo*, I hadn't felt fear like that in ages. I may not like the woman very much, but she is mine. Mine to claim, mine to possess, and above all, mine to protect. Engaged for less than a day and already some *pezzo di merda* is trying to take her away from me?

My blood boils for retribution, for Lei Wang's head on a fucking pike. But it's essential the Four Seas learn to respect Jia as their leader, and it'll never happen if I step in guns blazing. Which is exactly what I want to do right now. I want to light up the night with flames while the stench of burned bodies fills the air, their screams echoing across China Town. No one fucks with my future wife without becoming intimately acquainted with my gun.

I glance down at my hands, at the bloodied half-moons that have appeared across my palms. Damn it. Unclenching my fists, I wipe off the trickle of crimson on my slacks. Approaching footsteps lift my gaze to Dr. Pacetti and the over-sized medical bag in his hand.

"Mr. Guo seems fine, but it's likely he suffered a concussion from the blow to the head. He should be monitored for the next forty-eight hours, and if his condition worsens, he should be immediately taken to the ER." He lifts a dark brow. "Can you do that Mr. Rossi?"

"Of course, doctor." I offer him a pleasant smile. He's been working for my brother and me for long enough to know we avoid hospitals like the plague.

"Very well, then, if you need anything, you know how to reach me." He pivots toward the door and shows himself out. His generous monthly retainer keeps him at our beck and call, and the wad of cash we shell out is more than what he makes in a year at his private practice.

Jia emerges from behind the graffitied wall in a FIT sweat-shirt and yoga pants. It's the first time I've seen her without makeup and her hair wild and loose. Casual looks good on her, despite the pinched expression. My gaze lands on the scratch across her throat and that need for revenge bubbles up like fiery, molten lava. She must notice my reaction because her fingers come to her neck, slowly drifting across the wound.

"It's nothing," she murmurs.

"Did you let the doc look at it?"

"It's just a scratch, Marco."

It could have been worse, so much worse. Pools of crimson seep into my vision, and I blink quickly before the past can threaten to pull me under.

"Are you really okay?" The question I've been meaning to ask since I put down the Four Seas bastard finally emerges.

"I already said it's nothing."

"That's not what I mean. There's more than just the physical part of the assault."

Jia waves a nonchalant hand. "It's nothing I can't deal with." A yawn parts her lips, and she claps her hand over her mouth. "I'm exhausted." She ticks her head at the tattered couch I'm sprawled across. "And you're sitting on my bed."

I scoot over and toss her one of my million-dollar trademark smiles that has women consistently falling to their knees. "I'm good with sharing."

She snorts and attempts to shoo me off, but I hold my ground. "I don't think so."

"If you think I'm leaving you unprotected after what just happened, you've got another thing coming, spitfire."

"If you're worried about my safety, just leave me your gun, and I'll be fine." She eyes my handgun, dark eyes glittering.

"Not happening."

Jia slams her hands on her hips and glares down at me. "You are not spending the night in my apartment."

"Yes, I am."

She lets out a string of curses in Mandarin and damn, it's one of the hottest things I've ever seen coming out of that prim and proper little mouth.

I stand and loom over her, doing my best impression of my brother. Of the two of us, he's definitely the more intimidating one. "You better lower your voice or you'll wake your grandfather, and I'm fairly certain he'd agree with me."

"It's not fair," she hisses, crossing her arms over her chest and stomping her foot, like a petulant child. All it does is draw my gaze to her tempting cleavage.

"Life's not fair, you might as well get used to it."

With a final scathing glare, she plops down onto the worn cushions and stretches across the narrow couch. "Well, I hope you like the floor."

Merda. "Do you have a blanket or a pillow at least?"

She tosses me a lumpy cushion off the couch, then a throw-blanket. I eye both, and my mouth twists. Maybe I'll just make some coffee instead. I doubt I'll sleep much tonight anyway. Either way, I need out of this monkey suit.

Sliding the jacket off my shoulders, I release a faint groan as my back cracks once I'm free of the oppressive material. I must have really been out of my mind if I hadn't even attempted to take it off hours ago. The crisp button-down shirt comes off next, and I heave out a sigh of relief as I stretch my arms and glance up at the industrial rafters. The studio may be tiny, but at least the high ceilings give it a less claustrophobic feel.

When I glance down again, I catch a pair of dark eyes raking over my bare chest, lingering on the masterful dragon tattooed into my skin. The hint of a smile curls my lips as Jia's gaze darts away. *Caught ya.* "Uh, uh, uh, no peeking, Jia, not until we're married."

"I was not," she hisses and rolls over, burying her head in the pillow.

I move closer, unbuckling my belt as I grow near and finally stop when my legs hit the couch. I toss my belt on the floor, and a tiny gasp escapes between the cushions. Reaching for my zipper, I draw it down ever so slowly.

Her breaths grow ragged and despite her back being toward me, I can make out the quickening tempo of her pulse by the rise and fall of her shoulder.

My slacks slough to the floor with a satisfying whoosh, and I remain rooted to the spot. The rising tension has my cock thickening, excitement rushing through my veins. If she would only turn around, she'd see exactly what sort of effect she has on me.

"Jia?" I whisper. *Turn around…come on, turn around.*

"What?" she mumbles into the pillow.

"I need your help with something."

She whirls around, and I'm so damned hard now her nose nearly bumps right into my cock. She releases a gasp and a squeal, her face twisting into an expression of pure horror, and I can't hold back the roar of laughter.

"Oh my God, you're such an ass," she hisses as she spins back around and covers her face with a pillow once again.

I buckle forward, the laughter a much-needed release after the tension of the day. Once the mad chuckles finally subside, I drop down between the couch and the coffee table, shoving it over for a little extra room. At least there's a fluffy white rug that might offer a tiny bit of padding against the hard floor.

"Must you sleep right here?" she snarls.

"No, I could sleep beside you if you weren't hogging the sofa."

"In your dreams, Rossi."

"Hopefully. I'll need something to envision while I get rid of this erection."

"You're vile!"

"You know, you could help me out. It's your fault I'm all worked up."

"Me?" She flips over to face me, her annoyance clear, and I prop myself up on my elbow to glance up at her. Her gaze trails my bare torso—there's no denying it this time—then darts to the outline of my cock. Her cheeks turn an enticing crimson before she rips her gaze away and fixes it to mine. "How is that"—she motions at my lower half—"my fault?"

"For men like me, there's a razor thin line between rage and desire. Surely, you must have noticed as the daughter and sister of two very fucked-up males."

If she's upset by my insult, she doesn't show it. A part of me is starting to believe this hatred toward Nico and me for her brother's demise is more for show than anything else.

"So killing that man earlier turned you on?" she hisses.

"Exacting my revenge turns me on, spitfire. The idea of snuffing out that *pezzo di merda* for daring to touch what's mine, that's what turns me on." I drop my gaze from those piercing eyes, down to the perfect bow of her lips, to her elegant neck and to the rest of her form where it's swallowed up by the oversized sweatshirt. I can already imagine what she looks like bare beneath…

"And I think it turned you on a little, too."

Her pupils dilate, lips curving into an *O* as she regards me. "You're wrong," she exhales, her tone laced with desire.

"Whatever you say, spitfire."

"And stop calling me that."

"Would you prefer honey? Sweetheart? Babe?"

"No," she snarls. "I'd prefer it if you didn't call me at all."

"That's going to make for a very long fifty years…"

"Fifty?" Her eyes dart back to mine.

"Well, you're in your twenties and I just turned thirty, so I figure we've got at least fifty good years of marriage—"

Her dramatic groan cuts off my calculations. "I'd rather die than be chained to you for half a century."

"Rude."

"Ugh, just go to bed, Marco."

"I'd be happy to—"

"Sleep! Just sleep."

"You're no fun at all, spitfire."

CHAPTER 18
TWO WEEKS

J*ia*

Muffled snores draw me from a deep, peaceful slumber. My head slowly rises and falls, like a boat gently rocking at sea. I pry my heavy lids open and find my nose nestled in a jungle of dark, curly hair, inches away from a gold cross.

What the heavens?

I gasp and inhale a heady dose of bergamot and cedarwood. No, no, no.

My arm is sprawled across a firm torso and a steel band is laced around my waist, holding me against the hairy Italian mobster.

How did this happen?

I try to extricate myself from his hold before he wakes and finds me curled in his arms like a fool, but even asleep his arm is like a steel trap.

"Good morning, *bǎobèi*." *Yéye* appears from around the

brick wall of my bedroom, a smirk playing on his wrinkled lips, and heat splashes across my cheeks.

"Get off me," I grumble and shove at the mass of unconscious male.

Marco's lids finally open a crack, and a devious smile crosses that unfairly handsome face.

"Morning, spitfire."

"When did you get on the couch?"

He shrugs. "At some point in the night. The floor was terribly uncomfortable."

"Well now I'm terribly uncomfortable because you took up the whole damned couch."

"You looked fairly comfortable to me, *bǎobèi*." My traitorous grandfather's eyes sparkle with mirth.

Oh, God, he must have seen me snuggling with the mob boss. *Yéye* always was an early riser. I pop up and scramble off the couch, tugging down my sweatshirt which had risen at some point in the night, showing off my navel.

"How do you feel, *Yéye*?" I finally manage once the heat of embarrassment settles.

Grandpa's fingers gingerly move across the bandage on his temple. "The headache has dissipated, and it seems the doctor did a fine job with the stitches."

"Good." I reach for his hand and give it a squeeze. I'd apologized a dozen times yesterday evening, but I will have to do it again today, now that he's fully conscious.

"I am quite hungry, though."

Oh, right. Food. I glance around to the kitchenette and find a half-naked Italian peering into my refrigerator.

"Damn, Jia, when was the last time you went grocery shopping?"

"That's exactly what I asked when I arrived," said *Yéye*.

Great, now they're teaming up on me. I huff out an exasperated breath and shoo Marco away from my fridge. "I'll just order some take out and—"

"Take out for breakfast?" Marco's eyes go comically wide. "Even I can make eggs." He weaves his arm between me and the open door and pulls out a carton of eggs. Turning it over, he squints at who knows what. "Still good for another two days."

So embarrassing.

He starts rifling through my kitchen, opening cupboards and drawers until he finds a small skillet. "Guess this will have to do."

"I'm not hungry," I grumble.

"How about you, Mr. Guo, scrambled or fried?"

Yéye shuffles closer and pulls out two plates. "Scrambled is just fine, Mr. Rossi."

What is happening right now?

My gaze darts between the two men who have ransacked my tiny kitchen. Marco moves fluidly around the cramped space as if he belongs there. How a man his size pulls it off is astonishing. He cracks the eggs, stirs, adds some salt and pepper, and pours it into the pan; all of it a graceful, elegant dance.

Maybe if I'd seen cooking orchestrated in this manner before, I would have shown more interest in developing my own talents.

Shaking my head, I hitch my thumb over my shoulder. "I'm going to take a shower. Enjoy your breakfast."

Both males offer a quick wave, and I disappear around the brick wall to the sanctuary of my bedroom. Whatever *this* was could not go on. I need to get Marco Rossi out of my apartment and out of my life. But first, I must find the traitor who sent that assassin for me yesterday and make an example of him.

Once I emerge from the shower, fully dressed, hair done and soft makeup in place, I feel slightly better. Until I walk in on my grandfather and fiancé, now thankfully dressed, sitting at the kitchen counter in the middle of a heated discussion about wedding venues.

"It must be a Catholic church," Marco snaps. "If I have to tie myself to your granddaughter for the rest of my life, it will be before the eyes of God."

I nearly choke on my spit. Despite the gold cross necklace buried in Marco's overabundant chest hair, I never imagined the ruthless killer to be a man of faith.

My grandfather turns to me, swiveling on the barstool. "Ah, there you are, *bǎobèi*, what do you think?"

I think it's too early to be having this discussion before my first cup of coffee. Ignoring the question, I reach for my favorite mug and fill it. Taking a sip of heaven in a mug, I groan from the explosion of sweet roasted coffee beans on my tongue. At least my future fiancé knows how to make a good cup of Joe.

"Jia?" *Yéye* asks again.

"I don't know," I mutter around a mouthful of liquid caffeine. "Do we really have to talk about this right now? I'd rather plan how we intend on punishing the man behind last night's attack."

"And we will," my grandfather replies, patting my hand. "But the sooner we plan the nuptials and bind our families together, the safer you will be."

I bite back the retort I'd used with Marco yesterday. My grandfather was nothing like my father. Losing *Nanay* had been difficult for him too, and I hated to bring up the dark memories.

"Mr. Rossi, do you believe we could be ready in two weeks?"

"Two weeks?" I nearly spit the coffee all over my sheer white top.

Marco's eyes widen, and for the first time since the engagement announcement, I catch a glimpse of fear in his gaze. Perhaps he is wary about this arrangement too. For some reason, it makes me feel better. "I don't know that we need to move *that* quickly..."

Yéye's eyes narrow. "Can it be done or not, Mr. Rossi?"

He clears his throat, and those darting eyes flicker to me. "If the lovely Jia agrees to the wedding ceremony at the church, I'm certain I can find a suitable venue for the reception."

"In two weeks?" His silver brows twist as he asks again.

"Yes, in two weeks." Marco's Adam's apple bobs in time with my own hard swallow. "I'll have my assistant get on it immediately."

"Wonderful." *Yéye* shuffles to the bathroom. "I'll leave you two to discuss the details."

"Two weeks?" I hiss the moment the bathroom door closes.

"Why delay the inevitable?" He shrugs and sips at what I swear is his third cup of coffee this morning.

Because if I have more time maybe I can find a way out of this arrangement.

A long moment of silence lingers between us. My thoughts are on retaliation, and I have no idea where Marco's feelings lie, but judging by the deep creases along his forehead, something is on his mind. Flower arrangements, maybe?

I nearly laugh out loud at my own mental joke before I remember I have to play nice with my fiancé, at least for the time being if I want his help. "Can I borrow your gun?" I reach for it, but he slips out of the way.

"Excuse me?" He drops the mug, and it clatters to the table.

"You said I needed to show the Four Seas who was in charge, so that's what I'm going to do."

"With one gun? By yourself?"

"What would you suggest?" I snap.

"A combined show of force, Jia. Find the men that are still

loyal to you, to your grandfather, and then challenge Lei Wang."

"How am I supposed to do that without triggering his suspicions?"

"Quietly and cautiously."

"I need to move quickly." I try to grab his gun again, but he swings his hips, deflecting.

He wags a long finger. "And if you need a gun, I'll get you your own. Do you know how to use one?"

"Of course I do." I may have played the role of the demure, obedient daughter, but *Bà* had insisted I learned to protect myself long before *Nanay* was killed.

"Fine, we'll go see my guy this afternoon, right after we move you into my hotel room."

My brows scrunch as I regard the mercurial male. "Hotel room?"

"I'm currently in between apartments. I have a week until I can move into my penthouse, so I have a suite at the Waldorf." He eyes my studio and shudders. "It's not much larger than this, but it has a pullout couch and at least I can request a roll-away bed."

"I'm not leaving my apartment because of one isolated incident." And who knows how many women he's brought to that suite? I refuse to be anywhere some simpering debutante could have been…

"Jia, with the security at the Waldorf, we'll all sleep much easier."

"I slept just fi—" I cut myself off mid-sentence before I admit to having the best night of sleep in my overprotective fiancé's arms.

"What about your grandfather? Don't you want what's best for him?" He leans against the counter and shoots me a smirk that I'm sure has all the women dropping their panties.

"Of course I do," I spit.

"There's twenty-four-hour room service. Isn't that reason enough?"

"Then take him with you, and I'll stay here." I plant my heels into the old wood floorboards. Despite all the chaos in my life, I still need to work on my designs and the grand opening of CityZen. There are still glass shards to be picked up and the pungent odor of smoke clinging to the walls. I may have been forced into this new role as head of the Four Seas, but it didn't mean I was giving up all my dreams.

"*Cazzo*, woman, why are you so stubborn?"

"I need to be near my boutique!" I shout.

Marco's dark brows knit as he attempts to process my outburst. He apparently didn't do all his research on his new fiancée.

"You know, my boutique downstairs? I'm supposed to open in a few weeks, and everything is a disaster." Ari was supposed to come help this morning, but I'd lied and told her I wasn't feeling well. The last thing I needed was my best friend finding me with the gorgeous but infuriating Italian.

Oh, God, Ari. I'd have to tell her about the engagement...

Marco drags a hand through his mess of dark locks. "How do you expect to plan a wedding, exact your revenge, and launch a new business in the same month?"

"Clearly, I hadn't expected the first two," I hiss.

He blurts out a string of Italian curses that I can barely follow. I've already learned the basics, but he throws in some new ones this time.

"Fine, spitfire," he growls. "I guess we're all going to get to know each other pretty damned well in the next week." He steps closer, dappled orbs locking to mine, and his musky scent invades my senses. "But when my penthouse is ready, we're moving in, even if your boutique isn't."

We'll see about that.

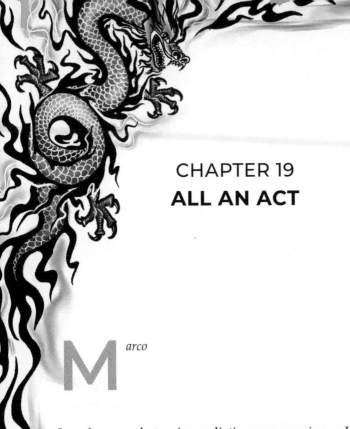

CHAPTER 19
ALL AN ACT

M *arco*

I crack my neck, tension radiating up my spine as I stare at the weekly report Jimmy just sent out. Despite having bought Jia a pullout couch with a queen-sized mattress, the stubborn woman refuses to share the bed. I'd hoped by giving her the bed like a gentleman, she would have invited me back in it. No such luck. So I've been forced to sleep on the floor for the past three days. Every muscle in my body aches, and the fog in my brain from sleepless nights just won't lift.

Heaving out a breath, I sink into the soft leather of my desk chair and scan the document on the screen. Red Dragons, Russians, *La Sombra Boricua*... The dark print blurs, and I simply can't focus. Reaching for my phone, I shoot off a quick text to my right-hand man. I don't see any of the information I'd asked for on this report; namely, who the fuck attacked my future wife?

That unfamiliar pinch in my chest returns at the grisly

image of Jia's cold, lifeless form. I blink quickly, burying the dark thoughts. I got there in time; I saved her. Not like with Isa... I slam down the wall I've fought so hard to build to keep the crushing weight of her loss from devouring me whole.

I can't let the rush of emotions free, or I'll never survive in their wake.

A sharp knock on my office door jerks my thoughts from the past, and I blink through the sharp sting in my eyes. "What?" I bark.

"It's me, boss." Jimmy's voice seeps through the door.

"Come in," I call out.

Maybe he finally has answers for me.

My colleague creeps through the open door, his footfalls silent as always. The man is a ghost, which is exactly why we hired him. He's also brutal and ruthless, but those were just added perks.

"Did you find out who sent the bastard to kill my wife yet?" I snap.

"Not exactly. But I did find out who didn't..." He slips into the chair in front of me and practically disappears into the black leather which matches his head-to-toe attire.

"What the hell does that mean?"

He flips up the bill of his dark cap so that his eyes meet mine. "I'm ninety-nine percent sure it wasn't Lei."

"How is that possible?"

"I've had eyes on him since the day he sent his guys to trash her boutique. I've questioned our inside guy, and I even snatched up one of Lei's men, and after hours of torture that would have had any man spilling his guts, he still swore they had nothing to do with it."

"Bullshit," I growl.

"I've been doing this for a long time, boss, and my gut says Lei wasn't behind this."

My fingers curl around the armrest, nails digging into the

soft leather. "I'll question him myself then." Fuck the stupid idea of letting Jia handle this on her own.

Jimmy's eyes go wide, the dishwater brown darkening. "You really think that's a good idea? I thought you were trying to keep your hands clean of this side of the business?"

"I am," I hiss, "but that woman is about to become my wife, and if I don't make it clear now, she'll be made an unnecessary target in the future. And I will fucking disembowel and mutilate anyone who lays a hand on Jia."

Jimmy's head slowly dips. "So you want me to pick up Lei Wang?"

"The sooner the better."

He slides to the end of the seat, but I stop him before he can get away. Jimmy hates coming up to the office, hates the attention it brings. He thrives in the shadows, skulking in the darkness.

"Wait a second. Can you summarize your report? I don't have the patience to read this crap. Anything I need to know?"

He shrugs, antsy to get out of my office by the way he squirms. "*La Sombra Boricua* is definitely up to something. They've been buying out properties across the Lower East Side, but no one knows why. Their operations have always been pretty bare bones. I even talked to Dante's guy about it. Apparently, the Valentinos have been surveilling the Puerto Ricans too."

Great, I detest the idea of having to reach out to my half-brothers for intel. But at least tension with them has subsided since the grand discovery that our father didn't exactly abandon us. It had been our mother who'd kept us away from him when we were kids. Which was why Nico and I aren't speaking to her at the moment.

Nico... that reminds me.

"What about my brother's housekeeper, Blanca? Anything new on her?"

He shakes his head. "We've been following her for weeks and still nothing."

"That's strange, indeed."

Jimmy releases a noncommittal grunt and heads for the door.

"Let me know as soon as you've got hands on Lei," I call out after him.

"Will do, boss."

My pace quickens as I spot the two-story brick building down the block. Though Jimmy protested my walk back from the office this evening, I wanted the time to collect my thoughts. Mel drove me crazy all day with wedding prep, despite the lingering tension between us, and that realtor I almost let suck me off on a stupid whim kept texting me to hook up. I finally had to tell her I was getting married so she'd leave me alone. At least there were some perks to this arrangement. Plus, I needed Jimmy out on the streets finding that asshole Lei Wang. Until I feel the crunch of his bones beneath mine and see his blood spattering the earth, I won't be convinced he wasn't behind Jia's attack.

From across the street, a blonde head bobs in the window, and I immediately recognize Jia's friend. Next to her, only a foot from the door stands Nicky, his broad frame eclipsing that of the petite female. He's been on Jia guard duty since the moment I left the studio this morning. My fiancée wasn't happy, but I didn't give her a choice about it. If she wanted to remain out of arm's reach, then she'd have a guard at her side at all times.

Arianna waves as I approach, tearing her gaze away from the big guard. Nicky unlocks the door and ushers me in.

"Everything good?" I ask as he bolts the door behind me.

"All quiet, boss."

"Hey, Marco…" Ari's silly grin and singsong tone confirm that Jia has let her in on our upcoming nuptials. I wonder exactly how much she's told the girl.

"Arianna." I give her a quick nod. "I appreciate you coming to help Jia with the boutique."

"Are you kidding me? This place is as much mine as it is hers." She twists her head over her shoulder and throws a glance in Jia's direction, and I follow her line of sight.

Jia's long hair is pulled into a messy bun with strands of raven hair framing her face. She's dressing a mannequin in a soft, gauzy top with long sleeves. Glancing at my fiancée's attire, it occurs to me I've never seen her in anything but long sleeves. She must have a thing for it as the style is rampant across her designs.

For the first time, I really look at the array of clothing hung from the cushioned hangers. Her style is unique, elegant but chic, with an interesting mix of fabrics and patterns. I'm not exactly a fashion connoisseur, but I'm certainly not completely clueless. She's got something rare here.

I slowly move through the sea of colorful clothing, my feet propelling me toward the woman in the back, who hasn't so much as lifted her eyes in my direction. Her lack of attention is strangely irritating. I've never met a woman who didn't want to fuck me.

I clear my throat as I grow near, but still, her eyes remain intent on the pins she's spearing into the mannequin. "You're not even going to say hi?" I finally snap.

Her gaze lifts to mine, a silver pin pressed between her full lips. And damn, I'm jealous of that fucking pin for getting to experience that mouth. "Hello," she mutters through clenched teeth.

"The shop is looking much better." I glance around the space and sniff the air. The toxic odors have all but vanished.

"Yeah, thanks for sending Nicky to help." She motions to the guard at the door, and I swirl around to catch his gaze.

Raising a brow, I shoot him a questioning glance and receive a quick shrug in return. I never instructed him to help with the clean-up job, he was only to serve as security. Knowing Jia, she probably roped him into it. A tiny smile ghosts across my lips as I imagine the little spitfire bossing the big guy around.

"Did you get a chance to select the wedding reception venue from the options Mel sent over?"

Her brow arches, and she really looks at me for the first time today. "No, I've been pretty busy." She drops her hands to her hips and narrows her eyes. "Did you confirm Lei's involvement in the attack?"

A wave of anger bubbles in my core, but I tamp down on it. "I'll have it by tomorrow," I grit out.

"Then you'll have my answer then too." She smiles sweetly, but her eyes darken.

"Jia, the venue is of the utmost importance. Even with all my considerable resources, putting on a wedding of this scale in such a short time is challenging."

"You'll have your answer when I have Lei's head."

I force a smile instead of the rebuttal poised at the tip of my tongue when I hear Arianna's dainty footsteps approaching. Good God, this woman will definitely be the death of me. Could this demure persona all be an act? Could Guo's grand-daughter be even more bloodthirsty than her brother?

"I'm working on it, sweetheart," I grumble.

She shoots me a scowl, and I can barely contain the smile. I love getting a rise out of her. "Work faster, honey," she snaps back.

"*Dio*, I can't wait to spend the rest of my life with you. It's going to be an absolute pleasure."

She snorts on a laugh. "You'll be lucky if you live past the wedding night." Flashing her teeth, she whirls around and disappears behind a wall of dresses.

CHAPTER 20
A MAN TO FEAR

J*ia*

Creeping around my own living room in a towel as I attempt to dress before *Yéye* or my infuriating new roommate wake, I grab a top and comfy yoga pants from the dresser. Marco's new apartment is supposed to be ready for us to move into the day after tomorrow which leaves me little time to work on the boutique. I'm fully aware I'm being ridiculous about refusing to move into a luxury penthouse, but I hate the idea of being supported by my fiancé. I spent enough of my life kowtowing to a man I despised simply because I was forced to live under his roof. I promised myself long ago I'd never find myself in that situation again, which is why I'm trying so hard to succeed on my own.

I step on a creaky floorboard and Marco stirs from his makeshift bed on the floor. After I refused to let him sleep on the pullout with me, he broke down and bought an air mattress. But at over six feet, the huge male swallows up the flimsy twin. His feet hang over the edge, and the mattress dips beneath his massive weight. He must be terribly uncomfortable.

A grin parts my lips.

The arrogant bastard deserves it.

With one last peek to confirm he's still asleep, I slide on my thong, drop the towel and tug my bra around my waist, keeping my back to Marco just in case. I wouldn't put anything past the conniving mob boss. Once my bra is on, I slip on the top.

"Mmm, nice ass, wifey." Marco's rough voice sends my head spinning over my shoulder.

He lifts his gaze from my bare cheeks long enough to grin up at me, eyes sparkling with amusement.

"You're an ass," I grit out as I tug the yoga pants over my thong so quickly, I lose my balance. With one foot stuck in the stretchy material, I keel over, the embarrassing moment moving in desperately slow motion.

My eyelids squeeze closed and I wait for the crack of my knees on the old floorboards, only it never comes. Instead, strong arms lace around my waist and my cheek hits a warm, bare chest.

"I got you, spitfire." Those mismatched orbs blaze down at me, and for an instant, I'm acutely aware of every point of contact: my cheek against his scruffy chest hair, his firm arms around my waist, my lower half pressed against... I jerk out of his hold as a particularly hard part of his lower anatomy jabs at my belly.

"Thanks," I murmur as I hold onto the couch's arm rest with one hand and finish pulling my pants up with the other. "But it wasn't necessary."

"So you would've rather I let you fall?"

"Yes... no." I cross my arms over my chest and stiffen my jaw. "I would just prefer you not touch me at all."

"That's going to make our wedding night rather challenging."

My heart catapults at my ribcage.

"But there's nothing I like more than a challenge." He shoots me a wink before plopping down on my couch.

With his shirt off, the exasperating male is all tanned skin and rippling abs stretched across the new sofa he forced me to buy. My traitorous gaze traces the dips and valleys of his torso before focusing on the Chinese dragon imprinted across his flesh. The riot of colors is mesmerizing, the artwork truly beautiful. It has nothing to do with the half-naked male beneath the design.

"You know," he whispers, the jagged edge to his tone drawing my attention away from his chest, "maybe we should give it a go before the big day. It could take some of the pressure off and release some tension…"

"Absolutely not," I snap and whirl around toward the kitchenette so I can put some much-needed space between myself and my future husband. I cringe at the word even in my head.

Reaching for a mug from the top cabinet, I stretch up, but a big hand beats me to it. Marco looms over me, holding my *I wear heels bigger than your d*ck* mug and grinning like an idiot. "Oh, yeah?"

"Shut up. Ari gave it to me as a joke." A huge joke since I could count the number of dicks I'd seen on one hand.

"I bet my cock is bigger."

Heat races across my cheeks as vivid memories of the sharp outline of his erection the first time he spent the night parade across my vision.

He chuckles. "And I dare say, you may agree."

"I never said that. I've never seen—" I smush my lips closed.

"Oh, I'm pretty sure you got a nice peek the other night."

I raise my hand and squeeze my eyes closed. "Just stop!" God, please just make this stop.

Marco pours the hot coffee I had the surprising presence of mind to automatically prepare last night, and I eye the enticing beverage like a starving woman. He holds the mug just out of reach, smirking like a fool.

"Give me my coffee."

"I'll give it to you for a kiss."

I snort on a laugh, the request so ridiculous I can't even hide the surprise. "What are you, fifteen?"

Marco drops the cup on the counter and whirls on me. The move is so fast I don't have a second to react. His hand curls around my neck, and he spins me so that I'm trapped against the counter. With his nose less than a centimeter from my own, his frosty breath dances across my lips.

My breath hitches, my chest rising and falling beneath his dark gaze as his fingers tighten around my throat. "Let's get something straight, spitfire. I like to joke, I enjoy the teasing, but ultimately, you are *mine*. I will have you in every way possible. If you want to wait for our wedding night, fine, but don't think for a minute because I treat you kindly and play around that I'm not a man to fear. I don't want to be that man with you, but I will be if you do not obey me. Are we clear?"

I grit my teeth, but my head bobs up and down regardless as I curse myself for not always keeping the gun I forced Marco to get me nearby. I have zero qualms about using it on my future husband. In fact, I plan to keep it under my pillow for the length of our marriage. However short-lived it may be.

"Crystal clear," I rasp. Then I reach for the mug where it now rests behind my back and toss the scalding coffee at my fiancé.

He leaps back, releasing me, and lets out a curse as the hot liquid dribbles down his bare chest. Those eyes turn murderous.

"*Bǎobèi*, is everything all right?" My grandfather shuffles around the wall that separates the bedroom from the rest of the studio.

"Just fine, *Yéye*. As it turns out, my fiancé is a bit clumsy in the morning and spilled some coffee on himself." I reach for a paper towel on the counter and dab it across Marco's chest. The erratic pounding of his heart vibrates through the thin sheet, and I dab only a few more times before making a hasty retreat toward my grandfather.

"Mr. Rossi, are you in need of any assistance?" *Yéye* watches Marco from across the small space.

"No, I'm just fine," he grits out before he storms by and disappears into the bathroom. The sharp crack of the door slamming sends my heart jumping up my throat.

"*Bǎobèi*..." My grandfather slants me a look.

"What?" I return one of pure innocence.

"Please remember how important this alliance is. I truly believe Marco Rossi is the best man for you, otherwise, I would not have entered into this agreement. It was not a decision I took lightly."

I dip my head, familiar with this tone. It brooks no argument. "Yes, *Yéye*, I understand." And I do understand, but it doesn't mean I agree.

He cocks his head to the side, and a relaxed smile curls his mustache. "How are the wedding preparations coming along?"

My shoulders slowly lift. The truth is that I have no idea. Marco and his assistant have been coordinating everything. My only task is to find a dress, which I've completely put off despite Ari's continuous pleading. I don't want some fancy princess ballgown for this sham of a wedding.

Yéye's hand closes around my shoulder. "May I accompany you to purchase your wedding dress? I understand you have yet to purchase it. And to be honest, it is a day I have long dreamed of, *bǎobèi*."

My eyes sting at the sincerity in his gaze and despite every instinct urging me to say no, my head dips, nonetheless. "Tomorrow, okay? Ari is coming in a minute to help me with the shop."

"Very well." He shuffles toward the kitchenette and picks up the mug from the floor.

Embarrassment pushes my feet forward and jerks my mouth open. "I can do that, *Yéye,* please don't bother."

"But why should you clean up the mess if it wasn't of your doing?" His knowing gaze sears into me. I've never been able to lie to my grandfather, and clearly after all these years, I'm no better at it.

"It may have possibly been a little bit my fault." I drop down to the floor with a handful of paper towels and clean up the puddle of dark brown liquid.

Grandpa's soft chuckle forces my gaze to lift. "Marrying a man does not mean putting aside who you are, child. And a real man would never expect that of you. You are strong—a bit too headstrong for your own good—but you are wise beyond your years, and anyone who doesn't see how incredible you are, is surely blind." He offers his hand, and I take it with my free one before he pulls me up off the floor. "Marriage is the delicate balance of two people who may not always see eye to eye but walk hand in hand."

The problems between Marco and I are far more complicated than simply not being able to see eye to eye, but I keep that thought to myself. Instead, I nod like the obedient granddaughter while secretly plotting my fiancé's demise.

Perhaps I'm looking at this all wrong. Maybe Lei shouldn't be the object of my vengeance, but rather a tool for my freedom.

The bathroom door creaks open, and heavy footfalls beat across the old floorboards. Marco appears around the wall with nothing but a towel wrapped around his narrow hips. Drops of water dribble down his shoulders, but I force my gaze to remain at eyelevel. There's something in his agitated state that has my hackles raised.

"What's going on?" I blurt when he rushes to his duffle bag in the corner and rifles through its paltry contents.

"Jimmy's got Lei."

CHAPTER 21
A KISS

M*arco*

"I'm going with you." My obstinate fiancée blocks the front door as I tug the shirt over my head, having already slid on my boxers and pants under my towel, preserving my future wife's innocence for a little longer.

"The fuck you are," I snarl before I remember the elder Guo standing only a few feet behind me. I've tried to be on my best behavior around the old man, but his granddaughter is wearing away at my final shreds of restraint. Spinning toward her grandfather, I search for backup. "Surely, you will agree it is best if Jia remains here."

"Jia, I believe Mr. Rossi is right—"

"No," she snaps, and I'm not sure who is more startled by her reply, her or her grandfather. "*Yéye*," she continues, her tone modified to a softer one, "Lei has insulted me. As the *lǎodà* of the Four Seas, it is my right to be present when an outsider questions my men."

An irritated growl vibrates my throat as I see the old man caving.

"And you…" The little spitfire whirls on me and jabs a finger into my chest. "You said you were merely the enforcer, and it was my duty to handle the Four Seas."

"That was before that *pezzo di merda* tried to kill *my* future wife."

She lifts to her tiptoes and, even though she's still several inches shorter, glares up at me. "I'm more than capable of fighting my own battles, and I will be much more than just *your* wife."

Dio, she's so fucking hot when she's angry. It took every ounce of restraint I had to walk away from her earlier when I had her trapped against the kitchen counter. If her grandfather hadn't interrupted when that little wildcat poured her coffee all over me, I would've tossed her over the couch, spanked her ass raw, then fucked that naughty streak right out of her.

"Fine." I loom closer, so damn close I can smell the sweet scent of jasmine that clings to her skin. "You want to come and watch me torture a man to within an inch of his life?"

"Yes," she snarls.

"Let's go, then, spitfire." I yank on the knob and hold the door open, hoping she'll back out. "Wait a second, I thought Arianna was coming to help you work on the boutique."

"Damn it," she hisses, and her lips screw into a pout.

"Maybe next time then—"

"No!" She pulls out her phone and her fingers fly across the screen. "That's what assistants are for, right? She can handle the shop for a few hours."

Merda.

Jia spins for her purse and drops a kiss on her grandfather's forehead. "We'll be back soon."

"Be careful, *bǎobèi*," he calls out, but she's already whizzing past me.

I throw her grandpa a reluctant shrug, and he responds

with a sly grin. Why do I feel like I'm the only one who's going to get utterly screwed in this relationship? And not in the good way.

Max pulls the limo up to the old electronics store we commandeered from the Four Seas last year when we were making some strategic moves in China Town. It's ironic that this is where Jimmy chose to bring the Four Seas' former right-hand man.

My driver for the day rolls down the window separating the back of the car from the front, and my fiancée slides to the edge of the seat across from me. Shockingly, she barely spoke a word the entire ride.

"You want me to go in with you?" Max asks.

I requested to borrow Max today instead of my usual driver, Rick, because of my brother's driver's rather specific skill set. "No, I want you to stay in the car with Jia."

"What?" she shrieks.

"You heard me." My steeliest glare does nothing but irritate her more.

She leaps toward the door and wraps her hand around the handle before I get my arms around her. "Let go of me!"

"Not until you stop fighting me."

"Never!" She kicks and squirms as I move to pin her body beneath mine in the backseat.

"Damn it, Jia. Why do you want to see this?" I wrap my fingers around her wrists, holding them in one hand. "I thought you wanted nothing to do with this life?"

"I don't! But it's not like I have a choice, do I?" she spits. "You can't protect me from everything, Marco. I'm not going to be your little kept woman."

With her wiggling like mad and my body pressed against hers, an unexpected wave of heat surges below my belt. She fights against me and gets one hand free and slashes her nails across my cheek.

"Get off me!" she howls.

The bite of her nails only awakens the beast I keep buried beneath my layers of charm. Nico may have always seemed like the darker one, but I've simply done a better job at hiding my true self. Losing Isa broke something inside me, and I hadn't ever been able to mend the pieces.

The more she struggles the harder my cock gets, straining against my slacks. Her cheeks flush, and I know it's not only from the exertion of the fight. Her pupils dilate, the pitch night growing darker. "You like it rough, spitfire?" I purr as my hips instinctively begin to move against her.

A satisfying rush of air parts her lips, and she instantly freezes as my cock rubs across the apex of her thighs. With only her flimsy yoga pants, she must feel every inch of me.

"No," she hisses, but the coarse hitch to her tone says otherwise.

"Must I fuck you into obedience?"

"No!" Still, I could swear she rocks her pussy against my hard length. Or maybe it's just wishful thinking.

"If I let you go do you promise to behave?"

"No," she spits. "I'm going in there with you whether you like it or not."

"Do I have to cuff you to this car to ensure compliance?"

"You wouldn't dare…"

"I would, and I will." With my free hand, I reach for the compartment in the door and pull out a pair of metal handcuffs.

A long minute of silence lingers between us as she eyes the manacles swinging from my finger. "How about that kiss you wanted? It's yours if you let me go with you," she grits out.

Well, that's unexpected. My stupid cock grows harder still.

"Done." The word pops out before I can think better of it.

Her eyes widen as if she hadn't expected me to agree. Hell,

I really shouldn't have. Her tongue slides out, moistening her lower lip, and anticipation unfurls in my gut. *Dio,* I don't remember being this excited about kissing a girl since I was in junior high.

My cock strains so hard against my slacks I consider unzipping them just to relieve the pressure. That probably wouldn't go over well with my fiancée.

"Just do it already," she mutters.

I waggle a finger. "I was promised a kiss from you, not the other way around."

"Ugh." Squeezing her eyes closed, she lifts her head so her lips barely brush mine.

"Eyes open, spitfire, or it doesn't count. I want you to see exactly who is claiming your mouth. It's only a matter of time before I claim every inch of you with my tongue, from that pouty lower lip to the soft swell of your breast to that sweet pussy."

She releases a sharp gasp, and her eyes snap open. "No one has ever dared talk to me like that."

"Get used to it, wifey." My mouth captures hers before her next breath. As much as I would like her to give into me, restraint is not exactly my strong suit. My tongue pushes through her clenched teeth, and as our tongues tangle, a soft moan rises between us. I ravage every inch of her mouth, acquainting myself with her taste. She only fights me for a moment, her palms pressed against my chest before she surrenders to desire.

Because her words may say one thing, but the way her body reacts to mine tells another story. I'm fairly certain if I were to run my finger across her panties right now she'd be soaked for me. This little virgin wants to be fucked, and I cannot wait to make her mine and mine alone.

I nibble on her lips, sucking and claiming as she melts under my touch. I resume rubbing my cock against her apex as I kiss her harder, and this time a more powerful moan escapes those swollen lips. She arches her back, giving herself to me and *Dio*, I'm so turned on by her surprising reaction I'm like a horny teen seconds from coming on myself.

Fisting her decadent raven locks, I tilt her head baring her throat. I'm an instant from tasting the sensitive flesh at her neck when a car zips by blaring a horn. The lusty spell shatters, and Jia plants her hand on my chest, shoving me back.

With a frustrated groan, I sit back and adjust my slacks. My cock tents the black trousers and Jia's gaze roams straight to the proof of my desire. She sits up, her cheeks burning a deep ruby that matches the natural shade of her lips.

"Well, that was unexpected," I mumble.

She doesn't utter a word, only presses her lips into a hard line.

"You ready to see Lei?" I offer my hand.

Her head dips, but she doesn't take my chivalrous offering. Instead, she barrels by me and nearly slams the door in my face.

CHAPTER 22
NEVER SUCCUMB

J *ia*

Oh, this is bad. So bad. Damn it, Jia, get a hold of yourself. So Marco Rossi can kiss? So my body is a traitorous little bitch? It doesn't mean anything. I reach the front door of the old electronics store and draw in a deep breath to still the pounding of my heart. I'm just winded from the sprint up the street. It has nothing to do with Marco's tongue or his ridiculously hard erection pressed against me.

Because what would that say about me? That I was actually attracted to my fiancé? No way in hell. It's simply been so long since a man has touched me... And let's be honest, I haven't gone past second base since college.

It's just out of control hormones.

Wrapping my hand around the rusty door handle, I bury the heated thoughts and focus on why we're here today. I catch a glimpse of my reflection in the dingy glass door and mutter a curse. If I hadn't been so worried about my fiancé leaving me behind, I would have changed into something more appropriate than an oversized long-sleeved shirt and yoga pants.

Marco's musky scent reaches my sensitive nostrils an instant before his hand wraps around mine, and he jerks the front door open. "Let me go first, spitfire."

"I don't think so." I tug my hand out from under his and dart in front of him. Too bad I have no idea where I'm going as I march through the dusty relics of the past. Radios, CD players, and a dozen outdated VHS systems line the rickety shelves of the abandoned shop.

A muffled grunt catches my attention, and I quicken my steps to the back of the store. A door is ajar, and a stifled male voice seeps through the crack. Barreling through the door, I find Lei, already bloody and beaten, shackled to a chair in some sort of abandoned stockroom. Dozens of tiny cuts litter his pale chest and his shirt lies in a pool of blood on the floor. His weary eyes lift to mine, and he mumbles something, but with the gag across his mouth I can't make out a word.

"Let him speak," I bark.

Marco looms behind me, his dark presence blanketing me in a burgeoning strength I didn't expect. A man slips out of the shadows, ink tattooed across every inch of exposed flesh, and his eyes raise over my shoulder to the big Italian behind me.

"Do it, Jimmy," Marco mutters.

The male's lips twist in disapproval, but he moves behind Lei all the same and begins to loosen the gag. The ring of black fabric falls around his throat like a necklace—or maybe more accurately, a noose.

"I did not do this, lǎodà, I swear to you!" A trickle of blood drips from the corner of his lip.

"That's what he's been saying since I grabbed him." This Jimmy guy shrugs and circles Lei. Beside the chair sits a small table covered in tools of our dark trade. Growing up in a household where torture was commonplace, I don't balk at the weapons. Each blade is spotted in droplets of dried crimson, including the brass knuckles my fiancé is currently eyeing.

Marco reaches for the glinting metal and slides them over his fingers. "Let's see if I can't get a different response out of him." His gaze slants to mine, and I nod. Though I've heard the effects of torture, been subjected to the screams ricocheting around my home since I was a child, I've never witnessed it in person.

A strange tangle of dread and excitement whips around my insides as Marco inches toward Lei.

"Should I gag him again, boss?" Jimmy's shifty eyes lift from his bruised knuckles.

"No," I interject. "I want to hear him."

"Lǎodà, please, I beg of you, I am one of your own. The blood of the Four Seas runs through my veins, much like yours. Do not allow this stranger to disrespect what your grandfather built."

I squeeze my eyes closed and slowly shake my head. "Do it, Marco," I hiss.

The crack of bone against flesh snaps my eyes open. Lei's head hangs back, a bloodied gash across his cheek. Marco pulls his arm back and swings again. Blood spurts across his dark shirt, soaking the material as he makes contact, splitting Lei's lip.

Marco creeps closer, his broad form towering over my brother's best friend. "Now, tell us again, Lei, did you send that man to Jia's home?" he growls.

"No…" He spits and blood coats the grimy tile floor. "I already told you."

"I don't believe you," Marco snarls before he lets his fist loose again. Bones crack and a sharp cry bursts from Lei's lips. There's no doubt in my mind that my fiancé has broken his nose.

"Why would I want to kill you, Jia?" Lei's unfocused gaze meets mine. "I've wanted you since we were children."

My head snaps back as if his words had delivered a punch.

"Why do you think I requested a change in the rules? I only wanted to be with you."

"Then why did you send those men to break into my boutique?" The question erupts before I can stop it. It was as if he knew exactly how to get to me and what would hurt the most.

"I only wanted to scare you, so that you'd make the right decision."

"You wanted to frighten me into submission?" Anger curls my fists at my sides, and I'm seconds away from punching the asshole myself. "That's the problem with men like you, Lei, you think you can get what you want by bullying others. I will never succumb to you, to any male."

A wry grin curls his lip, and already, I regret that slip of the tongue. "Like your fiancé?" His eyes lock on Marco's, and he spits again. If the Italian mob boss wasn't so quick on his feet, the smattering of blood and saliva would've landed on his shiny loafers.

Marco's hand snakes out and wraps around Lei's throat. "Watch your mouth, *coglione*. The only reason you are still alive is because *my* fiancée wishes it."

A harsh laugh bubbles from Lei's mouth, and more crimson-coated spit dribbles out. "You seriously believe he will allow you to rule the Four Seas?"

"Yes," I grit out.

"Then perhaps you are not as wise as your grandfather believes."

Rage simmers through my veins, and darkness creeps into the corners of my soul.

"You will spend the rest of your life as a pawn for the Italian mafia, and you will take all of us down with you. You will never be the true *lǎodà*, but rather only a female to warm the bed of a powerful man. That is your destiny, Jia, nothing more."

That fury rolls through me, the thundering of my heart like a war drum in my ears. My hand moves of its own accord, reaching for the knife on the side table. I bury the blade into Lei's chest before I take another breath. I twist and stare into eyes wider than the sun. A sun fully eclipsed by the blood of the dragon.

"Holy shit," Jimmy hisses.

Screams and shouts resound across the room, but they blur into the distance, as if underwater. That familiar, warm presence surrounds me, and I'm vaguely aware my fingers are being pried off the knife.

"Come on, Jia, let go. I've got you." That voice is so soft, so soothing I'm certain it cannot possibly come from the rowdy Italian. But then that pungent bergamot and cedarwood scent reaches my nostrils and slowly my fingers uncurl from the hilt.

Marco stands in front of me, blocking my view of Lei. Based on the shrieks alone, I guess Jimmy is trying to get the blade out. Good luck. I sunk it in right between his ribs, a spot that would prove lethal in no time if left unattended.

"I think you've seen enough for today." Marco laces a strong arm around my shoulders and tucks me into his firm side. I don't fight it, the anger dissipating along with the rush of adrenaline.

I allow my fiancé to lead me through the shop as Lei's screams echo all around us.

"Max will get you home, and I'll be back shortly, as soon as I settle this with Lei." His gaze dips to mine, and the fury reflected in those mismatched eyes mirrors my own. "I'll make him pay, Jia. No one disrespects my fiancée and lives beyond the day."

"No…" I mutter, my head slowly moving from side to side. "I don't want him dead. Not yet. I want him to witness how wrong he is. He needs to see that I will never bow down to any man." I squirm free of Marco's hold and narrow my eyes. "I do not belong to you, and I never will. Are we clear?"

His chin slowly drops to his chest. Then he takes a step toward me, pinning me against the shelf of antique electronics. It wobbles beneath our combined weight, but somehow holds steady. "I respect your desire to rule over these men, and I will stand by your side and provide whatever assistance I can. But it is not in my nature to stand by and do nothing when something or *someone* I value is threatened. And as my future wife, you will become of great value to me. Maybe you cannot accept that now, but one day, you will." That heated gaze bores into me, a tempest of unreadable emotions swirling below the surface. We remain like that for an endless moment before he spins away and stalks back into the stockroom.

CHAPTER 23
HAPPY WIFE, HAPPY LIFE

M *arco*

Jia trudges around the studio, her typically light, ginger steps leaden today. Who would've thought moving into a luxury penthouse would be such a death sentence? Despite knowing the move-in day would come for over a week now, she has yet to pack a single box. It's clear she intends to keep this crappy studio even after we're married.

Which I should be happy about…

After years as a more-than-content bachelor, having some space to myself and away from my forced marriage should make me giddy with joy. Instead, the idea of being away from her has me pissed off as all hell. In what world would anyone choose this dump over a Park Avenue penthouse?

"The movers are going to be at the apartment any minute now, Jia. I have to meet them there."

She pops her head around the brick wall and shoots me a

glare. "So go without me. I already told you I can manage myself."

Pushing off the sofa, I round the corner into her bedroom. "You're seriously only going to bring one piece of luggage?" I eye the bright orange suitcase spread out on her bed.

"That's all I'll need for now."

Yéye emerges from the bathroom and shuffles toward me. The old man has had his suitcase packed and by the door since yesterday. He's clearly as tired of the tight accommodations as I am.

"I'll still need to come to CityZen every day, so why move everything now?"

Her grandfather's lips twist into a scowl. "You intend to keep the studio, *bǎobèi?*"

"Of course, I do. I'm getting a deal from the landlord for both spaces. And anyway, even if I did want to move, my lease isn't up for another six months."

"I'm sure I could get you out of that," I interject. "I have plenty of money."

"As do I, but I refuse to touch a single penny of my inheritance. It's dirty money and I want no part of it. And besides, I don't want out of my lease," she counters. "If I have to work late, I can just stay here instead of having to travel all the way up to Midtown."

"I have a driver!" I roar, my nerves getting the best of me. "I literally pay him to drive us around."

"Not *us*—you." Those midnight orbs lock on mine, filled with so much defiance, my stupid cock gets hard just thinking about wiping that disobedient smile off her face. *Dio*, not for the first time I find myself thinking of what I wouldn't give to throw her across my lap and spank that perky ass raw.

I could if I just got rid of the old man...

Tossing the thought aside for now, I heave in a deep breath. "We are going to be married in less than a week whether you like it or not, Jia. What's mine will be yours."

A devious smile reaches all the way up to those bottomless orbs. "Great, what about that black Amex?"

A smirk tugs at the corners of my lips. "We'll talk about it once you become Mrs. Marco Rossi."

She snorts on a laugh before fully giving into the amusement, hinging at the waist at the force of her wild cackles. When she finally straightens a long minute later, wiping tears from her eyes, she lifts to her tiptoes and jabs a finger into my chest. "I will *never* be Mrs. Marco Rossi. I'm keeping my maiden name for business purposes."

My palm itches to plant one on that pert little ass so insistent on defying me.

Guo stares at me from across the room, waiting for my reaction. Does he want me to keep his granddaughter in line? Is this some sort of test?

"Whatever you want, spitfire," I grind out. "But the Amex will be in my last name, so it's your call." Shrugging, I move to the door. If the moving van arrives to the penthouse before me, I'll be S.O.L. I may not have much to add to the furnished apartment, but I've collected a few personal items Nico has been storing for the past few months.

"Come now, *bǎobèi*," the elder Guo calls out.

With a huff of frustration, Jia stomps to her bedroom. The whine of the zipper closing around her luggage brings a victorious smile to my face.

A familiar blonde stands at the front door of my new apartment, and I let out a muttered curse as I step out of the elevator. Raquel, the realtor, swings the keys from her finger, taunting, and wears a *please-fuck-me* grin.

As appealing as a much-needed release sounds, I'm no cheater. I may be a lot of things, but disrespecting a woman like that isn't in my nature. I may have slept around, but I was

very clear with the women up front that I did not do relation-
ships. And when I nearly allowed Raquel to suck me off, the
arrangement with Jia had yet to be made.

The little dark-haired spitfire might not wear my ring yet,
but she is already mine in all the ways that matter.

"Well, hello there, Mr. Rossi," she purrs as I approach.

Thank *Dio* Jia and her grandfather were still downstairs
waiting with the movers. The last thing I needed was my
fiancée crossing paths with this woman.

"Hello, Miss Raquel. You certainly didn't have to come all
this way to bring me the keys. You could have left them with
the doorman."

She closes the space between us and drags her finger down
my shirt. "I was hoping we could both come..." Her tongue
darts out and slides across her bottom lip.

Clearing my throat, I take a big step back and her finger
falls from the button she's toying with. "I'm sorry if you
misunderstood, but what almost occurred between us last
time, will never happen."

"Oh..." Her full lips pucker, and images of my cock in her
mouth leap to the forefront of my mind. Nope, definitely not
the lips I want. If anything she would be nothing more than a
warm hole to distract me from the frustrating Jia who'd
already gotten under my skin. And now, damn, am I strung
tight. "Are you sure?" She inches closer and her hand snakes
out, cupping me through my slacks, and my cock doesn't even
stir at the possibility.

"Raquel..." I rasp out before jerking her hand away. "This
won't happen. Ever."

"But why?" she whines.

The elevator dings, drawing our attention and forcing
Raquel to take a step away. Jia and her grandfather emerge
from the elevator with my driver, toting their luggage.

"Oh," the realtor blurts. She spins toward me and mouths,

"You really do have a girlfriend?" I guess she didn't believe me when I'd told her I was getting married.

But at least she's somewhat discreet. I nod slowly, and her smile only broadens. "Well, here you go, Mr. Rossi." She hands me the keys and whirls toward the approaching pair.

Jia's already scowling, and Guo doesn't look any happier. They bickered the whole ride over here.

"I hope you enjoy the penthouse," she calls out.

My fiancée rewards her friendly comment with a sneer, and the old man simply dips his head, the picture of resignation. As soon as the elevator doors glide closed behind Raquel, I release a breath and spear the shiny new key into the keyhole.

It's been a while since I've had my own place and despite my initial reluctance, I'm actually quite eager now. I hold the door open for Jia and Guo, and Rick hangs back with the luggage. "Go check it out," I call out as Jia moves through the grand foyer. With high ceilings and floor-to-ceiling glass that highlights a bird's eye view of Midtown, both my fiancée and her grandfather appear mesmerized. "Then I'll show you the master."

Jia whirls around and snaps her jaw shut. "I'm not sleeping in the same room as you."

Guo's eyes meet mine as he blanches, then looks between his granddaughter and me. Without uttering another word, he shuffles off toward the hallway that leads to the guest bedrooms.

Traitor…

"Jia, we are going to be married, and I expect—"

"You expect *what*?" she growls, marching toward me and digging her heel into my shoe.

"Son of a bitch!" I howl and leap back.

She glares up at me, arms knotted across her chest. "You expect me to part my legs for you at your beck and call? No wait, let me guess, you think my pussy now belongs to you because of this antiquated arrangement?"

"You will be my wife," I snarl, "in every extent of the word."

"I've heard of many sexless marriages."

An uncontrollable, wild laugh titters out. "Yeah, after years of marriage, not in the beginning." That's exactly why I'd always refused to tie myself to one woman. "That's why men cheat and—"

"Oh, so you're blaming the wife for a husband not being able to keep his dick in his pants?"

"No, that's not what I'm saying—" I release a frustrated growl. "Damn it, Jia. This doesn't have to be so fucking hard."

"You're right, it didn't have to be, but you and my grandfather made it this way when you took away my choice. I should have been consulted about this wedding. Even my brother told me about his intentions before he tried to sell me off to your twin."

"Did he give you a choice in the matter?"

She grits her teeth, flashing me a feral smile. "Of course he didn't, but at least I wasn't blindsided. Not like this."

"Are you ever going to get past this?"

"Ever? It's been just over a week, Marco!" She stomps around the foyer, throwing her hands up. "Excuse me if I can't bottle up all my feelings in a nice neat little corner in the far recesses of my soul like some people."

Her astute observation catches me off-guard. Only a week with me and she already knows me better than any of the women I fucked for months, even Mel who I'd lived with. "Fine, take your own damned room," I growl, "until we're married. Then all bets are off." I pause for dramatic effect then jerk my thumb over my shoulder in the direction her grandfather disappeared. "There are three bedrooms down that hallway."

"And what's that way?" She points across the great room to a small glass spiral staircase.

"That's the loft. The *master* loft," I amend.

Jia's heels click-clack across the white marble of the sprawling living room, then she disappears around the open-concept kitchen.

"Jia?" I bark. "That's my room..." I race behind her, but she's taking the steps two at a time. If I wasn't so annoyed, I would've been impressed by the ease in which she darts up the narrow steps with those heels.

When I reach the loft, she's splayed across the plush comforter of the king-sized bed. Her hand glides across the Egyptian cotton, and a smile parts her ruby lips. "Oh, yes, this will do just fine."

I'm so damned hard-up, I consider pinning her to the mattress and fucking her until she's begging to come. She must notice the dark gleam in my eye because she scrambles to the edge of the bed and sears me with a murderous gaze of her own. "Get out of my room."

"You're out of your fucking mind, spitfire."

"You just said I'm to be your wife in every sense of the word, right?"

I nod warily.

"Happy wife, happy life... you've heard that one, haven't you, *coglione*?"

I'm impressed with not only how quickly she's picked up the Italian word for asshole, but also with her pronunciation. "No, I'm afraid I'm not familiar with that saying," I grit out.

"Well, you're about it to learn it."

I stalk toward her, unable to keep my feet still or my twitchy hands off her for a second longer. My fingers wrap around her throat, and she releases a satisfying gasp. "Must we have this discussion again? No one says no to me... And it will certainly not begin with my wife."

"I'm not your wife yet," she bites back and tries to stand.

I shove her back onto the end of the bed and rub my thumb across the soft indentation in her throat, exerting a bit more pressure. She draws in a sharp breath. "I can make our marriage a tolerable one—hell, even an incredible one—or I can make it misery for us both. But I need you to understand that I *always* get what I want." I inch closer, placing a palm on either side of her thighs and run my nose across the shell of her ear. "And what I want, my lovely fiancée, is you, on your back, with your legs spread wide for me and only me."

Her breath hitches, and I know her well enough now to realize it's not from fear. This woman isn't the slightest bit scared of me. Which is something that should frustrate me, but instead, I'm only intrigued. What has she survived to inherit those balls of steel?

My hand drifts from the satin comforter to her thigh. Her silk dress has ridden up her hips, well past her knee. I brush the inner side of her leg with my thumb, just below her hem, and goosebumps ripple across her milky white flesh.

"Never," she whispers.

I'm so enthralled by the feel of her, I forget the course of our discussion. "You're a liar," I murmur against her ear before I nibble at her lobe and earn another breathy sigh. "I'll let you have the master bedroom, for now, but only because it will make things easier once we *are* married."

I straighten, and I swear her body crumples forward as I release her. Those rebellious eyes remain fixed to mine, mouth screwed into a pout. I drop my gaze to her thighs and get a flash of silk panties. Better yet, a faint wet spot on the pale, pink fabric.

A wicked smile hitches up the corners of my lips, and an unexpected flutter kicks at my ribs. Just a few more days and that woman will be mine, body and soul. And for the first time in my life, I cannot wait to commit to something.

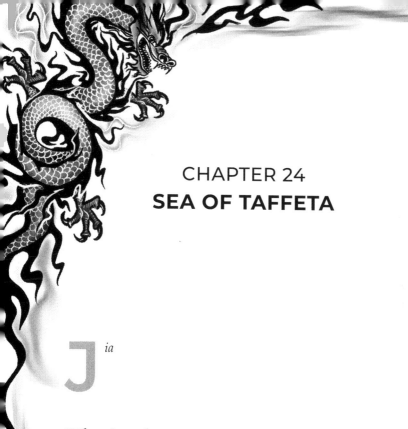

CHAPTER 24
SEA OF TAFFETA

J*ia*

"What about this one?" Ari pulls out a blindingly white gown with flashy sequins across the bodice. It's so loud a passing satellite could see it from outer space.

"Nope, don't think so." I stare out into the sea of taffeta and tulle in the bridal showroom in the hottest part of the garment district and curse my best friend for having convinced me to go on this little outing.

I should have just bought some random white dress online and called it a day. Who needs a fancy ballgown for a fake marriage? I've barely seen my fiancé since I moved into his penthouse... thankfully. Marco was gone this morning when I awoke, and I stopped by the boutique before meeting Ari and *Yéye* for this shopping disaster, thereby avoiding all potential proximity. If all goes well, I hope not to have to see that man until I'm forced down the aisle. Even better if he doesn't show up at all, but somehow, I doubt that is going to happen. After yesterday's argument on *my* bed, I've determined I need to stay far away from him, despite the way my stupid body reacts whenever he's around.

Yéye clears his throat, drawing my attention from the onslaught of thoughts twisting my insides. He sits on the upholstered couch watching the action from afar. He insisted on attending this farce, probably to ensure I came home with a dress.

"At least try one on, Jia." Arianna rifles through the never-ending racks, and all the white blurs across my vision.

Besides my obvious reluctance to marry the Italian mob boss, finding a gown with long sleeves is difficult. They are all either too conservative or too old-fashioned, too frumpy or too traditional. The scars on my arms only make this arduous process ten times worse. I wish *Nanay* was here, I wish my father hadn't been such a monster, and most of all, I wish I wasn't getting married!

Yéye shuffles over as if he's noticed my impending melt-down and places a calming hand on my shoulder. "Is there truly nothing here you like, *bǎobèi*?"

I shake my head, tears brimming in my eyes. God, what is wrong with me? I feel like I'm spiraling, like my entire life is slipping from my control.

Get it together, Jia. Sweeping the tears from my eyes, I delve into the racks beside Arianna once more, adamant on finding something at least semi-decent. What does it matter anyway? Clearly, this will never be the wedding of my dreams.

One of the sales ladies darts by, and grandfather stops her with a quick wave of his wrinkled hand. "Please bring the dress now."

The skinny blonde drops everything and nods. "Yes, of course, Mr. Guo." Then she scurries across the showroom and disappears through a door marked *Alterations*.

I spin toward my grandfather and lift a curious brow. "What dress, *Yéye*?"

"I had your grandmother's wedding gown shipped here when I made the arrangement with Mr. Rossi." He shrugs, a sly grin on his lips. "Just in case..."

A strangled sound erupts from my throat as the timeworn black and white photo surfaces to the front of my mind. Then to my *nǎinai* in her elegant gown, looking the picture of sophistication at her own arranged wedding. She used to carry the old picture with her everywhere, tucked in her variety of purses.

Emotion tightens my throat, and I try my best to swallow down the ache. "Thank you," I finally whisper.

"She would have been honored for you to wear it, *bǎobèi*. I believe she kept it in the hopes that one day she could pass it on to you. She loved you so very much."

My grandmother had only sons, and I was her only granddaughter. As much as I loved my mother, I would never wear her wedding gown with the knowledge of what a terrible marriage she and my father had. But *Nǎinai* loved *Yéye,* and he adored her. If it hadn't been for my grandparents, I never would've known what a happy marriage looked like.

"And I loved her," I barely manage.

Grandpa awkwardly tugs me into his chest and delivers a surprising display of public affection. Even Ari's eyes go wide over his shoulder.

The blonde saleswoman rushes by with gowns haphazardly flung across her arms. She pauses just long enough to catch her breath. "Mr. Guo, room three is ready for your granddaughter, and the seamstress will meet you there to make any alterations needed."

"Very well, thank you."

"Ooh, yay!" Ari claps her hands. "I can't wait to see you in your grandma's dress."

A smile lifts the corners of my lips, and for the first time since this arranged marriage bomb dropped, I'm excited. Ari tugs me to the dressing rooms, and *Yéye* follows a few measured steps behind.

When we reach room three, a buzz of excitement has my heart pumping faster. I step inside the chamber, and there, hanging from the wall is my *năinai's* dress. The endless lace stretches from the sophisticated high neck to the sheer long sleeves and intricate, sweeping train. Seeing it in person after so many years of staring at a grainy, worn picture is surreal.

I step closer and hesitantly reach for the delicate lace. *Năinai* was married at nineteen so this gown is over sixty years old, and still the fine fabric not only seems intact but in perfect condition. There's no yellowing, no frayed edges.

"It's beautiful," I whisper.

"Absolutely perfect!" Ari stands behind me, admiring the smooth lines of the gown.

The embroidery along the arms is sheer, perfect for our summer wedding, but the brocade appears elaborate enough to cover my scars. To this day, I'm uncertain if my grandfather knows of the tortures I suffered under my father's hand. Forcing away the dark thoughts, I turn to the exquisite gown. Now, to see if it fits. The curve-hugging bodice was tailored for my petite grandmother, and though I'm far from tall at five foot four, I have a few inches and a couple pounds on her.

Right on cue, after a quick knock, a woman pops her head into the dressing room. "Hello! I am Olga, and I will be assisting you today. Would you like any help with the gown?"

My head bobs. I'm scared to touch it, terrified I'll remove it from the hanger and it'll disintegrate in my fingertips.

Yéye stands and dips his head in my direction. "I will give you a moment."

The seamstress rushes in before I can reply to grandpa, then pauses in front of the dress. "It's truly superb. They simply don't make gowns like this anymore."

My smile grows wider, and I begin to relax as Olga carefully removes it from the hanger. As she does, I take in the daring deep-V of the back. Wow, *Năinai*, you little vixen.

"How many days until the wedding?" the woman asks as she signals for me to undress.

My heart's happy pitter-patter halts as I quickly count. "Three." The answer pops out on a sharp exhale. I can't believe it's nearly here, and I don't know a single detail about the event. Marco's assistant has coordinated the entire affair, and whenever she's reached out for my opinion, I ignored her. Maybe that was a mistake. The only thing I do know is that the ceremony will take place at St. Patrick's Cathedral and the reception at the Waldorf. Since Marco's brother owns a penthouse at the hotel, he was able to secure the last-minute venue. I'm sure it cost him more than just money.

"So soon!" Olga squeals as I step into the dress on autopilot, covering my arms until they're hidden beneath the lace.

"I can't wait!" Arianna claps her hands again.

I shoot her a scowl, and she tamps down on her excitement. Though I didn't share all the dirty details with my friend, she knows this is a marriage of convenience and nothing more. Still, she's ridiculously thrilled about the whole debacle.

As the lacy fabric brushes my skin, goosebumps ripple across my flesh. I hazard a quick glance at the mirror over Olga's shoulder as she pulls the gown up my torso. Oh my God, I'm really doing this. I'm getting married…

"Go open the door!" Ari calls out from the elevator bank. "We've got the dress…"

Năinai's gown was like magic. It molded perfectly to my form, as if it had been made for me. Even the seamstress couldn't believe that not even a single bit of alterations was needed.

With the tight deadline for the wedding, we really lucked

out. And now with my grandma's dress in hand, at least something would feel real about this arrangement. Maybe *Yéye* and Ari were right and I need to give this marriage a shot. My grandparents had been happy, perhaps there is hope for the mob boss and me after all.

As I approach the entrance to Marco's apartment, my steps lighter than they have been in a while, I find the door ajar, and voices drift out into the hallway.

One voice, a female, sounds vaguely familiar, but I can't quite place it.

I inch closer and the talking stops, the silence now overpowered by the increasing tempo of my pulse. What the... I whip the door open, and a furious scream lodges in my chest.

Marco leans against the kitchen counter with the realtor's tongue jammed down his throat.

CHAPTER 25
GRAY

M*arco*

Fuck. I can feel Jia's burning gaze from across the room before she utters a sound. I shove raunchy Raquel off for the third time since she came by to personally deliver a second set of keys for my *girlfriend*. The woman has no shame and simply cannot take the hint that I'm not interested. Clearly, this woman can't take no for an answer.

"Jia!" I spring for her, but she lifts a hand, pure venom carved into her jaw.

"Don't fucking touch me," she hisses as I reach for her arm.

"Let me explain—"

"There's nothing to explain. It's not like I expected your manwhoring days to come to an end just because of our sham of a wedding. I just didn't expect to see it in *our* apartment." She spins out of my reach and races around the back of the kitchen. Her footfalls slap across the steps a moment later as she disappears up into the master loft, and I just stand there like an asshole.

A lethal tempest of fury, pain, and ice-cold fear twist in my gut. What if she leaves? What if she calls this whole thing off? A few days ago, and I would've been thrilled by the prospect... but now? *Cazzo*, what has this woman done to me?

Raquel's head twists in my direction, and I swear a spark of hope lights up her face. She must have caught that sham wedding part. Bad news for her, though. She and I were not happening. Ever.

"Please leave," I bark at my all-too-eager realtor.

"But—"

"No *buts*. Get out of my house and *never* come back unannounced. What almost happened between us was before Jia and I were engaged, before we were even together, as I keep trying to tell you. And it will never happen again." I wrap my fingers around her wrist and haul her to the door just in time to find Guo and Arianna walking in. *Merda.* "If you have any business to conduct with me in the future, Miss Raquel," I add to the realtor, a bit more politely now that we're in company, "please go through my assistant, Melanie, at Gemini Corp."

She rips her hand free from my grasp and saunters toward the elevator. Before the elevator doors close behind her, she offers a flirty smile. "I'm always available, Mr. Rossi, whatever your needs may be."

I heave out a grunt and slam the door. Good God, the woman is relentless.

Mr. Guo and Jia's best friend stare at me expectantly as I stalk back inside. *Shit.*

"Everything all right, Mr. Rossi?" Guo cocks his head, eyes thinning as he scrutinizes my disheveled state.

"Just fine. I need to speak to your granddaughter, if you'll excuse me for a moment." I nearly make it all the way around the kitchen before calling out over my shoulder. "Please help yourselves to whatever you want in the refrigerator and make yourselves comfortable."

Then I'm racing up the steps and sorting through the best way to explain—no, grovel to my future wife. Thankfully, the master loft has no doors, so Jia has no option but to hear me out.

When I reach the sprawling, modern chamber, I find my fiancée in the closet yanking off the shirts I'd spent the last hour hanging.

"Hey! What are you doing?"

She whirls at me, dark eyes murderous. "What does it look like I'm doing? I'm moving your clothes. I may be forced to marry you, but I refuse to share the same bedroom with a man who is fucking other women."

"I'm not!" I howl.

"I just caught you with your tongue down the freaking realtor's throat!"

"It wasn't *my* tongue! She attacked me."

"Oh, you poor baby! How did you ever survive?" Her eyes narrow as they focus on my shirt collar. "You've even got battle scars to prove it."

I flip up the corner of my collar and cringe at the bright pink lipstick. "It's not what it looks like. The reason her lipstick is on my collar is because I turned my head when she tried to kiss me the first two times, and her lips landed on my shirt instead. The last time she got a little aggressive, which was at exactly the moment that you walked in."

She rolls her eyes so damned hard only the whites show. "You're pathetic."

"It's the truth!" I drag my hands through my hair and suck in a steadying breath. "Damn it, Jia, I haven't been with a single woman since our engagement was announced." And I have the blue balls to prove it.

She begins a slow clap that only aggravates my fired-up nerves in the way that only she seems capable of doing.

"Would you like a medal? You made it through two whole weeks without sleeping with another woman? That's truly impressive, Mr. Rossi. Well done."

"And I didn't kiss the realtor either!"

"Well, it didn't look like you were trying very hard to pull away until you saw me."

"Yes, I was! Did you miss the part about the first two attempts? Not to mention when she tried to put her hand down my pants—" Damn it. Too far.

A shriek bursts from her lips and she shoves me out of the closet, grabbing my shirts as I stagger back. "Take your clothes and get out of my room."

I plant my feet into the carpet and, despite her punches and an occasional kick, I stand my ground. "I'm not going anywhere, spitfire," I growl. "As a matter of fact, I think I'll sleep in here tonight."

"You will not!" She throws another punch. I don't deflect it; I just stand there and take it.

"It's not the night before our wedding yet. There's no reason why I can't sleep in my own damned room with my fiancée."

"You don't get to call me that when you still smell like that woman's cheap perfume."

As I stand there while she continues to wail on me, a realization surfaces: Jia's jealous. For the first time since this whole mess started, she's showing me actual emotion. Emotion for *me*. If she truly didn't care about me at all, then why the dramatics? We'd never discussed the parameters of our fake relationship, but there's more than just anger in her eyes. It's clear she's hurt.

And *cazzo*, that understanding has me downright giddy.

My fingers curl around her wrists and drag her flush against me. I keep her steady against my chest with one hand in spite of her squirming. My heart kicks at my ribs from the faint contact with her flesh. With the other hand, I grip her chin and force her eyes to meet mine. "Listen to me, spitfire. I don't cheat. I may have been sleeping around with a few women before we met, but they were all very aware of it. When I commit to something or *someone*, I'm all in. If you want this marriage to be real, then trust that I will be as devoted and faithful to you as I have been to everything that's real in my life. I put my heart and soul into Gemini Corp, into making myself into the man I am today, and I'll do the same for this relationship, but only if you're willing."

Some of the fire in her eyes diminishes at my tempered tone. Her chest still heaves with every breath, and I can't keep my gaze from dipping to the taunting neckline. *Dio*, she's tempting when she wants to kill me.

"I don't know," she finally mutters, a long minute later.

I release her and take a step back, all the intensity deflating from my lungs.

"I don't know that I can trust you, Marco. You've still done little to earn it."

Gritting my teeth, I fold my hands behind my back. I don't find that to be at all true, but I keep my mouth shut all the same. Maybe she really does just need more time. Maybe she needs to hear me say it...

"I don't need Raquel; I don't want other women. Your lips are the ones I dream of every night, spitfire," I whisper. "I dream of claiming that mouth, devouring those lips until they're swollen, then filling them up with my cock."

She gasps, and a satisfied grin stretches across my face. *Dio*, I love riling her up.

"We could be good together, Jia, really good. You just have to give it a chance."

She releases a breath and lowers her fighting stance, her arms falling to her sides. "... And if I can't?"

Those words sting more than a dozen knife wounds. "I don't know. I guess we'll have to find another way to make this arrangement work."

"Like we each live our own separate lives in private?"

"Is that what you want?" I bark, the question coming out harsher than intended. I never thought she would be the one to need her desires fulfilled outside of our marriage.

"Maybe," she murmurs.

Merda. That one little word is like a hot blade right between the ribs. I stagger back a few steps then whirl around, no longer able to face her. As I march to the steps, my pulse thrums across my eardrums in a furious rhythm. Why am I so stupid? Why would I give up everything for one piece of ass? If she wants an open marriage, I should be thrilled.

Before I reach the top of the staircase, I double back and swing my head over my shoulder. "I'm going out for the night. You'll have the place to yourself. Arianna and your grandfather are waiting downstairs so I wouldn't think on it too long."

The soft rush of her bare feet across the carpet stills my own footfalls. "Where are you going?" she blurts.

Without turning to face her, I mutter, "I'm not sure yet, but I need to think. And I find that difficult when I'm around you. Before I met you, things were very clear, black and white. Now all I see is gray."

I wait for a long minute, but she doesn't speak, so I force my feet down the stairs and forbid myself to look back.

CHAPTER 26
SOME SPACE

J*ia*

"What are you still doing here? It's almost ten." Ari marches into the boutique, buried beneath a tower of fabric. A rainbow of materials spills across the drafting table as she throws me a narrowed glare. "You're getting married the day after tomorrow. You shouldn't still be here hunched over a desk. You should be celebrating with your family and friends, or at the very least, relaxing."

"Ha, that's funny. What family? What friends, Ari? One doesn't invite people you actually care about to a fake wedding with a mobster. It's all a political arrangement, a big show. The heads of the most notorious crime syndicates will be in attendance, and we'll be lucky if it doesn't end in a bloodbath."

Ari's nose scrunches, her lips screwing into a pout. I've never been so blunt with her before. She's heard bits and pieces, but I try to keep my friend out of it as much as possible.

"I'm sorry..." She inches closer and tugs me into her side. "I'm really sorry that your wedding day isn't going to be the dream one all little girls hope for." She pauses and nibbles on her bottom lip, clearly hesitant to say what she wants to say next. "But I don't think Marco is that bad. I've seen the way he looks at you, the way he talks to you, and that's not a man who only thinks of you as a business arrangement."

I huff out a breath and sink into my desk chair. I'd told Ari all about that slutty realtor, and my friend is so naïve, she believed Marco's explanation. *Women are always throwing themselves at men like him.* And maybe, she's right, but it doesn't make it hurt any less. That is what I'm the most upset about. He fucking hurt me. After *Bà*, I vowed never to be hurt by a man again.

"Marco hasn't been back to the penthouse since our fight last night," I murmur.

"He's probably just blowing off some steam."

"Or getting a blow job from that all too willing realtor."

Ari shakes her head, a rueful grin on her lips. "No way. That little homewrecker has nothing on you, Jia."

I don't need Raquel; I don't want other women. Your lips are the ones I dream of every night, spitfire. Marco's sincere expression flashes across my mind along with the echo of his words. He couldn't be serious. *We could be good together, Jia, really good. You just have to give it a chance.* It's laughable, right? He can't possibly be serious about having a real marriage. How can I trust the eternal playboy to change his ways? And why can't I get his words and that desperate look in his eyes out of my mind? They'd been playing on repeat since yesterday, plaguing my sleep and haunting the waking hours.

Sure, I'd been at the shop all day, but I hadn't been able to accomplish a single thing. After pacing the quiet penthouse all morning, I'd ventured downtown for a distraction with one of Marco's minions on my heel. I thought for sure he would return while I was gone, but according to grandpa, he still hasn't. So where is my fiancé?

I stare at my phone carelessly flung on the desk, desperate for a message to come through. I even texted the idiot with some lame question about the wedding, and he still hasn't responded.

"Come on, Jia, I'll walk you out." Ari curls an arm through mine and hauls me out of the chair. "That big, scary, sexy guy is out front waiting."

I snort on a laugh as I picture Nicky standing guard by the front door. Poor guy has been there all day. And judging by the text messages he's been receiving on the hour, my fiancé is keeping tabs on my whereabouts. So why can't—I pull free of Ari's hold and dart to the front door.

"Where's Marco?" I snap at the burly guard.

"Sorry, Miss Jia, I have no idea."

I sear him with my most intimidating glare. "Next time he texts you, ask him."

"Um… I don't think I should—"

Rising to my tiptoes, I do my best to loom over the guy, which is pretty much impossible at my measly five foot four compared to his towering six foot five. "Listen here, Nicky, if you're going to be my personal bodyguard, we're going to be spending a hell of a lot of time together. I can make that time miserable or tolerable. Which do you prefer?"

The big guy swallows hard.

"You think Marco is scary? You haven't seen anything." I flick my gaze to my clutch and the sleek gun stashed inside that Marco acquired for me.

"Miss Jia…"

"Don't think I wouldn't do it, Nicky. Don't forget who my father was."

He blanches, his deep caramel skin morphing into a sickly pallor. Lucky for me, *Bà* was known to be a loose cannon, and everyone knows the apple doesn't fall far from the tree. "I'll let the boss know you're looking for him," he mutters.

"Fine," I grit out as Arianna saunters up, clearly amused at the exchange.

"So, we ready to go?"

Nicky nods and holds the door open. "After you, ladies."

I storm around the penthouse in my fluffy robe and slippers like a tornado ready to strike, slamming cabinets, whipping doors open and stomping across the pristine marble. It's been two days, and I have yet to hear from my fiancé. Despite my threats, Nicky hasn't caved on disclosing his location. Worse, our wedding is tomorrow.

Marco has ignored my text messages, my phone calls, even my rather desperate voicemails. What if I really was in trouble? I glare across the foyer at Nicky who avoids my attention, pivoting toward the door.

He's the reason Marco has made no attempt at contact, because his little spy has had eyes on me the whole time. So of course my fiancé isn't worried about my safety. The two of them must be laughing their heads off at my enraged state.

The familiar shuffle of approaching footsteps forces my wild pulse to calm. *Yéye* has already made his concerns for my state of mind apparent, and I hate worrying him.

"Everything all right, *bǎobèi*?" He scans the whirlwind of open cabinets, the barstools in disarray, and the line of dirty coffee mugs along the sink.

"Yes, of course, grandfather."

"Are you searching for something, perhaps?"

My sanity? God, how can this man affect me so much?

"It's only that I haven't spoken to Marco today, and I thought with our quickly approaching nuptials, he would have returned to the penthouse by now."

"I see…" A knowing smile curves his lips.

"Have you spoken to him?" I blurt.

He slowly dips his head.

"Seriously? And you never thought to mention it?" I slam my jaw closed before I say something I'll regret. In the past few days, I've practically annihilated the line of respect toward my grandfather. My poor mother must be rolling over in her grave.

Yéye squeezes my shoulder, his typical show of affection, and offers a reassuring smile. "Your future husband is only attempting to give you some space."

"Is that what he said?"

"Yes."

I hiss out a frustrated breath and plop down onto a bar stool. Leaning on the marble island, I focus on slowing my manic heartbeats and take a few sips of the lukewarm, leftover coffee. When I've finally gotten control of my temper, I turn to *Yéye* who's pouring a fresh cup for himself. "Did my fiancé happen to mention if he'd be returning home before the wedding?"

"He will not, *bǎobèi*, at my urging."

I nearly spit out a mouthful of the cold coffee. "*Why?*"

"It's not good luck to see the bride before the wedding day."

A completely unladylike snort erupts. "*Yéye*, this isn't a real marriage."

"Because you haven't opened your mind or heart to the possibility yet." He folds onto the barstool beside me and takes my hand. "I did not take this decision lightly, Jia, much like my father before me. When they chose your grandmother as my wife, it was after considerable thought. Look how well that turned out. It may seem to you that this wedding to Marco is simply a strategic one, but trust me when I say I would not have agreed to any of it if I did not truly believe Mr. Rossi to be a good man. More than that, a good man *for you*. He will treat you as you deserve, *bǎobèi*, you must only give him the opportunity."

Clearly, my perfect fiancé failed to mention to my grandfather that I caught him with his tongue down the realtor's throat.

"I cannot trust him, *Yéye*."

"Maybe not right now, but in time, I am certain he will prove himself to you."

Another snort threatens to break free, but I manage to suppress it this time.

"Now come, we must go to the Waldorf. Your bridal suite has been prepared, and you are to spend the night there. Your future husband has arranged for the wedding glamour team to meet you there in the morning."

I gulp. How did this all happen so quickly? I was supposed to find a way out of this and now, I'd wasted the past two days pining over my missing fiancé instead of planning my escape.

CHAPTER 27
OUT OF CONTROL

M *arco*

I slam the empty crystal tumbler on the bar top and heave out a breath before signaling to the bartender again.

"You sure, Mr. Rossi?" The young blond guy eyes me warily.

"I'm getting married tomorrow, Sean. I'm fucking celebrating." Alone because my twin is too busy obsessing over his girlfriend to spend a minute with his damned brother.

The bartender doesn't move, his eyes narrowed on the row of empty glasses in front of me. So what if it's only noon?

"I've got a room upstairs, kid. I'm not driving anywhere. Just give me the fucking whiskey, or I'll have your pretty boy ass fired."

He dips his head and scrambles away, and I heave out a sigh of relief when he's back a moment later refilling my glass. As I sip the smooth, smoky liquid and twirl the cubes of ice around, my thoughts flicker to the dainty red box in my pocket, and my spirits sink lower.

Damn Nico for forcing me to buy a stupid engagement ring.

Jia despises me, she wants an open marriage and nothing to do with me. Why the fuck would a fifty-thousand-dollar diamond ring change anything?

The damned box burns a hole in my pocket, its weight against my thigh irritating the hell out of me. Plucking it free, I slam the little box onto the mahogany bar. The gold piping along the top glistens beneath the dim lighting. I flick the lid and the enormous princess cut diamond winks at me.

It would look perfect on Jia's long, slender finger. My grand plan was to go back to the penthouse and offer it as an apology. Only, every minute I waited, the more nervous I became. What if she refused it? What if she refused *me*?

So instead, I drank more.

She hates you, you *coglione*.

I flip the lid shut, cursing under my breath, and bury the ring in my pocket.

A rush of female voices jerks my attention to the entrance of the Waldorf's lobby bar. A gaggle of young women saunter toward me, inquisitive gazes latching on.

"O.M.G, it *is* him," one of the girls squeals.

"I told you," says another.

The four females in bright sundresses surround me, oblivious to my deepening scowl.

"You were in last month's *New Yorker* for Manhattan's most eligible bachelors," says a blonde.

"Caught me red-handed." I finish off the remainder of my drink and stand.

"Oh, no, please don't go." A brunette places her hand on my forearm. "We just got here."

"And that's why I'm leaving." I signal to the bartender. "Put it on my tab, Sean."

"Sure thing, Mr. Rossi."

"Why do you have to go?" The brunette's hold tightens.

"Because I'm getting married tomorrow." I narrow my gaze and flash her a tight smile. "So kindly remove your hand from my arm so I can be on my way."

"Unbelievable." A familiar voice echoes through the foyer, and a tangle of excitement and trepidation swirls in my gut.

I push past the circle of females to find Jia with her grandfather in the lobby. She glares up at me, pitch irises smoldering.

"So this is you giving me space?" she hisses. "Getting drunk with a bunch of girls in the middle of the day?"

"No," I grit out. "I was getting drunk by myself. They just showed up about a minute ago."

"I bet." She knots her arms across her chest, the disgust in her eyes palpable.

"Fuck, I just can't win with you, Jia," I snarl. "I'm really trying here, but you're making it impossible." I pace a tight circle, dragging my hands through my hair. "We're not even married yet, and you're already driving me crazy. I don't know if I can do this…"

"*You* don't know?" she snaps. "That's exactly what I've been saying from day one. This was a terrible idea!"

"I couldn't agree with you more."

"Then why are we even doing this?" She throws her hands in the air, her cheeks flushed.

"Fuck if I know."

"Mr. Rossi," Guo whispers, "perhaps we should take this discussion to a more private location."

I glance around the lobby and meet half a dozen curious gazes. *Merda*.

"And need I remind you," the old man whispers, "this arrangement has already been finalized with a binding contract. If you'd like to discuss any of the details in private—"

"No. I've said all I needed to say, and your granddaughter

has made her intentions perfectly clear." I spin to Jia, to her puckered lips, to the fury in those midnight irises. "I'll see you at the altar."

"Marco!" Her voice echoes behind me, but I can barely make it out over the wild thrashing of my pulse.

I need to get the hell out of here. I need to shoot at something or fuck the shit out of someone before I lose my damned mind. Marching out the gilded doors of the Waldorf, that godforsaken ring stabs at my thigh with each frenzied step. I should go back to Cartier and return the cursed diamond.

My assistant Mel had already procured two plain wedding bands for the ceremony. That was all we needed anyway. That reminds me... *Mel*. My feet compel me forward, each step more rushed than the last.

I'm not married yet. I didn't even get a bachelor party, and I deserve a night of fun.

Mel's apartment is a short walk from the Waldorf, but even after the frantic five-minute march, the haze of booze begins to lift. By the time I reach the building, my resolve is faltering. I stand at the door for an endless moment, my finger an inch from the buzzer. But fuck, it won't move.

I wasn't lying to Jia the other day. She's the only woman I want, the only person I can't get out of my mind. My stupid cock twitches at just the thought of her. He's so stupid he doesn't understand we don't have a chance. What am I going to do, force myself onto her on our wedding night? I'd never... And just because we'll be married doesn't obligate her to fuck me.

Dragging my hand through my hair, I spin on my heel and barrel into a familiar form. Mel's groceries go sprawling across the sidewalk and I hiss out a curse.

"Geez, Marco, watch out."

"Sorry." I drop to the ground beside her and refill her recyclable shopping bags.

Once I've gathered the array of fruit, yogurt and energy drinks, I straighten and draw in a steadying breath.

"What are you doing here?" She brushes an errant strand of blonde hair behind her ear.

"Nothing... Um, I was in the area and—"

She sniffs the air, then inches closer. "Are you drunk?"

"Not exactly." I shrug, but even I can smell the Macallan on my breath.

"So you got drunk and came to see me?" Her eyes widen, almost comically.

Was I that much of an asshole while we were together?

"Maybe," I mumble. "Before I realized what a dick move that would be."

"On the night before your wedding..."

"...Right."

She draws in a sharp breath and motions to the door. "What are you doing, Marco?"

"I don't fucking know. I'm so out of my league here." I tug at the wild ends of my hair, wishing I could rip them out. I've never felt so out of control. I jab my hands into my slacks' pockets, and my fingers brush the ring box. Fury pummels my veins, and there's nothing I want more than to toss the fucking diamond in the nearest dumpster.

She must read the turmoil in my gaze because she steps to the door and unlocks it. "You can come in if you want to talk. I'm sure this marriage thing must be hard on you."

The crazy thing is that it isn't the marriage part that has me in a tailspin. A few days ago, sure. But I've come to terms with it. Now, what's driving me mad is how much Jia *doesn't* want this. Women have always thrown themselves at me. I've never been denied.

Leaning against the door, I shake my head. "Nah, I think I'm good now, but thanks for the chat, Mel. And I'm sorry if I was a total ass while we were together. You didn't deserve that."

A rueful smile parts her lips. "That's the thing, Marco, we were never really together. You never gave us that chance." Before I can get another word out, she slips through the door and disappears down the hall.

I stand there, motionless, for a long moment considering her words. I'd been so fucked up after Isa, I never gave any woman a chance. I buried my head between the legs of any female I could have and drowned the pain in meaningless sex. I never wanted to be hurt like that again, and the only way to accomplish that was to never let anyone in, never allow myself to become attached, to love.

The blaring horn of a passing car snaps me from my mental musings. I look up just in time to see the barrel of a gun emerge through the cracked window of a black SUV.

CHAPTER 28
A REAL MARRIAGE

J*ia*

I stare at my reflection in the full-length mirror, attempting to find a woman I recognize beneath the elegant lace gown and flawless makeup. The high collar of embroidered lace accentuates my long neck, and the intricate updo only elevates the air of sophistication. The sheer sleeves feel light yet cover enough of my scars to ensure I fit the image of the perfect bride. I'd been primped and powdered from the moment I was awoken at six in the morning until two seconds ago when the stylists finally left.

"I cannot stop staring at you, Jia. You look gor-geous!" Ari lifts her flute overflowing with champagne and toasts the air between us. "Are you sure I can't get you a drink?"

"It's not even eleven…"

"I can put orange juice in it if you want. It can be breakfast." She tosses me a smirk.

The idea of food, let alone alcohol, has my stomach tied in

knots. In an hour, I'll be standing in front of a priest vowing to live a life with a man I despise until death do us part. What I hate the most is his insistence on going through with this sham of a wedding before the eyes of God. Couldn't we have just gotten this farce over with at the courthouse?

"Come on, Jia, it'll help loosen you up." Ari offers her flute. "Just a sip?"

I take a reluctant taste, and the soft bubbles coat the back of my throat. I can barely get it down. Handing it back to her, I shake my head, mouth puckered. "I just can't right now." The last thing I need is to throw up across the altar.

Then again, maybe it's just what I need...

"Mr. Rossi, no. I'm afraid I must insist." *Yéye's* gruff voice seeps through the door that leads to the sitting area of the immense suite. "You know it is bad luck to see the bride before the wedding."

I spin to the doorway as the shouts grow more enraged.

"I have to see Jia, Mr. Guo. It's urgent."

"What the hell?" I march past Ari and open the door a crack.

From the sliver of space, a pair of mismatched irises meet mine. "Jia, please I need to talk to you."

"Can't it wait?" I grit out, still pissed about finding him at the bar last night surrounded by a freaking entourage of beautiful blonde and brunette co-eds.

"No," he hisses.

"An hour from now, we'll have the rest of our lives to make idle chit-chat."

"Someone shot at me yesterday."

Those five words send my heart on a tailspin. "What?" I jerk the door open and Marco's eyes widen to the size of glistening full moons as his gaze rakes down my body. "*Yéye,* please give us a minute."

My grandfather nods and disappears back into the sitting area. Ari squeezes my shoulder and follows him out.

"*Cazzo*, Jia… You are… breathtaking…" Marco regards me for a long moment, a storm of emotions brewing beneath the bejeweled surface. His hand slides into his pocket, and a bulge catches my eye. For once, it isn't his inappropriate arousal, but rather something more square and bulky.

I take a minute to search his body for evident wounds, but when I find none, I find I still can't tear my eyes away. I slowly peruse the sleek black tuxedo that molds perfectly to his form, to the broad expanse of his shoulders and those muscled upper arms straining against the fine fabric. His hair is slicked back, the typical wild ends smoothed down today, and his face is clean-shaven which only accentuates his high cheek bones and sculpted jawline. God, the man is terrifyingly beautiful.

Forcing my gaze back up to meet his, I focus on why he's come. "Wait, you said you were shot?"

Marco blinks quickly, and that tempest of emotion subsides. "Some *pezzo di merda* took a shot at me through the window of a blacked-out Hummer yesterday." He creeps closer, one hand still shoved in his pocket. "Coming that close to death… I don't know, it just made me think. I was up all night tossing and turning, trying to figure all this shit out." His expression softens, and a hint of a smile curls his lips. "I don't want to go into our marriage with everything so up in the air." His broad shoulders lift, and a full grin softens the harsh lines of his jaw. "I understand how you could have misunderstood the situation at the bar last night, and maybe going MIA before the wedding wasn't the best idea—but fuck, Jia, I'm way out of my league here. I just don't know what to do."

My heart flutters around my ribcage like a silly butterfly. God, one smile from this man has the power to erase all his past wrongdoings. It's much too dangerous. I swallow hard, shoving all the pointless emotions to my darkest depths. "Do you know who's behind the shooting?"

He looses a frustrated breath. "No idea. I lucked out, honestly. I was just outside Mel's apartment and who knew her building has bulletproof glass doors? If I hadn't managed to dart inside, there would be no wedding today…" His words trail off as I fix on the earlier part of his explanation.

"What were you doing at Mel's apartment?" I blurt at the same time he asks, "Did *you* try to have me killed?"

We stand there, gaping at each other, the warm and fuzzy feelings from a second ago, vanished. The mistrust is so thick in the air it's suffocating.

Oh my God, how can I marry this man?

I'm a second away from asking how he could possibly think that of me when I remember I'd considered the very same thing. "No," I grit out. "I did not hire someone to kill you." I glare up at him, hands on my hips. "Now, what were you doing at her apartment the night before our wedding?"

"She's my assistant," he stammers.

"So that's why you were there? To hammer out last minute wedding plans?" I've heard the rumors floating around the office of Gemini Corp. As I had no intention of ever allowing Marco in my bed, I tried to ignore the fact that he's likely screwed half the administrative staff including his executive assistant.

His mouth twists into a frown, and the blade in my heart twists along with his lips.

"Why I originally went doesn't matter. I couldn't go through with it, okay? I was drunk and pissed and, yeah, maybe I went there looking to blow off some steam, but I didn't do anything with her. Damn it, Jia, don't you understand? I want you… I want my damned fiancée, my wife. I have since the moment I saw that pouty, bottom lip and the fire in your eyes."

His words strike a chord, and hot tears burn the back of my eyes. I wish it were that simple. "And can't you understand why I don't trust you?" I cry.

"How can you if you never even give me the chance?"

I snort on a laugh. "That's bullshit, Marco."

"No, it isn't. You're the one who's never given this relationship a shot. It didn't have to be like this between us, Jia. You made it this way." He finally pulls his hand out of his pocket and drags it through his hair, mussing up the perfect dark strands. "Now, before we cement our union before the eyes of God, tell me what you want. Do you want this to be a real marriage or not? Because I need to know what I'm committing to now. Like I said the other day, if you want an open marriage, fine, but let's make it clear before we say our *I do's*."

Did I want an open marriage? No. I didn't want any of this. I wanted to marry a man who loved me, not one who was forced into a business arrangement.

"I don't know," I grind out. "I need a minute to think about it."

"Then I guess that's your answer because I know what I want, and it's you. But if you're not willing to commit, I'm certainly not going to force myself on you. Well, except for the wedding night, I suppose. We must make sure it's all official in the eyes of the church. But trust me, after that, there's plenty of willing pussy in Manhattan." He spins on his heel before I can get another word out.

I stand there gaping, a tangle of hurt scraping across my insides. Even if he had stayed, I have no idea what I would have said.

God, I despise him. But what I hate even more is that I don't hate him as much as I should.

Before Marco disrupted my neat little world, I knew where I stood, I knew what I wanted and where I was going. Now, the Earth spins beneath my feet, and everything I thought I knew is whirling off its axis.

Tears fill my eyes, and this time, I'm too exhausted to hold them back.

Ari must hear my quiet sobs because her soft footfalls brush the floor an instant before she appears beside me and draws me into her arms. "Oh, sweety, don't cry. You're going to smear all that beautiful makeup."

I snort on a sob.

After letting me cry on her shoulder for a long minute, she holds me out to arm's length and sweeps her thumbs beneath my eyes. "Luckily, it was waterproof, and you still look as beautiful as ever."

"I don't feel beautiful," I mutter.

"What did Marco say?"

"He wants a real marriage, and I said I wasn't sure what I wanted. He got pissed and stormed off, and he's probably going to screw the first woman he runs into after the ceremony."

"Oh, stop, I really don't think he'll do that."

"I'm not sure, Ari... I've never seen him so worked up. It seems almost as if he cares." Worse, I'm starting to. Too bad I just gave him permission to fuck whomever he wanted. And knowing my fiancé and his old manwhoring ways, he'll be more than happy to take me up on the offer.

CHAPTER 29
COLD FEET

M *arco*

The faint tune of the grand organ fills the church, extending high up into the soaring rafters of the Gothic cathedral, distracting me from the rush of murmurs from our gathered guests. But none of the sounds succeed in drowning out the mad thundering of my heart. *Cazzo*, why the fuck am I so nervous?

Jia already agreed to an open marriage. I should be pleased. This whole production is just for show. Tomorrow, I can go back to my old life. The only difference will be that I'll have a new roommate. It's certainly not the worst thing that could happen. Except, really, it is.

Standing at the back of the church, I rub my sweaty palms on my slacks and attempt to draw in a steadying breath. The cathedral is packed with hundreds of attendees, including the leaders of the most notorious crime families of Manhattan. Guards line every nook and cranny. If this weren't such a high-profile, public event, the results would be catastrophic. I can't remember the last time the Italians, Chinese, Irish, and Russians were all in the same room together, not to mention all the up-and-coming players, the Puerto Ricans, the Polish, even the Japanese.

All here for us. To witness the historic joining of the Geminis and Four Seas.

A firm grip clasps around my shoulder, and I nearly jump out of my skin. "Whoa, relax, *fratello*, it's just me." Nico appears at my side, and my manic pulse simmers. "What has you so on edge?"

"Oh, I don't know, *coglione*. Maybe it's the wedding thing, or perhaps it's the powder keg we're sitting on." I tick my head at the horde of attendees. "Did you really have to invite the Russians?"

"What would be the point of this strategic alliance if we didn't show it off?"

"Right," I hiss.

"How is your beautiful bride?" He smirks, eyeing row upon row of the who's who in organized crime.

"Reluctant," I murmur, and even I can hear the bitterness lacing my tone.

"I don't believe it... after all this time, the charming Marco Rossi hasn't been able to win her over?"

"Fuck you, Nico."

"Hey, boys, play nice." Maisy materializes from the arched entryway, looking stunning in a deep ruby gown that matches her fiery hair. "It's Marco's wedding day, Nico, give him a break. He already looks like he's about a second from puking." She throws me that concerned, motherly look. "Are you going to be okay?"

"Yes, I'll be fine," I grit out. "I just want to get this over with."

Maisy presses a quick kiss to my cheek and gives me a reassuring smile. "I'll go check on Jia and make sure she's not getting cold feet. Don't worry, everything is going to work out just great. I know it."

"I wish I shared your eternal optimism, Mais."

With a quick squeeze to my hand, she scampers down a candlelit corridor, disappearing into the bowels of the old cathedral. Nico's gaze trails her retreating form for a long minute, the yearning in his eyes only tightening the constraints around my ribcage.

"Just go with her," I growl.

"No, no. I'm here for moral support."

"I was about to say the same thing." An irritatingly familiar voice echoes across the vestibule.

I slowly turn to find my half-brother Dante with his wife, along with his brother, Luca and his fiancée, Stella.

"You know, you really didn't have to come," I grumble.

"And miss the opportunity to revel in your happy day?" Dante's smirk is begging to be punched right off his face.

"Dante…" Rose, his wife, reprimands. "You promised to be on your best behavior."

"You both did." Stella, Luca's fiancée, waggles a finger, showcasing an enormous engagement ring.

"And we will," Luca replies. "We're very happy for you, Marco." He gives me a tight smile which I barely manage to return.

Dante slaps me across the back and flashes a shit-eating grin. "You're going to love married life, *fratello*. You can fuck your wife all day and night, *and* you have someone to cook and do the laundry."

Rose smacks him on the arm, and he lets out a dramatic *oof*. "Behave."

My half-brother is all talk. He adores his wife and worships the ground she walks on. I've never seen him let her do an ounce of dirty work. That's what the staff is for.

Which reminds me…

"Nico, did you invite Blanca to the wedding?"

He nods. "As we decided. Maisy made quite a show of it, actually."

"You still think she's up to something?" Luca asks, the look of boredom lifting.

"The Puerto Ricans definitely are," Nico replies. "I'm just not certain if Blanca has anything to do with it yet. I spoke to Esmeralda, the head of *La Sombra Boricua,* and she denies any involvement with the recent attacks to our warehouses."

Luca's head dips. "I've had the same conversation with her. We've always had a good relationship so I don't see why she would lie now."

"Okay, boys, enough of this work talk." Rose steps between us and laces her hand around Dante's. "We're here to celebrate, and I want to make sure we have a good seat."

Clearing my throat, I tick my head toward the front of the church. "My assistant blocked off the first two rows for family. Feel free to use those." And since I'd chosen not to invite my mother because we weren't speaking at the moment, and my father was dead, we didn't exactly have many bodies to fill those seats.

A beaming smile stretches across Rose's lips, and my own mouth twitches at the sight. "Thanks, Marco. You're the best." I may not be a big fan of my half-brothers, but I can't deny they have good taste in women.

"We'll see you at the reception." Luca dips his head and pulls Stella into his side as he follows Dante and Rose down the aisle.

The tap-tap of heels across the stone floor turns my attention away from my half-brothers to the wedding planner marching toward us. "We're ready to go, gentlemen. Please take your places."

Nico inches closer and throws his arm across my shoulders. "You see? Everything is going to be just fine."

"I blame you for this by the way," I snarl. "It should have been you walking down that aisle, not me."

"Oh, stop, Marco. A few months from now, you'll be thanking me."

"We'll see about that." I squirm free from his hold and trudge down the damned aisle to take my place by the priest.

"Hey! Wait for me." Nico rushes behind me, and already I'm regretting making him my best man. The *coglione* didn't even throw me a damned bachelor party.

All eyes turn in my direction as I stalk past, and I can't even muster a smile. Instead, I don the practiced cold mask and pray this will all be over soon. The walk to the altar is endless, each step more difficult than the last.

Merda, I can't remember the last time I was this terrified about anything.

When I finally reach the marble step, I genuflect and make a quick sign of the cross. The priest's eyes meet mine, and guilt squeezes my chest. I've done many terrible things in my life, but nothing feels quite as wrong as this.

"Don't worry, I have the rings." Nico presses his palm to his jacket.

The wedding bands were the last thing on my mind. I'd left the engagement ring I'd bought for Jia in the hotel room safe. I'd walked into her suite this morning with every intention of getting down on one knee and starting this marriage out on the right foot. Then everything had gone to hell as usual with us.

Could she have possibly sent an assassin?

I didn't want to believe she was capable of that, but then again, she was related to Qian Guo, both iterations. She'd never wanted this marriage and disposing of me would not only achieve an end to the arrangement but also garner some notoriety for the new *lǎodà* of the Four Seas.

The familiar tune of the wedding march blasts from the enormous brass organ overhead, and all the hushed murmurs fall away. My ribs strain, assaulted by the jackhammering of my heart. The doors at the back of the church open, and Jia fills the archway. I thought she looked stunning before, but now with the sunlight streaming in through the stained-glass windows, her beauty is ethereal. Her porcelain skin is aglow, so radiant my breath hitches at the sight. It's as if her entire form is illuminated by the sun itself.

My eyes chase to hers, and the excitement vanishes. Those dark, impenetrable eyes are cast in shadows, empty, devoid of emotion.

She's miserable, and I'm smiling like an idiot. Like she is my real bride, and we are actually in love.

Dio, I'm a fucking *coglione*.

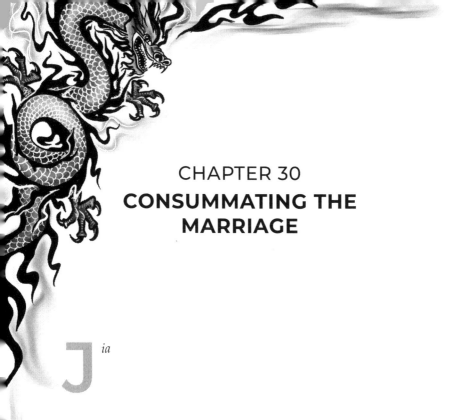

CHAPTER 30
CONSUMMATING THE MARRIAGE

J*ia*

My muscles tense as Marco's penetrating gaze pierces into my darkest depths from across the lengthy expanse of the cathedral. *Yéye* must feel my anxiety because his hold around my arm tightens as he urges me forward.

But my glittering stilettos are rooted to the spot.

I cannot do this.

"Come, *bǎobèi*, everyone is waiting," Grandfather whispers.

I attempt to will my foot forward, but it refuses to comply. My entire body is rigid, frozen in this terrifying, visceral moment. My fight or flight reflexes kick in and if I could only compel my legs to move, I'd sprint out the doors of the cathedral before anyone could stop me.

But that dark gaze rakes over me, and I'm a hopeless captive.

Marco's head slowly dips, and the faintest hint of a smile tips up the corner of his lip. It shouldn't affect me like it does, but somehow, the ice coating my veins thaws, and I take a wary step forward, clutching the bouquet of jasmines in a death grip.

Yéye takes advantage of the sudden movement, and we're suddenly whizzing down the aisle, all the curious stares and unfamiliar faces a blur. My gaze locks on the gilded cross above the altar, and somehow, my legs continue to propel me forward.

I blink, and we've already arrived at the first step. *Yéye* brushes a kiss to my cheek and hands me over to my uncertain future. Marco's hands grip mine, and I'm surprised to find moisture coating his palms. It's so unexpected, I hazard a glance up and meet those stormy eyes.

A tight smile melts the hard set of his jaw for an instant before we turn to face the priest. He begins to speak, but the mad drumbeat of my heart muffles his words. My head begins to spin, my lungs struggling for air. I think I'm having a panic attack. Instead of allowing the darkness to swallow me under, I focus on Marco's unwavering gaze.

That look is so raw, so turbulent, and yet it anchors me to the present. My own emotions are a tangled mess, the rush of nerves and fear crashing against the undeniable attraction and desire. Had I made a terrible mistake agreeing to an open marriage?

Clenching my teeth, I resolve to remain strong. Even if I hadn't, I doubt the philandering male would've kept to our wedding vows. The idea of Marco with another woman sends fire surging through my core and jealousy tearing at my insides. Yes, I need to hold onto that. To the fury, the anger. It makes me strong. The uncertainty, the onrush of feelings, they only make me weak and vulnerable.

I think back to the vow I'd made when I'd been ambushed by my grandfather into this nightmarish arrangement: I'll kill Marco Rossi the first chance I get. As I stare into those mercurial eyes, my heart pinches.

And I'm certain in that moment, I could never do it.

I may resent the man and distrust him, but I could never be the cause of those darting eyes closing for all eternity.

As if Marco has plucked the thought right from my mind, his hands tighten around mine. He inches closer, and I blink quickly, certain I must be imagining it.

"...and now you may kiss the bride." The priest's words pierce the chaos of my scrambling thoughts, and all the oxygen rushes from my failing lungs.

Marco's mouth captures mine, stealing the remaining air, and my head spins. His lips are soft, moving tentatively at first, but when I don't immediately pull away, he deepens the kiss. For a second, I'm back in the limo when I offered a kiss in exchange for a visit with Lei while my fiancé tortured him. That kiss had been an inferno, fueled by anger and desire. This one, in contrast, is almost tender, a gentle flame that warms rather than burns.

And my heart staggers at the difference.

When I finally summon the wherewithal, I pull away and draw in a much-needed breath of air not tainted with Marco's intoxicating, musky scent. Applause echoes around the cathedral, snapping me from the emotion-fueled haze.

Marco spins us toward the guests and raises our interlocked hands triumphantly. I barely muster a smile as the thunderous applause rages on. Once it finally dies down, we're moving again. This time it's my fia—husband ushering me down the aisle at a hurried pace instead of my grandfather. Oh, God, *husband*?

The myriad of faces rush by in a whirlwind as guards move in around us. Once we reach the vestibule, we're hastily escorted to the classic silver Bentley parked outside.

"Why are we running?" I murmur.

"Aren't you anxious to put an end to this farce?"

I nod slowly as the driver yanks the door open. Of course, I am. But maybe for an instant there, I wished it hadn't all been an act. I slide into the backseat and curl against the far door. "Where are we going now?" It's embarrassing, really, that I have no idea of the order of events for my own wedding.

"There will be a cocktail hour at the Astor Salon featuring a variety of hors d'oeuvres, then we'll move into the Grand Ballroom for the plated eight-course dinner."

"*Eight?*" I grumble. This nightmare of an evening would drag on forever.

"What's wrong, spitfire? Are you anxious to get our wedding night started?"

"No…" I hiss and press closer against the door to put as much space between us as humanly possible.

"You do understand that in order for the wedding to be valid, we must consummate it, right?"

I clear my throat, drawing out the silence for a lengthy moment. "I am aware of the Catholic traditions." I pause and nibble on my thumb. "But then again, an open marriage is not permitted under the eyes of the Lord either, so I'm not sure any of this is necessary in keeping with this sacred ritual."

He grinds out a rueful laugh, shaking his head. "So even on our wedding night, you'll deny me? Do you want me to celebrate the grand occasion with someone else?"

"Fuck you," I spit.

"I'm trying…"

"God, I hate you."

"Same here, wifey."

"Don't call me that!"

"Well, what should I call you, then? You didn't approve of spitfire either. Honey? Babe? Boo?"

"Let's just live in silence." I lean against the tinted window, the beginnings of a headache thrumming along my temples.

"Fine."

The remainder of the car ride through the bustling Manhattan city center is spent in silence. I have more than enough to consider with my spiraling thoughts. When the

Bentley finally pulls up to the Waldorf, the thrashing anxiety begins again.

The driver circles the car and opens the door on Marco's side. My new husband slides out, and I briefly consider jumping into the front seat and making a quick getaway. Would anyone catch me? Could I make it to the Canadian border?

Yéye's weary gaze fills my mind and I toss all thoughts of escape out the window. This is my duty. Not to marry this man or be his perfect wife, but to lead the Four Seas. That would be my focus from now on. Not to mention my boutique. Tomorrow, I'd divert all my attention back to opening my shop.

Just because Marco and I are married, it doesn't mean my life has to change much. Sure, I'll be living in a posh penthouse and running a notorious crime syndicate, but besides that, everything could stay the same.

You're delusional, Jia. I really must have been because that inner voice sounds a lot like my dead brother. All these weeks I haven't even thought twice of him. Maybe it was only an excuse to hate my future husband...

Marco's head appears through the door, a line of irritation furrowing his brow. "Are you coming or what?" He throws his hand out, palm up.

Heaving out a breath, I glide across the leather seat and ignore his offered hand. Guards already line the front door of the Waldorf. Only invited guests are permitted to enter the hotel today due to the infamous VIPs. Besides the crime bosses, the guest list includes a list of the city's most influential political and business elite: the mayor, some senators, a few congressmen, and a whole host of CEOs. The only reason I know any of this is that I'd had Marco's assistant send me the list of invitees last night. It had been partially out of curiosity, but more so to get a chance to chat with Marco's ex. It was silly and petty, or at least I'd thought so until my new husband let it slip that he'd been on his way to rekindle an old flame when he'd nearly been shot.

Asshole.

Fighting hard to hold onto the anger, I march up the red carpet and through the front door of the hotel. Marco walks a few steps behind me, and even at this distance, I can feel his fury.

I still don't understand what he's so upset about. He should be relieved I'm allowing this open arrangement. Despite his claims otherwise, I'm certain his desire to be with me only stems from my virginal status. Once he's had me, he'll grow tired of the novelty and want nothing more than to be let loose. I'm sure of it.

His hand latches around mine as a camera flashes an inch from my nose. "Smile for the camera, Jia," he mutters.

"I am." I shoot the photographer a feral grin.

"Just remember, you're going to have to look back at these pictures for the rest of our lives." He lowers his voice and leans in so that his warm breath skates across my ear. "Assuming you don't try to have me shot again."

"I didn't," I grit out. "So you should probably find out who did."

"Trust me, I will." He drags me into the lobby, and my team of stylists swallows me whole, forcing my husband to release my hand.

I'm powdered, perfectly groomed, and fussed over again, while Marco stands a few feet away, murmuring to one of the guards. The typically tight security is doubled today with every inch of the lobby crawling with men in black uniforms and earpieces.

As soon as the stylists back away, Marco is at my side once again. "You ready to go in?" He offers his hand, and this time, I take it.

"Do I have any other choice?"

CHAPTER 31
PERFECT

J *ia*

"Did it really have to be eight courses?" I grouse around a mouthful of tortellini. Marco sits beside me, shoveling the pasta into his mouth. He's been oddly quiet throughout the lengthy meal. We are only on the fourth course, and already, I'm certain I'll burst. I haven't eaten a thing all day and of course, now I'm ravenous. Also, I have no idea how I'll get out of my wedding gown tonight without help.

I doubt my stylists will be accompanying me back to the bridal suite. My stomach flip-flops at the thought. The idea of being alone with my new husband has a tangle of nerves, fear, and inexplicable desire flooding my chest. I refuse to consider what the last part means.

"Yes," he finally mumbles. "The wedding meal is supposed to be a feast, to regale the guests with your wealth and provide the couple with sustenance for a long wedding night." He smirks and for an instant, the joking, light-hearted mob boss I met resurfaces.

"Well, at this rate, I might fall asleep before we make it to our suite."

"*Our?*" His enigmatic irises sparkle to life.

I snap my jaw closed, annoyed with myself at that slip of the tongue.

"I assumed you'd force me to sleep in my own room," he continues.

At least he didn't say someone else's room. Waving a dismissive hand, I spear another tortellini drenched in the creamy sauce. "The bridal suite is huge. It would be wasteful to spend money on another room."

"I have lots of money, spitfire."

"It doesn't mean you have to waste it, *honey*."

His grin grows wider until it unfolds into a beaming smile, and God, I hate how all resolve crumbles at the sight. He points his fork at me. "I believe I like 'honey.'"

"Then I'll think of something else." I throw him a sweet smile and shove more tortellini in my mouth before our banter turns downright civil.

The wedding planner rushes over as I swallow down the last bite. "Finish up, it's time for the first dance."

"Now?" Why couldn't we have done that before the damned fourth course?

"Yes, Mrs. Rossi, now."

Mrs. Rossi? I cringe at the sound. "That's Guo," I snap.

"Apologies, Mrs. Guo. And to you, Mr. Rossi, for the interruption, but the orchestra is playing the song you selected next."

"The song *you* selected?" My gaze swivels between the planner and Marco.

"I picked one at random," he mutters.

Oh. That is unexpected. Now, I'm beyond curious…

Marco scoots his chair back, the sharp squeal against the

burnished wooden planks screeching over the pause in the orchestra music. A few curious gazes swivel in our direction as I stand, and Marco laces his fingers through mine.

With an increasing number of heads turning in our direction, I can't help but lean into his towering form to hide from the inquisitive gazes. To keep from meeting their stares, I take in the Grand Ballroom for the first time tonight.

The impressive space is adorned with intricate details that suggest a long-gone era of grandeur. The ceilings soar high above, lavishly decorated with ornate crystal chandeliers. The light casts a soft, ambient glow throughout the room, reflecting off the golden hues of the wall trimmings. The walls themselves are lined with paneled silk and velvet draperies, adding a touch of royal decadence to the atmosphere.

It's truly breathtaking.

I'm still amazed Marco's assistant was able to pull off the grand occasion in only two short weeks. And they say money can't buy you happiness…

When we reach the polished wood dance floor, the orchestra picks up a familiar tune. I'd fully expected a classic ballad from Frank Sinatra or Etta James, but instead the eight-piece orchestra plays their rendition of *Perfect* by Ed Sheeran.

Marco's arm laces around my waist, and a thousand tiny blades pierce my heart as he starts to hum the tune.

"I didn't know you were an Ed Sheeran fan." It's the last thing I would have expected from the playboy mafia boss.

He shrugs. "The guy knows how to write a love song."

"And what do you know about love, Mr. Rossi?" I curl my arms around the back of his neck because apparently Ed Sheeran is also a sorcerer.

"Not much, apparently, Mrs. Guo." A rueful smile hitches up the corner of his lips as he pulls me flush against his chest.

He guides me across the dance floor, my body moving effortlessly with his. For an instant, everyone else disappears, and it's only us and the magical notes and heart-filled words of the song. My chest heaves, brushing against his with each breath. His eyes darken as they latch onto my peaked nipples through the fine lace.

God, my emotions are so all over the place right now. I've never felt so out of control. One moment I'm certain I could murder Marco Rossi and the next, I cannot wait to fall into his arms.

"Jia, I..."

I press my finger to his lips, cutting him off. "Let's talk about it later, okay?" All of our discussions tend to take an animated turn, and a public fight with my new husband wouldn't exactly solidify the united front we're attempting to portray.

His head dips, and his nose accidentally brushes mine. My gaze lifts to meet his and our mouths hover only a heartbeat away. My breath hitches as thoughts of that kiss at the church whirl to the forefront of my mind. How is it possible to despise someone so much and yet be so attracted to them in the same instant?

The clinking of glasses rings out, a symphony of tinkling crystal, and Marco's mouth melts into a devious grin. "I guess we should make the audience happy."

"I don't know..." I rasp out, but my traitorous lips have already inched closer.

"If the Triad is to back off, we need to make them believe our arrangement is a solid one."

"And a kiss is going to do that?"

"Fuck if I know, spitfire, but it sure as hell would make this performance more pleasant for me." Again, with that smirk.

"Why would you enjoy kissing a woman who despises you?" Despite the bite of my words, my body leans into him as we smoothly move across the dancefloor.

"Maybe I like a little challenge..."

And a challenge he would get.

"Come on, just kiss her already!" From over Marco's shoulder, I catch sight of his half-brother, Dante, practically bashing his fork against the champagne flute.

"Ass," Marco mouths as he spins around to glare at the notorious Valentino.

"Fine," I grit out. "Just do it, or they'll never stop."

"*Dio*, you really know how to charm a man." His bottom lip juts out as if he's truly offended.

Rolling my eyes, I capture that pouty lower lip, drawing it between my teeth. Whoops and cheers explode around us as I nibble on the pillowy flesh.

"You better not draw blood," he mumbles against my lips, and I'm honestly shocked I'm able to make out the garbled words.

His hand creeps up my bare spine and his fingers dig into the hair at my nape before he dips us so low, the top of my elaborate updo nearly touches the lacquered parquet. How he manages to sustain the kiss while sweeping me across the floor is pretty impressive.

"This bare back is truly scandalous, Mrs. Guo." His fingers dance along my bare skin as he whispers. "I may have to tear the eyes out of every guest in this room for daring to look at what's mine."

When we finally straighten, I'm completely breathless from the fiery kiss and the risky dance move. The lyrics of the end of the song echo in the background, and Marco mouths the words. I'm not certain he realizes he's doing it.

"Now I know I have met an angel in person
And she looks perfect
I don't deserve this
You look perfect tonight"

My heart pinches, and a wave of regret batters my insides as those mesmerizing eyes lance into mine. Why did I say I wanted an open marriage? Because I'm too embarrassed to admit the truth? That I may actually like this man… I'm such an idiot.

"There, that should keep them off our backs for a little while, at least." That trademark smirk falls into place as the song comes to an end, and he releases me, leaving my body cold at the sudden absence of his.

Which reminds me... "Why did you choose that song?"

He shrugs and starts to back away as the dancefloor begins to fill with our guests. "I told you, it was random."

"Well, I liked it."

His eyes widen as he regards me. "At least I managed to do one thing right."

I open my mouth to respond, to tell him he's done more things right than I care to admit, but a shot rings out, stealing the words from my lips.

CHAPTER 32
LET HER GO

M *arco*

Merda! My heart lurches up my throat as gunshots ricochet across the dancefloor. Screams and cries fill the air, but all my focus is on Jia. Her eyes are wide as she stares at me, her mouth curved into a capital *O*. Then both our gazes drift lower, to the blood blossoming across the pristine white lace of her gown.

"Jia!" I shout and pull her into my arms. She glances up at me, two midnight spheres wide with fear. *Cazzo*, why did I ever let her go? Lifting her up, I cradle her slender form against my chest. Deep crimson blooms across her torso, and panic claws at my heart. "I've got you, spitfire. You're going to be fine."

Shots crackle in the air as our bodyguards spring into action, absolute chaos ensuing. The wedding guests are running, trampling over one another to reach the exit. Nico races toward us with Maisy, Jimmy at his heels. My brother's right-hand man holds a gun in each hand, his expression savage.

"Fuck," Nico hisses as his wild gaze lands on us.

"Oh my golly, is she okay?" Maisy's bright-green eyes go impossibly wide.

"Of course she's not okay, Mais," I growl. "She's been shot."

Nico steals the handkerchief from my pocket and presses it to the wound.

Merda, why didn't I think of that?

Jia's pale lids flutter, and paralyzing fear constricts my ribcage. "Jia, stay with me. Keep your eyes open." Fuck! If I hadn't been so busy screwing around, I would have had time to find out who shot at me yesterday. Now, Jia had paid the price for my failing.

I'll find the assholes behind this and kill them all. No one hurts my wife. I'll burn Manhattan to the ground if that's what it takes.

All the cries blur around me, the manic pounding of my heart drowning out everything else.

"Marco!" Nico's shout jerks me from my downward spiral. He's standing in front of my face, waving his phone. "Dr. Pacetti will meet us at your penthouse in five."

"No, fuck that. I'm taking her to the hospital."

"Are you out of your mind? You know I cannot let you do that."

"My *wife* was shot at our wedding, *bastardo*! You don't think that's going to make the front-page news either way? I won't risk her safety to keep Gemini Corp out of the public eye."

Maisy sneaks in beside me and whispers, "I'll call the ambulance. Go out the back."

My throat tightens, and I'm about a second away from kissing my twin's girlfriend full on the lips. Instead, I muster a quick, "Thank you," before darting toward the door of the grand ballroom.

Nico shouts behind me, but his voice is drowned out by the pandemonium. As I race through the crowd with my palm pressing the handkerchief to the wound, barreling over Red Dragons and Four Seas alike, it occurs to me I should find Jia's grandfather. If anything happens to him, she'll be devastated...

But I can't stop to look for him now.

I resolve to send Jimmy a message to find the old man as soon as Jia is safe. Speeding down the hallway of the hotel, I ignore the warm blood coating my sleeves and my sticky fingers. Jia will be fine. She *must* be. Pushing through another set of doors, I run into a wall of black suits. One of the men I immediately recognize: Max, my brother's driver. The big guy dips his head, and I exhale sharply.

"Come on, I'll escort you both safely outside." Signaling at the other men to stay put, he moves into step beside me, and a hint of relief slows the manic thundering of my pulse.

"Thanks," I mutter.

"Just following orders, Mr. Rossi."

"My brother?"

He nods.

The hint of a smile tugs at my lips despite the fear. Nico might be an asshole most of the time, but even he understands. Maybe more than I do. I glance down at Jia and my damned heart crumbles. Blood soaks the front of her beautiful gown. Squeezing my eyes closed, dark memories of the past rush to the surface.

Vacant eyes staring into the night sky.

Cool, frosty skin beneath my cheek as I hold her icy body to mine.

Isa...

"No," I grit out. "I won't lose you, spitfire."

The wail of the ambulance echoes at a distance before we

reach the back alley of the Waldorf. Max shoves the double doors open and I sprint out into the dim alley. The brilliant blue and red lights light up the narrow passageway an instant later.

The rest happens in a blur, my mind too plagued with fear to process any of it.

"Sir, you have to let her go." A paramedic glares at me, but my arms only tighten around Jia. "I can't help the woman until you release her."

"She's my wife," I mumble.

"Fine, sir. Now hand me your wife so I can help her."

Another paramedic appears beside me, this one a female. Her hand squeezes my upper arm as if attempting to pry Jia from my unyielding hold. "Come on, sir. We need to tend to that wound."

The male gets in my face again as he paws at Jia. "Do you want her to die?"

Die. Die. Die.

The word ping-pongs across my skull. Slowly, I shake my head.

"Then give her to me. You can ride with us in the ambulance to the hospital."

I attempt to do as I'm told, but I've lost all control of my bodily functions. I'm numb.

"Come on, boss, let me help you." Max pries Jia free of my death grip, and I watch, frozen, as he hands her over to the paramedic. Everything moves so incredibly slowly now—the sirens, the shouts—everything muffled, as if I were underwater.

I'm drowning.

Suffocating in fear and guilt.

Jia is hauled onto the stretcher and then loaded into the back of the ambulance. The paramedics are shouting instructions, numbers, and vitals that I can't understand.

The female EMT sticks her head out of the back of the truck

and ticks her chin at me. "Get in now if you want to come with us."

I stand there unmoving, my soles rooted to the cement for an endless moment.

"Boss! Hey, boss!" Max grips me by the shoulders and gives me a good shake. "You have to go now."

I blink quickly, and my head dips as I try to spur my legs into action. Max gives me a little push, and my feet finally move. The lady paramedic holds out her hand, and I grab on, then she hauls me into the back and the doors slam behind us.

The steady hiss of oxygen and intermittent beeping from the heart monitor has my own blood pressure skyrocketing. I pace the small hospital room, pissed off as all hell that they haven't moved us to the suite I'd requested yet.

Tugging at my bowtie which still hangs loose around my collar, I finally rip it free. Over the past few hours, I've shed bits and pieces of my tux. Jia's gown is in tatters, but I asked the paramedics to save the remains. I know how much her grandmother's dress means to her, and with her sewing skills, I have no doubt Jia could return it to its former glory one day.

If only she would wake up.

She lies so still, enveloped in an oversized robe. *Yéye* had insisted upon the thick terry cloth as opposed to the typical hospital gown. *My granddaughter is always cold, Mr. Rossi. Something you should learn about your new wife.* If she survives…

The surgeon said the surgery went well. The entire bullet was removed and no fragments had splintered off. The damned projectile had been only inches from her heart. I'd spent all night racking my brain, attempting to figure out who the fuck was behind this so I could tear their spine out through their throat, then stomp all over their disemboweled remains.

Jia had been the target. There was no doubt about it; that is unless the shooter was just totally incompetent. I stood within a foot from her when she was hit. Plus, I'd been shot at the day before, so clearly someone wanted us both out of the picture.

It had to be the same shooter, right?

"How is she?" Nico's voice jerks me from the jumble of my inner thoughts. And also, *cazzo*, how had I not heard him come in? He hands me a bouquet of bright flowers in a pretty vase, and all I can think is that they're not jasmine. Jia and her light, floral scent invades my nostrils. Even my memories of her natural perfume are so damned vivid.

I glance over my shoulder at Max stationed outside the hospital room door. At least someone was on guard.

"The same," I mumble.

My brother and his girlfriend had come by last night with Mr. Guo to check on Jia once Nico had done damage control. The tabloids had already gotten wind of the fiasco, and rumors were flying.

I try to care, but at the moment I couldn't give a shit. All I care about is seeing those dark eyes alive with light again. Even if they are filled with rage.

"When does the doctor expect her to wake?"

"She should have woken up by now…"

Nico's chin dips and he inches closer, squeezing my shoulder. "Love sucks, huh, *fratello*?"

"Love?" I blurt, massaging the void in my chest.

He points to Jia then me. "Isn't that what this is?"

I shake my head, a rueful smile curling the corners of my lips. It's been so long since I felt it, I wasn't sure I'd recognize the feeling even if it smacked me in the face. "I don't know," I finally mumble.

"It sure looks like it to me."

"Because now that you have Maisy, you're the love expert?"

He shrugs. "It does change your view on things."

"Did you punish your girlfriend for disobeying you and calling the ambulance for me last night?"

His grin twists into a scowl. "No…"

"My, my, you really have changed, Nico." I slap my brother on the shoulder as I pass him, resuming my pacing.

"Marco…" That voice sends me spinning on my heel, the delicate female timbre already possessing a straight line to my heart.

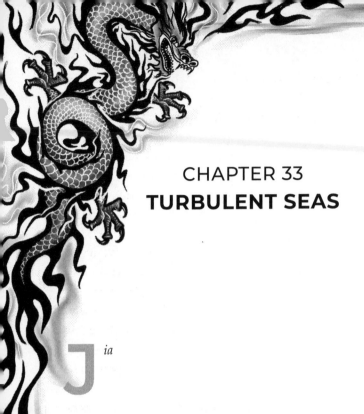

CHAPTER 33
TURBULENT SEAS

J *ia*

Fuck, everything hurts.

I blink quickly until the haze lifts, and I can make out the two men in my hospital room. "Marco..." I rasp. My voice sounds raw, like I've been gargling glass.

Marco darts across the room and appears at my bedside before I can blink. Something dark and unreadable flashes across those peculiar irises. Fear? Pity?

For a second, the depth of emotion steals the words from the tip of my tongue. Then my mind flies back in time to the chaos of the wedding. "Where's my grandfather?" I blurt, trying and failing to sit up.

"He's safe." Marco sits on the edge of the bed, hovering at the very end by my feet. "He was here last night, but I sent him home with Rick to get some rest. I practically had to force him to leave your side. I'll have Max call now to tell him you're awake."

"Poor *Yéye*. He must have been so worried…" I rub my arms and the soft terry cloth covering the scars provides immediate comfort. Had Marco seen them last night?

"He was."

"We all were." Nico appears behind his brother and offers a surprisingly pleasant smile. I don't believe I've ever seen one from the intimidating man. "I'm happy to see that you are awake. You had my brother sweating." A smirk lights up his deep blue eyes.

My gaze pivots to my new husband. Now that I've had a minute, I take in his disheveled state. His hair is a wild mess, sticking up in crazy points, dark circles mar the soft skin beneath his eyes, and he still wears the bloodied tuxedo shirt from yesterday, though it hangs open and it seems like a few buttons have come loose.

"I should leave you two to catch up," Nico whispers as he begins to back out of the room.

Marco's weary gaze doesn't deviate from mine, nor does he offer a goodbye to his brother. Once the door closes, he heaves out a breath and slides closer. His hand reaches out tentatively, before his warm fingers close around my icy ones. "*Cazzo*, spitfire, not even a day in and you try to make a widower out of me?"

A rueful chuckle squeezes out, and pain rushes up my torso. Shit, that hurts. Note to self: no laughing. Marco must notice my grimace because he bites out an apology.

"Damn it, I really can't get anything right with you, can I?"

"Getting me shot on our wedding day definitely doesn't bode well…" Pure misery etches into the hard set of his jaw and guilt spears me in the chest. "I didn't mean that. I know it wasn't your fault. I don't actually blame you for this—"

"You should. I'm your husband! It's my duty to protect you." He releases my hand and leaps up, dragging a hand through his hair for surely what has to be the thousandth time from the looks of it. "Fuck, Jia, when I saw that blood, I almost lost my shit. It was ten times worse than all the times I've been shot combined."

I raise a hand and sear him with a steely gaze. "First of all, don't get all caveman on me just because we're married now. I'm more than capable of protecting myself, as I've said many times already."

"I know, but—" He paces a quick circle before dropping back onto the bed. He jostles the mattress beneath his massive weight, and I wince again. "Damn it, I'm sorry. Again." He sucks in a breath and then slowly releases it. "I'm clearly not good at this husband shit."

Repressing a chuckle, I shake my head. "We both have a lot to learn, apparently."

His head dips, his fingers tangling with mine once more. Then his eyes lift to mine and that tempest of emotion flares. "I promise to find the person responsible for this and personally eviscerate them."

"Only if you let me go with you."

The hint of a smile curls his lip. "Deal, wifey."

"And you never call me that again."

His grin only grows wider.

I squeeze his hand before prying my fingers free. "Can you please call *Yéye* now and tell him I'm all right?"

"Yeah, I can do that."

"Thank you."

He rises and pulls his phone from his pocket. "You know, I think I like you all shot and vulnerable."

"Well, don't get used to it. As soon as I'm healed, I'll be back to my ball-busting ways."

"I wouldn't have it any other way, spitfire."

The days are a blur of HGTV, lukewarm chicken noodle soup and Jell-O. I absolutely hate being stuck in this hospital room, even if it is a suite. The doctors and nurses poke and prod at me under Marco's watchful eye.

The man has taken it upon himself to enlist as my personal bodyguard. Despite Nicky or one of the other Gemini sentinels constantly perched at the door, my new husband hasn't left my side. He doesn't work, he doesn't sleep, I'm not even sure he pees.

I reach for the magazine on the bedside table and Marco leaps up, handing it to me. It's been like this for days. He waits on me hand and foot, helps me shower and dress, which makes it very difficult to keep my scars hidden, but somehow, I've managed. I had to draw the line at taking me to the bathroom. There are some things that newlyweds should *not* share.

"Do you want something to eat? Are you thirsty?" Marco loiters at the foot of my bed.

"No, I'm fine."

"Are you sure?"

"Just sit down, Marco. You're driving me crazy."

He slumps down on the couch beside my bed, a frustrated sigh parting his lips.

After flipping through a few pages of the gossip magazine, I can feel his pointed stare. It's impossible to lose myself in the smutty tabloids with him watching my every move. With a huff, I point at the flat screen hung on the wall. "Why don't you find a movie for us to watch?"

He jumps up, reaching for the remote on the coffee table. "Sure, absolutely. What are you in the mood for?"

"Anything but a Romcom."

He smirks, the tight set of his shoulders finally relaxing. The man has been a walking ball of tension for days. Judging by the bits and pieces of conversations I've overheard, Marco is nowhere near finding out who was responsible for the shooting. And it's killing him.

"So, horror, then?"

"That sounds about right." Dropping the magazine back on

the nightstand, I snuggle beneath the down comforter Marco had Nicky bring from the penthouse.

As he scrolls through Netflix, he folds his massive frame onto the small couch. I don't know how he's been sleeping on it for days. It's no wonder he hasn't actually slept. Then again, compared to the floor of my studio, it's a step up.

God, I've really put him through hell since we met. A hint of guilt creeps up.

His head swivels to mine, distracting me, as the pointer pauses on a familiar title. "*Scream*? It's a classic."

"Sure, nothing like a light horror flick to get over a near lethal injury."

Marco's face crumples, and I immediately regret the bad joke. "We can watch something else—"

"No, it's fine. Just put it on." I try to sit up straighter and wince, the movement jostling the stitches. Marco is beside me before I can blink, readjusting my pillows. "You don't have to do that. I'm okay, I promise." He skulks back to the couch and lies down, his feet dangling over the edge.

Another stab of guilt pricks at my wound, and this time, it's not the stitches. For a hospital bed, mine is remarkably roomy. Before I can think on all the reasons why this is a bad idea, I scoot over to one side and pat the empty half. "Why don't you come lie down?"

His dark brows shoot up, nearly reaching the tumble of wild locks falling across his forehead. A long minute of silence fills the cold room. "Nah, I don't want to accidentally squish you or something…"

"You won't; I'm not some fragile little flower. Just get over here. I can't stand seeing you so uncomfortable."

He snorts on a laugh. "Me? You're the one that was shot, Jia." The bitter edge to his tone lingers in the air between us.

"And I'm on plenty of pain meds," I hiss. "Now get your ass over here, *honey*, so I can squeeze your hand at the scary parts."

The hard set of his jaw softens, the tempest of emotions in that dark gaze settling. Painstakingly slowly, he rises, eyes intent on mine, as if he's waiting for me to change my mind. After hovering beside the bed for an eternity, he finally folds onto the mattress beside me. He's so close to the edge I'm scared he'll roll off if he breathes too hard.

So I thread my fingers through his and tug him a little closer. "I'll warn you now, I have a tendency to dig my nails into skin when I get scared."

His gaze pivots to mine, and a slow smile melts across his face. "Do your worst, spitfire. I can handle it."

Bright sunlight streams through the floor-to-ceiling windows, highlighting the soaring peaks of downtown Manhattan's sleek skyrises. An entire week later, and I'm finally home. As *Yéye* leads me into the penthouse, I can't believe I actually just called this place home. Maybe I hit my head when I was shot?

No, it must be the endless days stuck in that hospital room —or rather, the suite my overbearing husband had insisted upon. He'd also insisted on spending every night on the tiny pull-out couch. Despite the high-end suite, after a week, those four walls were starting to close in on me.

Marco watches as *Yéye* leads me to the pristine white leather couches of the living room. Those intent eyes follow me everywhere. I don't think he's let me out of his sight for more than an hour this entire week. He worked from the hospital room the past few days, conducting conference calls from the bathroom, had elaborate dinners delivered, and even hired an aesthetician to give me a facial in bed.

To say he's been doting on me would be an understatement.

I'm fairly certain he's going above and beyond to make up for the fact he still hasn't figured out who tried to kill me.

Or him.

The infallible Marco Rossi doesn't allow anyone to touch what's his and live to tell about it. And yet, here we are a week later with no answers. It's done a number on his pride.

I sink into the soft leather, and a twinge of discomfort purses my lips. Even after all this time, the wound is sore. I'd only been released after my husband flashed his million-dollar smile and fat wallet. Gemini Corp is one of the hospital's biggest donors. The doctor had made me promise to take it easy for at least another week.

Yéye folds down beside me and offers a smile. "I am happy you are home, *bǎobèi*."

"Me too." And it's actually not a lie. A familiar scent fills my nostrils, and a smile instantly threatens to surface. A vase filled with jasmine blossoms sits on the coffee table, perfuming the air, much like the one that had been delivered to the hospital. Did my new husband know they were my favorite?

Marco's heavy footfalls slap across the marble as he approaches, and a prickle of awareness skates over my skin. It hasn't escaped my attention that this will be the first night we'll spend alone together in our bedroom since our wedding. And we have yet to consummate our marriage.

"I have an important call I need to take in my office, but I've already ordered lunch. It should be here any minute." He ticks his head at the imposing male standing by the entrance. "Nicky will get the door."

"Okay, thanks."

"Yes, thank you, Mr. Rossi, you have been quite hospitable." *Yéye* squeezes my hand and turns to me. "My stay is nearly coming to an end, *bǎobèi*. I fear I may have already overstayed my welcome."

"No, not at all!" I bite my tongue to keep from crying out, *please don't go!*

"You're welcome to stay as long as you like, Mr. Guo." Marco offers a surprisingly pleasant smile.

"I'm certain I am no longer needed here."

"You are!" I blurt. My grandfather has been covering the day to day running of the Four Seas in my absence, and now that it's time to take the reins, the idea of it has anxiety churning in my gut. "We haven't even found the person responsible for the shooting."

Marco's expression darkens, his jaw clenching so tight a tendon flutters across his cheek. "I haven't exactly had time with you in the hospital—"

I raise a hand, cutting him off. "I'm not saying it's your fault, only that we could still use my grandfather's help, right? No one knows how to run the Four Seas better than he does."

"Yes, of course," he grits out.

I can practically see his fragile male ego deflating and for once, I actually feel badly about it. Because my new husband has been nothing but dedicated this past week.

Before I can open my mouth, Marco whirls on his heel and stomps down the corridor to his office. *Damn it.*

I blow out a frustrated sigh and tip my head back to stare at the high ceilings.

"Marriage is never easy, *bǎobèi.* And the circumstances in which you've begun yours make it even more challenging, but I have faith that all will work out as it should."

"Right…"

"I will remain only a few days more. Now that you are home, I am confident you and Mr. Rossi will learn to successfully navigate the turbulent seas of marriage along with running an empire such as yours side by side."

I hope he's right.

CHAPTER 34
THE BEST THANK YOU

M *arco*

"I don't give a fuck, Jimmy!" I roar over the phone. "It's been seven days and the bastard who tried to murder my wife is still out there. How could you have no leads?"

"I already told you that all the cameras at the Waldorf were wiped clean. With the number of crime syndicates invited to the wedding, there are a shit load of suspects. Not to mention the fact that it could have been someone who snuck in."

"Then question the guards on duty again. I want them all interrogated until the fuckers spill. Someone has to know what happened that day, and no one better fucking sleep until you find that person."

"Got it, boss."

I jab my finger at the call end button, fury rushing my veins. I've never felt so powerless and, *Dio*, I hate it. If there was one thing about this damned marriage I thought I would be decent at, it was protecting my damned wife.

Now I feel like a fucking *coglione*.

That seething anger bubbles up, tangling with weeks of pent-up energy and sexual frustration. I stalk out of my home-office ready to rip something, anything apart. When I reach the kitchen, darkness blankets the city, the twinkling lights of the skyline streaming into the great room.

Cazzo, what time is it? How long have I been holed up in my office?

Jia's familiar form materializes on the couch, and I halt my mad stomping. Her eyes are closed and she's curled up beneath a blanket. *Yéye* is nowhere in sight, but since it's well past midnight, he's likely already gone to bed.

The fury ravaging my entire being wanes as I step closer, and my eyes land on the simple platinum wedding band around Jia's finger. My thoughts fly to the engagement ring I never returned. The red box still sits unopened, hidden in my underwear drawer.

With all the chaos of this week, I haven't had time to bring it back to Cartier. Maybe I shouldn't... I fold down onto the couch beside her and brush a strand of raven hair behind her ear. My little spitfire has been playing nice this week, but it's only because she's injured.

Now that things would return to normal what would happen?

Would she still insist on an open marriage? Would she at least allow me to fuck her first?

I've dreamed of sinking my cock into that sweet pussy since the moment I first laid eyes on her. Just the thought of it has my dick hardening.

Shaking my head, I heave in a breath. Cold shower and bed. That's what lies in my future. But first, I have to get my wife upstairs. Gently lifting her off the couch, I cradle her in my arms. A faint sigh purses her lips, and she leans her head against my chest.

My heart kicks at my ribs. *Dio*, this woman has my heart

and balls in a chokehold.

Nico's words at the hospital a week ago flit to the surface of my mind: *Love sucks, huh,* fratello?

As I carry Jia up the stairs, I consider the last few months since this woman bulldozed into my life, and a smile threatens. After Isa, I vowed never to love again. I would never allow myself to be that vulnerable. Her death nearly destroyed me.

When I reach the loft, I tiptoe the final steps to the massive bed. The bed I haven't slept in once since I moved into this damned apartment. Gently lowering Jia onto the silky sheets, I hold my breath so as not to wake her. Despite the pain pills, she hasn't been sleeping well. She tosses and turns at night, sometimes crying out.

It kills me to see the fierce woman plagued by nightmares.

I'm all too familiar with the feeling.

Briefly contemplating removing the sheer-sleeved sundress she wears, I reconsider, knowing how pissed she'd be at me having undressed her in her sleep. Instead, I pull the comforter up and tuck it around her sleeping form. Her chest rises and falls slowly, the slight movement entrancing. I spent the past week in the hospital watching her sleep like a psycho. She's not the only one who needs rest.

Before I consider the ramifications, I lean closer and brush a kiss to her forehead. Another faint sigh tumbles free, and my stupid heart pinches. This damned, fiery woman will be the death of me, I'm sure of it.

Forcing my gaze away from her peacefully sleeping form, I slowly back away and disappear into the closet. Stripping my clothes off, exhaustion sets in, bone deep. Fuck the shower. It can wait until tomorrow. I've suffered through blue balls for months; another night isn't going to make a difference.

Once I'm down to only boxers, I saunter back into the bedroom and head for the bed. I'm too tired to go back downstairs to the guest room, and this is my damned bedroom after all. I gingerly crawl onto my side of the mattress and the moment my head hits the pillow, my lids begin to close.

Until the feel of a warm body snaps them wide open.

Jia curls into my side, eyes still firmly closed. Her arm winds around my waist, and she mumbles something in her sleep I can't quite make out. Her warmth seeps into me, flooding my veins.

Fantastic, now I'm hard again.

Sunlight streams in through the gap in the curtains, directed straight at my eyes. I groan and attempt to roll over, but Jia is still curled into my side. So much for a good night's rest. I'd barely slept, scared to move and jostle her wound. And still, her mere presence insured I awoke with a raging boner.

Now I'm tired and horny as fuck.

On the bright side, at least Jia seems to have slept peacefully.

A dull throb pounds across my shoulder from remaining in the same position all night. Who knew Jia's head was so heavy? Okay, I have to move... Carefully, I slide her head farther down to my chest, freeing my arm.

Not ideal, but better at least.

The ties of her sundress have fallen off her shoulders, revealing the swell of her breasts, and my cock twitches at the sight. Fuck, it's about time for that cold shower. As I contemplate the best way to extricate myself without waking her, she begins to stir. Her arm glides down my bare torso and her slender fingers graze my hard-ass cock.

For the love of all things... I grit my teeth as her lids begin to flutter.

Jia lets out a yawn, her fingers still dangerously close to my raging erection. She finally glances up at me, and her eyes widen in surprise.

"Morning, spitfire," I rasp out.

"M—morning..." She glances around the bedroom, but she doesn't move. "How did I get here? Those pain pills must have been stronger than I thought." She drags a hand through her tangle of dark locks. Shockingly, she doesn't yell at me for crawling into bed with her either.

"You fell asleep on the couch, so I carried you up last night."

"Oh." As if she finally notices the precarious location of her hand, she pulls her arm back and rolls onto her back so her body is no longer pressed against mine. But her eyes roam to my visible arousal and remain there for an endless moment.

I wait for her squeal of disapproval, but it never comes. Instead, she just lays there, staring at it. "It's time for that cold shower," I finally mutter when the silence lingers on dangerously between us.

"Wait..." Her hand falls onto my bare chest again. "I've been meaning to thank you. You've been surprisingly decent since... everything."

I nod slowly. "It's the least I could do."

"No, it's not." She sucks her lower lip between her teeth. "Given the arrangement, there was nothing keeping you at my bedside while I recovered. You're free to do as you will. But you didn't..."

"Nope." I tick my head at my cock. "As you can clearly see, I'm a little hard up."

A rueful chuckle slides past her pinched lips. The faint line between her brow furrows as if she's contemplating something big. She sucks in a breath and blurts, "I'd like to help you with that."

I'm sure I've heard wrong, but judging by the deep blush on her cheeks, maybe I didn't. My eyes bug out. "What?"

She doesn't say a word as her hand wraps around my cock over my boxers.

"Oh, fuck," I groan. "Jia—"

"Let's not look too much into this," she murmurs, those darting eyes meeting mine. "It's a thank you and that's all."

"Well, *cazzo*, this is the best damned thank you I've ever gotten in my life."

Her hand strokes my cock over the linen, and my balls tighten, but it's not enough. I want to feel her skin against mine.

"If you're going to do it…" My hand closes around hers and tugs it beneath the waistband of my boxers. "Do it right, wifey."

She shoots me a glare, and her hand slows its glorious strokes. "Don't call me that."

"Okay, okay, just don't stop." I jerk the boxers down my thighs and lean back against the pillow to watch as her hand glides up and down my thick head. Beads of cum already glisten along the tip, and I'm sure this will be embarrassingly quick. Somehow, my cock knows the difference between my rough hand and the gentle touch of a woman's. And especially *this* woman's.

Cum slickens my shaft, and her hand glides more smoothly, back and forth, and heat surges through my veins. Her free hand slides down to my balls, and a groan tears free. "Mmm, Jia, your hands are amazing."

The hint of a smile curls her lip. "Don't get used to it. This is a one-time concession, an award for good behavior."

"If you do this on the regular, I'll be a really good boy. I can sit, come, shake… whatever you want, spitfire."

Her head falls back as a laugh spills out, and *Dio*, it's the most beautiful sound.

"I'm embarrassingly close," I pant and hand her my discarded boxers.

"What am I supposed to do with these?" She throws them back at me. "You hold them."

Fair enough.

She doubles her efforts, and liquid lightning surges from my spine and runs down to the tips of my toes. Squeezing my eyes closed, I reach for her blindly and my hand closes around her breast. She gasps, but her hands don't stop. In fact, they move faster.

I toy with her nipple, and she releases a satisfying moan which only gets me more worked up. "Mmm, spitfire, I cannot wait to coax more of those sexy sounds out of you once you're healed."

"Good luck," she whispers and with one final, expert stroke, the orgasm slams into me.

All the air squeezes from my lungs as my balls tighten and ropes of warm cum shoot out. I barely have the wherewithal to reach for my boxers before I get sprayed with my own damned giz.

Once the frenzy subsides, my head falls back against the pillow, and a satisfied smile melts across my face.

Jia kneels triumphantly beside me, one breast nearly exposed.

"Well done."

"I know." She smirks and shimmies to the end of the bed.

My hand juts out, fingers wrapping around her arm. "Where do you think you're going?"

She pauses about halfway across the mattress and cocks her head over her shoulder. "I have a busy day ahead. I've abandoned my boutique for long enough, and I'll have to show my face at the Four Seas headquarters eventually. It's time they realize their new *lǎodà* is back."

"Jia… that doesn't sound like resting to me." I inch closer. "You heard what the doctor said, you have to rest." Carefully, I tug her back and force her down onto the mattress.

"Marco—"

"No squirming. We can't have you busting those stitches." I

move down her body as she stares up at me, back against the mattress, dark eyes pulsing.

"What are you doing?"

"It's my turn to thank you for thanking me." A devious grin pulls at my lips as I spread her legs and kneel between them.

CHAPTER 35
JUST DO IT ALREADY

J*ia*

Marco looms over me, still completely naked, that Chinese dragon glistening across his muscled torso and fire blazing in those mismatched irises.

No. No. No. This was not the plan. The hand job was bad enough, but this is crossing a whole other line. I can't even explain what came over me this morning. It was pity, that had to have been it. And maybe the best night of sleep I've had in forever. Since the wedding, I've been plagued by nightmares and somehow, snuggled in Marco's embrace, I finally slept in peace.

"My wound," I blurt. Because that's the reason we shouldn't have sex. *Ha!* How about the other thousand reasons this is so wrong?

"Relax, spitfire. I'm not going to fuck you. Well, at least not with my cock." He slides his tongue across his bottom lip, and a blazing inferno lights up between my legs. Speaking of hard up, how long has it been since I've had a release? I may be a virgin, but I still have a vibrator and know how to use it. With all the drama lately, I haven't had a minute to tend to my own needs. His nostrils flare, and lust pulses through my core. "I just want to taste that sweet pussy."

Before I can spit out my rebuttal, his hands close around my knees and pry them open. His fingers glide up my thighs and goosebumps explode across my flesh.

"Marco," I grit out.

"It's just tit for tat, Jia, relax. Like you said, it doesn't have to mean anything, right?" His eyes sear into mine, and my breath hitches. "I just want to give my new wife a little pleasure. It won't change anything. You can continue to hate me, and we can keep living our separate lives... but maybe, we can give into occasional moments like these, too." His hopeful gaze is almost too much to bear. Also, damn, do I want this. "What do you say?"

"Okay." The word spills out without my approval.

His gaze turns feral as his head disappears beneath the floral print of my sundress. I squeeze my eyes closed as his fingers dance up to the waistband of my panties. He slides the lace down my thighs, and anticipation tightens my core.

I should have been drunk for this, or at least a little tipsy. I'm much too aware of every touch, every sensation. Marco's warm breath against my inner thigh, the coarse hair on his leg brushing my knee, but mostly those devastating lips blazing a trail toward my now exposed pussy.

"Mmm, spitfire, I've been dreaming about this sweetness since the day I saw you through the window of your boutique all those weeks ago."

"What? When?"

His warm tongue lavishes my inner thigh, and every nerve springs to attention. "Doesn't matter," he murmurs against my skin.

My back arches at the gentle vibrations of his words, the

anticipation of that tongue driving me to the point of insanity. Even the slight ache from the wound beneath my breastbone doesn't take away from the blossoming pleasure. He continues to tease, licking and nibbling the sensitive skin only millimeters away from my throbbing center.

"Oh, for the love of all things, just do it already!" The command bursts from my lips and my eyes snap open, heat racing across my cheeks.

Marco's head pops up from between my legs, a devilish grin plastered across that unfairly handsome face. "All you had to do was ask, spitfire." He dives back down, like a man on a mission, and that sharp, wet tongue finally lavishes my center.

An embarrassing moan spills out and my eyes close again, hoping to somehow hide from the mortification. A chuckle vibrates against my folds, the warm sound reaching all the way to my spine and sending a tremor tumbling through. His tongue finds my clit, and my hips buck.

Oh, my…

I clench my teeth to keep from mewling like a cat in heat.

That tongue circles, each pass more devastating than the last. I'm strung up so tight I'm a second from exploding. Fiery energy builds, a blazing inferno on the point of combustion.

Marco's head pops up again, and I nearly mutter a curse at the sudden lack of his tongue. I was so damned close. My arousal glistens on his chin, matching the luster in his eyes. He drags his tongue across his bottom lip and savors *me*. "I must have done something right in this life to have been rewarded with a wife whose pussy tastes like heaven." His smile is downright sinful, and it's enough to push me over the edge alone.

"Just stop talking and keep going," I rasp out.

His head falls back and a laugh roars out. It's deep and genuine and sends my heart staggering. When the laughter finally falls away, he pins those mesmerizing eyes to mine and grins. "You feel okay? Nothing hurts?"

I slowly shake my head. For the first time in a week, I haven't thought about the shooting or my wound.

"I'm glad you're enjoying it."

"It's not bad…"

"Liar." With his eyes still fixed to mine, he slips a finger inside me and I'm so wet, he glides right in. "Damn, you're so tight, wifey."

The sudden intrusion is so unexpected, a squeal escapes. Then he starts to move, pumping in and out of me, and my hips take up the tantalizing rhythm. His thumb finds my clit as his finger continues to thrust, and again, that rush of heat consumes me.

"Eyes on me, spitfire. I want you to remember exactly who gave you the best orgasm of your life without even using my cock."

My breath hitches. I'm a writhing, wriggling mess, the intensity of his gaze only heightening the desperate tangle of sensations.

He glides a second finger inside, and the feeling of utter fullness nearly sends me plummeting over the edge. "We have to get you ready for me, spitfire."

My eyes widen as I regard him, genuine fear lancing through my chest. Now that I've had a front row view of his cock, I'm not certain he's the best option considering my virginal status. I must tense up because his cocky smile falters.

"Relax, it's not going to happen today—but trust me when I say it *will* happen. And not only because we should consummate the marriage." His eyes smolder as they regard me. "But because you are my wife, and I will claim every inch of you once you're ready."

With his thumb still teasing my clit, those fingers pumping in and out, and my orgasm looming closer, I simply bob my head. Because the truth is, I want him. I want my infuriating, philandering, arrogant husband to be my first. Possibly my only.

As if the silent admission frees something inside me, the fire blossoms and my fingers dig into the silky sheets as raging energy rushes my veins.

"Come for me, Jia. Me and only me."

The orgasm tears through me with the force of a wild tempest, igniting every nerve and setting my senses ablaze with an intoxicating rush of euphoria. My eyes close at the rush of sensations but Marco's reprimand snaps them open again.

"I said eyes on me, spitfire." His irises are two pits of smoldering heat, one the most brilliant blue and the other the darkest midnight.

I do as I'm told because apparently, I become mindless in the midst of an amazing orgasm. Wave after wave of pleasure crashes over me, the vibrations encompassing my mind and body. I've never felt anything like this. Clearly, I've been missing out. The handful of guys I hooked up with in college did not know there way around a clit. But my new husband...

Another thrill skates up my spine as my gaze deviates from his and drops to the once again erect, enormous veiny beast between his legs.

My head falls back against the pillow as the final tremors fall away. I suck in a deep breath, refilling my lungs. That orgasm has literally stolen all the air away.

A smug grin curls Marco's lips as he crawls up the bed beside me. "Tell the truth, spitfire, was it the best you've ever had?"

Like I'd ever give him the satisfaction. "It was fine."

Another wild roar of laughter bursts free. "Right..." He brings his finger up between us and pops it into his mouth. His tongue swirls around his thick digit before his cheeks hollow as he sucks. "Mmm, I could get used to this sweetness."

Oh. My. God.

I've never been with a man who speaks like this.

"Have you ever tasted yourself?"

My lips pucker as he offers me his middle finger. The one which was just buried deep inside me. "No, thank you."

"You're missing out, spitfire. You taste like spiced honey, a hint of fire with a sweet finish."

Another blast of heat streaks below my belly button. I clench my thighs to smother the lusty sensations. "I'll take your word for it."

As the conversation falls away, I glance over the edge of the bed in search of my panties. They're nowhere in sight. Then it occurs to me, Marco is still completely naked beside me, and his big, thick cock looks ready to go again. Worse, there's something about the look in his eye...

"I think I need to change the dressing on my wound."

The happy, flirty man disappears, and he snaps straight up on the bed. "Let me see. Did you tear a stitch?"

"No, I'm fine. It's just a little sore."

He mutters a string of curses, and that damned guilt rears up. "Are you sure?"

"Yes. It wasn't you," I mumble. "I just need a minute to myself."

His head dips, jaw tensing before he slides off the bed and collects his discarded clothing. As he rises, his eyes meet mine once again. "There's nothing I can help you with?"

Gritting my teeth, I slowly shake my head. Because the truth is I'm afraid to spend another minute alone with this man. After that groundbreaking orgasm, my emotions are all over the place. And I'd hate to do or say something stupid...

"Fine," he grumbles. "I'll see you downstairs."

The moment he disappears down the spiral staircase, I flop back down on the mattress and heave out a breath. Why did I ever think casual sex with my husband would be a good idea?

CHAPTER 36
A MAD MAN

M *arco*

Circling the kitchen like a mad man, I slam cabinets, yank drawers open then closed, ransack the refrigerator, but nothing helps. I don't know what I'm looking for. I'm not hungry, I'm not thirsty, but I reach for the coffee all the same.

A nervous energy courses through my veins, one I cannot control.

It's been over a week since someone shot my wife and, still, my incompetent men have found nothing. It's time to take matters into my own hands. Lifting my hand to eyelevel, I run my index finger beneath my nose. A full day later, and I can still smell my little spitfire's spiced honey scent. *Cazzo*, I'm hard just thinking about my fingers inside her, those sounds I forced out. She can deny it all she wants, but I'm certain no one has ever made her come like that.

I'd worked late last night, and by the time I got home, she was already asleep. I snuck into bed beside her, and if she felt me, she didn't say anything. I half-expected her to kick me out, but instead, a soft sigh escaped her lips as I curled around her.

Now it isn't just my cock, but my damned heart growing fuller. The hold this woman has over me is dangerous.

Nicky clears his throat, the big guard appearing at the foot of the kitchen. "Hey boss, Rick just called. He's on his way back with Mrs. Rossi."

Mrs. Rossi. I nearly choke on a laugh. Jia would have Nicky's head if she heard him call her that.

"Thanks," I murmur before returning my attention to the coffee I just poured. The tightness in my chest begins to dissipate, and I refuse to accept the possibility that my wife's absence was a contributing factor.

Jia was gone when I awoke, and I nearly lost my shit. Why she insisted on going to her damned boutique this morning was beyond me. Even with my guys and the elder Guo with her, I hated the idea. But she'd been adamant the day before, and I knew my wife well enough to know that forbidding it certainly wouldn't stop her. So instead, I agreed like a whipped *coglione* as long as she took an entire entourage of guards.

I hadn't expected for her to leave so early though.

She was clearly trying to avoid me, and her plan worked. A stupid grin curls the corners of my lips. She's absolutely impossible.

My phone rings, jerking my attention from thoughts of my wife.

Jimmy. Finally.

"Tell me you have something." I grit over the phone.

"I do, but you're not going to like it."

"Just spit it out."

"Dante got a lead."

Fuck. Of course, it had to be my half-brother.

"What does he want in return for the intel?"

"Shockingly, nothing."

"Not possible."

"That's what he said, boss."

I drag my fingers through my hair, tugging at the ends. My relationship with Dante has certainly been less strained over the past couple months since we called a truce between the Kings and Geminis, but there's no way he's doing this out of the goodness of his heart.

"Fine, set up a meeting," I growl. "Today."

"Will do, boss."

The moment the call drops, the hum of a familiar voice reaches my ears. Even through the reinforced front door, I recognize Jia's melodious timbre. My heart rams against my ribs, and my feet propel me to the entrance.

I open the front door before Nicky makes it halfway down the hall. Jia stands in the foyer, her long, silky locks pulled up into a messy bun. Despite the beads of perspiration glistening along her brow, she looks hot as fuck.

Which reminds me…

"Aren't you hot in that long sleeve shirt?" It hasn't escaped my attention that she constantly wears long-sleeved tops and dresses, but now that we are living together, I've realized it's all she wears.

She exchanges a quick glance with her grandfather, but it's so swift I may have imagined it. A tendon in her jaw flutters before her eyes narrow as they regard me. "Skin cancer, you've heard of it, right? I'd like to avoid it."

The sharp edge to her tone surprises me since we've been on rather good terms since her return to the penthouse.

"Got it," I mutter as she stalks past me with Guo at her heels. "How's everything at the boutique?"

She releases a frustrated huff and grabs a bottle of water from the fridge. "Awful. I'm so behind. Even with Ari's help while I was in the hospital, I'll never get all the designs done in time for the grand opening of CityZen."

"Grand opening? You have a date in mind already?"

She nods. "September first, for Labor Day weekend. I've been working on the fall line for months."

"Why didn't you tell me?"

Jia gnaws on her bottom lip. "Honestly, I thought I would've escaped from your clutches by now."

An unexpected chuckle tumbles out.

She flashes me the back of her hand, showcasing the simple platinum wedding band. "But the whole getting shot thing put a crimp in my plans, and here I am, still shackled to the mob boss."

"And you love it, wifey."

She rolls her eyes, but the hint of a smile curves her full lips. For a second, I'm so completely enthralled I nearly miss the text message from Jimmy.

Jimmy: Dante's available now. Meet at his office in 15.

Merda. Shoving my phone back into my jacket, I rush to the door. "Sorry, I have to run. An important meeting just came up."

"You have to go right now?" Jia lifts a curious brow.

Spinning back to face her, I shoot her a smirk. "Why, are you going to miss me?"

"Of course not."

"Right…"

"I was just wondering if it had anything to do with me or the shooting?"

It only takes me an instant to decide to lie, but apparently, the pause is enough to trigger her suspicions.

"Marco, if it is, you have to take me." She erases the space between us and jabs a dainty finger at my chest.

Guo, who's been exceptionally quiet, shuffles closer. "*Bǎobèi*, let Mr. Rossi attend to his affairs, and we'll attend to ours. It is nearly time for me to go home, and there is still much that must be done to stabilize the Four Seas."

Her mouth screws into a pout, but the threat of her grandfather's imminent departure is enough to silence her rebuttals.

"Fine," she grumbles, eyes intent on mine. "So you're actually going to allow me to leave the penthouse and meet with my men?"

"Fuck no," I grind out. "I still don't know if it was *your men* who tried to kill you."

Guo raises his hands, stepping between us. "I agree with your husband, Jia. We will simply conduct a video call with the Four Seas Council. It is tentatively scheduled for two o'clock."

I still hate the idea of Lei's beady little eyes on my wife, even if it is through video. But it's better than the alternative.

Jia glances at her watch and lets out a groan. "Fine, I guess that's good enough for now." Then she spears me with those starlit irises. "But if you discover anything that does concern me, you better tell me."

"Of course, sweety pie." I offer my best smile, and she shoots me a scowl in return.

"Keep working on those terms of endearment." She whirls on her heel and disappears into the great room. . Guo throws a knowing smile my way before following his granddaughter.

I have to pry the soles of my shoes off the marble to force myself out the door. I simply can't get enough of that little spitfire and her smart mouth.

The boardroom of the King's empire is strikingly similar to the one in Gemini Corp. It doesn't surprise me considering we're practically neighbors, the two soaring, modern skyscrapers standing toe-to-toe along the mid-town Manhattan skyline.

As expected, my asshole half-brother makes me wait.

We've pulled the same shit with him and Luca, so I'm not certain why I thought this exchange would be any different. I drum my fingers on the lavish mahogany table as the minutes grind on endlessly.

Finally, when I'm about a second away from walking out, the door creaks open. Both of my half-brothers appear in the doorway. Luca, ever the businessman, is in a sleek dark suit, while Dante looks like he just rolled out of bed in a white undershirt and sweatpants.

How Luca trusts his volatile brother to run his empire is beyond me.

Neither speaks as they stroll into the boardroom, and it occurs to me I should thank them for the intel they're about to share, but I just don't fucking feel like it.

The Valentinos tower over me, so I finally stand and reluctantly offer my hand. "I suppose I owe you a thanks for this."

"You can thank all of us." Nico appears in the doorway and struts in.

What the hell is my brother doing here?

CHAPTER 37
A NEW PLAYER

J *ia*

"I know Marco's up to something, *Yéye.*" I could barely focus on the call with the senior members of the Four Seas with my thoughts stuck on my sneaky husband.

He's barely left my side over the past week unless it was something to do with the shooting. And with the way he zipped out of here earlier, there's no doubt in my mind.

"Let him handle his business, *bǎobèi,* and we will attend to ours."

"But it is my business, *Yéye.* Whoever it was attacked *me.*"

"Though that is true, we do not know if it was retaliation against you, or your husband and the Geminis."

"Does it really matter? Aren't we supposed to be one, united front?"

The hint of a smile glistens across my grandfather's weary gaze. "I see you're already learning what it means to be married."

I shrug. It's not like it's been marital bliss… except for that spine-tingling orgasm I still can't get out of my mind. But the past week has been surprisingly peaceful. I guess getting shot puts things into perspective.

But a part of me is still waiting for the other shoe to drop.

Now that I'm nearly healed, will Marco stick to our open marriage agreement?

God, why did I ever say I wanted that? After the other morning, the idea of that wicked tongue on anyone else—I squeeze my eyes shut, nausea churning in my gut. I never expected these feelings… the jealousy, the possessiveness, over *my* husband.

I just need to talk to him. I need to put on my big girl panties and tell him I made a mistake. I don't want an open marriage. I want to give this a shot, if he is still willing. The confession, even if only to myself, is startling. My heart flutters, and an immense weight lifts from my shoulders at the realization. I *want* my husband.

Before my cowardice gets the best of me, I reach for my phone and type out a quick message.

Me: We need to talk when you get home.

Marco: … That sounds ominous.

Me: You better hurry back to find out.

Marco: I'll try my best.

There. Blowing out a breath, I drop my phone on Marco's desk, the one I'd commandeered for the video conference. *Yéye* watches me from across the slab of dark wood, the hint of a smile still lingering.

"I think the time has come for me to go."

"No, *Yéye*, please not yet." I slide to the edge of the massive chair and reach for my grandfather's hands.

"You do not need me here any longer, *bǎobèi*. You have your husband now. And if you truly wish for your men to respect you, you must take the reins yourself and prove to them what sort of leader you will be."

I nod slowly, my chest constricting at the idea of ruling those bloodthirsty killers. Even with my grandfather here, the Four Seas have been out of control. I cannot imagine what will happen upon his departure. "You're right," I finally mutter. "But that doesn't mean I'm pleased you're leaving."

He squeezes my hands. "I will still come to visit as always." Then his eyes drift down to my belly, hidden beneath the desk. "Besides, I hope to have a new grandchild to visit soon."

Heat floods my cheeks, and an embarrassing sound escapes my clenched lips. Once I've regained my composure, I manage to put together a sentence. "Not anytime soon. We only just got married."

"But you have consummated the marriage?"

Oh, God, please strike me down. I cannot be having the sex talk with my grandfather. Chomping down on my bottom lip, I shake my head.

"Jia, you must. Nothing will unite the Four Seas like a male heir. It's unfair, and I'm completely aware it's against all feminist values, but we come from an ancient, patriarchal culture."

"I know," I grit out.

"Then complete your duty, *bǎobèi*. The sooner the better."

I bite my tongue to keep all the rebuttals from bursting free. Who cares that I've just been shot? That my husband has an enormous cock and that I'm scared he'll break me? Or how about the fact that I'm terrified I'll catch more feelings for the bastard once we take that step...

Instead, like an obedient granddaughter, I nod again. "I will do my best, *Yéye*."

"Good. Now, help me pack. There is a flight in a few days, and I'm anxious to return to my quiet life."

I force myself off the chair and follow my grandfather out of Marco's office, but my heart feels heavier with each step. How am I supposed to survive this without him?

Soft footsteps echo across the quiet penthouse, snapping my eyes open and sending my heart leaping up my throat. Shit. I fell asleep. I glance at the clock on the nightstand and a twinge of anger blossoms in my gut. Despite Marco's promise to return home soon, it's nearly midnight. And I passed out waiting for him in a sexy negligee like a fool. Never mind the fact that it took me hours to find the only one I owned with the lacy long sleeves.

The footsteps loom closer, and I freeze. I should have raced to the closet to change, but now it's too late. He'll catch me and see that I'm awake. So instead, I sneak under the covers and close my eyes an instant before he enters the loft.

Marco steps closer, the musky scent of bergamot and cedarwood invading my nostrils. I force my lids to remain closed despite the feel of his warm breath against my mouth. Then he does something so completely unexpected, my eyes snap open in spite of my best efforts. His lips brush over mine, ever so gently, like the faint kiss of butterfly wings.

Our eyes meet, and all the air rushes from my lungs.

A crimson hue tinges his cheeks, and it's unfair how handsome he looks, with those sharp cheekbones, full lips and perfect olive skin. Even that five o'clock shadow only adds to his brutally rugged good looks.

"Ah, you *are* awake."

"I wasn't," I snap and pull the comforter up higher to hide the skimpy nighty. "You woke me up."

"I apologize." He clears his throat, but doesn't move, still bent over my side of the bed.

"Why did you take so long to come home?"

He folds down onto the bed beside me, smirking. "Did you miss me, spitfire?"

"Of course not."

"Liar." His grin only grows more obnoxious. "You know,

I'm starting to figure out your tells. When you lie, this tiny vein throbs across your forehead." He reaches for me, but I swat his hand away.

"So, where were you?" I clutch the comforter, a tiny part of me terrified of what he'll say. What if he was with another woman? I practically forced him into this stupid open marriage.

"Something urgent came up that I had to handle."

"Was it about the shooting?"

His lips press into a tight line before he finally nods. "It was."

I nearly leap up before I remember I'm trying to hide my scandalous sleeping attire. "What did you find out?"

"Why don't we talk about it tomorrow? You said there was something you needed to say?"

I shake my head, in no mood to discuss our relationship now. "No, it can wait. Tell me."

His shoulders sag and he looses a breath. "There's a new player in town. Or rather, a new offshoot of an old one, I guess…"

My brows slam together as I try to decipher that cryptic response. "What does that mean?"

"Dante believes it's *La Sombra Boricua*. They've been making moves in our key districts, burning shit and buying off our suppliers."

My mind flies back to my years of Spanish tutoring. "The Puerto Rican Shadow?"

He nods. "Esmeralda has long headed the crime syndicate from her home on the island. She's never caused any problems before. A few months ago, we had a slight misunderstanding, and I thought everything had been ironed out. I left Nico to deal with it, but it seems as if the head of her local operation is making a move on her own."

The Puerto Rican mob was never a big player. After years with my father in charge of the Four Seas and then with my brother taking the lead, I would've known if they had been. I may not have wanted to be involved in the family business, but it was impossible not to overhear details over the years. "Who?"

"We believe it's my brother's housekeeper, Blanca."

CHAPTER 38
LIKE A GOOD WIFE

Marco

"The housekeeper?" Jia balks.

"Crazy, I know." I still can't quite believe it myself. Nico's girlfriend had caught her a few months ago snooping around his computer, and he's had eyes on her since, but the woman is a pro.

She shifts beneath the comforter, and I catch a flash of red lace. "Why would the Puerto Rican mob want to kill me?"

"I don't think they do, other than to cause tension between the big crime families. If we assumed it was Lei and his band of rebels, we'd break apart the Four Seas from the inside out."

"And that would make us more vulnerable."

"Exactly." My hand nudges her leg hidden beneath the blanket, and she jumps at the brief contact.

The comforter slides down, revealing her shoulders and the sleeves of a crimson lace negligee. My brain short circuits for a second as all the blood rushes to my dick. *Cazzo*, she's wearing sexy lingerie?

She jerks the silky coverlet back up, but the damage has been done. When she texted me saying she wanted to talk, I assumed it was bad.

"Are you trying to seduce me, spitfire?" I slide up the bed, closer.

"No…" she mumbles.

"Then let me see what you're wearing." Whatever it is, it's a far cry from the typical oversized sweatshirts she wears to bed.

She curls into a ball, wrapping the comforter tight around her. "No. It's too late."

"That's not fair," I whine. "If I knew this was what you wanted to talk about, I would have been home hours ago. Fuck the shooting." A smirk crawls across my lips unbidden.

"You're such an ass."

My fingers creep up the coverlet and tug at the edge. "Come on, at least let me see."

Jia clutches the silky comforter in a death grip. "You lost your chance."

"Don't make me tear that thing off you, wifey."

Her eyes flash. "Do it, and you'll be spending the night in the guest bedroom."

That fire in her eyes has my cock straining against my slacks, and I'm about a second away from losing it. Rising to my feet, I loom over her, but she glares right back up at me, defiant as all hell.

"Jia, as your husband, I demand that you show me what you're wearing."

A laugh erupts from her clenched lips. "Oh, really? You *demand* it, do you?" She pulls the covers over her head, and wild cackles vibrate beneath the silky fabric. Once the last bit of laughter dies out, she re-emerges with a shit-eating grin. "I may be your wife, but you do not own me, and you certainly cannot demand that I do anything I don't want to."

Merda, I can't believe I'm about to do this. I'm sure all the blood has evacuated my brain because I've never done this for any female, any pussy. But damn it, I just can't get my wife out of my mind. Her honeyed taste, those sounds she made as she came on my fingers, the idea of being the first to have her, it's all I can think about.

I drop to my knees, and Jia's narrowed eyes widen. "Please, spitfire, show me the delicious, sexy negligee you're hiding beneath the covers, and I promise you a night you'll never forget."

Her dark brow arches and a hint of excitement streaks through those midnight orbs.

I press my palms together and fix my eyes to hers. "*Ti prego.*" Fuck, now I'm begging for sex? When did this happen?

A sigh parts her lips and devastatingly slowly, she peels back the comforter. Sheer ruby lace molds to her milky white skin and smoldering heat ravages my veins. Even the small white bandage across her sternum doesn't detract from her overwhelming beauty. A deep-V drops nearly to her bellybutton, the scrap of material barely concealing anything. Her nipples are peaked beneath the translucent lace, and it takes every ounce of restraint I possess to keep from capturing one in my salivating mouth.

"*Madonna, sei belissima. Cazzo*, Jia, you are more beautiful than the dawn breaking over the horizon, illuminating the entire city."

A silly grin parts her lips, and I realize how ridiculous I sound.

I cannot rip my gaze away from her as I take in every inch of porcelain skin. I follow the trail of lace from the dip of her shoulder down her arms, nearly reaching her fingertips. Again, I'm momentarily aware of the constant covering of her arms, but I'm too damned distracted by the lust pounding through my veins to dwell on it.

"So before I fucked up by coming home late again," I whisper, barely recognizing the soft, dreamy quality in my tone, "what did you have in mind for tonight?"

She shrugs, wisps of dark hair falling across her face. I reach for her instinctively and sweep the stray tendrils behind her ear. Her breath hitches as our skin makes contact, and I'm not sure how much longer I can keep from really touching her.

"Will you let me..." I let the rest of the question hang in the air between us as her head slowly dips.

That faint gesture is all it takes for the dam to burst. I leap onto the bed, pinning her to the mattress on all fours. She gazes up at me, a tangle of emotions I can't pretend to decipher flashing across the endless midnight. I capture her mouth, wrapping my hand around the back of her neck so I can devour those pouty lips before she stops me. Instead, she moans against my tongue as I ravage her, keeping myself suspended over her body to avoid the wound.

There's nothing I want more than to rub my hardass cock against her, to release some of the building pressure, but if I drop down on top of her, I could aggravate the stitches. So instead, my biceps burn from hovering just a few inches above her. I barely notice the strain, the pounding heat raging through my body consuming all my attention.

I want to bury my cock inside her so badly, the desire is all-consuming. I want to claim her as mine and only mine. Why the fuck did I agree to the open marriage? The idea of another man's hands on her drives me to the point of insanity. And I haven't even fucked her yet. Once I do, I'm certain nothing will ever be the same.

Jia wiggles beneath me, drawing my thoughts to the fire building between us. She angles her hips, desperate for that friction my cock is more than eager to provide.

"How are your stitches?" I murmur against her lips.

"Fine," she pants.

Her hips rock, meeting mine, and that faint brush with her pussy has stars dancing across my damned vision. Her hands come around my waist and settle on my ass, driving my cock between her legs.

Cazzo...

"Are you sure you're well enough—"

"Damn it, Marco, just fuck me already." Her dark eyes sparkle with desire. "I've waited over twenty years for this moment. I'm ready."

"*Dio*, I love it when you're demanding." My hands move to my belt buckle, but Jia sits up, pushing them away.

"Let me do it."

Merda, I'm going to come just from that commanding tone. With all my previous partners, I've been the one in charge. I never thought I'd like being the submissive one...

Her slender fingers make quick work of my slacks, then my boxer briefs, and my cock springs free. She eyes the thick, veiny bastard for a long moment, and I'm terrified she's going to reconsider.

My dick is huge. And it's not arrogance when it's true. I've spent enough time around the locker room in Palestra to know it's a fact. My brother and I are well-endowed. It must be our genes or something.

"We'll take it slow," I whisper, as she continues to size up my cock.

Her head dips before her fingers wrap around my shaft, and a tremor races up my spine. As she runs her hand up and down my length, I rip my shirt over my head and toss it to the floor. I'm completely naked, but she's still wearing that ruby teddy. Not that I mind, but I'd prefer to see all of her.

As she continues to stroke my dick, I reach for the lace at her shoulder and attempt to draw it down her arm. She freezes, every muscle in her body going taut. "Don't," she snaps.

My gaze lifts to hers, brows furrowed. A storm of emotions brews beneath the dark, impenetrable surface. "But how am I supposed to—"

Releasing my dick, she brings her hand between her legs and unfastens two snaps. The lacy fabric falls away revealing her pussy.

"Hmm, I guess that will work." I can't deny the frustration of being unable to see all of her though. Maybe she just needs to work up to it. Her body is perfect, what would she be embarrassed of?

The curious thoughts scramble away as her hand wraps around mine and brings it to the wetness between her thighs. A hiss purses my lips as I feel how drenched she is.

"Mmm, spitfire, you're already soaked and ready for me like a good wife."

CHAPTER 39
READY FOR ALL OF ME?

J *ia*

I want to be insulted by his degrading words, but my entire body is alight beneath his touch. And all I want is for this man to claim me with that enormous cock. In Marco's words, *if you're going to do it, you might as well do it, right,* right?

My virginity has loomed over me for years, much like the shadow of my father. I simply want to be rid of it, and I want my husband to deflower me. It's fitting, after all. And it would make not only *Yéye* but also my mother happy that I waited for marriage.

He cups my pussy before running his thick finger through the wet folds, and my back arches at the rush of sensations.

Marco's dappled orbs sear to mine, an unfamiliar emotion racing through the multi-colored hue. "You're wet all right, but I want to make sure you're ready for me, spitfire. I don't want to hurt you..." His gaze dips to the small bandage across my upper torso. He's been eyeing it from the moment I revealed the negligee.

I'm sure it's not exactly sexy.

"I already told you, I'm fine," I bite out before reaching for his erection. "Let's just do this."

His dark brows knit as he regards me. "Why are you in such a hurry all of a sudden?"

Because Yéye's leaving and I'm terrified of being alone. "You're the one that said we have to consummate the marriage, and it's our duty to create an heir."

Marco blanches, the fire in his eyes dissipating. His jaw drops before he mutters, "Excuse me?"

"Yéye said—"

He stiffens and sits up, removing that skillful digit and I release my hold on his shaft. "So that's why? Because your grandfather forced you to fuck me?"

"No..." Not exactly.

"Then why, Jia? A week ago, you said you despised me and that you wanted an open marriage. What changed?"

Anger pummels my veins as I stare up at the irresistible idiot. "I want you, okay? I find you attractive, I even find you slightly tolerable sometimes. You were kind and caring when I was stuck in that hospital for a week, and I don't know, maybe being shot put some things into perspective. The other stuff, the duty and what not, plays into it, but it's not the only reason. It's just a good excuse, I guess."

A stupid grin lights up his handsome face. "So I didn't need to beg? You really want this too?"

"Yes," I hiss.

"Say it."

"Say what?"

"Ask me to please fuck you." That cocky smirk only grows more intolerable.

"Dream on, honey." I reach for his cock and squeeze. "Now give me that unforgettable night you promised."

He smothers a squeal through clenched teeth and presses his lips to mine. "Your request is my command, spitfire." Then he pushes me back onto the mattress and nestles his hips between my thighs. "Can we talk about removing the lingerie?"

"No," I growl.

"Maybe next time?"

"If there is one."

"Oh, Mrs. Rossi, after tonight, you'll be begging me to fuck you all day, every day."

"Pretty arrogant words, Mr. Rossi. I hope you can back them up with action. And it's Mrs. *Guo*."

"What about Guo-Rossi?"

"We'll see after tonight."

"Fair enough." He disappears between my legs, and a warm tongue drags across my clit an instant later. His tongue flicks the delicate nub, then draws it between his teeth. I wriggle from the riot of sensations, but his palm flattens across my belly. "First, I'm going to fuck you with my tongue, then my fingers, and finally, my cock. By the time I'm done with you, Mrs. Rossi, you won't be able to walk."

"That's Mrs. G—" I begin to murmur, but the rest of the word falls away on a moan as he dips a finger inside me.

His tongue continues its maddening strokes as he thrusts with one finger, then adds in a second. I'm so full of him, so aware of our joined flesh, of his tongue circling my clit, his fingers pumping in and out of me, his hand splayed across my belly. Marco is everywhere.

The delicious tension builds, the steady thrusts increasing in tempo with the incessant circling. Fire scorches my veins, racing to my lower half.

"Marco," I groan.

He doesn't let up his assault, only doubling his ministrations as my hips buck beneath him.

"I'm going to come," I pant.

"Good," he murmurs against my heated flesh, the vibrations only pushing me closer to the edge. "It will only be the first time tonight."

His tongue finds the taut bundle of nerves once again, and he sucks on the swollen nub. The sun, moon and stars all sail across my vision as I reach for his dark locks and tangle my fingers through the silky strands. Then the hand splayed across my belly moves up to my breast, somehow still managing to carefully avoid my wound, despite the obvious uncontrollable lust. He pinches my pert nipple, and I explode.

"Oh, Marco," I moan as I come apart. Liquid fire surges up my spine, the overwhelming sensations licking up my core, and a tremor surges through every inch of my body. All the air escapes my lungs, and I just lay there, a quivering, whimpering puddle.

As I attempt to catch my breath, it dawns on me he's going to try to do this all over again with his cock. A thrill streaks up my spine. *Chill, Jia.* Sex for the first time will not be pleasant, or at least, that's what I've always heard from my girlfriends.

As if Marco has plucked the thought right out of my mind, he crawls over me, wedging his hips between my thighs. "Relax, spitfire, I'm going to take care of you."

Clenching my jaw, I nod slowly, the echoes of desire still vibrating my core.

He runs his finger across my jawline. "But you need to relax. If you fight me, it won't be pleasant because I am big and you're tight as fuck."

A whisper of fear tangles through the excitement.

His hand tightens around my jaw, and he forces my eyes to his. "I won't hurt you. If you're in pain, just tell me and I'll stop, okay?"

There's something about the look in his eyes that has a knot of emotion thickening my throat. Oh, God, do not cry, Jia. He'll freak out and bolt.

"Promise me you'll say something?"

My head dips, and I blink quickly to keep the mounting tears at bay.

"I don't want you to just smile and fake it, okay? I need you to answer me, Jia."

"Okay, I promise."

"Good girl." He cups my throbbing pussy, and tingles race through my core once again. His mouth moves over mine, and my body begins to relax, melting into his touch. As his kisses become more desperate, I feel his head prodding at my entrance. I'm still so wet, he glides over my slick folds, igniting another wave of desire.

"Eyes on me, spitfire," he whispers against my lips. "I want you to remember this moment forever. So when we're old and gray, you can tell our grandchildren about the night I claimed you as mine. Because this is it. Once you're mine, you'll never belong to another."

I nod quickly, the intensity of his smoldering gaze too much to bear. I don't dare ask about our open marriage agreement, or how I'm supposed to belong to only him if we're screwing other people.

Because in that moment, it is only him and me.

And he's right, I will remember this for the rest of my life, whether we remain together or not. Every woman remembers their first time.

Mouth capturing mine once again, his hips thrust in time with his tongue, and his thick head pries me open. A cry dies in my throat as a swirl of pleasure and pain consumes my lower half. Marco doesn't move, with only the tip inside me.

His anxious gaze locks on mine. "Are you okay?"

"Mmhmm," I mumble, teeth baring into my bottom lip.

"You don't seem okay."

"It just stings a little."

He releases a string of Italian curses and starts to pull back.

"No!" I shout and palm his muscled ass, driving him farther in.

He gently inches in, eyes pinned to mine. "You're doing a great job, spitfire, I'm about halfway in now." A reassuring smile softens the typical hard set of his jaw. "You ready for more?"

I nod slowly.

More pressure, but also a tiny hint of pleasure as his crown hits my clit.

"Almost there, wifey. You're such a good girl taking all my cock…"

I'm going to smack him in a second if he doesn't just do it already.

"Ready for all of me?"

"Yes!"

He pushes in the remaining inches, and we release a sharp hiss in perfect unison as he settles deep inside me. I stretch around his cock, somehow accommodating his ridiculous girth. Once he's in, I release the breath I've been holding.

Marco still doesn't move, his body hovering a few inches above me. "You look like you're in pain."

"I'm not."

"Then why are you clenching your teeth?"

"Because you're pissing me off."

A deep chuckle vibrates above me, and I relax, a smile melting across my lips. "*Dio*, you're going to ruin me, wifey."

"I was about to say the same thing." I tighten my hold on his ass and urge him on. "Just start slowly."

He nods and presses a gentle kiss to my forehead. His hips begin to move, and he inches out of me before easing back in. It's a painstaking process, but soon the sting is eclipsed by the blossoming pleasure.

"Is this okay?" he whispers against my lips.

"Yes."

"You sure you want me to keep going?"

"I said *yes*!"

He picks up the pace, and the brewing heat intensifies. His

cock glides in and out, in and out—and I thought his fingers were good. There's something about him being inside me, the connecting of our two bodies as one, and the significance of it all, that has my chest tightening with emotion.

What is wrong with me?

Heat springs to my eyes and despite blinking like mad, a tear spills over.

Marco immediately stops, panic washing over his face. "Fuck, did I hurt you? Is it the bullet wound?"

I shake my head, more tears running down my cheeks at the sheer terror in his eyes. Only it's not just fear, but genuine concern, as if my husband truly cares for me. The realization has a sob building in my throat.

So I do what I always do when I panic. I push him off, spring out of bed, and race to the bathroom.

CHAPTER 40
YOU'RE IT FOR ME

M *arco*

As a newlywed, I never thought I'd spend so many nights on the couch. I stretch out my legs and my feet hang over the edge, only heightening my frustration. First, at the hospital and now, in my own damned home. I waited for Jia to emerge from the bathroom for half an hour last night before finally giving up and marching downstairs. At some point as I tossed and turned on the leather sofa, I heard her quiet footfalls across the loft.

At least she finally came out of the bathroom.

I haven't heard her stir since. Even *Yéye* hasn't materialized from his room, and he's usually an early riser. Then again, it is only seven in the morning. But I've been up for hours. I'm not sure I can even say I truly ever slept. Besides my raging hard-on, I couldn't get the look in her eyes off my mind. Like the sex actually meant something.

And it did. To me.

I've been with more women than I can count, and it never felt like *that*. Fuck, is this love? It's been so long I'm not sure I remember what it feels like anymore. The craziest thing about all of it was that it was the most vanilla sex I've ever had. Hell, neither of us even came. And still, despite the awkward maneuvering, for those few blissful moments buried inside that warm pussy, it felt like I was finally home.

A home that belonged to me and no one else.

Being in foster care, I'd never had that. Not since I was a young kid and my *mamma* and *nonno* put Nico and me on that plane to America to find our father. Spoiler alert: things went to shit real quick when our father never showed up at the airport.

I bury the dark memories, reminding myself that Umberto Valentino wasn't the bastard I'd spent my whole life believing he was. If it wasn't for Dante and Luca sharing some old correspondence they'd found buried in our father's boxes, I never would have known the truth.

Faint footsteps draw me from musings of the past, and my head swivels toward the spiral steps. Jia descends slowly, wrapped in a red silk robe with brilliant dragons embroidered across the material. Dark circles line the soft skin beneath her eyes, and they're swollen and puffy as if she's been crying.

My chest aches as I take her in and before I can stop myself, I'm on my feet moving toward her. *Cazzo*, I'm in love. My ribs constrict, squeezing my failing organ at the visceral truth. I'm totally out of my mind in love with *my wife*. Her dark gaze rakes over me as I approach, and I halt abruptly only a few inches before I reach her, my arms longing to wrap around her waist and hold her close. Maybe she doesn't want me to touch her. Maybe I hurt her, and she's really pissed. "I'm sorry," I mutter.

"You have nothing to apologize for. I'm the one that freaked out and ran. *I'm* sorry." Her eyes meet mine, and my jaw nearly unhinges at the unexpected apology.

I release a breath of relief and reach for her hand. I'm pleasantly surprised when she allows my fingers to tangle with hers. "Are you okay?"

The hint of a smile curls the corner of her lip. "Just a little sore from your ridiculously large cock."

I bark out a laugh and draw her into my chest, squeezing her slender form tight against my own, nearly forgetting all about the wound. "Why didn't you just tell me to stop?" I whisper against the top of her head.

"Because I liked it."

I hold her out to arm's length because I have to see her face after that startling confession. "You did?" I don't know much about a woman's first time, because I never cared to, but from what I've seen in movies, it seemed painful.

Her intense eyes chase to mine, and the darkness from a moment ago lifts. "It hurt like hell for a few seconds, but then, it was starting to get better."

"Then why did you run?"

She pulls back her arm and slams her petite fist into my chest, right at the dragon's snout. "Because I didn't want you to see me cry."

"It hurt that bad?"

"No," she squeals. "I wasn't crying because of the pain, you idiot."

Dio, I don't think I'll ever understand this woman. "Then why?"

Her gaze casts down to the floor, one hand still pressed to my chest and the other toying with the long sleeves of her robe. "I was just emotional... I honestly don't know what came over me."

Hmm, interesting. She wouldn't be the first woman I've made cry during sex, but it was for completely diffcrent reasons the other times. "So...you enjoyed it?"

"Yes."

I reach for her chin, trapping it between my fingers and force her eyes to mine. "And you'd like to do it again?"

A lopsided smile curves her lips. "Maybe…"

My cock hardens at the thought. And wearing only boxers, the effect that one word has on me is painfully evident. Her gaze dips to my fully tented crotch.

"Not right now," she squeaks.

"Why not? Wait—I have an idea." I scoop her into my arms and carry her toward the stairs.

"Where are you taking me?"

"You'll see." I race up the steps, taking them two at a time as anticipation sends heat and a rush of blood to my throbbing cock. The image of Jia in the bathtub, all wet and covered in indecent bubbles has my footsteps quickening.

When we reach the master bathroom, I prop Jia on the edge of the marble tub and spin the faucets.

She wraps the robe tighter around her waist and glares up at me. "What are you doing?"

"Isn't it obvious? We're taking a bath." I drag my boxers down and they slough onto the marble floor.

She shakes her head, something like panic streaking across those expressive midnight spheres. "Nope, not happening."

"But why? You said you were sore… this will help. I promise, I won't even touch you if you don't want."

"I said no." She knots her arms across her chest and shoots me a narrowed glare.

"Come on, Jia, why not?" Turning off the running water, I drop down beside her. "Please, just tell me what it is. I want to understand you." I drag a hand through my hair, a mix of frustration and confusion elevating my pulse. "I'm really trying here…" I pry her hand from beneath her underarm and press it between mine. It's so small and delicate compared to my big, rough ones.

I watch as her expression of outright determination begins

to soften and then crumble. Her bottom lip quivers, and now I'm totally fucking lost. What did I do now?

"Jia…" I caress her cheek, running my thumb across her skin and catching the falling tear. "Please, tell me what's wrong. This is never going to work if we're not honest with each other."

"I hate this," she mumbles, and I jerk my hand back. A rueful smile emerges, and she pulls my hand back. "No, not that." She blows out a breath. "I hate this incessant crying. I despise you thinking I'm weak; I abhor the idea of you seeing my flaws."

"What flaws, spitfire? From where I'm sitting, you're absolutely perfect."

She snorts on a laugh, and on her, the awkward sound is the cutest thing I've ever heard. She draws in a long breath once the giggle subsides, and as if she's made up her mind about something, she fixes her eyes to mine. "Promise me that you won't think differently of me."

I don't think there's anything this woman could say or do that would keep me from wanting her, from loving her. "I promise."

"And that you won't overreact."

My brows furrow at that one. I'm not exactly known for my levelheadedness. "Damn it, Jia, just tell me." Modifying my tone, I add more softly, "Please."

Releasing my hand, she begins to unknot the tie of her robe. The red silk slides off her shoulders, and I'm so enthralled by the canvas of porcelain skin beneath: the full breasts, the firm torso and the smattering of dark hair between her legs, I nearly miss it.

As I double back to take her all in once again, my hungry gaze finds her twitchy fingers and moves up her arms.

To the dozens of shallow cuts across her forearms.

No, hundreds. Long ones, short ones, jagged ones, deeper ones.

A wave of red-hot fury pummels my veins as rage darkens my vision. "Who the fuck did that to you?" I roar.

Her eyes cast down to her tangled fingers and I immediately regret my outburst. Attempting to tamp down the burgeoning fury, I heave in a breath and school my expression into a mask of calm. Dropping to my knees, I crawl between her legs and capture her chin. This time, I don't compel her eyes to mine.

"Please, Jia, tell me who did this to you so I can crucify the bastard, rip him apart limb from limb and drag his remains up and down the Westside Highway."

She finally lifts her chin, her eyes willingly meeting mine. A tragic mixture of shame and despair darkens those bottomless irises, and my fingers curl into a fist at my side. "It was my father."

Undiluted rage rushes my chest, tightening my lungs. "Fuck!" I growl. "That *pezzo di merda*, mother fucker, worthless son of a *puttana*." The curses continue to fly as I leap to my feet and pace a tight circle around the bathtub. "How? Why?" I shout into the air, waving my hands like a lunatic.

"I don't know," she whispers, "because he enjoyed inflicting pain on others?"

"Fuck!" I snarl again. "If I can't kill him, I'll kill someone in his place then. Someone has to pay for this!"

A small hand closes around my forearm, jerking me from the bottomless downward spiral. "Marco, please, you promised you wouldn't overreact."

"How could I not? The man abused you, Jia! Your own damned father. The one person who is supposed to protect you."

"I know," she shouts back, her fingers tightening around my arm. "And that's exactly why I turned out this way. Why I cried last night, why I'm scared to death to trust you, why I'm fucked up in the head." She presses her finger to her temple in the form of a gun. "I can't do this…"

Ripping her hand away, I squeeze both between my own. "Yes, you can. So our families fucked us up a little? It doesn't mean we can't overcome it together."

"I don't know if I can."

Blinding realization hits me like a fucking freight train as I stare at this beautifully fierce but terribly broken woman. "That's why you wanted an open marriage? You thought if you gave me an out, you wouldn't suffer if I disappointed you."

Her fine shoulders lift. "In my experience, men don't change."

"You're wrong, and I'll prove it to you." I press a kiss to her forehead and draw her tight against my bare chest. "If you want an open marriage, you can have one, but there's no one I want but you, my wife. You're it for me, damn it, spitfire."

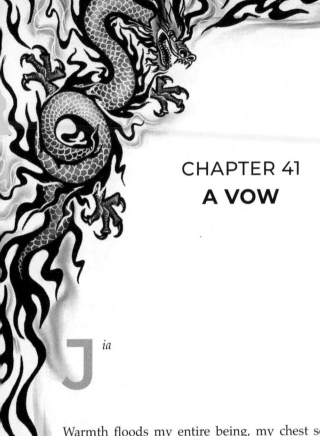

CHAPTER 41
A VOW

J *ia*

Warmth floods my entire being, my chest so full I'm certain it'll burst. Wrapped in Marco's arms, his musky, cedarwood scent invading my nostrils, it all feels like too much. A tangle of pain, embarrassment, anger, and now hope bloat my torso. My heart slams against my ribcage in a desperate effort to break through the skeletal barrier between us.

I never planned on admitting the truth, on allowing him to see my scars, but maybe it was time. Because can a wound really heal without ever seeing the light of day?

I want to believe Marco; I wish our marriage could work because maybe *Yéye* is right. Maybe Marco Rossi really is the man for me. But I'm terrified. Exposing myself to·him was more difficult than giving him my body.

My virginity had become more of an inconvenience than anything else.

But revealing my true self, scars and all, is humiliating.

That I allowed *Bà* to abuse me for years is mortifying. I was weak, something I vowed never to be again. And behind Marco's looming shadow, I fear I would become that meek little girl again.

"Talk to me, spitfire." Marco's gaze rakes over me, the depth of emotion in those multi-colored spheres stealing the remaining air from my lungs.

It's not as if I want to be with another man either. But he's right, the idea of tying myself, of placing all my faith and trust in him scares the shit out of me.

"Okay, you've left me no choice. I'm going to have to say it now, even if we are both naked standing in the bathroom."

I glance down between us and finally notice his erection wedged between our bodies. I swear the man is eternally aroused.

"I love you, Jia."

My eyes snap up, the unexpected declaration catching me completely off guard. "Wha—"

"I'm hopelessly, madly in love with you, Jia, *my wife*. I probably have been for a while, now, if I'm being honest with myself, since for as long as I can remember, I haven't wanted to fuck anyone else but you."

My heart staggers out a manic beat, and all the air evacuates my lungs. The sincerity in his eyes is breathtaking and startling all at the same time. I want to say *how can you love me?* I've been awful to him from the very beginning. More than that, though, I want to say *I love you too*, but how can I when I'm not sure I know what real love is? It's been so long since I felt it, I've forgotten what it is.

"I don't want an open marriage," I whisper instead. For now, it's the best I can do.

"Thank *Dio*," he mumbles against my lips. "Because the idea of another man's hands on you would send me to an early grave. Or worse, prison, because I'd have to murder anyone who dared touch my wife."

My wife. Somehow it doesn't sound so scary anymore.

I lean into him, reveling in his familiar scent. Then I rise to my tiptoes and brush a kiss to his lips. It's chaste and gentle, but his cock grows even harder, poking me in the belly. A flicker of heat courses below my bellybutton, and my hips tilt to meet his. "I think I'm ready for that bath now."

"Thank fuck." He scoops me into his arms once more and within two long strides, we're inside the oversized marble tub, the tepid water enveloping me in its embrace. He reaches for the faucet and runs the hot water, warming the lukewarm bath. Then he gently removes the bandage across my chest, scowling at the puckered skin beneath.

"It's fine," I whisper. "It doesn't hurt, I swear."

With a huff of resignation, Marco slides to the back of the tub, pulling me between his legs so my back is against his chest and his cock is wedged between my ass cheeks. He dips his chin to my shoulder, and his warm breath skates across the shell of my ear. "Have you ever been fucked in the ass, spitfire?"

A thrill races up my spine as his thick shaft glides along my crack. "No," I squeal, wriggling. "Let's work on one hole at a time, honey."

His tongue licks along my collarbone, sucking and nibbling. "Fair enough. But by the time we're old and gray, I will have claimed every inch of you, wifey."

"I think I can handle that."

His hand curls around my waist, then his fingers dance down my thigh and find my pulsing center. I'm already aching, but in the best way. His finger gently glides through my wet folds.

"Is this okay?" he whispers against the shell of my ear, eliciting a wave of goosebumps.

"Yes." My hips buck, forcing his finger deeper.

"Mmm, you're so tight, spitfire. Do you feel that? How your hungry pussy sucks my finger in?"

I nod, the fiery sensations already building.

"Do you think you can take my cock again so soon?"

"Umhmm," I murmur, that skilled thumb exerting just the right amount of pressure on my clit as his middle finger slips inside me.

"Good, because I want you to come all over my cock. I felt robbed yesterday."

A cackle erupts, but it's quickly overpowered by the building pleasure, and I chomp down on my bottom lip.

"You know, it just occurred to me I'm going to be your first for a lot of things. The first to fuck you in the bathtub, in the shower, on the balcony, the washing machine, all over this damned penthouse."

"But *Yéye*," I pant.

"You'll just have to be quiet, spitfire." His thumb quickens its movements and I grind my pussy against his palm, desperate for the friction. "Or not, whatever. You know your grandfather would be thrilled about us fucking."

He's not wrong there. *Yéye* can't wait for me to start popping out heirs. Which reminds me, we need to have the baby talk. We'd been irresponsible the other night, and married or not, I wasn't ready for kids.

I'm about to say as much when Marco slips a second finger inside me, and pleasure roars through my system, sending me sprawling over the edge. I grip his forearms as the unexpected orgasm rips through me, the tremors vibrating from the top of my head down to the tips of my toes.

He's toying with my nipple, only extending the flood of pleasure, when I finally regain my senses and glance up at him. A ridiculous grin parts his lips, that cocky smirk that used to irritate me so much causing my heart to trip on a beat.

"Good?" His warm breath flits through my hair.

"So good," I groan.

"Then get ready for round two, baby." His arm curls around the underside of my legs, and he draws me into his chest. Then he stands, not even bothering to dry either of us and darts into the bedroom, his wet feet slapping against the marble.

"Don't you think a towel would be nice?"

"What's the point? You're going to be drenched in a second anyway." He shoots me a wicked grin as he lays me across the mattress. His cock stands proud between us, and my core clenches in anticipation. I imagine his thick crown nudging at my entrance, and every nerve ending fires up in eagerness.

It has to be easier today, right?

Vaginas were meant to stretch. If a baby could come out of one, surely mine would get used to accommodating my husband's enormous dick.

"I'm going to go easy on you today, spitfire. But you have to tell me what's going in that little head of yours, okay?"

I nod, snagging my lower lip between my teeth.

He crawls over me, and I eagerly part my legs for him as he wedges his hips between my thighs. Those colorful irises lance into mine, the blue a most brilliant aqua and the dark one, a raging abyss of midnight. "It's easy for me to get carried away, and I don't want to hurt you. I will never be that man with you. I am not your father. Do you understand?"

Emotion tightens my throat, but I refuse to cry again. Marco's going to think I'm absolutely insane. "I understand. And I know you're not."

"Good. Because I still owe you that amazing night I promised." He glances at the clock and shrugs. "Or morning, whatever. I think the Geminis and Four Seas can manage without us for another day."

He runs his cock across my wet folds, and even though the echoes of the last orgasm are still vibrating through me, a new wave of desire crashes over me. "Yes, they can."

I tense for a moment, awaiting the sharp pain as he enters me, but instead his cock remains still, and he bows his head before brushing his lips across my forearm. Painstakingly slowly, he kisses every single cut, every scar, every wound my father inflicted. Shit, I'm going to cry again.

All the while, his thick crown nudges at my pussy, desire growing with each passing moment and somehow, I manage to keep the tears at bay. When he finally finishes his gentle ministrations, he hovers over me, eyes smoldering. "I vow to be the man that guards your heart, Jia, your unwavering protector. With every beat of my heart, I promise to cherish you, to love you fiercely and without reservation. For as long as breath fills my lungs, my devotion to you will burn as brightly as the lights across the Manhattan skyline, illuminating our lives with the promise of a love that knows no bounds."

"You're doing it on purpose," I choke out, a damned tear spilling over. "You're trying to make me cry, aren't you, you *coglione*?"

A deep chuckle rumbles in his chest, reverberating against my own. "No, spitfire, I just want you to know how loved you are, how absolutely cherished."

"I—"

He presses a soft kiss to my lips before whispering, "Don't say it until you're sure. Because when you do, I want it to be forever."

I swallow hard, once again blown away by the depth of this man's emotions. I never expected any of it from the playboy mafia boss. His lips claim mine, and I melt into his touch. While his mouth devours my own, capturing my attention, he thrusts his tip inside me. I gasp at the sudden intrusion, but this time there's no pain, only that thrilling sensation of Marco.

His eyes lance into mine, a question in that mesmerizing gaze.

"I'm fine," I whisper. "More than fine…"

"Are you ready for more of me?"

I nod, and he sinks all the way in. My entire core throbs

with pleasure at the feeling of utter fullness. Of finally feeling complete.

"Good girl, I knew you could take all of me."

I lift my hips, urging him on, and his cock slowly retreats before filling me to the hilt once again. I groan as his thick head brushes that elusive spot buried deep in my pussy. "Again," I groan.

He quickens his tempo, gliding in and out of me more forcefully. "Mmm, *Dio*, I love fucking my wife."

"I think I could get used to this."

Marco's mouth moves down my neck, blazing a trail to my breasts. He sucks my nipple, and my back arches at the explosion of pleasure. Then his hands curl around my ass and he drives himself impossibly deeper. His balls slap my ass as he quickens the tempo, and I reach around between us to stroke them.

He lets out a groan against my peaked nipple, the vibration reaching all the way to my core. "Mmm, spitfire, do you feel that? Your virgin pussy is so hungry for my cock." He hovers over me and glances between us, his shaft exposed and only his crown buried in my folds. He watches as he thrusts in and out, in and out. It's strangely erotic, watching him disappear inside me. As if we truly are one. "I want you to come for me, baby. I want to feel your pussy clenching around my cock, begging me to fill it up with cum."

Damn, why is that dirty talk so hot?

Instinct takes over, my hips rocking beneath him and eagerly meeting each thrust. He plunges deeper, filling me so completely I can't tell where he ends and I begin. And it's absolutely perfect.

It occurs to me again that we're not using protection and he literally just said he was going to fill me with his cum. I should say something... I don't want to get pregnant right now, do I?

"Marco..." I rasp out.

"I'm close, spitfire. I want you to come with me."

"But… babies… pregnancy," I mumble incoherently.

A feral grin spreads his lips as he pounds into me harder. Fiery heat rages between my legs and I'm so close now, the energy building to near combustion. I'm not sure I could stop now if I wanted to.

"I want it all with you," he whispers against my lips.

"Right now?"

"Whenever…"

Perhaps now is not the best time to have this conversation with both of us an inch away from orgasm and lust clouding our senses. What are the chances I'll get pregnant the first time, right?

Wrapping his arms around me, he pulls me into his lap, deepening the angle of penetration. "Oh, fuck," I groan. "Don't stop, I'm so close."

He resumes his thrustss, gripping my hips and lifting me up and down along his silky shaft. Each devastating drive pushes me closer to that fiery end, his head rubbing that taut bundle of nerves at my core and driving me wild. His mouth closes around my breast again and his hand runs down my torso until his finger finds my clit. Pressing the swollen nub, I hurtle over the edge of pleasure. With his mouth sucking on my nipple, his cock deep inside me and that devastating finger on my clit, I'm so full of Marco he's all-consuming.

I come with his name on my lips, the fiery sensations pummeling through me in an avalanche. A second later, I feel his cock twitch inside me, and his head falls back on a long groan as his orgasm roars through. We remain like that, clinging to each other for a long moment as the tremors continue.

Finally, with my legs like jelly, Marco lowers me back onto the mattress and settles over me. He hovers just a few inches over my exposed wound, his expression turning glacial every time it crosses his line of sight. '

In an effort to regain his attention, I cup his cheek and force his gaze to mine. "That was pretty good."

"Pretty good?" he scoffs. "Those moans sounded a hell of a lot better than 'pretty good'."

"What can I say, I'm not an easy one to wow."

"No surprise there, spitfire." He smirks, then slowly glides his tongue across his bottom lip. "It's a good thing I'm just getting started."

"Oh really?" I arch a taunting brow.

"By nightfall, your pussy will be aching, and you'll still be begging for more." He drops between my legs and drags his tongue across my center. "I was wrong before. I thought you were the best thing I'd ever tasted, but this, you and me, *our* cum splattered all over your pussy together, it's absolute heaven."

Those words alone have me ready to go again. I didn't think it was possible. So I spread my legs and give into the burning desire, the absolute pleasure, the incredible love I didn't know I was so desperate for.

CHAPTER 42
THE MILE HIGH CLUB

M *arco*

Three days of wedded bliss is all we're allotted before the Lower East Side explodes into chaos. With Jia still home recovering and the impending departure of the elder Guo, the Four Seas along with the other bands of the Triad squabble and fight like stupid-ass children. And the damned Puerto Rican mob steps in, taking advantage of the pandemonium.

They've ransacked warehouses, destroyed shipments, even hijacked cargo liners before they reach the docks. My fingers dig into the smooth leather armrests of the captain's chair on our private jet. If it wasn't for Jia's hand on my thigh distracting me, my blood pressure would be through the roof. And if it wasn't for my twin and his girlfriend·sitting across from us, my wife's hand would be down my pants, strangling my cock and providing a much more pleasant experience for us all.

Nico made the executive decision that it was time for us to

travel to Puerto Rico to meet with the head of *La Sombra Boricua*, Esmeralda, in person. I'm not anxious for this little reunion for numerous reasons. One: I hate the idea of putting my wife in danger, but of course, she wouldn't take no for an answer. Two: I should be at home right now fucking my little spitfire, instead of dealing with this nonsense. Three: Last time I saw Esmeralda, she held a gun to my head after I'd thoroughly fucked her. That last one may have been my fault.

I have no desire to see my past conquest while toting my new wife at my side. I debated telling Jia before we got on the plane about a hundred times, but somehow the timing was never right. How could I tell her with my cock buried balls deep in her sweet little pussy as she moaned my name? Which was how we'd spent the last three days, only emerging from our bedroom to scavenge for food and give *Yéye* a quick hello.

I don't think I've ever seen the old man smile so much. Who knew he'd be so pleased we were finally getting along?

Jia's hand creeps higher up my thigh, drawing my attention away from the torrent of my musings. My cock instantly hardens at her touch, and I hazard a quick glance toward my brother and Maisy. They've nodded off, the cute redhead asleep on his shoulder, both wearing matching earbuds. My eyes flicker to my wife and the mischievous glint in those dark irises.

I cup her hand over my cock, and her fingers wrap around me over my slacks. Only a few soft touches, and I'm hard as hell and desperate for more. I lean closer and whisper, "I've got another first for you, spitfire."

"Oh yeah, what's that?" Excitement sparkles in her gaze.

"The mile high club." I toss her a wink, and her grin grows more brazen. She may have been a virgin only a week ago, but damn, she's learned quickly. And she's so willing to try anything. I've already had her across nearly every surface of the loft and, once her grandfather departs, we'll have even more unclaimed territory to explore.

My hand wraps around the back of her neck, bringing her mouth to mine. As I claim that sharp tongue, I drag her into my lap so she straddles me. She's wearing a skirt and a scrap of lace covers her pussy. I can easily work around that.

I reach between us, unfasten my belt, and drag down the zipper of my slacks.

She freezes, eyes meeting mine as she reads my intent. "But your brother—" she murmurs against my lips.

"Is asleep," I answer as my cock springs free.

"What if they wake up?" she whisper-hisses.

"Those noise-cancelling earbuds are pretty powerful. And besides, I've walked in on them fucking so many times it's only fair, really."

She claps her hand over her mouth to smother a chuckle. "You're terrible."

"And you love it." I slip my hand beneath her skirt and find her already wet. I try to focus on that instead of the fact that she hasn't actually told me she loves me. I tell myself she needs time after all the fucked-up shit she went through with her father. Besides, I was the idiot who told her to be sure.

That damned ring is burning a hole in the hidden safe I moved it to at home. I've been dying to give it to her, but she has to say the words first. I need to know she's really in this. Despite all the amazing sex.

With her panties pushed to the side, I toy with her clit as my mind wanders. It isn't until she reaches for my cock and positions it at her entrance that I really focus. *Cazzo*, this woman has ruined me. I'm about to fuck my gorgeous wife mid-air, and all I can think about is if she loves me or not.

Damn it… I need to tell her about Esmeralda. There can't be any more secrets between us if this marriage is to truly work. And I'm so desperate for that.

"There's something I have to tell you." I keep circling that taut bundle of nerves, hoping the news will be more palatable this way.

Her eyes narrow as she regards me. "Okay."

"Esmeralda and I have history…"

Jia grunts, rolling her eyes. "Of course you do." She tries to squirm off me, but I hold her in place with one hand on her thigh and increase my attentions to her swollen clit.

Once I'm certain she won't bolt, I whisper, "It didn't mean anything." Cupping her cheek, I run my thumb across her soft skin. "Nothing meant anything before you."

Her gaze chases down to the minute space between our bodies, and fear blossoms. She's going to run. I rub her clit harder, anything to distract her.

"Okay," she murmurs an excruciatingly long moment later.

"… That's it?"

"What else can I say? Do I like the idea that you fucked the head of *La Sombra Boricua*? Of course not. Am I surprised? Also, no. I can't hold you responsible for all of your stupidities before we met."

Extricating my fingers from inside her, I frame her face with both my hands and press a kiss to her pouty lips. "I guess this is what a healthy discussion in a mature relationship looks like, huh?"

"I suppose so." She adjusts her stance and hovers over my thick crown. "Now, fuck me already, so I can get the thought of you with that woman out of my head."

Gripping her waist, I force her down onto my cock and we groan in perfect unison. She's so fucking tight, I feel like a damned school boy every time I'm inside her. It takes all my concentration not to come on the spot.

"Are you going to be able to be quiet, spitfire?" I whisper as she bounces on my cock. She's so eager, her pussy so ravenous for me.

Her head falls back. "Mmhmm."

"I'm not sure I believe you." My hands skate up her skirt, squeezing her perfect ass and she lets out a faint groan. With one palm urging her closer, my other one travels beneath the curve of her ass cheek. I run my finger through her wetness, dragging her arousal toward her puckered hole. The one part of her I have yet to claim.

She trembles at the touch, her hips rocking more forcefully against my cock. I brush the edge of her back hole, circling slowly. I've been priming her for days. She's soaked already and I'm certain she could handle it, but it's probably not the best place to test it out.

So instead, I insert only the tip of my finger.

She gasps at the unexpected intrusion, but she doesn't balk. She simply moves faster, gliding up and down my shaft before reaching between us to cup my balls.

"Fuck..." I groan as they tighten at her touch.

My free hand moves from her ass and skates beneath her blouse. I free her breast and rub her nipple until she moans.

"Mmm, I feel so full of you, honey," she whispers against my ear, her peaked nipples brushing my chest through her blouse.

"That's right, wifey. You're all mine. My cock in your drenched pussy, my finger in that tight asshole, and your perfect breast in my palm. You were made for me, all of you."

"Yes..." she groans.

"Get ready, because I'm going to fill you with my cum in a second. And I don't want you to clean up after. I want you to walk into Esmeralda's house with my cum dripping down your leg so she knows your mine and I'm yours."

A chill races up her spine, making her shoulders tremble. "I'm ready." She captures my lips, devouring them with unbridled enthusiasm as she rides my cock.

We haven't exactly been careful the past few days. Though we've talked about her going on the pill, we'd need to leave our bedroom to make it happen. I know how invested Jia is in the grand opening of CityZen and a baby would not make that easy.

On the other hand, my biological clock must have just

materialized because all I can think about is filling my wife with my seed. And the idea of her belly round with my baby has me at the point of orgasm. It's fucking nuts what love can do to a self-proclaimed eternal bachelor.

I thrust harder, meeting her with every rock of her hips and dip my finger farther inside that virgin hole. She lets out a faint moan through clenched teeth, and her head falls back. I can feel her pussy clench around my cock and it's all I need to fall right along with her.

Tremors ravage my body as the orgasm rips through me and I come inside her, the thick ropes dribbling down her thigh. *Dio*, I'll never get tired of this. I could live inside her and be a happy man.

Once the echoes of pleasure subside, she collapses against me, a beaming smile on that radiant face.

"Soon, I'm going to fuck that tight little ass, spitfire," I whisper.

Mischief dances across those darting eyes. "As long as it's good, you can claim every part of me, honey."

"Oh, it'll be good. Trust me."

She tries to scramble off, but I hold her down for another minute. "When we're at Esmeralda's let me do the talking, okay? I don't need you making any more enemies."

Her lips screw into a pout. "I can't make any promises."

I should have known better…

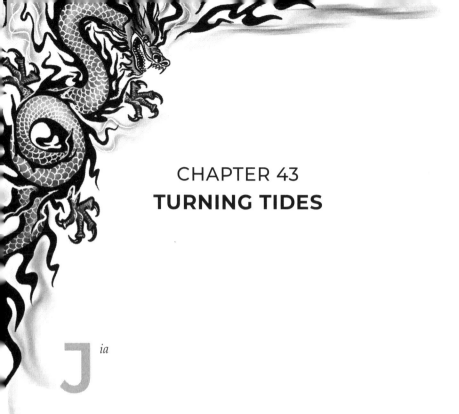

CHAPTER 43
TURNING TIDES

J *ia*

The sprawling compound of *La Sombra Boricua* looks more like a five-star luxury resort than the hideout of a notorious crime organization. A sultry breeze sweeps dark hair across my face, the towering palms swaying to the rhythm of the warm air blowing off the Caribbean Sea. The waves roll in, the soft rush lulling me into a false sense of calm.

Esmeralda may have been on good terms with the Rossies, but I know better than anyone how quickly the tides can turn in our dark world. As if Marco has read my thoughts, his hand tightens around mine, his thumb brushing across my palm.

The gentle touch sends a whisper of heat streaking below my bellybutton, reminding me of the cum between my legs. Marco wasn't kidding when he said he wanted me walking into Esmeralda's home with him dripping down my thighs. I should be mortified, but instead, I enjoy the wicked sensations it elicits. It marks me as his, and considering he's been with this woman not long ago, I'm feeling a little insecure, something I do not enjoy. Though I've never met Esmeralda in person, I have seen photos of her, and the woman is gorgeous.

A spike of jealousy jabs at my insides.

Stop it, Jia. Marco loves you, he married you. This time it's *Yéye's* voice that whispers through my subconscious.

As we walk up the coquina stone pathway, I draw in a breath and remind myself why we're here. Not to size up one of Marco's past conquests, but to discover who dared to ruin our wedding day.

"Remember, let me do the talking," Marco whispers.

"Of course, honey."

Maisy giggles, canting her head over her shoulder as she regards us. I send a quick prayer up thanking God she and Nico are heavy sleepers. Despite Marco's reassurances, I was more than relieved they hadn't awoken midway through our in-flight sexcapades.

When we reach the front door of the tropical bungalow, the guard stationed at the entrance opens it and ushers us inside. From the foyer, the turquoise waters of the Caribbean Sea stretch out before us. The view is so incredible, I nearly miss the leggy Latina sauntering toward us in nothing but a skimpy bikini. She's all perfectly tan and toned skin, with dark, wavy hair cascading down her shoulders doing nothing to hide her full breasts. The bikini top barely conceals her nipples.

Maisy stares so pointedly, I'm scared her eyes are going to pop out of her head. The feisty redhead had fought tooth and nail with Nico to be allowed to join us. Marco's brother had planned on leaving his girlfriend on the jet with a slew of guards, but she'd convinced him otherwise by the time we landed. I liked her from the start, but that power move had sealed the deal for me.

"Gentlemen, so lovely to see you both again in my home." Esmeralda presses a kiss to Nico's cheek, utterly ignoring Maisy.

When she approaches Marco, I glide between them, sticking my hand out. "A pleasure, Esmeralda, I've heard so much about you. I am Jia Guo, perhaps you've heard of me?"

"Guo-Rossi," Marco grumbles. "My wife."

"Ah, yes, of course." Her dark eyes sparkle in amusement as she regards us, her gaze lingering on my husband and the ring on his finger a little longer than I appreciate. "I apologize I was unable to attend the wedding, but in hindsight, I suppose it was for the best."

"About that—" Marco interjects, but Nico cuts him off before he gets the rest of the sentence out.

"Thank you for having us today, Esmeralda. We hate to inconvenience you, but the matter we'd like to discuss warrants an in-person visit."

Her lips curve into a devilish grin. "I told you that you were always welcome in my home, Nico." Then her gaze flickers to Marco. "You as well, despite your questionable behavior on your last visit, but I suppose all of that is over now that you're married."

"Very much so," he snaps before drawing me into his side.

I can't help but tense as I feel his body against me, my thoughts conjuring images of him with the Puerto Rican beauty. The logical side of me knows I'm being ridiculous, but unfortunately, logic has no bearing in matters of the heart.

"My husband is more than satisfied," I blurt.

Marco's eyes widen as his gaze snaps to mine. The hint of a smirk curls his lip before he schools his expression to neutral once again. Of course, he's enjoying this.

Nico clears his throat. "Back to the matter at hand…"

"Yes, of course, come sit." Esmeralda and a troop of guards escort us through the open doors to the patio. Beyond the sparkling pool, the crystalline waters of the sea roll up to her backyard. All five of us fill the tropical print patio chairs, positioned in a neat semi-circle facing the ocean.

"It's really beautiful here," Maisy murmurs.

Esmeralda turns her fiery gaze on Nico, then Marco. "If you'd like, the women can enjoy the beach while we discuss business."

Righteous indignation zips through my veins, compelling a slew of curses to the tip of my tongue. "The *women*," I grind out, "are more than capable of attending to the discussion. As I'm sure you're aware, I'm the head of my own organization, and it isn't like this is a social visit. Right, Maisy?" I'm not certain how involved she is in the day-to-day business, but she's the one who caught the housekeeper spying after all. Clearly, she's got a keen eye and a good head on her shoulders.

She nods quickly, red curls bouncing. "Yes, absolutely. We can always swim later... Or not at all." Her hand settles on Nico's thigh, and I wonder if she's feeling as insecure as I am in front of Esmeralda's predatory gaze. Had she slept with Nico too?

My new brother-in-law clears his throat once again, sliding to the edge of the cushion. "We need to discuss your operations in Lower Manhattan."

"And anything you might know about Blanca Alvarez," Marco adds.

A tendon in Esmeralda's jaw feathers, but she keeps her expression a blank mask. "Yes, I am familiar with Blanca and her family. They are prominent people in San Juan, with roots in Colombia."

"Great, the fucking cartel," Marco mutters.

"When did she join your operation?" Nico's question catches her off guard, and her smarmy smile wanes.

"How very astute of you, Mr. Rossi..."

"Well, we figured someone had to be leading the show in Manhattan." Nico motions at the sprawling shoreline. "And as you seem to prefer your tropical hideaway, it wasn't too difficult to connect the dots." He pauses, his eyes, nearly the brilliant blue of the sea surrounding us, blazing. "Was it your idea to plant her as a housekeeper in my own home?"

Her eyes widen, the dark spheres piercing. Her hand twitches before she folds it in her lap. She doesn't know.

I nudge my elbow into Marco's side as his head slowly dips as if he's come to the same conclusion.

Esmeralda uncrosses her legs and leans forward, dark gaze darting between both brothers. "I was not aware of this. Perhaps the leash across the ocean needs to be shortened."

"We believe she instigated the attack at our wedding." Marco's voice sharpens like shards of glass crackling across the tile. "As you can imagine, she *will* be dealt with. That level of disrespect will not be tolerated."

Esmeralda's shiny façade falters, and she reaches for a sarong haphazardly tossed on a neighboring chair. As she slowly wraps it around her curves, the tension thickens.

"Unless you tell us otherwise, we are going to assume you had nothing to do with it, correct?" Marco slides to the edge of the couch, mirroring his brothers position, his mismatched eyes seared to the woman.

"Of course not."

"Then it was just a coincidence you didn't attend?" I blurt.

"I prefer not to leave the solace of my island home, as you've said."

Marco grumbles beneath his breath.

"If you choose not to break ties with her," Nico continues, "we will have no other choice than to take matters into our own hands. And just so that we're clear, the Valentinos are onboard with whatever decision we make."

"As well as the Four Seas, obviously," I interject. "And I have no doubt that I could persuade the rest of the Chinese Triad to see it our way. Attempting to murder the new *lǎodà* is a sign of extreme disrespect."

She swallows hard, the faint sound echoing through the sudden stillness.

"An attempt on the life of my bride is not something I take lightly, Esmeralda," Marco growls and locks one hand onto my thigh. "The only reason Blanca's blood isn't painting the streets of Lower Manhattan already is out of respect for our past. The Geminis and *La Sombra Boricua* have always had a mutual understanding. I'd like to keep it that way, but Blanca continuing to breathe will not be part of the deal."

"Feel free to call Luca or Dante and speak to them directly," Nico adds, "but our half-brothers have promised their full support. And as Jia mentioned, the Chinese Triad will fall in line next. That would leave you with very few allies—or at least, trustworthy ones." He shoots her a grin, and with the smart twist of his lips, he looks so much like Marco it's unnerving.

"I will consider your terms," she finally mutters. "But it seems my options are limited."

"Trust me, Esmeralda, you do not want to make an enemy out of the Geminis." My husband leans closer, eyes locked on her, and a vicious snarl curls his lip. "And on a more personal level, you do not want *me* as your enemy. A newly married man out of his mind in love with his new wife is not one to be fucked with."

CHAPTER 44
STUPIDLY IN LOVE

M*arco*

Every tear that rolls down Jia's cheek is like a stab to the heart. *Dio*, why did people desire to be in love? It's the cruelest form of torture if you ask me.

Jia's grandfather pulls her into his arms once more, holding her tight and whispering foreign words. The only one I recognize is *bǎobèi*, treasure, the term of endearment he always uses for his granddaughter. The name certainly is on point. I never thought I would love again after Isa, and because of that, Jia falling into my life has been a true treasure. Because as hard as it has been, what we have now is one hundred percent worth it.

"Do you really have to go already?" Jia glances at her grandfather, eyes red and swollen.

"*Bǎobèi*, I leave you in good hands with your husband." He cocks his head over his shoulder and gives me a smile. The gesture speaks volumes. How this man knew I would be right for his granddaughter is beyond me.

I had no idea.

I was certain I'd fuck it all up.

And hell, I nearly did. I still might...

"But we haven't even made our move against Blanca and her *Sombra Boricua* offshoot, and then there's Lei Wang and his rebels—"

The old man raises a hand, cutting her off. "There will always be something, Jia. I wish I could lie to you and say a peaceful existence will come, but in this business, one always dances on the edge of a blade. And it is for that reason that you must enjoy every moment of your life to the fullest." He holds her out to arm's length before sliding a hand to her belly. He palms the flat contours of her torso, and a happy smile melts across his stern countenance. "I will be back to celebrate the birth of your first child."

"Oh, *Yéye,* we're not ready for that yet."

A knowing smile spreads his lips. "No one is ever ready for what fate has in store. Trust me when I say I will be back before long. I have a good feeling about this, *bǎobèi.* Your husband is a strong, virile man, and your womb is ripe for planting."

A nauseated expression crosses Jia's face, and she finally releases her grandfather. "Oh, please, *Yéye,* not the sex talk again."

"You're right, I must go." He reaches for his suitcase, but Nicky grabs it first.

"I'll take care of that for you, Mr. Guo."

The old man dips his head then turns to me. "You have a very special treasure to guard now, Mr. Rossi. I hope you take your duty seriously."

Reaching for Jia's hand, I tuck her into my side. "I will guard her with my life, Mr. Guo. I vow to keep her safe, cherish her, and adore her, above all things. You truly gave me a gift when you *forced* me into that marriage contract."

Jia punches me in the gut, and I buckle over just to appease her.

"And I couldn't be happier."

"Very good, Mr. Rossi. I will see you both soon."

Jia's gaze follows his trailing form until he and Nicky disappear through the front door.

The moment he's gone, I spin her into my chest and capture her mouth. Her lips are salty, the lingering tears still coating her skin. I kiss her tentatively at first, but the fire kindles between us in seconds.

"As much as I'm going to miss *Yéye*," I whisper against her mouth, "I cannot wait to freely fuck you all over this penthouse, spitfire."

"And I won't have to be quiet anymore." A rueful smile parts her lips and I fill it with my tongue. I'm going to fill it with my cock in a second. I'll have her so full of my cum, panting from all the orgasms in the next few hours, she won't have time to be sad.

"I love you, Mrs. Guo-Rossi," I murmur against her pouty bottom lip.

Her eyes meet mine, a tempest of emotion brewing in the sleek, dark night.

"And one more thing," I interrupt, "your grandfather isn't wrong about the baby thing. If we keep having sex without protection, you're going to end up pregnant."

"I know." Her gaze drops from mine. "I just had my period before we had sex for the first time, so technically, we should be in the clear. I shouldn't be ovulating for another week."

"I didn't know you were an expert on the menstrual cycle."

"I'm not, but Ari is. She refuses to go on birth control because she doesn't like the idea of those hormones in her body. Which I kind of agree with. So anyway, she tracks her period religiously and got me into the habit."

An unexpected thrill courses straight down to my cock. "So what are you saying? You want to keep having unprotected sex?"

"Or you could wear a condom."

I snort on a laugh. "With my wife? I've worn one for the better part of my thirty years!"

She shrugs, a hint of crimson tingeing her cheeks. "Then I guess we can try the natural method of contraception and just not have sex when I'm ovulating."

"How long is that?"

"It's about a five-to-seven-day window."

"Fuck no."

A rueful laugh purses her lips.

"You expect me not to touch you for an entire week every month?"

"We can do other things…" A mischievous grin reflects in her dark eyes.

"You'll let me claim your ass?"

Her head falls back in a cackle. "I was talking about oral pleasures, honey." She shakes her head, still laughing. "But I guess we could work up to that."

Those words have a straight line to my cock, and I'm immediately hard. Before I lose control and bend her over the bar stool, I pull her close and press a kiss to her forehead. "And if you do get pregnant? How will that work with the boutique, with our riskier professions…"

Her slim shoulders lift along with the corners of her lips. "I guess Yéye is right. We can only plan so much. Sometimes we just have to leave it up to fate." She nibbles on her bottom lip, anxious eyes lifting to mine. "As long as you're okay with the possibility of a baby?"

I heave in a breath and frame her face with my hands. "A few months ago, I would've run out of the room screaming— but now, I can't wait to have the full experience of wedded bliss. I want it all with you. Hell, I may even move to the suburbs so we can have that white picket fence."

"Seriously?"

I nod and brush my lips against hers. "I've never been so sure about anything in my life."

Jia's arms come around my neck, and she rises to her tiptoes. "I love you, Mr. Rossi."

My heart staggers, momentarily freezing before starting to pump again. I'm suffocating and soaring all at once. "Are you sure?" It's been a tumultuous storm, this arranged marriage, and it seems like I've been waiting forever to hear those three damned words.

"Yes, I'm sure, you *coglione*. As hard as I've tried to despise you, you've wormed your way into my heart. If I wasn't so stubborn, I probably would have admitted it long ago. You've won me over, Marco Rossi. I love you with my whole heart and soul; every beat belongs to you."

The last word barely falls from her mouth before I capture her lips. "*Dio*, I love you, wifey," I whisper as I devour her.

My hands are at the hem of her dress, tugging it over her head as she battles my belt buckle. The sight of the scars along her arms still has anger boiling to the surface, but I remind myself the *bastardo* is dead. I wish I could resurrect the man just so I could kill him all over again. How dare he defile her like that?

One thing is for certain, I'll be ten times the dad Qian Guo was. That's something, at least.

I drop to my knees and slide my fingers beneath the lacey waistband of her panties as I squirm out of my boxers. With *Yéye* living with us, we've never been nude around the penthouse. Now, I fully plan on changing that.

I rise, my cock hard and ready between us. "I think you should just throw away all of your panties," I murmur against her swollen lips. "It's just an extra step we should definitely do away with." My hand cups her wet pussy and a groan rumbles in my chest. "Mmm, *cazzo*, I love you and that warm sweetness."

Her hips rock into my palm, and a faint moan escapes as her hands close around my ass. "And I love your enormous cock and that incredible ass, Marco. It's seriously amazing."

"Now you're just teasing me."

She smirks as her hand glides around to my cock. "No, I really do." She kisses me hard then drags my dick between her legs. "I want you inside me already."

"Such a needy, bossy little thing." My hands close around her hips before I slide one hand beneath her thigh and curl her leg around my hip. With her pussy bared, I thrust inside her, filling her up in one go.

Her head falls back and moans rent the air, a tangle of us both.

"Oh, spitfire, fuck me, you are so tight and wet."

"I am fucking you." She meets every single thrust as I back her against the kitchen island.

"So sassy," I whisper. Reaching for her other leg, I wrap it around my waist and walk us toward the couch. Not that standing isn't fun, but I want to take my time and enjoy this. I drop her down onto the couch and throw her legs over my shoulders. Then I slowly withdraw, taking her all in. She's splayed out before me, the most beautiful pussy I've ever seen taking me in and in and in.

I'm home. Married. And stupidly in love.

CHAPTER 45
BADGES OF SURVIVAL

J *ia*

I never thought anything would take precedence over CityZen. My designs, seeing them come to life in an array of hues and textures, was what I lived for. Now, every moment I spend apart from Marco is torture. Even if I'm doing what I love most.

From my drafting table, I cast a glance across the boutique at Nicky. He stands guard at the door as always. He's become a permanent fixture in my little shop. And I'm fairly certain my dark shadow has a crush on my best friend. Behind the tinted sunglasses, I notice the flick of his gaze following Arianna as she flutters around the space. With everything still up in the air with Blanca and *La Sombra*, my initial instinct was to hold off on the grand opening of CityZen, but with the Triad dragging their feet, and the Kings and Geminis arguing over the splitting of Esmeralda's territory, it's already been a week since our visit to Puerto Rico, and we seem nowhere close to a grand finale.

I just want this Blanca woman dead.

The bitch tried to murder my fiancé, shot up our wedding, and then attempted to kill me. I don't care what Marco says about diplomacy and keeping the shaky peace, if someone doesn't bury a knife in the woman's chest, I will.

Revenge is not a dish best served cold in my opinion.

I tried that once, and I regretted every day that I wasted…

Shaking my head free of grisly thoughts from the past, I remind myself that the grand opening is a week from today. I must focus.

I stare at the brilliant lavender hue of the dress stretched out across the table, my eyes settling on the sheer sleeves. An unexpected flare of anger tightens my chest. Long sleeves have been an essential part of my wardrobe, to hide the shame, to conceal my scars, for as long as I can remember. But since revealing the truth to Marco, something has changed. I don't want to hide them anymore; I want everyone to see the scars for what they are. Badges of survival. I'd been abused by the one man who was supposed to love me unconditionally and protect me from harm, but I'd endured.

And I'd won.

Grabbing the scissors from the drawer, I tear into the fabric, and with each snip, my heart feels lighter.

"Oh my gawd, Jia! What are you doing?" Arianna stares at the ruined dress, bright eyes wide.

"I decided it needed to be short-sleeved." In a second, I'll do the same to the oppressive blouse I'm wearing, and my best friend will really think I've lost my mind. Even she has no idea of the truth. Over the years of our friendship, I've gone to painstaking lengths to hide these ugly scars.

But no more.

The jingle of the front door opening tears my attention away from the mangled dress to the male stalking through the entrance. My husband. I never thought I'd enjoy the feel of that word on my tongue. My mouth is uncontrollable, my lips splitting into a grin of their own accord at the sight of him in a dark suit.

"It's a good thing you're here, Marco," Ari breathes. "I think Jia's on the point of a major breakdown."

His expression darkens as he regards me, that heated gaze raking over every inch of me then finally falling to the ruined dress. "Everything okay, spitfire?"

I wave a dismissive hand and drop the scissors. "Yes, I'm fine. Ari is totally overreacting."

"She just cut the sleeves off that gorgeous dress!" she squeals.

Marco's eyes meet mine, the brilliant blue darkening to a deep navy while the midnight orb smolders with starlight. "Give us a minute, Ari. Why don't you and Nicky go grab a coffee?"

My friend's eyes meet mine, and I nod my approval. "Bring me back the usual, please?"

"Will do, boss." She smirks before rushing toward the big guard, already chattering away.

As soon as the chime signals their departure, Marco circles the drafting table and pulls me into his chest. "What's going on, spitfire?" His cedarwood scent envelops me as I bury my nose in his button-down shirt. The suit is odd for this time of the day. I make a mental note to ask why later.

Propping my chin on his chest, I lift my gaze to meet his. "Nothing. I feel oddly liberated, actually."

"That's why you took a pair of scissors to your newest design?"

"It was symbolic."

"Mmhmm." He eyes me warily.

"And actually, I have you to thank for it." I wriggle free of his embrace and reach for the scissors once more.

When I bring it up to my shoulder, Marco's hand wraps

around my wrist. His wedding band shifts, calling my attention to the white line beneath. There's something about the new tan line that offers a sense of permanence and brings an unexpected smile to my face.

"I think there are safer ways to make this statement." His fingers find the top button of the sheer red blouse, and he slowly undoes the first button. "First, remove the garment before cutting the sleeves." His eyes raze over me, each move deliberate as he works his way down my top. "I think it's very brave what you're doing, Jia, and if you'd like, I can help you destroy every single one of your creations once I'm certain there's no bloodshed involved. But I don't believe that's going to take away the pain..."

The final button comes loose, and Marco drags the blouse down over my shoulders. Bit by bit, my arms are exposed, the dozens of pale white marks crisscrossing my flesh unearthed.

His gaze turns feral as he focuses on the swell of my breasts. The lace bra leaves nothing to the imagination. Clearing his throat, he draws in a breath and fixes those enigmatic eyes to mine. His fingers trap my chin, holding my gaze steady. "Jia, your beauty is so overpowering that even if your entire body were riddled with scars, they would pale in comparison to your inner radiance. Your fierce spirit, your pure heart, your unyielding determination—these qualities draw others to you. They are what captivated me from the beginning. Embrace your scars proudly, because they have molded you into the remarkable woman you are today."

Tears fill my eyes and one escapes, then another and another.

"I am so proud of you, spitfire." He kisses each fallen tear. "You are quite literally perfect, which was why I chose that song for our wedding day. I was listening to the wise words of Ed Sheeran the first time I laid eyes on you in your boutique all those weeks ago. When the wedding planner asked me about our first dance, it seemed the most obvious choice."

Those damned tears threaten again, and I barely bite back the sob. "Why didn't you tell me?" Why did I waste all this time despising this man? The perfect man for me.

He shrugs. "It didn't seem like the right time then."

His mouth captures mine once again, and the pain of the past morphs into something else with each tender touch. His mouth moves from my cheek, across my jaw and down my neck. When he finds my breasts, I arch into him as his tongue swirls around my nipple. As he continues to devour me, his hands cup my ass and lift, spinning me around so I'm sitting atop the drafting table.

"Another first, spitfire." A sinful gaze darkens his features.

"Here?" I blurt.

He nods slowly, unbuckling his belt before dragging down his zipper. His pants and boxers slough to the floor in one swift move. His cock stands eager between us, a bead of cum already glistening on the tip.

His hands wrap around my thighs and jerk me to the edge of the table, then he slides them beneath my skirt. Anticipation has heat flaring between my legs before his fingers find my center.

"Mmm, good girl, no panties."

"You've torn through so many I figured it was becoming terribly wasteful."

"That is true." Pushing the skirt up to my waist, he takes me in, those piercing irises swallowing me whole.

I hazard a quick peak over my shoulder at the glass walls that make up the front of the boutique. If anyone passes by and glances in this direction, they'll get a front row view. Not to mention the possibility that Ari and Nicky could come back quicker than expected. I open my mouth to voice my concerns, but Marco's hungry mouth swallows all objections.

His thumb is at my clit a moment later, and I'm already too far gone to object. "That's my good girl, already drenched and ready to take my cock like an obedient wife."

I snort on a laugh. "Obedient, really?"

"Okay, more like obstinate wife?"

"That sounds more like me."

He dips a finger inside me, and my head falls back, a groan escaping. I've forgotten all about the passersby or unexpected guests. All I can focus on is Marco and the heated sensations lashing through my body. My hips rise to meet the thrusts of his fingers, eager for more.

"I want you inside me. Now."

"What a bossy little wife."

"Just fuck me already, Marco."

"Yes, ma'am." He positions his throbbing head at my entrance, and every nerve-ending riots at the feel of him. He pushes into me without restraint, filling me so fully another groan peals out.

"Oh, Marco…"

"That's right, spitfire, I've got you." Thrust. "I'll always be with you, always stand beside you." Thrust. "No one will ever hurt you again now that I'm here." Thrust. Fiery heat builds into a scorching inferno each time he sinks deeper inside me.

"I know," I murmur.

"Good." He captures my lips as he drives into me, faster, harder. "I want you to come for me, spitfire. Tell me that I'm the only man for you, the only man that has ever made you feel like this."

"You *are* the only man for me. I come only for you, *my husband*."

"*Dio*, that word is so sexy on your lips. And even more so when my cock is inside you, claiming every inch of that pussy. *My* pussy."

"Yours and only yours."

My hands wrap around his muscled ass, urging him deeper, his pulsing head nudging that elusive spot.

"Don't stop," I moan. "I'm almost there…"

Cupping my ass, he lifts me off the table and forces me up and down his thick shaft.

"Oh, Marco, oh fuck, I'm going to come…"

My toes curl and that raw energy courses through me, blossoming in my core and spreading like wildfire through my veins. I moan his name as his cock twitches inside me, and his warmth fills me to the brim. My breath hitches, my heart halts for a devastating instant. Everything stops but the raging pleasure. As the lingering tremors slowly subside, Marco lowers me back onto the drafting table, but we remain locked in each other's arms for a long minute.

He feels so good, so strong. I've never felt so safe as when I'm surrounded by Marco. His fingers trail up my arms, tracing the patchwork of scars. His jaw tenses and that raw fury flares.

"I want that *bastardo's* head for what he did to you."

Qian used to keep it in a box, but once my brother died, I had *Bà's* head buried with the rest of his body.

"Qian was a lucky man, getting to claim that *pezzo di merda's* death."

I nibble on my bottom lip as the secret I've carried for too long now weighs heavily on me. Maybe the dark confession would finally free me of him. And for some reason, I want to tell Marco the truth. I feel like he'd feel better about the hell I'd suffered.

"It wasn't Qian," I whisper.

"What?" His eyes fix to mine.

"I killed my father."

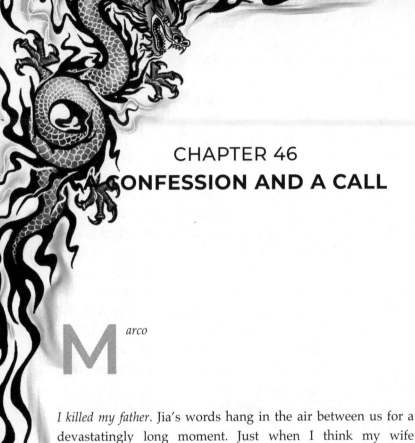

CHAPTER 46
CONFESSION AND A CALL

M *arco*

I killed my father. Jia's words hang in the air between us for a devastatingly long moment. Just when I think my wife couldn't possibly surprise me, she says that...

And me with my pants down, too.

The anguish in her eyes is palpable, a furious mix of pain and anger. But I don't catch a glimpse of remorse. Not that I blame her. The man clearly tortured and abused her for years, to speak nothing of the verbal assault she must have endured.

"How?" I finally manage.

"I shot him." Her answer is quick, her voice clear. Again, I don't detect a hint of regret. "And after that day, I promised myself I would never live beneath the heel of a powerful man again."

At once, everything is so much clearer. Her hatred of me stemmed from a much deeper one, that of her abusive father.

"What made you finally do it?" I pull up my pants and

hand her the discarded blouse. Perhaps, it'll be easier for her to confess the truth with clothes on.

"I guess I just snapped one day, as they say." She shrugs, fastening the final button. "My mother was dead, Qian was the heir and he was readying to take over the Four Seas. I suddenly found myself with nothing to lose. *Bà* came into my room one night, angry about my chosen profession. He forbade me to pursue my fashion career, and I just lost it. He came at me with the knife he used to inflict my punishment, slow, shallow cuts to ensure I didn't bleed out. It was a ritual of sorts to my father. He would force me to wear an apron so my clothes wouldn't get bloody. At first, it was to hide the truth from my mother, and then after she was gone, I believe it was for him." She heaves out a breath before continuing. "When he went to pull the apron from my drawer, I got my gun. I'd owned one for years, been trained on it as a teenager, but I'd never fired it at someone until that day."

Her shoulders begin to tremble. I inch closer and place my hands on her thighs, steadying her.

"I'll never forget his face when I pointed it at him. That look of surprise and betrayal will be permanently carved into my mind. Worse was the expression that came along with it, a hint of *pride*. Like he was happy that after all these years, I was finally standing up to him." Her hands find mine, fingers clutching my own. "How fucked up is that?"

"Extremely." I cradle her cheek, drawing her closer. "He was a terrible, horrible man, Jia, and he deserved to die for what he put you through."

"I know…"

"You never should have had to endure that. I only wish I could have been there to protect you from him. But I'm so damned proud of you for standing up for yourself and for becoming this incredible woman despite all of it. More than that, I'm now convinced I'm the luckiest man alive that after everything, you were finally able to put your trust in me. I probably don't deserve it."

She caresses my cheek, mirroring my pose. "I wanted to believe you were like him. I needed to in order to protect myself, but you made it clear from the start you were nothing like that monster. I just needed time, and I suppose it took being shot myself to finally see it." A rueful smile tugs up the corners of her lips and *Dio*, she's radiant.

I should be scared of the woman in front of me, of that quiet, demure demeanor and the murderer that lies beneath, but all I can summon is respect and admiration. Besides, we all get a little unhinged sometimes.

"So should I be worried you'll shoot me if I get out of line?" I kiss the corner of her lip as it twitches.

"Damn right, you should." She grabs my cock over my slacks, fingers biting into the material. "This is mine, and if you ever stray, I *will* punish you."

"I would never dream of it, spitfire." I lean into her touch despite the rough edge because I'm a total masochist, and I like this dark side of my new wife. It makes me feel less guilty about all the ways I plan on defiling her. I'm about a second away from splaying her out on the table again, when a horn blasts outside.

Merda, how could I have forgotten? "I have a surprise for you out front." She removes her hand from my now once again hard dick, and I'm kicking myself for ruining the moment.

"You couldn't have opened with that?"

"I got a little distracted when I saw you with the scissors, remember?"

"Point taken." She slides off the table, and I wrap my hand around her soft one, leading her to the door.

A van sits outside with a grumpy driver. "Where do you want it?"

"Just set it right over there." I point at the sidewalk in front of the boutique. "My wife will tell you where to hang it."

Jia's wide eyes flicker to mine. "Hang what?"

"You'll see."

The driver walks around to the back of the van and pulls out something big beneath a white sheet. A buzz of excitement and nervousness streaks through my veins as he unveils it. *Dio*, I hope she loves it. It's a custom CityZen sign in bright neon with bold text.

Jia's jaw drops as she takes it in, following behind the man as he lowers the huge sign onto the sidewalk. "It's perfect," she whispers as she crouches down in front of it to run her hand over the big, bold letters. She turns to me, tears in her eyes. "It's exactly what I wanted. How did you know?"

"I may have grilled Arianna for design details. She was very helpful."

She stands and leaps into my arms, pressing a kiss to my lips. "Thank you. It's the best gift anyone's ever given me."

Heat burns my cheeks at the intensity of her gaze. I'm not used to being this guy, this supportive husband. "And between Ari and Mel, they've got everything ready for the grand opening. You won't have to worry about a thing."

She melts into my embrace, those dark eyes twinkling. "Have I told you how much I love you, Mr. Rossi?"

"Not recently, no, wifey."

Jia smirks and captures my lips, pressing her body to mine. If she keeps this up, I'm going to have to take her back inside again and let the guy figure out how to hang the damned sign up himself.

The penthouse is too quiet without Jia's energy filling it. Despite Arianna and Mel taking the reins for the grand opening, she still spends all day at CityZen which drives me nuts. But not tonight. She promised to be home early.

I slip my hand into my pocket and meet the small box hidden within. I pull it out for the tenth time and flip it open. The diamond winks at me, the overhead lighting setting the princess-cut jewel ablaze.

I've wanted to give Jia the engagement ring for days, but the timing has just never been right. She's been so absorbed by the boutique's opening, and I've been preoccupied with Esmeralda and *La Sombra Boricua*. A part of me wanted that handled and behind us before giving her the ring and embarking on our new life together. Which is crazy, I realize, since we're already married and what difference does an engagement ring make after the fact?

But I want Jia to have the real experience. We skipped over all the fun stuff to race to the altar, and she deserves a true relationship with all the steps that come in between.

I glance at the clock in the kitchen and mutter a curse. It's only four, which still leaves me two hours until her return. The dining room table is already set, rose petals strewn across the white tablecloth. The candles are in place, but not lit, and the caterer will be arriving at seven.

Everything is ready, so why the fuck am I so damned nervous?

My heart pounds an erratic rhythm, and my fingers tighten around the little red box. I stuff it back into my pocket and start pacing.

You're a complete *coglione*. You are already married. It's not like she'll say no.

My phone buzzes in my pocket, pulling me free of my spiraling thoughts. I scan the screen, unfamiliar with the number on the text message that pops up.

Unknown: I have your wife. If you want to see her alive again, meet me at the warehouse on the corner of Grand and Madison and come alone.

Panic steals the air from my lungs as I read the lines of text over and over again. No. This can't be happening. I jab my finger at the screen, clearing the message and dial Jia.

"Pick up, come on, pick up."

Each unanswered ring spikes my pulse, elevating my frantic state. Sweat dribbles down my spine, and I'm pacing a tight circle now as darkness encroaches into my vision. When the voicemail responds, I jab my finger at the call end button and dial Nicky.

No answer.

"Fuck!" I growl and rake my hands through my hair.

One last call. But I'm already moving toward the door.

Arianna picks up on the second ring, and a hint of hope flares.

"Where's Jia?" I bark.

"Um, well, hello to you, too, Marco."

"I don't have time for this, Arianna, this is serious. Is she with you or not?"

"No," she murmurs, a whisper of fear now in her voice. "I left her and Nicky at the boutique to grab some more samples from the warehouse. Why? What's going on?"

I race through the foyer and spear my finger into the elevator call button, waving off the guard stationed at the door. "Get back to the boutique and call me immediately, Ari. I think she's been taken. I'm on my way to get her back."

"What—"

The rest of Arianna's words are cut off as I hang up and toggle back to the mysterious text message.

Me: Whoever the fuck you are, you're a dead man or woman. If you lay one finger on my wife, I'll make sure you and everyone you love dies an excruciating death. Are we clear?

Unknown: Meet me as indicated and no harm will come to your precious wife.

Me: Tell Jia I'm on my way, and I'm going to fucking destroy you.

I shove my phone back into my jacket pocket as the elevator descends to the first floor. Bypassing the main entrance, I go straight to the garage to get my car. When the asshole said come alone, I'm assuming he meant no driver either.

Before I reach my BMW, I shoot a quick message to Nico. In case this whole thing goes to shit, someone has to know what's going on.

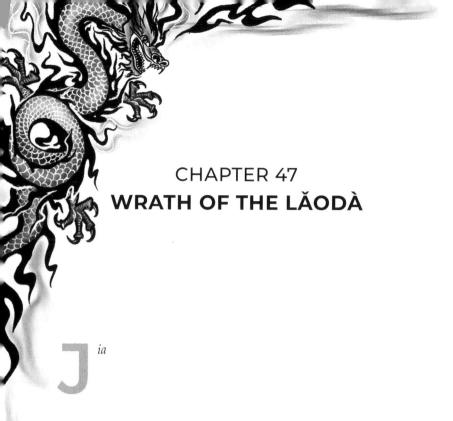

CHAPTER 47
WRATH OF THE LĂODÀ

J*ia*

Glancing up at the CityZen sign Marco had custom made for the big opening has my heart doing a silly dance. Everything is nearly complete, and my nerves are a wicked tangle of excitement and anxiety.

I clutch my cell and shoot a few pictures of the front of the boutique. "There's a little spot on the left. Right by the Z," I call up to Nicky, who stands on a ladder with a damp cloth, cleaning the sign. A stupid pigeon had the nerve to poop on the beautiful design, and I just couldn't stand the sight of it.

"Did I get it now?" the big guard calls down.

"Just a little more on top."

The click-clack of heels on cement turns my attention to a leggy brunette in a ruby-red Chanel skirt suit strutting our way. She's on the phone, chattering away with earbuds in and completely oblivious to Nicky and the ladder.

"Watch out!" I yell, but it's too late. She bumps the ladder, and the metal thing begins to tremble. I try to reach for it, but with my phone in one hand, the rungs slip right from my grasp. I watch with my heart shooting up my throat as Nicky falls, the ladder hitting the sidewalk with a sharp clang.

For such a big guy, I'm amazed by the guard's agility. He lands on one foot, staggers forward, but somehow maintains his balance. Too bad the same can't be said of his phone. It flies out of his pocket and hits the cement with a crash.

"Oh my goodness, I'm so sorry," the woman gushes. She scurries toward Nicky and pats him down, making sure to touch his chest and arms a handful of times. "Are you alright?"

A deep blush rushes my guard's cheeks. "Yeah, yeah, I'm fine. No worries, lady."

She bends over, giving him a bird's eye view of her ass cheeks and picks up his phone. "Oh no, it's broken! I'm so clumsy." Handing the mangled cell back to Nicky, she turns to me and offers a saccharine smile. "Give me your phone and I'll put my number in it. I insist on paying for a new one."

"It's really not necessary," I mumble as I step closer.

She bats her dark lashes at my personal guard and presses her palms to his chest. "I really insist. I'm just so embarrassed."

I barely resist the overwhelming urge to roll my eyes and turn to Nicky instead. "I'm sure Marco will buy you a new one."

"Yeah, of course he can," he says to his ogling admirer. "It's really not necessary."

Before I can stop her, the woman snatches my phone from my hands and begins jabbing at the screen with long, manicured nails.

Well, then. I guess she isn't taking no for an answer.

I glance up at Nicky over the pushy woman's shoulder and he shrugs, a shade of crimson still tingeing his cheeks. She hands the phone back to me a moment later, flashing a beaming smile. "There now." Then she spins at Nicky and folds her hands around his big one. "Please call me and tell me what I owe you. My name's Laura, by the way."

"A pleasure to meet you," Nicky mutters.

Then she spins on her stilettos and marches down the block so quickly she's nothing but a blur of Manolos and red Chanel.

"Well, that was interesting."

Nicky smirks and bends down to pick up the ladder. "Yeah…"

I still have my phone in my hands, so I open the camera app to shoot a few more pictures when a video fills my screen. What the hell?

Then familiar moans erupt, and two dark forms coalesce from the dimly lit video.

"What the fuck?" I screech, sending Nicky scrambling off the ladder. How are they together? Did the head of *La Sombra* make a surprise visit to Manhattan?

"What's wrong?"

I grasp my phone tighter, hiding the screen against my chest. Even as the rage starts to boil over, I have enough sense not to show Nicky a view of his boss fucking Esmeralda from behind. Her groans fill the air, and I'm filled with the most perverse need to watch.

I need to see it with my own eyes.

I lower the volume as I watch the muscles in Marco's perfect ass strain as he rails into her. He fists her hair in one hand, free hand groping her ass. It's like a car wreck, gruesome and so disturbing, but I can't tear my gaze away.

I'm going to kill Marco.

I'm literally going to chop off his cock and then shoot him in the face.

How can he do this to me?

Hot tears threaten to spill over, but I clench my jaw and find the icy calm. Blood of the dragon, right? I'll make him pay for this betrayal. As I continue to watch the nightmarish scene, my gaze settles on Marco's hand.

His left hand.

Which is curiously missing a wedding band.

That cheating bastard... no, wait. Clearing my head, I force a deep breath into my failing lungs. I pause the video and zoom in on his ring finger. The white band of skin beneath the platinum band is non-existent.

Which means... this isn't a recent video!

Nicky still hovers nearby, a wary expression twisting his lips. "What's going on?"

I try to ex out the video, but my phone seems frozen, stuck on this eternal loop from hell. That woman...

"We have to call Marco!" I shout at my guard who's the picture of confusion. "My phone's not working either." I race into the boutique then curse myself remembering Ari left for the warehouse, and I never bothered to put in a landline.

Something bad is about to happen, and I'm completely useless to stop it.

An hour later and a lethal mix of fear and panic has set in bone deep. I circle the kitchen island like a madwoman, unable to keep my feet from moving. I have to do something. I can't just stand here.

Marco is gone.

Despite Nico's assurances that we'll get him back, I'm terrified. I haven't been able to draw in a full breath since seeing that damned video of him and Esmeralda.

My gaze flickers to the dining room table, to the candles, the rose petals... I force my eyes away to keep from sobbing.

"Can I get you anything, Jia?" Maisy appears beside me, putting an end to my circling. "Some chamomile tea, maybe? That always helps soothes my nerves."

"I'm not just nervous, Maisy, my husband is missing!" I snap. "Tea isn't going to help." I bite my tongue, immediately regretting my harsh tone. My almost sister-in-law has been nothing but kind to me since we met, but I'm just so damned worked up.

"I know. I'm so sorry, sweety." She pats my arm gently, like I wasn't just a total bitch to her. "Nico's right though, we will find him."

"How can he just disappear like that?" I shout, again my tone is sharper than intended.

Nicky's dark eyes dart to mine from across the room, the big guard's mouth twisting. He's already apologized a dozen times for screwing up. The whole damned thing with the phones was a setup. But why?

Clearly, this has something to do with Esmeralda, but what's their plan?

Nico stalks into the kitchen from Marco's office where he's been camped out for the past hour. I'd finally found someone with a cell phone and called the operator to get the number for Gemini Corp. From there, I finally got a hold of his twin. That's it, I'm never going to be so dependent on my phone again. From now on, I'm memorizing everyone's phone numbers.

By the time I spoke to Nico, it had been nearly ten minutes after the incident with the woman in red Chanel. We returned to the penthouse to find it empty, and the dining room set up in a beautiful display.

My heart aches.

Marco was planning something special for tonight, and if we don't find him, I'll never know what it was. That thought alone has my throat thickening, emotion squeezing the airway.

No. I cannot lose him. I won't. He's the first good thing I've had in my life in years, and I refuse to give him up.

Maisy and Nico are right. We *will* find him.

"Maisy, can I borrow your phone?"

"Yeah, of course." She hands the cell over as the wheels in my mind begin to grind out an idea. "Do you want to call your grandfather?"

"No, I'm calling in my men. If Marco is out there somewhere, the Four Seas will find him or suffer the wrath of their new *lǎodà*."

CHAPTER 48
STRANDED

M *arco*

"You've got to be fucking kidding me," I grumble as I struggle against the ropes binding my wrists to the back of a metal chair. I scan my surroundings, my mind hazy and thoughts murderous. Darkness surrounds me, except for a sliver of light peeking in through the cracks in the doorway. The last thing I remember is walking into that damned warehouse, so out of my mind with worry for Jia, I let some asshole get the drop on me.

Jia. Fuck, where is she? Did they get her too?

"Jia!" I shout for no other reason than I'm pissed off as all hell. "Jia, where are you?" I yell for a few more minutes until my throat is raw. Then I sit back in the hard chair and mutter a curse.

I attempt to rub the back of my head, forgetting about the current predicament my hands are in, but the thick twine cuts into my wrists, instantly reminding me. I'm certain there's a golf ball size knot where someone hit me with the butt of a gun. My skull is pounding, and my mouth feels like I gargled cotton balls.

How long have I been out for and where the hell am I?

Squeezing my eyes closed and drawing in a deep breath to slow my thundering pulse, I attempt to focus. A faint breeze stirs the air beyond the four dark walls, accompanied by a rhythmic whooshing. The sound is so familiar... Once I've steadied my breaths enough that they no longer muffle the noise, a groan builds low in my throat. I shuffle my bound feet against the floor, and the scrape of sand against the soles incites a swirl of unease in my gut.

No, it can't be.

The rush of water is undeniable, the hiss and crash of waves along a shoreline.

Relax, *coglione*. Maybe I'm just in Long Island... It's much more plausible than—another breeze whizzes by and branches swoosh against the outside of my enclosure.

That sounds suspiciously like palm trees.

I sniff the air and a briny sea breeze fills my nostrils. Fuck. I'm in Puerto Rico. There's no doubt in my mind. Either Esmeralda or Blanca or one of their *La Sombra* henchman knocked me out and brought me here.

I must have been drugged.

That would explain the taste in my mouth and the jackhammer taking permanent residence in my skull. I'm going to kill whoever is behind this, even if it is a woman. I squirm in my seat, trying to wriggle free of the restraints. Fuck being a gentleman, this is a total outrage.

"Esmeralda, show your face! Or is it you, Blanca? If that's even your real name. Come face me, *cazzo!*" I shout some more, even though my throat feels like sandpaper, until I notice the light creeping into my prison is growing brighter.

Worn wooden planks surround me and a thatched roof sits

overhead. I'm in a hut… Some sort of tiki bar along the beach? Where's the damned whiskey?

With the sunlight seeping in through the cracks in the wood, my guess is it must be nearing dawn. Did my captor leave me alone out here or is there a guard stationed just outside the rickety door ignoring my shouts?

I guess we're about to find out.

Propelling my bound feet forward, I manage to scoot forward a few inches. Then again and again. Painstakingly slowly I manage to creep up to the door. At least my feet are only tied to each other and not the chair. Rookie mistake.

Drawing my knees into my chest, I kick the old door, pushing all my rage into the quick thrust. The hinges squeal and one of the boards cracks. Warm, golden light streams into the small hut, and I squint from the sudden influx. Two more good kicks and the door crumbles.

Take that, mother fucker.

I scoot the chair outside, the brilliant sun beaming down on me. Crystalline, turquoise water surrounds me, that rush of waves louder now. Swiveling my head from side to side, that pool of dread blossoms.

No. No. *No.*

An island? A tiny stretch of land, no bigger than my penthouse, encircles me.

That *puttana* left me on a mother fucking deserted island?

A growl squeezes through my clenched teeth as I shout a few curses up into the clear blue. How is this happening to me?

I'm being punished, right? I throw my head back and stare up into the sky. "I'm sorry, okay? *Dio,* I'm sorry for all the terrible things I've done in my past. If you want to punish me, fine, but please let Jia survive this. She's been through enough, and she doesn't deserve to be tortured."

Jia…

The idea of never seeing her again, of never touching her…

My heart quickens and my ribs contract, squeezing the air from my lungs. No. I have to survive this for her. I refuse to be the next in the long list of men who have disappointed her.

Squinting, I can barely make out land beyond the brilliant blue. Okay, so I'm stuck on an island, but there's land somewhat nearby. I can do this... I search the sandy beach, scanning the white powder for a shell, a rock, anything I can use to get these damned ropes off. Sweat pours off my brow, my shirt already damp from the exertion of fighting my way out of that damned hut.

A sparkle, buried in the sand, catches my eye. I slowly scoot toward it, moving through the dense surface much harder than from my original prison. When I finally reach the spot, a whisper of hope kindles in my core. Sea glass.

The edges have been dulled by the crashing waves, but maybe, just maybe, it'll be enough to cut my way free. If only I can grab it somehow. Positioning myself right in front of it, I attempt to kick it up with the tip of my shoe. I only succeed in burying the glass farther beneath the sand.

After multiple failed attempts, I want to scream.

"Okay, think, damn it, Marco." My toes. They'll have better traction.

Squirming out of my dress shoes with the laces still tied is no easy feat, but minutes later, I've done it. Only to have to repeat the painstaking procedure with my socks. The tight dress socks prove much more difficult to remove and twenty minutes later my shirt is soaked through with sweat, and I'm cursing like a madman. But my socks are finally off.

I don't even want to consider what I'll do if I actually manage to get the ropes off. Swim to shore? From the looks of it, I'm miles away from the nearest landmass. Something to deal with later. *Just get the damned glass,* coglione. My annoying inner voice sounds a lot like my twin, which now has me questioning my sanity.

Do I have heat stroke?

Am I too dehydrated?

I have no idea how long I've been on this damn deserted island.

None of that matters. Just free yourself from the ropes.

"I'm trying," I shout at my non-existent brother.

Stretching my big toe, I trap the sea glass and lift it toward me. Somehow, after multiple attempts, I manage to drop the makeshift weapon in my lap. Now what? My hands are still bound behind me, and I have to figure out how to get the glass within reach of my fingers.

The rumble of a motor jerks my attention to the horizon. A glistening white speedboat races toward the island, and that dangerous hope blossoms once again. The glass is still between my thighs as I turn my chair so I'm facing my approaching captor.

Dark, wavy hair billows on the breeze as a familiar form begins to take shape.

The fucking housekeeper. Unbelievable.

Blanca Alvarez appears atop the boat in nothing but a bikini and sarong along with two burly men. I size up all three of them before they set foot on shore. I can take two of them easily, the third person would be the problem, and given that the third person is a woman, doubly so.

Not a gentleman, I remind myself.

You're a husband, and your duty is to get home to your wife.

"Where's Jia?" I bark the moment Blanca's bare foot hits the sand.

"Relax, Mr. Rossi, your bride is just fine." She saunters closer, guards flanking her sides. Each has a gun holstered at his waist, but neither of them is holding it. They don't think I'm a threat. Or they hadn't expected me to be awake and moving around, more likely.

"Prove it," I growl.

"You're not really in any position to make demands."

"On the contrary, I'm fairly certain I hold all the power. Why else would you go through such lengths to capture me?" I shoot her a cocky smirk, the one I've perfected over the years.

Her lips twitch, and I already know I've got her. "I hope you're enjoying our lovely tropical weather." She stops a few feet in front of me and cocks a dark brow.

"I'd enjoy it a hell of a lot more if I wasn't tied to this damned chair."

"I'm sure you would. But I rather enjoy breathing, and I'm afraid you wouldn't allow that if I set you free."

"Try me. I've become an incredibly patient and understanding man since becoming a husband."

A sharp cackle parts her ruby-red lips. "I bet you have."

"What do you want, Blanca? Why am I here?"

"I want many things, Mr. Rossi, and I think you can help me attain them."

"As I said before, I'd probably be more willing to hear you out if I wasn't so damned uncomfortable." I struggle with the binds, wincing for added effect. "And I still haven't seen proof that my wife is alive and well at home in Manhattan. Without that, you don't get *merda*."

Blanca ticks her head at one of the big guys at her side. "*Llama la.*"

Luckily, I can pick up a lot of Spanish with Italian being my mother tongue. The guard takes his phone out and starts dialing. Then he flashes the screen in front of my face and presses the speaker button.

"Hello? Who is this?" Jia's voice rings out across the line, and I can suddenly breathe again.

"Spitfire—"

He presses the hang up button, cutting me off from the woman that has become everything to me. Pivoting my gaze, I glare up at the traitorous housekeeper. "What the fuck do you want?" I snarl.

"I want my own empire. I want to rule *La Sombra Boricua* and raise it to new levels of notoriety."

"That sounds like a you problem. What the hell do you want from me?"

"Growing up in Colombia, I'm no stranger to this world you thrive in. The Alvarez cartel was once one of the greatest in our nation."

"I'm not familiar." *Lie.* I simply refuse to give the woman what she wants.

"After years of struggling to become someone in my own family, that of five siblings with me being the youngest daughter, I decided to make my own move elsewhere. I've studied the crime families of Manhattan for a while now. I understand the inner runnings and what is required to attain the wealth and power I desire. While I hate to admit it, in order to achieve that, I need you. Or more specifically, the Geminis and Valentinos on my side. And just to sweeten the deal, you also hold the power to sway the Four Seas and the entire Chinese Triad in my favor."

CHAPTER 49
WELCOME TO THE FAMILY

J*ia*

I stand across the table from the most powerful men in all of
Manhattan, but I don't tremble, I don't waver beneath their
intimidating glares, because there's something I fear far more
than the males sitting in front of me. Losing my husband.

"Why should we involve ourselves in a Gemini mess?"
Jianjun Zhang glares at me from his seat at the head.

Hao Wei of the Golden Star sits beside him, twisting the
end of his trailing white mustache. Lei Wang sits opposite the
pair, scowling, still occupying the seat of my second. With all
the drama, I haven't had time to choose his replacement.
Clearly, no one is excited about the emergency Council
meeting I called a few hours ago.

"It is not simply a Gemini mess. I am the *lǎodà* of the Four
Seas, and Marco Rossi is my husband. You all sat there and
watched as I tied myself to the man only a few weeks ago. If

you had such issue with it, you should have expressed your concerns then."

A chorus of mutters explodes across the small room.

"What exactly do you expect us to do?" Jianjun asks.

"Whatever it takes to get him back." I force my chin up and swallow down the emotion constricting my throat. Today, I must be strong. Today I am not a weeping wife, I am the *lǎodà* and the blood of the dragon runs through my veins.

"Do you have any idea who has abducted your husband?" Lei grits out the last word as if it's physically painful. "Where are we to start?"

"We have a strong lead—"

"*We?*" Hao Wei raises a silver brow.

I throw my thumb over my shoulder at my brother-in law standing outside. "Nico Rossi and the Geminis; the ones you refused to allow entry to the meeting."

"The Council is a sacred institution of the Triad," Jianjun snaps. "It is not open to outsiders." He folds his hands in front of him, forcing that mask of calm.

"Well, those *outsiders* have answers that will affect all of us."

"What are you getting at?" Hao Wei asks.

"*La Sombra Boricua* has been creeping into our territories, as silent as their namesake, sowing seeds of discord, uniting our enemies, and preparing to move against all of us. Esmeralda lost control of her followers stateside, and Blanca Alvarez is stepping in. Her family is one of the most ruthless cartels in Colombia."

"So you believe they are the ones behind your husband's capture?" Jianjun mutters.

"Yes, we are certain." I pull Marco's cell from my pocket, and my fingers tighten around it as if I could somehow hold onto him. "We were able to trace the phone, then the location from which the message was sent. It's a remote spot along the western coast of Puerto Rico."

"And you expect us to travel outside the country to find your husband?" Lei barks.

"No!" I shout right back.

He stands, snarling. "We already scoured the streets all day and night at your beck and call."

"As you should. You would have done no less for my father or brother. And you *will* do as I command. I am here today hoping to unite the Triad for the good of us all." I throw my shoulders back and suck in a breath as my gaze moves between each of the males. "I will handle *La Sombra's* leaders myself. I simply need all of you to protect our territories here. I need your support and a vow to do whatever is necessary to ensure the safe return of your *lǎodà's* husband."

Lei's mouth twists, jaw clenched in a tight line.

I keep my eyes steady on him, on all of them. I only need one to agree, and the others will fall in line, I'm certain of it. *Come on, come on.*

"Do I need to remind you of the vow you made upon joining the Four Seas and the greater Triad?" I sear Lei with my steeliest glare.

"No, *lǎodà.*"

I continue anyway. "'I vow to protect our family with unwavering courage, to keep our secrets close, and to carry out our missions with skill and discretion. I commit to the prosperity of our organization, to support my brothers in times of need, and to sacrifice for the greater good of our community.'" The entire room stills at my words. "Do I need to remind any of you?" I pin Jianjun in my gaze, then Hao Wei, then complete a slow circle of the rest of the room.

Lei rises, head bowed. "I stand with you, *lǎodà*, as I always have, along with my ancestors before me."

I nod in acknowledgement, biting back the thank you perched on my tongue. *They owe you this, you must command their attention, you are their supreme leader.* My father's voice echoes through my mind, the many lessons I listened in on as a child as he instructed my brother in his destiny as heir.

Little did they know I was always listening, watching, waiting.

And now my time has come.

Hao Wei stands next, as leader of the Golden Star, his business typically restricts him to the outer boroughs. "I see no reason not to assist in whatever manner feasible, especially if the threat of *La Sombra* is legitimate."

The door whips open and a menacing Italian storms in. "Trust me, it is."

"What the hell are you doing here, Mr. Valentino?" Jianjun snarls. Marco's half-brother, Dante, darkens the door, a feral grin on his face.

"Apologies for the intrusion, Jianjun." Luca appears a moment later, moving in front of his brother. Of the two, the younger Valentino has always been the more diplomatic, the smooth businessman. "We have urgent information for Mrs. Rossi."

Nico shoves his way into the room, the three big males now crowding the tight space. My head spins to Luca, then jumps to Dante, and finally, Nico. "What is it?"

"We've got her," Nico announces. "We found Blanca Alvarez."

"Thank God," I murmur. "Where is she and where's Marco?"

"In Puerto Rico, just like we thought." A smile of relief tips up his brother's lips.

Luca turns to Jianjun, expression carved in stone. "We need the Red Dragons to keep *La Sombra* busy while we make our move."

I'd nearly forgotten the Valentinos and Red Dragons had struck an alliance months ago. My gaze pivots to the stern leader of the most powerful leg of the Triad. Would he take an order from the king of the Kings?

Jianjun's lips thin before his head dips, the move so faint it's nearly imperceptible.

"*Bene*. Very well, then." Luca turns to me, a faint smile tugging at his lips. "Let's get your husband back."

When the private jet lands along the gravel stretch of runway in Puerto Rico, my heart skips all the way up my throat. I've attempted to remain hopeful, to still all the dismal thoughts from entering my mind. With the Kings, Geminis, and Triad working together for the first time in history as far as I know, there's no way I won't get Marco back.

It's only been twenty-four hours, and already it feels as if I'm missing a piece of my heart. *Please let him be okay.*

We've gone over the plan a dozen times and still, I'm terrified. So many things could go wrong. I was shot only a couple weeks ago, and I'd been lucky. In this life we lead, everything is fleeting. Why did I waste so much time hating Marco for no reason?

I should have given him a chance...

Muttering a curse, I toss the pointless thoughts to the back of my mind. It's too late now. I can't change the past, but I can make sure we make the most out of every day to come.

The flight attendant opens the door, and everyone is out of their seats in a wave of movement. Nico moves to my side, his dark brows in any angry tangle. "Are you certain you wish to come? Marco will kill me if anything happens to you."

I pull my gun out and cock the trigger. "I'll kill you if you try to stop me." Giving my new brother-in-law a sweet smile, I march past him toward the exit.

"She's going to get along just fine with the rest of the girls." Dante slaps Nico on the shoulder and saunters past, chuckling.

When the elder Valentino reaches me, I'm already darting

down the steps onto the gravel tarmac. He places his hand on my shoulder and I spin at him, eyes narrowed.

"Relax, tiger. I was only going to say welcome to the family."

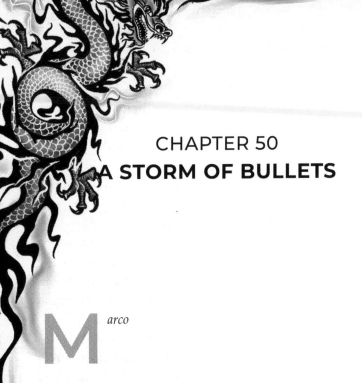

CHAPTER 50
A STORM OF BULLETS

M *arco*

"You're *loca, señorita*." Batshit crazy, actually, if she thinks I would help her take over Esmeralda's territory. I throw her a charming smile, the same one that has worked countless times before on many a beautiful, insane woman.

As she blathers on, I've been working on the ropes. Inch by inch, I've dragged the sea glass until the twine has frayed to a more manageable level.

"Why?" she snarls. "What makes Esmeralda more equipped to run *La Sombra Boricua* than me?"

"Nothing that I know of, but she knew her place. We maintained open lines of communication, worked well together, and she understood who ruled Manhattan. It certainly will not be *La Sombra*."

"Because the Geminis and Kings are in charge?"

"Yes, exactly." My smile grows more brazen. "Now you're

starting to understand." I pause and sear her with a narrowed glare. "Not to mention you shot my wife at our wedding, and for that unforgivable sin, you will die."

She tsks, shaking her head. "You and your brothers have grown weak. Don't you think I've learned things coming in and out of Nico's house? His head is too busy buried between Maisy's legs to secure Lower Manhattan."

"We've known about your treachery for months, Blanca. Everything you've learned since Maisy moved into the penthouse has been hand-fed to you by my twin."

Her eyes widen in shock, ruby-red lips screwing into a pout. She hisses something in Spanish to one of the guards, but it's too low and quick for me to catch. Still, a swirl of satisfaction rolls in at her expression. The guard stalks off the beach, heading toward the speedboat beached on the shoreline.

"Esmeralda would've known she'd been played… In fact, she almost took my head off a few months ago for the same reason." I wave a nonchalant hand. "Maybe I'll tell you about it one day."

"Oh, you mean the video of you fucking her?"

My head snaps back, the impact worse than if she'd actually slapped me. There's a video? Figures the little Latina vixen would film her sexual encounters.

"Your wife was pretty pissed when she saw it."

Fuck. "How dare you?" I roar and leap up, the fury compelling my arms to break through the binds around my wrists. My feet are still tied together, but not for long. I wrap my hand around Blanca's throat before the guard can pull his gun out. I drag her closer, pinning her back against my chest.

"Let go of her now!" the guard barks, finally cocking his pistol.

"Relax, *amigo*," I purr, keeping one eye on the other guard on the boat. He's oblivious to what's happening on the shore, but I doubt he will be for long. "I won't hurt your boss, yet; I just want off this fucking island." I twist my neck, my gaze swiveling to meet Blanca's. "This is what we're going to do. You're going to tell your man to drop his gun, I'm going to relieve you of any weapons, and then I'm going to take that little boat of yours and be on my way." I pause, flashing teeth. "*Comprende, señorita?*"

"*Vete ala mierda, cojudo,*" she spits.

"Such nasty words from such a pretty little mouth." I squeeze her cheeks, and her lips pucker. "Now tell him."

The rumble of an approaching boat spins my gaze toward the sound. The other guard on the speedboat does the same, and all hell breaks loose. Gunshots echo across the sandy shores of the island as five familiar figures coalesce on the newly arrived speedboat.

"Jia!" Her name explodes from my lips, along with the chaos.

Blanca wrenches free of my hold because I'm too damned distracted by the sight of my wife. She turns on me, freeing a small blade tucked into her bathing suit beneath the sarong. Swiping the knife at my chest, she lands a hit. The blade slices through my shirt, but the cut isn't deep, the sting barely forcing out a hiss.

A gunshot rings out just over Blanca's head, and I barely duck in time. Jia stands on the edge of the boat, her gaze murderous as she trains it at Blanca. "Get the fuck away from my husband!" she shouts.

The air thickens with the acrid scent of gunpowder and the shouts of men as another boat appears on the horizon. Shit, we need to get out of here.

I reach for Blanca's wrist and pry the knife from her grasp as bullets rain down from above. "I'll take that, thank you."

She snarls at me, her lips twisted into a furious scowl. But more bullets whiz by, forcing her and her guard to drop to the sandy ground. I run the blade across the ropes around my ankles and race toward the shoreline.

Bullets zip overhead, tearing through the palms and sending splinters of wood flying. Amidst the turmoil, the roar of the ocean serves as a grim backdrop, muffled by the pounding of my thundering pulse.

Nico and Dante stand side by side atop the front deck of the gleaming speed boat, a barrage of bullets spraying the air.

Luca's at the helm, directing the others, a gun in one hand and the steering wheel in the other. "Let's go, let's go!" he shouts. "Incoming in five!"

Jia leaps off the vessel, sinking into the brilliant blue waters, and races toward me. My heart kicks a desperate beat against my ribs as I take her in. *Dio*, for a terrible moment, I thought I'd never see her again. I reach the water's edge and drag her into my arms. She feels so strong, so alive against my chest. I capture her lips for a quick kiss, and salty tears mingle on my lips.

"*Dio*, I love you, spitfire," I murmur against her mouth.

"No, I love you, Marco. So, so much." Tears flood her eyes, spilling down her cheeks. I've never seen her so gorgeous. She steps back, her eyes scanning every inch of me, mirroring my efforts. "You're bleeding!"

I press my hand to the wound across my chest. "It's nothing, she barely nicked me."

"Marco…" Fear flashes across those expressive spheres.

"I swear it's nothing." As if to prove it, I claim her lips once again, reveling in her sweet taste. *Dio*, if anything had happened to her…

"Come on, you two, get over here!" Nico yells. "There will be plenty of time for that when we get home."

Dante and Nico jump off the bow of the speedboat, peppering the beach with bullets. I scoop Jia into my arms and spring into the shallow water. Bullets fly past our heads, a deadly assault between my brothers and Blanca's guards. If it wasn't for their precise cover, we never would've made it aboard.

I toss Jia onto the boat, then pull myself up. Nico and Dante climb up next, still shooting. Luca revs the engine and pulls back off the shore.

"Hurry," Dante hisses at his brother, throwing his thumb over his shoulder.

The other speedboat filled with *La Sombra Boricua* is on our ass. I hold Jia tight against me as Luca maneuvers the vessel out to sea. "Thanks for the assist, gentlemen." I glance at my twin, then my half-brothers. I never thought they'd show up today. Never thought I'd be thanking them for reuniting me with my wife.

"You can thank us when we get back to Manhattan safe and sound, *coglione*." Dante tosses me a cheeky grin. "*My* wife is going to kill you if I don't make it back by dinner."

"Hold on!" Luca spins the steering wheel and the speedboat careens to the right. With one arm around Jia, I grab onto the sleek white siding, then drop down to a crouch. The second boat filled with Blanca's men races after us, a cacophony of bullets resounding across the tranquil blue.

"Go faster," Dante shouts at Luca.

"I'm going as fast as this thing will go, *minchione*. You should've gotten a better damned getaway vehicle."

As my half-brothers bicker in Italian, I keep Jia tight against my chest, using my body to blanket her against the storm of bullets. I can barely feel the cut across my chest now that she's safe in my arms again.

"How the fuck are we going to get out of here?" I bark at Nico over the wind.

"Your wife took care of that." He turns to Luca and grins despite the hailstorm of projectiles. "As long as Luca can get us back to the airfield."

"I'm on it, *bastardo*," Luca growls back as he swerves across the whitecaps.

My gaze swivels to Jia and I cover her head with my hand. "What did you do?"

A mischievous grin tips up the corners of her lips and damn, I cannot wait to get my wife home and bury my cock into that naughty little mouth. Then every other place she'll have me. I'll have her coming so hard she'll forget all about this little unfortunate incident.

My thoughts flicker to the video with Esmeralda... how pissed is she about that? I thank *Dio* I made the right decision telling her all about it before any of this happened.

"So?" I prod when she doesn't answer right away.

"I enlisted the unwilling help of the Triad. Blanca should be getting a call from her associates in Manhattan any minute now."

"She's being modest," Nico cuts in. "Your bride called a meeting of the Triad Council and strong-armed all three syndicates to stage a three-pronged attack on *La Sombra* in Lower Manhattan. They'll never come back from this." He shrugs. "I almost feel bad for Esmeralda, but she dug her own damned grave when she let Blanca steal her throne right out from under her nose and forced us to clean up her mess." My twin casually leans against the back of the captain's chair as if the air wasn't riddled with bullets.

An explosion rings out, the sharp keening sound vibrating the brilliant blue around us and sending our boat tumbling forward on a tsunami-sized swell. "What the fuck?" I shout, clapping my hand over one ear while tightening my hold around Jia with the other.

With the deafening sound of the detonation still ringing across my eardrums, it takes me a second to notice the bullets peppering the boat have halted. I glance over my shoulder and find nothing but a fiery mess where the *Sombra* boat was.

"And you can thank me for that one." Luca throws me a grin over his shoulder. "I convinced Esmeralda it would be in her best interest to remain on our good side if she ever hopes to show her face in Manhattan again."

"Which I hope she doesn't." Jia's lips twist into an adorable pout.

A stupid grin melts across my face as I regard this fierce, beautiful woman who allowed me to make her mine. "Well done, *lǎodà*. I would expect nothing less of the fearless leader of the Four Seas." I capture her lips in a swift, fiery kiss. "Or anything less from my wife."

CHAPTER 51
THIS IS FOREVER

J *ia*

I watch the gentle rise and fall of Marco's chest, the sea of tan skin buried beneath dark tendrils of hair and that gilded cross nestled in the center. I've been thanking God every day since we returned from Puerto Rico with both of us safe and sound.

I also haven't been resting enough, spending all night just watching him sleep. To make sure he's still breathing, to make sure he's still here… I never thought I could love someone so much, so wholly, so completely.

When he was gone, it was as if he'd taken a piece of my heart with him. I inch closer so I'm flush against his side and tighten my arm around his torso. I've slept attached to him every night since our return two days ago. We've also spent nearly all of those forty-eight hours in this bed.

But today, we would finally have to leave the confines of our happy bubble because it's finally opening day for CityZen.

As if Marco senses the flurry of excitement thrumming through my veins, his lids flutter and he inhales deeply.

"Good morning, spitfire..."

"Good morning, honey." I roll onto his stomach and press a kiss to his mouth. My thighs are still sticky with his cum from last night, and as I straddle his hips, I'm greeted by his already hardening cock.

"This is how I want to wake up every morning," he murmurs against my lips.

"I suppose it could be arranged, if you're a good boy."

Marco chuckles, the warm sound reverberating through his chest into my own. "Only for my wife." He frames my face with his strong hands and captures my gaze. "*Dio*, Jia, I don't know what I would have done if I'd lost you. You have me so completely whipped it's embarrassing."

A faint chuckle seeps through as I regard him. "I guess this is what real love is, right?"

He nods. "I hate the feeling as much as I love it." He pauses to nibble on my bottom lip before continuing. "I've never felt so vulnerable, so afraid of losing everything. The human life is frail, fragile, so easily extinguished. In my line of work, it's the harsh reality we live. The idea of spending even a minute without you has become completely unacceptable. How are we supposed to continue doing what we do? And when we have children..." His hands drop to my stomach, cradling my belly.

"So what are you saying? You don't want to run the Gemini empire anymore?"

He shrugs. "It's not something I can just walk away from."

Just like I couldn't walk away from the Four Seas.

"But there has to be something we can do so I'm not tempted to tie you to this bed and never let you leave the safety of the penthouse again."

"I think I would be okay with that." I rock my hips against his cock, and he releases a satisfying shudder.

"There's something I've never told you…" His lids slowly close, then he shakes his head as if ridding himself of some dark memory. "I wanted to tell you after you admitted the truth about your father because it made me understand so much more about you, and I want you to know everything about me. It doesn't excuse the way I've acted toward women for the majority of my adult life, but maybe you'll understand why I got so fucked up."

I still, no longer grinding against his erection. I've never seen him so serious.

"You can tell me anything." I caress his cheek, reveling in the feel of the soft stubble.

"I was only a kid when I first fell in love—or at least, I was certain it was love until I met you. I was nineteen and Isabella had just turned eighteen. She was my world at the time. She was a foster kid like me and we'd met in the system years earlier. I'd already aged out and we continued to see each other, and things finally developed into a serious relationship. She was supposed to move in with Nico and me…"

Tears fill his eyes, and a sliver of my heart nearly breaks right off.

"We'd just started the Geminis back then. We were a rag tag group of kids without families, without love or guidance. Nico and I were hustling on the street to pay for college, anything to make a buck. We were stupid and got into the drug business because it was easy and paid well. Isa was just at the wrong place…"

His jaw clenches as his eyes flutter closed once again.

"She died because of me, in a damned dark alley with a gunshot in the chest. A bullet that was meant for me because I stiffed our dealer a hundred bucks. She died for a mere one hundred dollars. Do you know how fucked up that is?" A dark, rueful chuckle pierces the tense air. "I drop hundreds like dollar bills now. And Isa died because I was a selfish asshole."

"No, you weren't." I cradle his face with both my hands

now and sink down closer so our chests are flush. "You were just a boy trying to survive. That poor girl didn't deserve to die, but you can't hold yourself responsible for some drug dealing asshole with a gun."

"But she never would have been there if it weren't for me."

"And Qian never would have been in your sights if I hadn't killed my father." I snag my lip between my teeth. "And still, I blamed you for his death."

His head dips, and he releases a slow, pained breath. "After Isa, I vowed never to get attached, never to fall in love because it hurt too damned much. I'd already been abandoned by my mother and father. Isa had no fault in her abandonment, but still, I was left alone."

"Never again." I capture his lips, pouring every ounce of love I feel for this man into that kiss. "You'll never be alone again now that I'm here, and I vow never to leave you, for as long as we both shall live."

A rueful smile parts his lips as I echo the words of our marriage vows. "I love you, Jia," he whispers against my mouth before he sinks his cock inside me. "And now, I'm going to show you exactly how much."

When we reach the corner of Gansevoort, the street is closed off, hundreds of people filling the area in front of my boutique. "What the…?" My head spins to Marco.

"What? It's the grand opening of CityZen, right? We had to go big."

I try to peer over Rick's shoulder as he maneuvers the car through the immense crowd gathered. Not only are there people everywhere, but some sort of a stage stretches across Gansevoort Avenue.

I shoot my husband a questioning glance as a tornado of nerves lash at my insides. "What did you do?"

"What I had to do to ensure the success of my wife's new business." He pulls me into his side and rewards me with his trademark panty-dropping smile. It's a good thing I'm not wearing any. "Did you know that between the Valentinos and Rossies, we have a pretty decent portfolio of the fashion high and mighty?"

"You went to Luca and Dante?" I know my husband's relationship with his half-brothers is strained on a good day.

"Only for you, spitfire."

Rick pulls the car up to the back entrance of CityZen, the crowd parting at our arrival, and I see it. It's a runway filled with models and rows of seats lining both sides. Marco planned a full out fashion show for the grand opening.

"Oh my God, I love you!" I throw my arms around the back of his neck and squeeze so hard I take both our breaths away. "When did you have time to do all this?"

"I told you, Mel and Ari were on it. We're pretty damned lucky to have such fantastic assistants."

"And I'm beyond lucky to have the most amazing husband in the world." I smash my lips to his, reveling in his familiar taste and touch. If we only had a few more minutes, I would have thanked him more thoroughly, but there is always tonight.

When Rick opens the back door, shouts and applause ring out from every corner. Light bulbs flash as Marco and I step out, and a dozen paparazzi push mics into our faces. He ushers me through the mob, much more familiar with this sort of fiasco than I am.

We reach the stage, and guards move in around us as we rush up the steps, Nicky's familiar bulky frame slowing the manic fluttering of my heart. Then Marco hands me a mic, and heat flushes my cheeks, the mad drumbeat skyrocketing once more.

"Say something to your fans, spitfire," he whispers. A glint of mischief lights up his mismatched irises. "This is your show, after all."

Right. Drawing in a breath, I try to think of something smart and witty to say, but my tongue is hopelessly tied. I can already see the models showcasing my designs lining up behind me beneath the glittering lights.

It's so surreal.

"Thank you," I murmur against the mic. "Thank you all for joining us to celebrate the grand opening of CityZen. I hope you find as much joy in my designs as I did in crafting them. Each piece represents a journey of personal catharsis, a revelation that allowed me to embrace my true self—with its scars and flaws and all."

Marco's arm tightens around my waist as heat pricks at the back of my eyes. I'm so overwhelmed with emotion I can barely speak. So instead, I hand the mic over to the emcee Marco has hired for the event and press my palms together before dropping my chin to my chest. "Thank you, again," I mouth over the roar of applause.

The fashion show was a hit, the grand opening of CityZen completely phenomenal. I sold every single piece I'd prepared for the event and I'm so keyed up by the enthusiasm, I have new ideas popping into my head non-stop.

I stand atop the runway with Marco at my side as the crowd has finally dissipated. The lights are still on, beaming rays against the stage. Nico, Luca, and Dante and their significant others litter the area, drinking from the full bar set up along the sidewalk. Arianna is already busy setting up the deliveries with Mel's help.

My phone buzzes again, and though I've been ignoring most of the messages, this one I read because it's from *Yéye*.

I've been sending him pictures all night and he even Face-Timed with me to see the fashion show live.

I smile at his congratulatory message before the sound of my husband clearing his throat draws my attention away from the screen. I glance up and see... nothing.

"Down here." Marco's rough voice immediately sets my heart fluttering.

He's on one knee, holding a red velvet box in his hand.

Oh. My. God.

"What are you doing?" I choke out.

"Something I should have done months ago." An unsure smile lifts the corners of his lips. The hesitant look is so unlike my typically smirking husband it has my heart floundering. "I bought you this ring before the wedding, but I was too much of a coward to give it to you. I was terrified you'd deny me, and even more panicked that you'd actually accept."

A smile sneaks across my face even as the tears begin to well.

"I may not deserve to be your husband, but I'm a lucky *bastardo,* and I get to be anyway. I swear I will spend the rest of my life trying my damnedest to make you happy and become the man worthy of you. I vow to love you to the fullest of my ability, protect you until my dying breath, and cater to your every whim and desire. I will be your partner, your best friend. The man you should have had beside you all along. I love you, Jia Guo-Rossi. Will you spend forever with me, for love this time?" He flips open the little Cartier box, revealing a gorgeous princess-cut diamond with shimmering baguettes along the band.

My head bounces up and down as tears blur my eyes. I leap into his arms as he stands, nearly knocking him over.

I'm barely aware of applause echoing around us, but it all blurs in the background over the desperate drumbeat of my heart. I crush my lips to his as he pins my legs around his waist. "I love you, Marco, so much. This is real and this is forever."

EPILOGUE

T*wo Months Later*
Marco

The familiar melody of the church organ hums in the background and, unlike last time, the sound doesn't send panic racing through my veins or my feet wanting to sprint toward the door. I stand in the vestibule in a navy tux with my wife by my side, trailing my fingers down her bare arms. She's a glorious sight in a sleeveless, shimmering ruby gown, her beauty so radiant no one has wasted a second on the faint scars crisscrossing her arms.

I'm so damned proud of her.

My half-brother, Luca, on the other hand looks as if he's a second from spilling the contents of his stomach. Beads of sweat line his brow and his typically tan skin is a pale shade of olive. Dante wears a shit-eating grin, enjoying every moment of his brother's torture. He slaps Luca on the back and whispers, "This is why I eloped." But the loud, obnoxious Italian can't whisper for shit, and I'm certain half the crowd has heard him.

"Just wait until Rose is in the delivery room, *coglione*," Luca hisses back. "Then we'll see who's laughing."

Jia glances at Dante's wife, her swollen belly peeking beneath the layers of plum ruffles of her maid of honor gown. Something unreadable flashes across those dark spheres, but it vanishes as quickly as it appeared.

"Oh, quit it, you two. Don't freak Rose out." Maisy stands beside her best friend and gives her a squeeze. "You'll be totally fine when the time comes."

Rose shoots a glare at her husband. "Oh, I better be or there will be hell to pay. And I'll never let your cock anywhere near me again."

Maisy giggles, her cheeks burning a deep crimson as Dante scowls. Nico watches his fiancée like she's the most amazing thing he's ever seen, and the cute redhead probably is in his eyes. I get it now. Maisy finally let him propose about a month ago. My twin was mad about her from the start, but since she'd been recently divorced, she forced him to take things slow.

I can see the anticipation in my brother's eyes, just waiting for the moment he can walk down the aisle with the love of his life. I never thought I'd see the day.

As I stand there in the huge church once again, I can't believe how far I've come. How far all of us have come. In the span of a year, I met my half-brothers, nearly destroyed their business, bolstered my own, discovered my father hadn't exactly been the bastard I thought he was, been forced into a business arrangement with the Four Seas and ended up falling in love with my wife.

It's been a hell of a ride.

I'm still the CEO of Gemini Corp and now Co-CEO of City-Zen, not to mention handling our back-alley businesses, the Geminis and the Four Seas. Jia has managed to successfully run both operations with little help from me. The Kings and Geminis are at peace, and the Chinese Triad is as close to peace as possible, and we've managed to keep the flagrant killing to a minimum. Squabbles inevitably arise but due to the Kings' alliance with the Red Dragons and my wife as head of the Four Seas, we've reached a sort of status quo.

A temporary cease-fire.

With the next generation of Valentinos and Rossies in the making, one can never be too careful. Supremacy is one thing, but stability is far more valuable in the dark chaos of our world. Especially when there's so much more to lose now.

"You okay?" Jia's voice tears me from my thoughts.

"Yeah, just reminiscing about the last time we were here."

"And how miserable you were?" She lifts a challenging brow.

"On the contrary, I remember it as the day my life really began."

A smile settles across her delicate features, only making her more beautiful. "I'm glad to hear you say that because there's something I have to tell you—"

The wedding march blares, and Maisy appears between us, cutting Jia off. "Come on, we have to take our seats. I absolutely have to get a good picture of the bride as she walks down the aisle. That dress is just so fabulous, Jia!" As she continues rambling about Stella's dress, created by my wife, of course, she shuffles the four of us toward the pews in the front.

Luca and Dante walk a few steps behind us, slowly making their way to the altar. I'm relieved I'm not on center stage today. I much rather watch the happy couple from the sidelines, my life with Jia firmly in order for once. Everything is perfect.

A wave of oohs and ahhs fill the cathedral, and I turn around just in time to see Stella in a billowing white gown. Jia created something straight out of *Cinderella* with the endless layers of satin, tulles and lace. I catch a quick glimpse of my half-brother's face and unexpected happiness fills my heart at the sight of the overwhelming joy in his.

And they say villains don't get a happy ending...

Jia

I can barely keep still from the excitement. I had hoped to tell Marco the news the moment we stepped into the church where we'd been married only a few months ago. I thought it would be the perfect place, but we'd been surrounded by Rossies and Valentinos since we arrived.

After the ceremony, I rush Marco down the pathway to the car where Rick awaits with the back door open. For once, I actually pray for traffic on the way to the reception at the iconic New York Public Library so we'll have more time alone. Maisy told me the venue was chosen because it was the location of the first event the billionaire bachelor had taken Stella to when their love story began.

I slide into the backseat and wipe my sweaty palms on the sides of the silk ruby gown I designed for the wedding. For the first time in as long as I can remember, I crafted a dress for myself without sleeves. A dress that would show my scars to the world. But I walked through that church with my head held high today, with my love at my side, the man who makes me stronger. I never would have had the courage to do that without him.

I only hope I have the courage to confess the truth now.

A part of me wants to believe Marco will be thrilled, but the other part is petrified it's too soon. As it is, we both have so much on our plates...

"Are you going to tell me already or should I force it out of you?" Marco's warm breath tickles the shell of my ear as he wraps an arm around my bare shoulders.

I whirl at him, nearly bumping his nose. "Hmm?"

"You said you had something to tell me earlier, and that vein in your forehead has been twitching since we left the penthouse." A smirk teases up the corners of his lips as he takes my hand. "So please tell me what's going on, spitfire, before I start to worry."

His big hand envelops mine, the feeling of safety and protection mirroring exactly how I always feel when I'm with Marco. Together we can do anything. And let's be honest, anyone would be a better father than *Bà*. Only a few months with Marco and I'm certain he'll be the absolute best because he, too, knows what it's like to have a father who failed miserably.

"I'm pregnant," I blurt. I guess *Yéye* was right, and he'd be back to meet the new heir before long.

Marco's eyes grow large and round, and I prepare for the oncoming rage, but instead, his smile only splits impossibly wider. "I knew your all-natural method would do nothing against my Italian super sperm."

I choke on a nervous laugh as he pulls me into his lap. "Yeah, well maybe the fact that we didn't exactly adhere to the no-sex-during-ovulation rule had something to do with it."

He chuckles, the happy sound relieving some of the blossoming tension.

"So you're not angry?"

His hand cups my belly, his warm palm moving tentatively over the barely-there bump. "Why would I be angry, spitfire? I told you a while ago I wanted it all with you. I'm not stupid enough to think this wouldn't happen with the constant fucking. If I'd been really concerned about it, I would've put on a condom."

A relieved sigh slips out as I press my lips to Marco's. "God, I love you."

"Not more than I love you." Then he slips his hands beneath my dress and clutches my thighs. "So if this baby is coming in nine months, we better make sure we get in all the orgasms we can now." His thumbs brush my bare pussy, and a groan rumbles his chest. "Mmm, damn, I love it when you don't wear panties, wifey."

"Only for you, honey." I offer a sweet smile as I drag his zipper down and free that enormous cock. The one I was so terrified of at first and now can't seem to get enough of.

He lifts my hips and I easily settle down on top of him, that thick head hitting all the right nerves when he thrusts deep inside me. I let out a moan as I rock against his hardness, rubbing my clit to his shaft.

"Promise me nothing will change when we have this baby," I rasp out as the orgasm begins to build. There's something about pregnancy that has me horny as hell, every touch magnified, my senses on high alert.

"Nothing will change," he murmurs as he bounces me harder on his cock. "Except I'll probably love you even more, seeing your belly full with my child. *Dio*, it's going to be so fucking hot."

I toss my head back and laugh, the onslaught of sensations overwhelming. "I'm so lucky *Yéye* chose you to be my husband, Mr. Rossi."

Marco stops his mad thrusting and fixes that enigmatic gaze on mine. He's never looked more sincere, more serious than in this moment. "No, Mrs. Guo-Rossi, *I'm* so lucky that he chose *you* for *me*."

Read on for a special sneak peek of *Ruthless Guardian*, the first story in the **Ruthless Heirs** series where you'll meet the next generation of Kings! The release date is currently set for December 10th and you can preorder it now.

For all the updates make sure to join my VIP mailing list! Come hang out in my FB group Sienna Cross's Heartbreakers and you'll also get the chance to win an ARC and get exclusive sneak peeks of what's to come and the *Ruthless King* prequel story for FREE!

Each novel in the Ruthless Heirs series will feature a sinfully gorgeous heir and the person who makes them fall to their knees. If you haven't read *Ruthless King,* start Luca and Stella's story while you wait for the new one!

SNEAK PEEK OF RUTHLESS GUARDIAN

Chapter 1
Isabella

"Get down!"

I feel the subtle shift in the atmosphere—a tension that tightens the air an instant before gunshots explode across the swanky bar. Waves of gunfire follow instantly, shattering the rhythm of the night as screams erupt around me. I nearly choke on my martini as a big hand clamps over my head and shoves me beneath the high-top table.

"Stay down, Isabella, and don't move until I come back for you!" my bodyguard, Frankie growls in my ear. He blankets me with his massive form for a long minute before he releases the gun at his hip and leaps back up to return fire. "Stay hidden, do you hear me?"

I nod, instinctively.

Bullets pepper the air, tiny missiles of death echoing over the pounding bass. The clink of glasses and bursts of laughter pervading the posh Manhattan bar are gone, replaced by blood-curdling shrieks.

My heart kicks at my ribcage, and I'm filled with the most

overwhelming urge to scream myself. Why can't I just have one normal night? One night to celebrate my graduation from NYU with my friends.

"Shit, Bella! Are you okay?" Serena drops down to the ground beside me, cocktail still clenched in her fist. Wisps of blonde hair fall across her bright blue eyes as she regards me. Guards now surround the table we're hidden beneath but still, her hand shoots out attempting to cover my head. I swat her away.

"Don't you dare, Serena. I'm not yours to protect. My life is no more valuable than yours."

"I don't know about that, cuz. I'm pretty sure your father would say otherwise."

"And I'm pretty sure your father would kill my father if you died trying to protect me."

She smirks, flashing me ruby stained lips. "Touché."

"Come on, huddle closer." I reach for my cousin, who also happens to be my best friend, and tug her beside me. Down on all fours in my sleek black mini-dress, I make a barrier of the surrounding chairs, and Serena pulls a silver handgun from her sparkly clutch. It's just another Friday for the Valentino mafia princesses.

Serena rises to her knees, her head nearly bumping the underside of the table thanks to that long torso of hers. She points the barrel through the slats in the chair and aims at the half a dozen men blocking the door.

"Maybe you shouldn't," I hiss.

"Why not? I can help and take a few of the guys out."

I quickly shake my head and strands of dark hair whip across my face. "What if you get one of *our* guys in the crossfire?"

Serena sticks out her bottom lip, pouting. "Fine…"

While Serena chooses to focus her talents at the shooting range, I prefer to work out my stress and occasional rage at the gym with hand-to-hand combat. Give me the feel of flesh and bone cracking against each other over a gun any day. Krav Maga is my current obsession, but I'd taken classes in nearly all the martial arts from the day I could walk. Papà had insisted.

When your father is Luca Valentino, the head of the ruthless Kings, the most notorious crime syndicate in all of Manhattan, there's no such thing as being too prepared or a quiet girls' night out. It doesn't help that we chose The Velvet Vault, a bar owned by our cousin whose father, Marco Rossi, is the boss of a rival organization, the Geminis. The Valentinos and Rossi's may have found peace, but that doesn't mean every other criminal association in New York City didn't want our parents dead.

And us, by association.

From beneath the table, I can just make out Frankie's black loafers, partially concealed by his dark slacks. Blood already splatters the leather. I blink quickly, chasing away the deep crimson staining my vision. Beside my guard stands a slew of Kings, our fathers' henchmen and our typical entourage. The barrage of missiles echo across the mostly empty bar, most of the patrons having raced out of here the moment the battle began.

"Bella!" A familiar voice surges through the chaos of ricocheting bullets. "Bella, where are you?"

"Down here," I whisper-hiss, waving my hand from under the tabletop.

Matteo crawls toward us, a gun clenched in each fist. My cousin shoots a round over his head before holstering his weapons and turning his attention to us. Apparently, he has no qualms about accidentally taking out my dad's men. Then again, given the tumultuous nature of our fathers' relationship, I'm not that surprised. His dark eyes raze over me, searching for blood. I know the look, I've seen it in Papà's gaze more than I care to remember.

"What the hell's going on, Matty?" Serena barks.

"Fucking Alessandro. He messed with the Russians last week so I'm guessing this is payback."

This lovely establishment is owned by our other cousin, Alessandro Rossi. Which is the only reason I'm occasionally allowed to frequent the place. Normally, no one is stupid enough to mess with the Geminis.

I guess all bets are off when the Russians are involved.

"Where is he?" I ask. "And where's Alessia?" Not that I'm a big fan of either of the twins, but they are my cousins—half-cousins—but still. From the Rossi side, Matteo is the best by far.

Matty shrugs. "Last time I saw Ale, he was texting Uncle Marco."

Serena snorts on a laugh. "Calling Daddy to clean up his mess? Figures the cocky bastard would be a chickenshit when things got real."

"I know he can be an asshole, but he's blood, cuz." Matteo wraps an arm around me, tucking me into his side. Everyone in the family coddles me, Luca Valentino's *principessa*. Princess and heir to the Kings' empire.

"Speaking of blood," I add before peeking between Frankie's legs. My guard has been stationed in front of the table spraying the air with a continuous volley of bullets. "It's a good thing you didn't bring any of your siblings out tonight. Your mom would've killed you if anyone got roped into this mess."

"Which is exactly why I didn't tell any of them I was coming here for our early graduation celebration." He presses a finger to his lips. Matteo has four younger siblings, the biggest family in the Valentino-Rossi crew ranging from Matty's twenty-four to Rex's twelve. I love the guy and all his brothers and sisters, despite who his father is.

"All clear!" Frankie's gruff voice puts an end to our casual conversation. It's a testament to the life we live, that the three of us can chat so nonchalantly while a full-on shootout resounds in the background.

After all these years, I've grown accustomed to the chaos. That, and I know Frankie has my back. He's been my personal bodyguard since the first day I left the penthouse without my parents back in grade school.

"Finally," Serena mutters, crawling out from under the table and pulling me along with her. "I better not have ruined my new Dolce & Gabbana dress, or I'm sending Alessandro the bill." She straightens to her full height, towering over me, even with my heels. With long, blonde hair and those ocean blue eyes, she looks every bit like her mom, my feisty Aunt Rose.

Matteo stands, leaning against the chair and runs a hand through his disheveled dark locks. "Don't worry, we're good for it."

"Where is Ale anyway?" I rise to my tiptoes to see over Frankie's broad shoulders. The rest of the Kings' men and the bar's security team are circling the bar, assessing the damage and righting fallen tables and chairs. At least there aren't any bodies. From our side anyway. I can't say the same about the Russians. I squeeze my eyes closed, avoiding their bloodied, mangled forms. They may be our enemies, but I've always lacked the bloodlust that's supposed to run through my veins.

"Over there." My guard ticks his head toward the modern glass bar that runs the length of the wall behind us. Or at least what used to be the bar. Shards of glass glisten across the black marble floor shimmering beneath the soft glow of lights.

Alessandro and Alessia pop up from behind it, and if it weren't for the bloody gash along Alessia's forehead, I might have laughed. I've never seen my perfect cousin in such a state. Wild, wet curls tumble over her shoulders, her fuchsia dress splattered with an assortment of liquors from the mirrored shelves above. Ale is in no better condition, soaked from head to toe in his beloved alcohol. Above them, the rows of top shelf liquor bottles dribble pathetically, riddled in bullet holes.

"Fucking Russians," Alessandro growls as he throttles his gun and walks around the bar, glass crunching under his boots.

"This is all your fault," Alessia whines at her twin brother, wringing alcohol from her hair. "Pa is going to kill you for getting The Velvet Vault shot up like this. You know he hates when Gemini Corp gets drawn into the press alongside mob shit."

"It wasn't my fault," he mutters.

Serena releases a sharp cackle, her head falling back dramatically. "I'm sure you were the innocent one in all of this."

"Shut up, Serena. If this place closes down, where are you going to go trolling for your fuck buddies?"

"Oh, you wound me so. At least I can get some…"

"Alessandro, stop," I hiss. "Both of you, relax. Everyone's just on edge because of the shooting."

"And it's time for us to go, Isabella." Frankie moves to my side, squeezing my shoulder. "*Signor* Valentino is not pleased. And no one wants to see your father pissed."

I glance up at those dark eyes, the faint crinkle on the edges of the rueful smile.

Great. If The Velvet Vault closes, where the hell will I go for these brief moments of freedom? Unlike Serena who actually has her own apartment, it's not like I can bring a guy back to the penthouse I share with my brother and overbearing parents. Papà would strangle the guy before he set foot into the foyer.

"Fine," I grumble.

Serena pulls me into a hug, then holds me out to arm's length and straightens the strap of my dress. "I'm sorry this night was a complete disaster. I never should have dragged you out. Tell Uncle Luca it was a freak incident that will never happen again."

"If he ever lets me leave the penthouse again."

"Isabella, it's time." Frankie motions to the entrance across the dancefloor, the thick velvet curtains hanging askew, and the velvet rope sprawled across the floor.

Matteo presses a kiss to my cheek, and Alessandro and Alessia offer half-hearted waves as my guard escorts me toward the door.

"He's never going to let me out again," I groan.

Frankie cocks his head and offers a reassuring smile. "Never is a long time, *piccola*." Little one. He's called me that for as long as I can remember, and now despite having just turned twenty-three and about to embark onto a long, difficult journey at medical school, when I hear the nickname, I'm that insecure little kid again hiding behind *Papà*'s looming shadow. Frankie tousles my hair and moves into step beside me as we cross the sticky dancefloor. I refuse to look down, preferring to ignore whatever it is I'm walking through. "Don't worry, I'll talk to him."

"Thanks, Frankie. Of all the bodyguards to be stuck with, you're the best."

He chuckles, the warm sound vibrating his barrel chest. "I'm the only one you've ever had, *piccola*, so I sure as hell better be."

I step onto the red carpet, the soles of my Jimmy Choo's sinking into the plush material, and a shadow streaks across my peripheral vision. The velvet curtain glides back, and I'm greeted by the barrel of a gun.

A gasp slips through my clenched lips as time slows. Everything blurs but that hand on the sleek weapon, that finger on the trigger. A shot fires, and the scream dies in my throat.

I hope you enjoyed that little sneak peek of the brand new series, Ruthless Heirs! The first book, Ruthless Guardian, will be out in December and you can preorder it now :) While you're waiting, check out the other books in the Kings series. And make sure you join my FB group Sienna Cross's Heart-breakers or my VIP mailing list! You'll get a FREE copy of the *Ruthless King* prequel story, *Ruthless Blood* and see how Stella and Luca first met!

ALSO BY SIENNA CROSS

ACKNOWLEDGMENTS

I'll let you in on my dirty little secret… Sienna Cross is my pen name, one I've been dying to launch for a while now. I never would've even attempted it if it wasn't for the support of my husband. He's the only one in my family who knows about naughty Sienna. Thanks for pushing me to do all the things, honey!

A special thank you to my awesome V.A., Sarah, who has been such a huge help and also vault when it comes to keeping all of this a secret. And thank you to the incredibly talented Samaiya for the gorgeous art (you really make the story come to life!) and to my lovely editor Rachel who always makes me laugh at her comments and makes the editing process less annoying. And of course my beta readers, Katelin, Alex, Anca, and Sarah (again!), and my ARC team, you're all amazing! Some of you have been with me for years and I really appreciate all your feedback (thanks for keeping the secret too!)

And the biggest thank you to my readers! I could never do this without you :)
   ~ Sienna

ABOUT THE AUTHOR

Sienna Cross was kidnapped by mobsters, saved by her super-hot step-brother, then forced into an arranged marriage with a billionaire. From there, things got really interesting... She loves to write about dark, morally-gray alpha males and the captivating women that bring them to their knees. For all the inside info, join Sienna Cross's Heartbreakers on Facebook, like her page, and follow her on Instagram and Tiktok. She has a thing for stalkers ;)

www.siennacrossbooks.com

Made in the USA
Monee, IL
14 August 2024